D0398118

The

SECRETS
WE
KEEP

CONTENT WARNING

My Dear Reader,

This book contains material that some may find potentially triggering or traumatizing, including:

- Sexual assault, verbal abuse, and gaslighting of a minor or minors
- Suicidal ideation and self-harm
- Bullying and victim-shaming

If you need to take breaks while reading this book, please do. I really mean that. Also, please consult the resources list on page 341, should you feel the need.

All my best,
Cassie

ALSO BY CASSIE GUSTAFSON

After the Ink Dries

The
SECRETS
WE
KEEP

Cassie Gustafson

SIMON & SCHUSTER BFYR

NEW YORK LONDON TORONTO SYDNEY NEW DELHI

An imprint of Simon & Schuster Children's Publishing Division
1230 Avenue of the Americas, New York, New York 10020

Text © 2022 by Cassie Gustafson
Jacket illustration © 2022 by Beatriz Ramo
Jacket design by Krista Vossen © 2022 by Simon & Schuster, Inc.

SIMON & SCHUSTER BOOKS FOR YOUNG READERS
and related marks are trademarks of Simon & Schuster, Inc.
For information about special discounts for bulk purchases, please contact
Simon & Schuster Special Sales at 1-866-506-1949 or business@simonandschuster.com.
The Simon & Schuster Speakers Bureau can bring authors to your live event.
For more information or to book an event, contact the Simon & Schuster Speakers Bureau at
1-866-248-3049 or visit our website at www.simonspeakers.com.
Interior design by Hilary Zarycky
The text for this book was set in Adobe Caslon Pro.
Manufactured in the United States of America
First Edition
2 4 6 8 10 9 7 5 3 1
Library of Congress Cataloging-in-Publication Data
Names: Gustafson, Cassie, author.
Title: The secrets we keep / Cassie Gustafson.
Description: First edition. | New York : Simon & Schuster Books for Young Readers, [2022] |
Audience: Ages 14+. | Audience: Grades 10-12. | Summary: Told in flashbacks, dark fairytales,
and present-day prose, fourteen-year-old Emma, whose best friend has accused her father of
heinous crimes, must testify against her friend's word, and her carefully constructed "truths" about
what she may or may not have witnessed between father and friend start to crumble.
Identifiers: LCCN 2021052662 (print) | LCCN 2021052663 (ebook)
ISBN 9781665906944 (hardcover) | ISBN 9781665906968 (ebook)
Subjects: CYAC: Sexual abuse—Fiction. | Secrets—Fiction. | Best friends—Fiction. |
Friendship—Fiction. | LCGFT: Fiction.
Classification: LCC PZ7.1.G882 Se 2022 (print)
LCC PZ7.1.G882 (ebook) | DDC [Fic]--dc23
LC record available at https://lccn.loc.gov/2021052662
LC ebook record available at https://lccn.loc.gov/2021052663

For Mom, Megan, and Aunt Cathy—my childhood
superheroes—with endless love and appreciation.

And for the Emmas and Hannahs of this world. I see you.
I hear you. I believe you.

The

SECRETS
WE
KEEP

You remember the beginning

You remember your childhood as remarkably unremarkable.
Though you lived in a big city, you were educated at home by your
mother, so you'd grown up a bit sheltered and socially awkward.

Then, on the verge of adolescence, you remember the day a
scandal drove you and your family from San Francisco up to rural
Oregon and a town called Prosper. There, in the vastly different
landscape of small-town public school, you did not fit in with your
new classmates, possessing neither the right surname nor the code
to unlocking the secrets of local etiquette—or so your peers were
quick to inform you.

You remember how, for two long years, your only friendship
came in the form of the countless fairy tales you devoured, all
the while convincing yourself that you preferred the company of
bound books to that of your schoolmates anyway. Thus, your life
remained remarkably unremarkable . . .

Until several weeks into high school, when new girl Hannah
Garber—older, bolder, unapologetic—blew into your life.

You remember that, despite the twelve months and grade level
separating you two, your connection with Hannah was immediate
and fierce, outsiders united. At long last, you had a true friend
alongside whom to navigate all the beauty and cruelties of the

world, a kindred soul so entwined with your own, it was as if you had both spent the whole of your lives searching for each other.

You remember strolling the high school courtyard arm in arm like royalty, ignoring the pitiful murmurs that had once dragged you down, all while vowing to each other—through bonds of breath and blood—that your friendship would last forever.

Forever, you whisper-promised. *Forever.*

And you remember that, for much of that first year in each other's company, this was how it remained: twin souls cultivating a remarkably remarkable coexistence together, both of you unwavering in your certainty that nothing could tear you apart.

Until the day everything changed.

arrest

Friday

It's the white Nissan that does it, waiting at the high school's curb when I get out of class. Something's wrong. Sure, not finding Hannah at her locker where we had agreed to meet felt off too. But it's the white Nissan—Mom's old white Nissan, parked where Hannah's mom's charcoal-gray SUV should be—that twists my guts into an inky black snake.

I stand motionless in the middle of the patchy lawn, a group of upperclassmen whooping as they file past, their jackets pulled tight against the foggy chill. Everyone's eager to clear school grounds on this early-release Friday, like the teachers might change their minds and pull us all back into class. But my eyes see only Mom's Nissan and its embarrassing layer of dirt and pollen, idling where it shouldn't be.

As I near the car, I check over my shoulder for anyone watching—or Hannah, as if she would magically reappear after being called from our third-period geometry class and never returning despite promising me she would—but none of my schoolmates pay me any attention. I glance at my phone. No new messages, not even from Hannah.

Mom blares the horn and I flinch, nearly dropping the phone.

As I open the car's rear door, the snake in my belly coils tight, its bloodred eyes alert and dangerous. Something's most definitely wrong. I feel it hanging in the air, heavy and perfectly still. My brother, Kyle, peers at me from his booster seat, still in his Star Wars pajamas from this morning, his small face as white as a sheet. Kyle's much younger than I am, made more obvious now by his innocent eyes, the size of half-dollars, and the line of thick yellow snot trailing from his nose. In the rearview mirror, Mom's gaze reflects back at me, all puffiness and smeared mascara. Frozen tear streaks have cut pearl-colored tracks through her usually pristine beige foundation, and she's still in one of her work shirts—a ruffled, floral blouse. My insides thrum with heat, hand suspended on the door handle. I glance again behind me, but no one's looking. No one's coming.

"Get inside, Emma. Close the door," Mom snaps, her voice strained and hoarse.

But I remain frozen in the mist, a cold chill creeping under the collar of my fleece. "What's wrong?" I ask.

A pause that lasts forever.

"Your father's been arrested."

The words wrap around my throat and squeeze.

Is this real? Can it be?

"Don't ask questions," Mom adds.

But a question slips from me anyway. The wrong question. "What about the party?"

Today's the Friday before Easter, the annual Cats Club egg-dyeing event. It's tradition for our small community service group to dye boiled eggs after school, then meet again Easter Sunday morning to hide them for the town's big egg hunt. Of course, it's also just an excuse to throw a party. Named after our high school mascot, the Bearcats, Cats Club is mostly made up of uncool freshmen like myself who didn't have anything else to do when the school day ended, plus nerdy sophomores who couldn't find a better alternative to put on their résumé—or whose parents couldn't. Hannah's the obvious exception to that, of course. As an outgoing sophomore who couldn't care less about people's opinions of her, she could be popular if she wanted.

And then there's Justin, my crush since last year, a gorgeous guy in Hannah's grade whose mom helps run the group and who's drop-dead hilarious. My heart flip-flops at the thought of him—his smooth brown skin and tight dark curls. Truth be told, this afternoon is not just a party to me. Sure, the prospect of getting to spend a whole afternoon around Justin is always welcome, but also, and more important, I finally get to hang out with Hannah again, since she's been so busy lately. I've already packed a mini duffel of treats to share and planned what I'm going to wear.

What about the party?

My brain repeats my question, one I immediately regret saying aloud but can't swallow now.

"Honestly, Em," Mom splutters, "what's wrong with you?"

I absorb the question in the center of my chest. Bull's-eye. She's right, though. To just find out Dad's been arrested, then ask about a party? Linger over thoughts of Justin and Hannah? What *is* wrong with me?

Making as little noise as possible, I slide in next to Kyle and click my seat belt shut, choosing as usual to sit in the back next to him over taking the front seat. Kyle had stayed home sick from first grade today because of his cold, and Dad had stayed with him while Mom had gone to work. So did the cops come to the house, then? Had Kyle seen Dad get arrested? Who'd called Mom? I want to know all this and more, but I don't dare ask.

I eye Benny, the astronaut LEGO guy, gripped fiercely in my brother's small fist. I know I should talk to Kyle, comfort him, tell him stories until his fist relaxes and the color returns to each tiny finger, but the image of Mom's eyes, raw and undone, keeps me silent. Instead I stare out the window and cover Kyle's closed hand with mine, squeezing it to tell him everything's okay, even though it's clearly not.

As we pull away from the curb, my gaze snags on a figure outside—my homeroom and Honors English teacher, Ms. Saeed. She's standing in a swarm of students on the school lawn, almost exactly where I'd stood just a second before, the brilliant canary-yellow of her sweater contrasting like sunshine against her olive-brown complexion and raven hair. And yet, the last glance I'd had of Ms. Saeed before rushing out of class was of her settling behind her desk, ready to tackle several stacks of homework. So what's she doing out here now?

A breath later, I have my answer. The mass of students shifts, and a woman standing next to Ms. Saeed emerges into view. She's got a small top bun of mousy blond hair perched on her head, and her white face is flushed Froot-Loop pink in the cold. Drawing even more attention to her brilliant cheeks are the purple jacket and bright scarf she's wearing.

Beside this woman, Ms. Saeed's gaze scans the departing cars before locking her eyes on our passing Nissan, which she points out to this plum-jacket-wearing woman. Plum Jacket Woman follows Ms. Saeed's pointed finger before taking a single step toward our retreating vehicle. Inside, I duck a little, even though I don't know if either of them can see me through the car window. Still, I feel oddly exposed as this stranger rakes us with her stare.

Mom takes no notice, her glare fixed dead ahead, one foot pressed firmly against the accelerator.

This woman's looking for us—for me?—I'm pretty sure, but I don't risk pointing that out to Mom, afraid to stir her wrath but also because something about the woman's stare makes me not want to be found.

Still, who is she? What does she want?

Your father's been arrested.

Your father's been arrested.

It's the phrase my mind has latched on to this time—to torment me with all the way home like an evil curse until this inconceivable fact has properly sunk in. I must need this reality check, though, because as we turn onto Main Street, my mind starts attempting to conjure an absurd fairy tale in its place, one where we'd get to drive home with my mother's mascara still intact. And before she'd even fully park, I'd bail out of the car and race up to my room to grab my mini duffel. Then, by the time I'd return back outside, Hannah's mom's clean SUV would be freshly idling in the driveway, an impatient Hannah yelling out the passenger window for me to hurry my ass up even as I'd hop in, dragging my duffel behind me, before we'd zoom off to tonight's party.

The fairy tale dissipates as reality sets in once again: Dad's been arrested. I'm not going to any party.

I picture that duffel now, resting parallel to the wall of my immaculate bedroom, just where I left it: navy with wide purple flowers, the inside already stuffed with Chips Ahoy cookies (Justin's favorite), caramel squares (Hannah's), and Sour Patch Kids (mine), all of which I would've pretended I just had lying around. Resting at the bottom are old sheets the club parent leaders had asked us to bring to cover tables while egg-dyeing, and above that sits the best part of all—my carefully folded, brand-new, official concert T-shirt featuring Corey Starr, Hannah's and my favorite musical artist. On the graphic, still stiff and pristine, Corey stands in profile, holding a mic, head bent low as if in prayer, hair falling in dramatic slashes across his forehead. Across the back is every tour stop he's hitting on his upcoming REVOLT Tour, including Portland, which is so close to us I can taste it, even if we hadn't managed to get tickets for the show.

In spite of this, Hannah and I had still bought the shirts, specifically to wear together this afternoon, in an unspoken agreement that Justin would tease us for it, both for matching and for Corey Starr's boy-band face on the front. She'd picked them out and ordered them. I'd just needed to scrounge up enough cash for my part.

Hannah: my very best friend—my only real friend—ever since she moved here at the beginning of the school year. Dauntless and daring. My whole world.

Hannah: who was supposed to meet me at her locker after school, who never came back after third period, who's been strangely too busy to hang out, apart from at school, for *weeks*.

Hannah: the ghost haunting the stillness of this car and lurking in every shadow of my house.

Your father's been arrested.

Your father's been arrested.

As the scarlet-eyed snake settles, heavy and slimy in my belly, I realize suddenly that everything's changed, that somehow I maybe even feared today would come. Because I'm positive, without daring to ask, that Hannah's absence and Mom's presence—that Dad's arrest—go together like fingers intertwined.

You remember a good father

You remember, many years back, when you could hardly wait for your father to come home from work so he could play with you. And when that front door opened, you wouldn't even let him set his briefcase down before you leapt into his arms. You would boast to him that you'd learned to spell the word "tomorrow"— two *r*s but only one *m*—as you presented your latest masterpiece, a Technicolor rainbow butterfly you had created with Wikki Stix, cupped in proud, sweaty hands. Then you'd drag him out to the shared courtyard of the apartment complex in San Francisco where you lived back then, showing him the Robinson Crusoe fort you'd erected in the giant guava tree, complete with a blanket canopy and metal bucket hanging from twine to "carry supplies" up and down. You'd make him stand next to the tree, placing item after item into the bucket so you could demonstrate just how well your pulley system worked.

And when it got dark outside, after you'd been called in for a dinner of creamy tuna-fish casserole with peas and crunched-up potato chips on top, you remember feeling scared and not wanting to go get your blanket down from the tree, where you'd forgotten it. What if a monster got you? You still needed that blanket to fall asleep, even though your mother insisted you were far too old for such childishness. And even though Dad could have made you go get it yourself, he'd venture out into the unknowable night to retrieve it, every time.

You remember snuggling under the covers, breathing in the cold, foreign scent of your newly rescued blanket as your father settled next to you on your bed, a stack of books between you. And when you picked up Calvin and Hobbes, you would take turns reading the captions until it got to a Spaceman Spiff page. He would read those ones because they had such big words, and your father did the best alien and Spaceman Spiff impressions anyway.

And when you were through reading parts of every last book in the stack, he would rise from the bed, kiss the top of your head, and tell you how much he loved you. Then he would turn on your globe night-light, shut off the lamp, and close the door behind him, leaving behind only the impression his body had made on the comforter, still warm.

seized

The state of our house steals my breath. I take a shaky step in retreat onto the back porch before Mom pushes at my backpack, propelling me forward into the entryway. The screen door bangs into place behind us, pressing Kyle into Mom's legs as I stand transfixed, taking in the chaos.

Our house is never sparkling clean, even at the best of times. And on the rare weekend I do invite Hannah over, I usually spend hours beforehand washing dishes plastered with days-old food, wiping grime off countertops and dead horseflies from the windowsills, and sweeping clouds of dust bunnies from filthy corners. Luckily, though, we live far enough outside of town that Hannah coming over is often out of the question, so I rarely have to make excuses. In fact, it's a relief we almost always wind up at her house—or, at least, we used to, up until recent weeks.

I push away the panic slithering through me at the thought, the one that's been eating at me lately that I haven't allowed to take full shape till now. Hannah not meeting me after school like she said she would, disappearing from class and never coming back . . . This is not the first warning flag, just the biggest. It's tied to feeling that, in the last few weeks, Hannah's been pulling away—always having something going on outside of school so I can never go over to her house, but also not wanting to come to my house either.

I get why she wouldn't want to come here given how much nicer her place is in comparison, but even last week, when I grew desperate enough to ask her over because I wanted to make sure she and I were okay, Hannah had made every excuse in the book not to come, though she hadn't been able to look me in the eye as she did.

So maybe it's not my dirty house she's been trying to avoid.

Maybe it's me.

But this time, my house isn't just messy; it looks like it's been ransacked. To my left, kitchen drawers have been ripped free and placed in haphazard stacks on the floor, their contents tumbling down the sides. Cupboard doors hang open with boxed pasta and canned green beans scattered across the counter. To my right, the dining room table's been pushed off-center, chairs askew. And in front of me, the medicine cabinet outside the small bathroom has barfed tiny pill bottles and boxes of Band-Aids onto the floor.

I slip my hand into Kyle's, who's scooted in close.

"What happened?" I ask, and thankfully Mom's need to talk overrides her annoyance at being asked another question.

"Bad men," Kyle whispers, at the same time Mom answers, "Police search. Don't know what they think they were looking for." Her lips are thin, and I realize I haven't seen my mother this unmade since the last time she'd stayed in bed for over a week. That was a few months ago, when I'd only catch glimpses of her holed up in my parents' bedroom, her washed-out face and sad eyes trained on yet another episode of *Outlander* when she should've been at work.

Mom runs Shazam!'s makeup counter, at the local beauty supply store in the next town over, which means that showing up with a full face of makeup and selling it is quite literally her job, one she usually takes very seriously. But this last time—just like every other time when I'd start to get more worried and think she wouldn't get better—she had once again reemerged, all done up. I'd never felt so relieved to see that many shades of pink.

I realize I've been staring when Mom snaps, "Don't just stand there. Help clean this mess up."

"Do I have to?" Kyle asks, his large eyes staring up at me. I want to run and get him a tissue, but I'm strangely nervous to move, like this is a crime scene and I'll destroy evidence of a break-in. But of course, it's the police who made this disaster, so there's no one to call and report this to.

The sharp lines of Mom's face soften as she looks down at Kyle. "No, sweet. Why don't you go play with your LEGOs, and Em will bring you a snack in a bit, okay?"

Kyle releases my hand with a soft "Yeah, okay," then runs his sleeve across his nose, smearing the snot before shuffling away. Kyle never shuffles, usually hurtling himself around like a pinball, but the whole house feels stifled somehow, like having our possessions tossed in all directions has dampened everything.

Watching him retreat, I hear Kyle's "bad men" response echo in my head. So he was in the house when the police came.

"They must've just left," Mom's saying about the cops, one hand on her hip, the other pushing hair from her eyes. "God only knows what they took," and I recall the way she'd searched the driveway when we'd pulled in.

My insides warm. Who'd been through our house, then? Just

the police? More people? They must've seen how filthy it is. I hadn't known they were coming, hadn't cleaned anything . . .

It's an absurd thought, which registers immediately. The police tore apart our house and arrested my father. Our home's level of tidiness hardly matters. Still, I can't shake my lingering embarrassment.

Gesturing at my backpack, I mumble, "I'm gonna . . . ," then wait till Mom nods.

"Hurry up," she says.

As I make for my room, I pass through the dining area. The doors to the hutch stand open, the dishes shoved aside. Even the silverware drawer looks attacked, forks tumbling into the spoon section. The small bookshelf where the mail lives has been pushed away from the wall, exposing cobwebs and piles of dust that make my skin crawl. The metal doors of the wood stove also stand open, dusty ashes from inside now scattered across the dining room floor.

What were they looking for? I step around the ashes and right the candle in the center of the table before glancing through the doorway into Mom and Dad's room. I pause midstep. A blank space yawns where Mom's home computer usually sits. My heart, already weighed down by all the chaos, grows as heavy as my backpack. The police took it?

On the far corner of the dining table, I find my answer on a sheet of paper with the Prosper Police Department crest on top and a list below labeled *ITEMS SEIZED.*

The paper trembles as I scan the list:

—1 desktop computer (Dell), plus monitor, owner: family
—1 cell phone (iPhone), owner: Brian Clark

—1 laptop (HP), owner: Brian Clark
—1 tablet (iPad), owner: Stirling Community College; user:
  Brian Clark
—19 file folders, contents writing and paperwork of Brian Clark

So they'd also been in Dad's upstairs office and taken all his things.

Then, at the bottom of the page, the last item steals the warmth from my bones:

—1 diary, owner: daughter

Two thoughts rise in a bubble of dread: *Diary? What diary?* and *Did they not know my name or just couldn't remember it?* As if that's even the point.

Then the image of a journal flashes in my head, the one my aunt Jane gave me two birthdays ago.

Oh no.

"What's that?" Mom demands from behind me.

I jump, jamming the police form into the front pocket of my jeans where it turns into a spiky wad. "Nothing, just trash. Um, I'm gonna go put down my backpack."

She crosses her arms. "You said that already. So hurry up."

"Yeah, I did! Be right back!" My voice is too high, false-bright, but Mom doesn't comment.

My journal can't be gone. Still, I need to make sure.

Sprinting away, I pass the living room with two couches' worth of displaced cushions and an upended rug whose corner's been flipped in a loop. My fingers itch to fix the cushions, flatten the rug against the floorboards, but I fly past, the balled-up list in my pocket pressing with insistence against my thigh. I blow past Kyle's room, where, startled, he looks up from his LEGO pile, a spaceship and Benny frozen in his grip, but I'm already taking the stairs two at a time before hauling left and catapulting through my doorway.

I skid to a stop on the smooth, varnished floor that's unique to my room. Easing my backpack to the ground, I take in the space—the slanted ceiling where it hangs low over my bed, then rises at a steep pitch across the room; the furniture and floor—before finally locking eyes on the far wall where my Corey Starr concert poster hangs. Hannah gave it to me for my half-birthday in February, something she insisted we celebrate for each other since we both have August birthdays and she hadn't moved here till early September.

This room is my space. My safe space.

Someone's been in here, too.

If the open dresser drawers aren't evidence enough, my bedding gives it away, comforter loose and crumpled, though I'm absolutely certain I'd tucked those bedsheet corners in snug before scrambling to catch the bus this morning.

My bookshelf's been messed with as well, the books I'd so carefully alphabetized no longer in order, instead stuffed back in at random, now perpendicular to the still-shelved ones. The potted succulent Hannah had also brought to school for my half-birthday—that we'd named Hector and I'd carried with embarrassed pride from class to class all day—sits in a pile of spilled sand.

Yet, unlike downstairs, whoever was in here had tried, if in haste, to piece the plant back together, close dresser drawers, and remake my bed. I picture a cop bumping the small gold pot, then throwing out a Hail Mary hand and catching it right before it could explode across the floor. In the process, they'd sent loose sand flying in all directions, sand that's now scattered across the floorboards, piled deep in the cracks and overflowing in parts like small mounds of dusty Sahara. It's also covering the top of the bookshelf, finger marks raked through the half-swept sand. I try to scoop some of this sand back inside the pot, but most of it rains onto the floor. *Do succulents need their roots covered to survive?*

My bones hum with panic. It's so filthy in here. Everything is. Crap all over the place. It'll take *forever* to clean. Just my room, let alone the entire house!

At least Hector's safe, I tell myself, squeezing the gold pot to my chest so I don't start crying. My gaze drifts to my window past the scratchy tree to the muddy cow fields surrounding the house.

Swallowing my dread, I turn, nudging my backpack aside with my foot. My mini duffel's no longer parallel to the wall, zipper only halfway up. From across the room, I can tell by the lumps inside that it's also been rifled through, not carefully packed like how I'd done it when I'd placed each item inside one by one over the past week.

Setting Hector down, I crouch beside the duffel, running my fingers over the soft fabric of my Corey Starr concert T-shirt that's sticking out. I'd saved up over three months' allowance for this shirt so Hannah and I could match, and yesterday after school we'd done a small dance together over FaceTime, celebrating the small miracle of them arriving just in time for the egg-dyeing party. Last night I'd cut off its price tags and gently removed the poke-y plastic bit stuck in the fabric, setting the pieces in my otherwise empty trash can. Below the shirt, I hear the crinkle of the candy bags and cookie package, then Justin's gorgeous, smirking face appears in my mind. Guess they'll all have a great time tonight without me.

Will Hannah be there? Will they all know why I'm not coming?

Tears spring to my eyes as I drop the shirt and rise to face my rumpled bed, then my nightstand. Though the top drawer is mostly closed, a traitorous inch proves the drawer's been opened because I'd never leave it like that. Gaps creep me out, along with cracks or bizarre clusters of holes like honeycombs. On top of the nightstand, my lamp sits at an odd angle, the seam of the lampshade now facing out. My book, *Grimm Tales*—an illustrated collection of original Brothers Grimm fairy tales—is no longer parallel to the nightstand's edges like I'd left it.

Closing the distance, I rotate the lampshade and straighten the book, then pull open the drawer.

It's just as I feared. My mini book lamp, metal pencil tin with its rainbow of highlighters, pens, freshly sharpened pencils, and army of bookmarks all look disturbed, moved, touched.

I slam the drawer shut, moving on to the next one. It's the same. Though my stack of library books and tiny glass bowl full of paper clips and thumbtacks are still inside, it's all been touched.

Most important of all, my journal's gone, the one the police called a diary.

But it's just full of random fairy tales I wrote. *Nothing important,* I tell myself, even as my stomach churns with heat. And the pages I ripped out . . . *But they can't possibly know.*

Despite the fact that it's clearly gone, I dig through the nightstand anyway, then cross to the dresser, searching every disheveled drawer before returning to my bed, straining to lift the mattress to eye level and in the process almost whacking my head on the sloped ceiling. It's not there. My journal is gone. The police really did take it, then.

I think back, knowing the offending pages don't exist anymore, that there's nothing besides the gaping hole of torn paper, but maybe the police could somehow know what those pages had held, what I'd written, and that's why they'd taken the journal as evidence. Or—panic descends from the sky—maybe they'd somehow thought the fairy tales were true.

But they couldn't think that. Even so, I search back in my mind over the many months of writing out draft after draft of each fairy tale onto scratch paper, then carefully transcribing the perfect final copy into the journal, word by precious word, before tossing the latest rough draft in the trash as shredded confetti.

They're fairy tales, nothing real.

The panic's smothering me now, and I drop the mattress I'm still holding. Something clatters to the floor by my pillow, and only then do I remember what I'd hidden under there.

Oh my god.

Scooting the bed away from the wall, I'm for once not concerned about scraping my varnished floors as I dive behind the bed and grope around. At last, my hand closes around the plastic hilt, and I pull it free, examining the serrated blade of the small knife I keep under my pillow. They didn't find this. They wouldn't know. *How could I have explained?*

My vision darkens, and I fight to suck in air. The room spins— my beautiful, immaculate room with its glistening floors and neatly packed drawers, all torn up because the police were in here searching, taking computers and journals full of ridiculous fairy tales that weren't theirs to take.

And Hannah . . . ? Where'd she go today?

Hot tears squeeze from my eyes. She just disappeared and didn't return, so Mom came instead with her unmade eyes and Kyle gripping Benny too tightly. Now Dad's in jail and the inside of my house looks like a bomb went off.

I squeeze the knife as the tears come fast.

Hannah, where'd you go?

Pressing my eyes shut, I gulp in huge pockets of air, trying to steady my ragged breath and shove away the crowding thoughts, but they're coming so fast.

The doorbell rings, and my eyes fly open. It rings again, and I hear the distant crack of floorboards as Mom heads to answer it. I dash across the room and shove the knife deep into my duffel, then spread the Corey shirt back over the top for good measure. Dragging my fists across my eyes, I wipe them free of all traitorous tears. I take one more glance at the impossible mess surrounding me, then hurry for the stairs.

Because anyone coming over right now can't be good.

You remember life before Hannah

You **remember** **almost** **three** **years** **ago** **when** **you** **moved** **to** Prosper and became the new girl in a claustrophobically tiny junior high. Though you had no previous schools to compare it to, unlike the bustling sea of the city, here you were a small fish in an even smaller pond.

You remember that first day when several of your seventh-grade classmates surrounded you at lunch and rapid-fired questions at you—*Where are you from? What's San Francisco like? What street did you move to?*—but after that first day, their interest in you had evaporated like raindrops on a hot sidewalk, and they'd deemed you no one special. Back then you'd had such high hopes for junior high: to be surrounded by kind, like-minded peers who'd accept you, admire you, even. Yet the one person you hung out with was another outcast named Robyn, though she wasn't in any of your advanced classes and you had little in common.

But then you remember the day your only friend, brimming with excitement, told you her family was moving to Idaho. Her words pounded over you, heavy as a raging waterfall.

You remember the first lunch without Robyn, the sinking feeling in your gut when she wasn't waiting for you near the painted eagle mascot, and you remember thinking you would've done anything to see her face once more. Each lunch period, as everyone else claimed their picnic tables, you remember settling beside a spidery cinder-block wall and reading every fairy tale retelling you could get your hands on from the dusty library on Main Street.

But then you discovered the school library—a shared building between the junior high and high schools.

You remember the first time you wandered past the library door and saw kind, elderly Ms. Patterson sitting at her desk. And when she caught you staring, you remember how she had beckoned you inside, beaming her radiant smile at you. You remember how, from that moment on, the library became your lunchtime refuge, how Ms. P was always waiting an extra fifteen minutes to see if anyone—you—would wander in again. And since you always did, she'd stay at her desk with you and eat the food she'd packed instead of leaving for the teachers' lounge.

Then you remember when, at the beginning of freshman year, Ms. P was out sick for a week, and her substitute had locked up the library during lunch. You remember pulling hard on the door like a little kid, but it wouldn't budge, which made your chest squeeze with a tight pang of panic that felt like a heart attack.

You remember wandering back outside, the heavy weight of your bagged lunch and the school library book you'd wanted to exchange weighing you down, feeling pathetic for once again having no place to go. You were in high school now. The landscape of the school grounds had changed—different picnic tables—as had your rank as freshman, but really, nothing else had. Again, you wondered, had homeschool truly been so bad?

At last you remember sitting by a small crab-apple tree next to a trash can and trying to pretend like you didn't mind the smell of sunbaked garbage or the fact that everyone was staring—especially after you put your hand through a rotten crab apple and several girls from your advanced biology class had erupted in laughter.

You remember that week of school being torture without Ms. P, even though you knew that, as kind as she was, she didn't quite count as a friend—the whole week dragging by like a recurring nightmare . . .

Until that unassuming Thursday when she showed up: Hannah Garber, the newest new girl.

Your savior come at last.

stranger

The color purple is the first thing I notice about the person standing at our front door. It's Plum Jacket Woman from the schoolyard, I realize, the one who'd watched our car drive away. Here she is again with the same flushed cheeks, except now she's wearing a calculating expression as she peers at Mom like a barrier she'll need to puzzle her way around.

It's begun to rain. Dark spots mark the woman's coat, and her hair bun is beaded with droplets, but if the tension in Mom's shoulders is any indication, this woman won't have any luck entering our house today.

I should've known it was a stranger because only strangers come to our front door. It's made of solid oak and swells more with every rainstorm, which is almost constantly in our damp, foggy town, so the door's near impossible to open and close well. And given the overgrown grass and scraggly plants choking the brick stoop—not to mention the explosion of spiderwebs across every pane of glass lining either side of the entryway—it should be obvious that this isn't our main entrance.

I step off the last stair and, behind the cover of the front door, gently close the door to Kyle's room without looking in. This reappearing woman can only mean more trouble.

"Kathleen MacNamara." The woman emphasizes her name, as if repeating herself. "I'm a social worker here in Stirling County, and I'm here to speak with you and your children, Emma and Kyle?" Her gaze flits past Mom and around the door to where I stand, frozen.

A social worker here to talk to us. Definitely *not* good. My thumb runs over the front pocket of my jeans, feeling the bulge of the crumpled police form, which I only now realize I forgot to hide.

Kathleen's eyes haven't left me. "In fact," she continues, "I tried to catch you and Emma before school let out today, but I must've just missed you both." She smiles pleasantly, holding out what I realize is an ID badge, though Mom doesn't take it.

Mom's return smile looks strained, but maybe it's because I know what to look for. "Now's not a good time." Mom tries to close the door, but Kathleen stops it with a dainty-looking shoe before it can shut. Still, I'm shocked. I've never seen Mom shut the door in anyone's face before. Artificial smile or not, she's normally much better at performing in front of strangers.

Into the gap, Kathleen says, "I'm sorry to do this, Mrs. Clark, but I must insist. I have a court order signed by a judge, allowing me to enter your home and speak with you and your children. Now, if you would please let me in?" It's another one of her question-not-questions, which Mom must hear, because she releases her hold on the door with a tired sigh. Then Kathleen's inside our house, closing the door behind her, though it takes a few tries because of the swollen doorframe. When it's at last shut and we're all crammed together in the small entryway, I'm beyond regretful at having come down to investigate.

It begins to rain in earnest outside as Kathleen produces a

folded sheet of paper. She hands it to Mom, who frowns down at it while Kathleen takes in the living room mess. I notice how well her manicured nails match her jacket, how the scarf she's wearing looks like a falling-leaves speed-painting project, and how tightly her leather briefcase is tucked under one arm. She turns to me then, her face breaking into another warm smile, but I don't trust it. I don't want her here witnessing my house in this condition, let alone following me home from school like a spy and cornering us like this. What information is she trying to gather with her court order? More important, what information would she be willing to use against me, against my family? My instincts say: *everything*.

Be careful.

"Emma?" Kathleen asks, though she must already know it's me. I nod once while in my head I command, *Don't drop your guard for a second.*

Mom passes the paper back to Kathleen. "Well." Mom's tone has shifted to almost cordial, and I realize with relief that she's at last registered the severity of all this. "We can talk in here." Mom's gesturing to the living room disaster with a huff of a mirthless laugh. "If we can find somewhere to sit."

But Kathleen's already shaking her head. "I'm sorry, Mrs. Clark, but I must speak to the children individually. First Emma, then Kyle, then you. All right?"

Mom's expression hardens even as Kathleen adds, "It's all part of official protocol, I assure you."

Mom turns her dark gaze on me, but Kathleen speaks first. "Emma, let's talk in your room, if that's okay with you?"

The knife. A jolt of alarm zaps through me before I remember it's hidden. Kathleen can't possibly know where, let alone that it even exists. Then I feel the weight of the police form in my pocket. I need to get rid of that as well, just in case. *Give her nothing.*

I realize Kathleen's waiting for a response, so I jab a thumb behind me. "Um, sure. It's up here."

I know good manners would dictate climbing the stairs together, me a few steps ahead, but I don't have that luxury. Instead I turn, heart thundering, and race up the stairs two at a time. They're old and narrow and slippery as hell, so I know it'll take her a bit longer to make the journey, which should buy me a few extra seconds.

Bursting into my room, I shove the balled-up form into my duffel, then zip it all the way shut, squeezing the zipper with my fingers as it closes to minimize the sound. I drop the duffel just as Kathleen's head surfaces from the stairwell, face turned in my direction, hand sliding gingerly up the handrail. Her shiny shoes look even more delicate against our rough wooden floors as she clears the landing.

I wish I'd thought to close the other doors in the hallway as I watch her take in the surrounding rooms, a horrifying mess even before what the police did to them—the bathroom a heap of toiletries and towels, Dad's office with his laptop gone and his filing cabinet a wreck of drawers, and the guest bedroom with its unmade bed clearly visible.

I kick the duffel against the wall for good measure, then hover, feeling awkward. By now, Kathleen's replaced her observing face with her pleasant one as she nears my room.

Sand sticks to my shoes, the grit making me shudder, as I back up, letting her enter. "The police," I say, crossing my arms and hunching in on myself as we both look around. "It's not normally this dirty." I pray she notes that in her report.

Kathleen eyes the room, surprise lighting her face. The walls are bright lavender in here, unlike the dingy wallpaper everywhere else that's bubbled and torn from the foundation settling. And whereas the rest of the house has dull, splintered floors, mine are sanded smooth and glossy with varnish.

"May I?" Kathleen gestures to my rumpled bed. "May I sit down?" she clarifies.

"Oh. Uh, sure." I'm hovering again, wondering if I should close the door or sit next to her on the bed. Clearly Kathleen wants to talk in private, but I don't want to shut us in my room, and sitting beside her would feel far too intimate.

"Emma," Kathleen begins, settling onto my comforter while leaning forward because of the slanty ceiling. "Do you know why I'm here?"

I glance toward my duffel once, twice, before giving up and sitting cross-legged on the floor next to a small Sahara sandpile. "Because my dad got arrested?" Saying it aloud feels harsh and still so unreal. Turning away, I focus instead on my fingers plowing sand into the nearest floorboard crack even though it means I'll have to vacuum out every grain of it later, at least once. I also know I should be salvaging as much sand for Hector as I can, but I can't stop myself now that I've started.

"That's part of it, sure," Kathleen says, matter-of-fact. "I'm a social worker. Do you know what we do?"

"You . . . help people?" I say it because I know it's what she wants to hear. I'm rewarded with an earnest nod.

"That's right, and I'm here to help you. Your father's been

arrested, and because of the nature of the allegations against him, I need to ask you a few questions. Though some of these questions may be uncomfortable to answer, understand they're important and that I have to ask them. That there's a reason I'm asking them, Emma, okay?"

"And I have to answer your questions?" I blurt out, heat flooding my face. Why would I ask this woman that, with her court order and badge? Of course I have to. Besides, do I want her to file me as "uncooperative" like she may already do for Mom?

I glance up, expecting a frown, but her pleasant expression hasn't changed.

"Yes, legally you do have to answer," Kathleen says, "and I ask that you cooperate fully so I can help you, okay? I can only help if you let me."

I try not to notice her elbow on my nightstand that's pushing my book off-center, but my eyes fixate on it, even as she pulls a folder and pen from her briefcase, consulting some papers.

"Okay, Emma, let's start with your father. What's your relationship with him like?"

I swallow hard, stomach lurching.

"Uh, good," I say, sounding like Kyle, which is to say six years old.

She nods, encouraging, but I don't elaborate. "Could you expand on that, please?" she prompts. "How does your father treat you?"

"He treats us great," I say too loudly, too quickly. "He's a great guy, a great dad." Could I say "great" any more times?

She pauses, making some notes on her paper, seeming to wait for more. When I don't offer anything up, she asks, "And your mother?"

Pause. "Mom's . . . harder to warm up, but she cares about me. Me *and* Kyle. She's so good with him. Very loving." I only hope the answer doesn't sound forced, because it's true. Mom's a good mom. She tries.

More nods from Kathleen, and then she leans forward. "Emma, have either of your parents ever hurt you or Kyle? Verbally, physically?" Her eyes find mine on the last word, her expression unwavering, and I tear my gaze away.

Be careful, my brain repeats. *She's monitoring. Every. Word.*

But it's more than that. Kathleen looks like she already knows the answer. Or thinks she does, at least, which sends sparks of annoyed panic through my blood. Because how could she possibly?

In a sudden rush, I wonder if Hannah's talked to Kathleen too. If Hannah's told her anything, like about the splinter incident. Because it wasn't like that. Not like Hannah had made it out to be. My dad was just trying to take care of me—to be a good father— and he had, no matter what Hannah thought.

You remember splinters

You remember the summer before you started seventh grade, just after you moved to Prosper. You'd rushed barefoot up the stairs and skidded to a stop in your room, where a thick splinter the size of a toothpick pierced your big toe, driving in a full inch. Hot with shock, you dropped to the floor and stared in horror at the sliver of wood pushed deep under your skin, only just visible like a rigid worm.

You remember hobbling downstairs, calling out in desperation for your father since your mother and little brother had gone out. As you did, blood surged across the upturned pad of your foot and dripped down the side, marking a small trail behind you. Your father, meanwhile, had sprung from his room where he'd been napping and rushed into the dining room to meet you. There he held your foot, examining the wound as you sat in a chair and shivered from the blossoming pain.

You remember his words: *This is going to hurt*, and his forearm pressed tightly against your calf, pinning your foot against the table. All the while, you faced away, gritting your teeth and trying to balance like a clumsy flamingo. You remember him dipping an X-Acto knife in rubbing alcohol, and then, with the concentration of a true surgeon, slitting open the skin of your big toe along the length of the splinter. You remember his painstaking gentleness as he extracted the thick shard of pine from the cavernous cut, working to remove any remaining fragments.

Even though the extraction had hurt much more than you would ever admit, you remember the deep sense of gratitude you felt for your father, who had known just what to do: disinfect the wound, run a line of ointment across the gauze square, and press the large Band-Aid in a firm but gentle hand around your toe so that you hardly even flinched, following it all up with several lengths of medical tape.

You remember him helping you mount the stairs and slip your injured foot into a sock. Only after he'd done this did he survey your room and the offending floor with crossed arms and the proclamation: *This floor's not safe. We'll need to get you a rug.*

And even though, days later on YouTube, you found a more permanent solution with floor sanding, you remember how much his concern had meant to you. Because in his actions and his words, all you could hear was the promise behind them:

I am your father. I will always keep you safe.

accusations

Have either of your parents ever hurt you or Kyle? . . . Physically?"

I shake my head fast at Kathleen's question, even as the memory flashes through my mind—of Hannah's face twisting in horror when I told her about Dad removing the splinter on his own. Up to that point I'd been proud of his response, but her expression had wilted the boast right off my face. *Why didn't he bring you to the doctor?* she'd asked, horrified.

Sure, a doctor's office—bright, clean, and full of numbing creams—would have been preferable, but it wasn't a visit we could easily afford. Besides, Dad had taken care of it, and wasn't that all that really mattered? And yet, if even Hannah hadn't understood that he was just doing his best, how am I supposed to make Kathleen, an adult stranger, see that now? What chance do I have to convince her that he's a sound father, that he's innocent, *especially* with the possibility that Hannah may have already convinced Kathleen that he's not? Can't any story—any memory—be twisted to make the person in that memory look bad?

"No, Mom and Dad have never hurt us," I say in a steady voice, hoping to erase any doubt and trying like hell to squash the irritation-edged fear in my voice. "Verbally *or* physically."

Kathleen nods, writing something down, then directs her next question to her papers. "Do you understand the nature of the crimes your father has been accused of, Emma?"

I almost nod, but then I realize no one's actually told me anything definitive, only what I've sort of pieced together myself. I think of Mom's bloodshot eyes in the rearview mirror. "Not really. Mom's been too upset to talk about it."

"That's understandable." Kathleen leans forward. "Well, Emma, your father's been accused of being 'inappropriate' with a minor, touching them in a sexual and criminal way. Were you aware of this?"

I still, insides thrumming with heat, then shake my head hard.

She scribbles something. "Okay. Has your father ever been inappropriate with you, Emma?"

"No. Never inappropriate," I say, feeling suddenly dizzy from all this head shaking.

"Are you sure, Emma? This is very important. Do you understand how important this is?"

"Yes," I say, firm. "I understand. And I'm sure. Very, very sure."

Kathleen nods again, but it's a disbelieving sort of nod, and in a flash I hate her. Why ask all these questions if she's not even going to believe me when I answer her?

"Okay," she continues, oblivious to my inner outburst. "Have you ever witnessed your father behaving inappropriately with anyone else? Acting in a way he shouldn't?"

For the first time since Mom told me he'd been arrested, I imagine Dad sitting in jail and wonder if he's sad, if he's wearing an orange jumpsuit or his regular clothes. The image overwhelms me. "No," I choke out, just above a whisper. "Never."

Kathleen pauses the length of a mile, and I know I'm not doing enough to persuade her. But, at last, she moves on to her next question, asking if I've ever felt scared or nervous around my parents.

I tell her no, that I never have, that they're amazing parents, very caring. "She's just really stressed," I say regarding Mom, and for some idiotic reason I almost tear up. All I want is for Kathleen to know that Mom's not a bad mom, that even though our house isn't sparkling clean, Mom tries. She does. "She yells sometimes," I add, because no parent is perfect. Because whose parent doesn't have a temper that occasionally trips over itself and rages out of control? "But not all the time," I insist, hoping I haven't gone too far.

A sudden fear strikes me. Is Kathleen here to take Kyle and me away?

I hesitate, trying to figure out how to shape this into a manageable question. "What's going to happen to my dad?" I blurt out instead, a fear that's been hammering my brain all afternoon, but one I knew better than to ask Mom.

Kathleen takes her time answering, readjusting her scarf, her hair bun dangerously close to the slanted ceiling. "Well, right now he's going through the booking process at the county jail. He'll be fingerprinted and photographed, and presumably meet with a lawyer. Then he may be released on bail and, in that case, get to come home, most likely tonight. That's why I'm here. To make sure it's okay that he comes home, though of course he wouldn't be allowed to enter either your room or Kyle's, and he couldn't be left alone with either of you, along with some other rules."

I try to process this information and the fact that my father can't come into his own kids' rooms, even though he's in charge. Can they really do that? Command him out of whole sections of his own house, let alone enforce it?

"What other rules?" I ask.

Kathleen tap-taps her pen. "Well, he wouldn't be able to use the internet or be within a thousand yards of schools, or playgrounds, or anywhere else minors congregate. And no friends are allowed to come over here, okay? Nor anyone else under the age of eighteen. At least for now."

No Hannah. Like my dad's a monster who lunges at teen girls.

No Hannah. Like he can't be trusted.

No Hannah.

"And you're not allowed to talk to Hannah about the case," Kathleen adds. "If it has anything to do with your father, or the case, or how she's involved, it is not to be discussed. Okay, Emma?"

My heart almost stopped at the "not allowed to talk to Hannah" part, so the rest seems like a small sacrifice. That is, until the "how she's involved" part finally registers. So Hannah *is* involved somehow. Part of me already knew that, knew that something had to break. Still, the weight of this confirmation sinks my gut like a stone.

But why did Kathleen mention Hannah specifically? What, exactly, does Kathleen know, or think she does?

Kathleen's waiting for me to acknowledge that I understand her rules, so I give her a tight nod. Then, because this always, *always* happens when I'm overwhelmed, I feel the tears resurface. I force out the brittle words that've been caught in my throat. "You're not . . . going to take us away, are you? Kyle and me?"

Kathleen's expression shifts from pleasant to unreadable as she straightens. I hold my breath as her top bun brushes the ceiling. "That's never our goal, Emma, but it happens sometimes if it's in the best interest of the children—or young adults, like yourself," she adds, like including my age bracket will somehow make me feel better, "if those minors would be better off elsewhere."

"But we wouldn't," I blurt out. "Be 'better off elsewhere,' I mean." My chest floods with heat. How can I make her see? "He's innocent, my dad. He didn't do it. Whatever they say he's done."

"Okay, Emma." She leans forward again, elbows tucked between her knees, peering down at me like I'm a little kid. "I didn't mean to upset you. I'm only here to collect the truth. To make sure you and your brother are both well cared for. That's all."

I hate her so much, repeating my name like she knows me, pretending she cares, like she's here for my well-being even as she tries to find reasons to take Kyle and me away from Mom and Dad. From a sudden and terrible place deep inside me, I picture her sitting up fast and smacking her head on the ceiling, and it makes me viciously glad.

"Kyle is," I rush on. "Well cared for. We both are. Nothing's wrong. We're fine here. Our parents are great. More than great." I keep repeating myself but can't seem to stop.

Kathleen smiles again, but this newest version has lost some warmth. She doesn't believe me, isn't convinced, thinks our family's messed up, I can tell. But if Kyle and I were taken away, then where would we go? What would we do? How could I protect Kyle?

Kathleen can't be trusted.

She roots around in her briefcase and pulls out a small card, rising as she hands it to me, ducking around the sloped ceiling just in time. "Emma, thank you for answering my questions. Here's my information if you need to get ahold of me for anything."

I rise to my feet and take the business card, dusting sand from my jeans as I stare down at the glossy text: *Kathleen MacNamara,*

Social Worker, Stirling County, and below, a phone number with an extension. "Thanks," I whisper, but I don't really mean it. I want her gone already.

Her hand finds my shoulder, and it's all I can do not to flinch away. "Call me anytime, Emma, even just to talk." She holds my gaze for a beat too long, then adds, "I'll see you soon." I try to puzzle out these last words as she gives me her fortieth smile of the day, its full warmth restored. Then she gestures to the door. "Now, would you mind showing me to Kyle's room?"

I shove down my anger, my confusion, and lead the way out. But in the hallway, I pivot back around. "Can I stay with Kyle while you talk to him?"

"I'm sorry, but that's not allowed." To her credit, Kathleen does look sorry, though it doesn't make me like her any more.

Still, I nod and turn for the stairs, then spin back around, our faces too close now. I duck away. "He's really shy. He may not want to talk to you."

"That's okay. I have a lot of experience with shy kiddos."

But she doesn't know Kyle like I do. No one does. I keep my voice low as I lead her down the stairs. "He's just . . . extra sensitive. And scared."

"Thanks for the heads-up," she replies. "I'll keep that in mind. Remember, I'm here to make sure everyone's safe."

I keep him safe! I scream in my head, then shove open Kyle's door. He looks up, startled, from where he lies on his stomach propped up on his elbows, like he's been caught red-handed even though he's only playing space LEGOs, with a few pirates mixed in now.

"Kyle?" I say. "This nice woman wants to ask you some questions, okay?"

He looks between us. "Why?"

"So that Dad can come home," I say, hoping it's not a lie. "So be good and answer her questions, and I'll be right outside, okay?"

He eyes Kathleen with suspicion, face pinched in a frown. "Do I have to?"

"Yes, but I'll be right outside when you're done. Then I'll help you put together that vampire castle you've been wanting to build!" I add in a rush, wishing it can be true while also knowing I have to help Mom clean the house.

I leave before he can protest, feeling horrible as I half close the door, wanting to stay and listen to their conversation but forcing myself into the living room instead. Mom's there, righting the metronome on top of the piano, both of which we got as hand-me-downs from a great-aunt, before replacing the sheet music above the piano keys. Why would the police bother with books of sheet music? What could anyone possibly hide in there?

Mom's eyes snap to me, then down to my hand, and I realize, too late, that I'm still holding Kathleen's business card. Mom snatches it away, peering close. "What did she ask you?" she demands in a whisper. "What did you say?"

"Nothing." I follow behind her as she storms to the kitchen and tosses Kathleen's card into the trash. "Nothing," I say again, but she won't look at me.

In silence, I follow her back into the living room, kicking the corner of the rug into place and stomping on the resulting hump till it lies flat. I want so badly to go upstairs to my room. My fingers itch to sweep away the sand on the floor, vacuum all the cracks, and straighten up the rest—starting with the book on my nightstand that Kathleen's elbow just knocked askew—till my room is perfect like when I left it, but I know Mom would throw a fit. She'd call me selfish for starting there when the rest of the house is such a disaster, and she'd be right. Besides, I need to be down here for Kyle, to check on him whenever Kathleen's done.

Still, I feel the mess of it all—upstairs, downstairs—pressing on me like a lead jacket.

Halfway through reorganizing the old records, I hear the creak of Kyle's door. Skirting around Kathleen, I hurry into his room and see him frowning down at his LEGOs in a way that makes me both furious and heartbroken.

Kathleen's heading toward Mom, so I drop to the floor beside Kyle and pick up a random pirate, intoning my best pirate-y voice. "Arr! I'm a space pirate!" I wave the piece at his spaceship, but Kyle's frown only deepens.

"And I'm on the attaaaack!" I continue.

His face turns up to mine, confused. "But you don't have any weapons."

"I don't need no stinkin' weapons!" I blunder on. "I haves . . . pirate toots! And I'll blast yeh into the next galaxy with 'em, matey!"

I know it's beyond immature, but I also know it'll make Kyle laugh, and it works. His grave expression falls away, replaced by a trying-not-to-laugh twist of his mouth.

I've never been so thankful for childish fart jokes as we play on, waiting for the plum-wearing, pleasant-smiling, question-not-question-asking Kathleen to be done with us and leave us in peace.

You remember meeting Hannah, becoming friends

You remember a month or so into your freshman year when you met Hannah Garber for the first time at lunch—a girl with big opinions and even bigger boobs. You remember she looked eighteen, not fourteen like you, with your nonexistent boobs, though you later found out she was just one year older than you. You'd seen her in your geometry and Honors English classes already—classes you'd tested into despite your freshman ranking—but of course you hadn't talked to her.

And even though Hannah didn't have the right surname either, you remember the confident way she moved, proving Hannah Garber didn't give a damn about surnames. Hannah also didn't bother to act intimidated, so none of the guys thought to intimidate her. And when several freshman girls tried to tease Hannah about her strawberry-blond ringlets at lunch—despite Hannah's superior sophomore ranking—you remember Hannah giving them the sharpest, most unimpressed stare, and that it was they who grew uncomfortable and looked away first.

You remember observing this last interaction from the base of your tree and over the top of your novel, a gorgeous *Beauty and the Beast* retelling that Ms. Patterson had found for you and which you'd already read twice. But when Hannah threw a glance in your direction, you ducked behind its pages, as if it were a shield.

You remember Hannah calling out, "Hey, bookworm!" from her bench a few feet away, though you didn't respond, uncertain how to safely distinguish an enthused greeting from the beginnings of an insult. Then you felt something hit your foot and glanced down to investigate before it dawned on you that the looking itself gave you away. But you could not un-look at the plastic bottle of orange Crush soda that had just rolled against your shoe from new girl Hannah Garber's direction.

And you remember Hannah's impish grin and warning—"Careful when you open it"—as she rose from the bench and walked toward your tree. "It might explode."

You remember reaching down with a shy smile and picking up the bottle, then twisting it open too fast. An orange geyser of soda burst forth, and with it, laughter from two newfound friends.

You remember that before Hannah Garber, your clothes, music preferences, book choices, and any and all words that fell from your mouth felt unacceptable. You felt unacceptable . . . until Hannah crash-landed into your life, gave you a place to belong, was the best thing to ever happen to you. So proud were you to have her as your best friend, despite how different you were— short and petite to Hannah's tall and curvy. And though you both had the same milky white complexion, yours was as plain as unflavored yogurt while hers held an enviable spatter of freckles and the ability to tan without scorching. Whereas you had learned to live inside a turtle's shell, Hannah seemed to have no shell at all, and you remember her explaining once how to act indifferent, like her: *Pretend they're all cockroaches, and picture yourself squashing them into the dirt when they're mean. They'll read it on your face.*

You remember Hannah talking you into joining Cats Club with her, though it was less of a request and more a mere mention that she was considering it. To this, you promptly echoed that you'd been considering it as well, even though of course you hadn't been, and even though the idea of a social club made your stomach churn; you knew that Hannah was worth it and would make it bearable—possibly fun—by leading the charge.

And so together you joined, wearing your matching blue sweatshirts to school with pride, your first names embroidered on the front, daring someone to make fun of you. And you remember during that first sweatshirt-wearing lunch when Brooke, from Hannah's grade, had dared. But she'd hardly uttered a word before Hannah had yelled, *What's that, Brooke? I can't quite . . . hear you!* all while cranking her phone's music ever louder, drowning out Brooke and making her look the fool. You remember laughing so hard, your side hurt for the rest of the afternoon.

You remember most how, after school each day, you and Hannah would walk together to the corner store in town and empty your pockets of crumpled dollars and loose change in exchange for your favorite treats—hers, chocolate or caramel; yours, sour and gummy. And despite her contributing more money every time, she'd always insist on splitting the loot exactly in half. Then the two of you would walk to Hannah's house, cackling with laughter from inside jokes while your lips smacked over Milk Duds and sour gummy bears, for the world was your queendom and you two its queen bees.

Except, you also remember never wanting to have Hannah over to your house because you were afraid of what she'd think about the shabbiness, the mess. But then one day she did come over, and she didn't even seem to mind the state of your home, which made you love her all the more fiercely.

But it was shortly after this when you realized it wasn't the shabbiness or the mess inside your house that you had needed to fear all along.

caught

The sun's almost set as I sit on the living room rug beside Kyle, my back against our gray couch. Next to me, Kyle pieces together the vampire LEGO creation I promised I'd help him build—yet another kit, since LEGOs seem to be the one thing Mom never balks at spending money on. It's getting harder to see the pieces, though, and I know I should turn on a lamp, but I can't summon the energy. My mind's stuck on Mom, who just received a phone call, then disappeared into her room before I could properly eavesdrop. I only heard enough to know it's Aunt Jane calling, Dad's older sister who lives in the next town over, but not much else. And even though today's been an exhausting, never-ending unearthing of horrible things, somehow all the not-knowing, the hushed conversations behind closed doors that I can't manage to listen in on, seem equally terrifying.

It had taken most of the afternoon after Kathleen left to shove our things back into cupboards and drawers, righting furniture and cleaning up seemingly endless mini disasters. I still have homework to finish if I'm going to stay ahead of it this weekend, not to mention cracks in my floor I need to vacuum again and books I need to double-check that I re-alphabetized correctly. Then I can hide in my room in peace and be alone with my thoughts. But I told Kyle I'd play LEGOs, and the tiny pieces always get caught between my floorboards, so we can't do it up there. Instead, we sit here, me pretending to construct the spired roof of a haunted castle. I stare down at the six plastic figures—two blocky monster fighters, a lord and lady vampire, and two brown bats. They stand in a perfect line off to one side, not quite holding hands.

Why hasn't Hannah texted me back?

My gaze drifts to the green couch across the way, its cushions now shoved back into place.

A few hours ago, as soon as I'd been able to get away on the pretense of straightening up the upstairs, I'd run to my room, carefully closed the door, and texted her.

Hannah Banana! All good?

What I really meant was *Are we good?* but how do you say that in a text? And of course we're all right. Best friendships can't just evaporate.

But Hannah did today, my brain reminded me. *Evaporated into thin air.*

So I'd sent a second text—

Can't make the Cats party today. SO BUMMED. You there now?

—which also went unanswered. It was like my fingers wouldn't let me type what my brain was screaming: *Where did you go earlier? Why didn't you come back like you said you would? The things they're saying about Dad . . . What exactly did you say to them all?*

Now twirling my phone on the living room floor, I will it to ping to life with a text from Hannah—any text. Around and around a knot in the wood it goes, just past the rug's fringe, as I try to tune back in, straining again to catch Mom's hushed phone conversation happening in her bedroom while also following along with Kyle's quiet but intense chatter about his LEGO construction. But it's no use; I can't catch a single word from Mom.

Cats Club is probably painting eggs at this very minute, in full party mode without me. I should be there right now with Hannah, both of us trying to find reasons to talk to Justin, not here at home waiting on a text from her, trying to eke info from the next room, stuck in all this not-knowing.

The thought hits me like a slap: Does Hannah even have her phone, or did the police take that as well? Maybe they're waiting to see if I'll text her and say something incriminating.

As my gaze flicks to the green couch again, its cushions sagging in the center, my phone slips from my fingertips and skitters away, stopping to rest against a corner of the rug that's starting to unravel. I grab for the phone and imagine taking a pair of scissors to the rug, snipping the offending threads and pulling them free. It's then that I notice the mint green Tic Tac resting in the crack between the floorboards. Dad's mint green Tic Tac.

Mom emerges from her room and wanders back into the dining room, past the doorway, her voice loud enough to hear at last. "I know, Jane. I know. It's absurd, the whole . . . Oh crap. I think it's the bail bonds guy calling. Let me call you back. Yes, yes. I will. Bye."

Dad always carries a pack of Tic Tacs in his pocket, which shake like a maraca when he walks. Does he have them with him in jail right now?

"Hello? Yes, this is she." A breath-holding pause. "But I've sent the payment in twice already."

No, they take your possessions from you. I saw that on an

episode of *To Catch a Criminal*. Dad's Tic Tacs are probably in a sealed bag somewhere, along with his tattered wristwatch and favorite fountain pen.

"Yes, twice," Mom repeats. "If it hasn't gone through yet, then . . . Oh, you got it. Well, that would've been nice to know."

Mint green. That's what kind it is. I can almost feel it rolling around my mouth, feel the burn of cool spice on the tip of my tongue.

"Okay then. So how does this work? When will he get released? I don't exactly . . . Well, it's not like I've done this before."

I could use a LEGO piece, maybe, to lever it out of the crack. A long, skinny piece. The Tic Tac would go in the garbage, of course, not my mouth, along with the strands I'd snip from the rug.

"Wait, tonight? That soon? I thought it would . . ."

"It's not supposed to go that way," Kyle's voice breaks in.

"What?" I ask. My mind's still caught between its two halves—the half that stretched itself across the worn floorboards and into the next room to rest beside Mom, and the half here, stuck on a Tic Tac and an unraveling rug. A second flicks by, then another, as my thoughts rejoin like elastic. Kyle comes into focus. He's fixated on my hand, a frown souring his small face, freckles on full display. To my surprise, I'm holding the perfect LEGO levering piece—a thin black spire that's attached itself sideways to the castle roof and nowhere near the Tic Tac.

"It's not supposed to go that way," Kyle repeats. "You're doing it wrong."

"Then how's it supposed to go?" I snap, unable to squash the irritation from my voice. I hate the thought of upsetting him, but I need him to be quiet long enough for my mind to slip back into the next room so I can overhear more of Mom's conversation and know what the hell is going on. Then I can snip off those loose threads from the rug, pry the mint green Tic Tac free, and throw it in the garbage. But it's too late. Mom's already disappeared back into her bedroom.

Kyle sighs like an old man to let me know he's exasperated with me. His small fingers pluck the spire off and place it on top. "Like this, see? It lines up with the others."

"Whatever," I mouth, even though I know it'll hurt Kyle's feelings. LEGOs are not—could never be—*whatever* to Kyle.

"Sorry, I gotta pee," I say, climbing to my feet. "Be right back." I'm too antsy to sit still anymore. But more than that, I'm nervous about the decision I've just made. If Hannah won't text me back, then I'm going to call her. Right now.

I slip into Kyle's room because it's nearest, pushing the door most of the way closed. And finally, finally, I allow my brain to loop fully back to where it's been trying to go all day: to Hannah this morning, sitting beside me in geometry, doodling flowers onto the corner of her homework. Suddenly Patty, the office lady with a helmet of hair-sprayed hair, had buzzed into our classroom, interrupting Mr. Barnham, who was writing practice quiz questions on the whiteboard. Patty had called out Hannah's name and announced, with lots of *I'm sorry to interrupt*s, that Hannah was needed in the front office and should take her stuff with her. She wasn't coming back to class.

Hannah had turned to me then, unworried, smiling big, and whispered in her overly dramatic way, *Ugh, must've forgotten a dentist appointment or some such crap. But fear not! Mom and I will be back by 2:15 sharp to snap you up. Miss you, love you, bye!* before triple-tapping her pouty lips in a three-blow kiss sent in my direction.

She'd swung her bag plastered with GRRL PWR and Corey Starr buttons over her shoulder, and then she was gone.

I'd believed her when she'd said she'd be back, that we'd go to Cats Club together. She'd seemed extra happy this morning, exuberant, even. So, had I missed something? Because, thinking back, I keep returning to the look on Hannah's face as she'd bounced out the door. She'd looked almost . . . relieved. Like she'd known something was going to happen and was glad not to have to witness it. But that couldn't be right, could it? If Hannah had known *beforehand* that this was coming, wouldn't she have at least tried to warn me—that, maybe even in that exact moment, they were getting ready to pull my dad from our house and arrest him?

Would it make it any better if she hadn't known ahead of time? Would it make it worse if she had?

Don't best friends tell each other everything, even the horrible things?

But my brain halts there, erecting a brick wall in front of that question so fast. Because of course that's not true.

This I know, and yet I can't stop thinking about how, for the rest of the school day today, I'd continued to go through the motions like everything was normal, not knowing they weren't. I'd even stopped by Ms. Saeed's desk before my last class with a stack of library books I'd just read, Post-its marking every page I'd happened to find a vocab word on. I'd gotten twelve extra credit points, and Ms. Saeed had laughed, saying she'd have to cut me off on the extra credit soon. Yet all the while . . .

Hannah's face. Knowing. Relieved.

If she did know, she most definitely owed me a warning.

Hypocrite, my brain snarls from behind the brick wall.

Shut up! I hiss back. *Shut up!*

Forget Kathleen's rules. I've already decided I need to hear from Hannah's own lips exactly how the police got involved, and just how "involved" Hannah was, what all she knew. And above even that, I have to make sure she and I are okay.

After another glance at Kyle's mostly closed door, I click on Hannah's contact and wait. One ring, two . . .

"Em?" she answers in a whisper, and my pulse leaps.

"Hannah." The name drops from my mouth like a prayer I didn't know I'd been reciting all day.

"Hey . . . ," she says, sounding quiet, almost shy, which is immediately off because Hannah is never quiet, nor shy, around me or anyone else. Of course, it kind of makes sense right now, but still. I hoped it could be different with us in that nothing would be different. But that, of course, is an impossibility after today's events. If anything, I should be mad at her.

Still, I try to fill my reply with as much reassurance as I can. "Hey back."

"Sorry . . . ," she begins again. "About today, I mean. The not-coming-back part? I thought I would, but then my—"

Kyle's door bursts open, and I jump, the phone slipping from my hand. It falls, crashing into a bin of LEGOs and landing faceup.

Mom's standing in the doorway, a hand planted on her hip, her face remade with creamy foundation and penciled-in eyebrows, dark mascara and soft rouge. We both stare down at my phone, where Hannah's contact photo—one of her cross-eyed, tongue sticking out of her purple-lipsticked mouth—blazes up from the screen. Below, the thirteen . . . fourteen . . . fifteen seconds of our call time tick away.

The look on Mom's face cuts off any possible explanation I'd been trying to invent in my head.

"Hello? Em?" a tinny, distant Hannah says, even as Mom swoops to retrieve the phone.

"What were you *thinking*, calling her? What would your father say?" Mom snaps, punching the end-call button.

I stare at the floor, ashamed, because no one even had to tell me. Not Mom. Not Kathleen. Hannah's the reason Dad got arrested, and here I am hiding in my little brother's room, calling her.

"Get out," Mom snaps. "I have to go pick up your father, and no, you can't come. You need to stay here and watch Kyle like you were supposed to be doing right now."

I flinch at her words even as relief flutters through me. I didn't really want to go with her to pick up Dad, though that probably makes me a horrible person since I'm sure he could use some friendly faces right now.

Trailing behind Mom, I stare at my phone squeezed in her grip.

Hannah hadn't sounded upset on the phone. She'd apologized and had even been trying to explain this morning. I tell myself it's a good sign.

"Think you can manage to take care of your brother and not burn the house down? Or do anything else reckless?" Mom demands. "Here, I'll make it easier on you." She shoves my phone into her purse.

Kyle's paused on the living room floor, small shoulders hunched like they always get when Mom raises her voice. His gaze is fixed

on the LEGO vampire he's just snatched up—a snarling, wicked thing—even as an endless stream of snot runs from his nose.

I nod once to Mom's question. Then I grab a tissue for Kyle and plop back down beside him on the fraying rug, just an arm's length from the mint green Tic Tac still nestled between the floorboards, begging to be tossed in the trash.

As gravel crunches outside in the driveway and Mom's Nissan pulls away, I realize I'd do anything to be anywhere that isn't here.

You remember summers with Aunt Jane

You remember the small cabin Aunt Jane would rent on the coast of northern Oregon every summer of your childhood, inviting you along for several blissful weeks in June. The tradition started the year you turned seven, when Aunt Jane first made the long road trip down to collect you, a road trip that continued—albeit shortening—after your move to Prosper. And each time you'd first step foot inside, you would revel in the fact that the cabin's interior always smelled the same—of cedar and seaweed, salty ocean breeze and suspended tranquility.

You remember Aunt Jane nicknaming you her "Mini-Me," which, over the years, morphed into "M&M's." You remember her taking you on long beach walks to hunt for agate rocks, clear and as hard as amber; or tiny, pearlescent periwinkle shells; or glimmering shards of beach glass and pottery, but only the well-tumbled pieces. These treasures you and your aunt would scoop into old peanut butter jars to set side by side in the large bay window where they'd reflect the midday sun.

You remember the fresh bread she'd bake several times a week, the heavenly aroma of which you'd wake to in the early morning hours before being gifted a thick slice from the middle of the still-warm loaf that you'd drown in melted butter and sticky honey. This

you'd gobble down, then beg for more like a chirping baby chick. You remember the empty yogurt containers you'd use to collect blackberries from the brambles that grew in the ditch down the length of the winding drive, berries your aunt would help you transform into bubbling, doughy cobblers you'd eat by the bowlful for dessert one night and breakfast the next.

You remember the faded, water-stained maps of nearby harbors tacked to the wall, the homemade wind chime in one corner comprised of clattering clamshells and woven grass reeds, the mason jars repurposed as water glasses resting on the sill above the sink with a line of masking tape and a name to identify its owner. You remember the sand sprinkled throughout the cabin that would stick to your feet no matter how many times you swept it back out the door. You remember the many mugs of hot tea and card games of gin rummy your aunt Jane and her "Mini-Me" would play well into the night. But mostly you remember sinking into your bunk by the dreaming window, watching the scattered stars twinkle above you as your aunt relayed adventure after adventure from her past, your father's, their childhood together, before you'd drift off to sleep, full of food, warmth, and a profound sense of safety.

You remember how important that cabin became to you, especially in recent years—a sanctuary, a respite. An escape. In fact, the only summer you'd ever even considered declining your aunt's invitation to go was this coming summer because you couldn't imagine spending even a few days away from Hannah, the girl who had breathed fire into your life, even if it meant the end of sandy walks by day, of stargazing by night. That thought alone could bring tears to your eyes . . .

If you let it.

favor

It's pitch-dark by the time Mom gets home with Dad.

Kyle and I are up way past his bedtime. I'd felt too stir-crazy to read a chapter from his beloved LEGO Ninjago books, so instead we're watching his favorite show, *Dragons: Rescue Riders*, in the living room when we hear tires crunch gravel in the driveway. Pausing the show, we rush into the back entryway to meet them. The rear gate swings open, and Mom's and Dad's silhouettes appear, their footsteps creaking on the porch. Kyle bounces on his toes, impatient, till the back door cracks open at last, and Dad slips through with Mom trailing in his wake, pressing the door shut behind them.

A rush of cold air hits me as I blink at Dad, a paused grin on my face, trying to make sense of his appearance. Dad's complexion is drawn and ashy-white, his hair standing up in random spots like he's raked it with his hands all day, something he always does when his mind's overly full. This part I understand. It's what he's wearing—his faded flannel pajamas and wool-lined leather slippers from several Father's Days ago—that throws me off. Then it dawns on me: it must be what he was in when they came to arrest him today. As an administrative assistant at Stirling Community College, Dad usually works from

home in the mornings, lingering over his coffee and responding to work emails in his pj's on his college-issued iPad. It's my job to make sure Kyle and I catch the bus since Mom's almost always at the store well before that, except for today, when Kyle stayed home sick. I guess the police must've not even let Dad change into normal clothes before taking him away.

Kyle reaches Dad first with a leap and a bound into his arms, the weight of him making Dad "Oof!"

"Daddy!" Kyle yells, gripping Dad's neck like it's been years since he's seen him instead of hours. Kyle's been so anxious and distant all afternoon, despite my best attempts at distracting him, but of course, after being the one to watch Dad get hauled out of the house this morning, Kyle's mood was understandable. Now his relief's contagious.

"Guess I don't have to change into pajamas!" Dad's exclaiming. "Had to spend the whole day in this getup!"

I force a laugh, embarrassed for him, for our family, but so glad to be done with today.

Dad's eyes fall on me, and his too-jolly smile falters. "Emma-Bean," he says, pulling me into him with his free arm, kissing my hairline. I breathe in his scent, my muscles relaxing in his tight embrace. But then Kyle's too heavy to be held in one arm and Dad has to pull away to reinforce his hold. "You okay?" he asks. His face is wide open and vulnerable, so full of the need for reassurance that it guts me.

I nod fast. "Fine! So glad you're home!"

"Well," he says, trying to put down a spider-monkey-of-a-Kyle who won't let go of his neck. "What do you say to some hot cocoa before bed?"

Mom's already moving to put the kettle on, seeming eager for a task, her purse with my kidnapped phone still pinched under one arm.

He comes to my room several hours later, long after the house has quieted and the shadows have dragged their shifting shapes across my floorboards. The moon's heavy outside, as bright as stadium lights, though it's not the light that gives Dad away. I can sense his presence in the doorway for several stretched seconds before he whispers my name into the darkness. "Emma."

I flick on my lamp, pretending to blink sleep from my eyes, even though I'd been anything but asleep. My mind's so full of Hannah, wondering if she'd texted or called while Mom's had my phone on lockdown.

"Dad?" I ask, like I don't already know it's him. *You're not supposed to be up here, alone,* I think but don't say. I glance at his socked foot resting halfway across the doorjamb, then avert my gaze.

But he must've seen me because he pulls his foot back. "I didn't mean to wake you. I just wanted to check on you and make sure you're okay. After today." His voice is the "professional" one he uses when talking to his boss, the college dean. It's his phone-answering voice—official but still a bit self-conscious somehow.

Nodding, I will my hands to unclench the comforter. "I'm good. Promise."

He nods as well, folding his arms across his chest, leaning into the doorframe. "Well, your mother also mentioned a social worker who came by to talk with you. I hope you weren't . . . scared by all this business." The embarrassment slips from his mouth and floats over to where I sit up in bed, settling across my shoulders.

Oh. That. "It was . . . fine," I say. "She just, you know, wanted to make sure you and Mom were good parents. Which I told her you were, of course."

"Oh right," he says. "Is that all?"

"Yeah," I lie.

He nods again, stance relaxing. "Well, I just came by to give this back to you." Hesitating for a breath, he steps through the doorway and hands me something, then retreats a few paces but remains inside my room. I glance at the back of my phone, the silver sparkle case warm from the heat of his hand. How long had he been holding it? I force myself not to check the screen for messages in front of him, wondering if he or Mom had tried to get into it, if they'd managed to.

"Your mom also mentioned you were talking with Hannah on the phone earlier."

I swallow hard, staring at his jawline where his black stubble looks almost purple in the weak lamplight. The way he'd just said Hannah's name came out softer than the rest of his sentence, almost gentle.

He's closer now, halfway to the bed, frozen midstep. I wonder if he's angry, thinking I've been disloyal somehow by talking to Hannah, so his next question throws me off.

"How is she?" The casual tone of his voice doesn't match the way he's leaning forward, hands shoved under opposite armpits.

"Fine, I guess." My eyes fall to my lap, to my locked phone cradled there. "We . . . We barely said hello on the phone before Mom freaked out that I was talking to her. . . ." I hesitate, wondering if Dad thinks I'm bad-mouthing Mom now, if he's on her side or mine in this case. "We haven't really talked since school this morning," I hurry on. "Hannah and I."

He nods, too quick and eager. "I'm worried about her, you know? Don't know what's gotten into her to say such awful things, but I can only hope she gets the help she needs."

His words sound worn out, as if he's repeated them multiple times, and I wonder if he has, on a half dozen phone calls on his way home from jail, maybe, or even just in his head.

I don't respond, allowing myself to wonder for the first time if he blames Hannah for all this, or me, since Hannah's my friend, because I'm the one who brought her into this house. And it's not lost on me how very much his attitude toward Hannah has changed overnight. From the first moment I'd invited Hannah over and introduced her to Dad, he'd taken it upon himself to be extra nice to her, even taking her through some of the remodeling plans he had envisioned to "fix up the place," going so far as to ask her opinion on paint colors for walls I knew he'd never get around to painting. And Hannah had leaned in, proud to be consulted like an adult, calling him "Mr. Clark" till he'd insisted on "Brian."

Later that same day once Hannah's mom had come to get her, Dad had asked me about Hannah's homelife, and when I'd explained what a loser her dad was, largely absent and aloof despite only living a half hour away, he'd nodded like it had been obvious. *Bright girl*, he'd remarked, *though she's starving for attention. Clearly lacks a solid father figure.*

And Hannah's remark? *You're so lucky*, she'd gushed at me after meeting Dad that first time, and many times following. *What I wouldn't pay to have a father who gave a shit about me. My dad wouldn't notice if I tripped and fell off this freaking planet!*

I'd always stay silent when she said stuff like this, caught between immense pride that I had something Hannah Garber could ever covet and some other unnamed emotion that felt like murky ink seeping through my blood.

"Emma?" Dad asks now, and the earnestness in his voice makes me look up. He's tracing the grain of the wooden floorboard with his socked toe. "How old is she?"

I don't need to ask who "she" is.

"Fifteen," I blurt, confused by the question but happy it's one I can answer without double-crossing anyone. At least, I think so. It's not a secret anyway. "She turned fifteen back in August, right before we met, but then we celebrated her half-birthday a few months ago."

"Right. That's right." He's nodding, then swallows, taking a half step forward. "Would you, uh . . . Could you do something for me? A favor?"

My insides warm. He's not mad, nor does he hold it against me that Hannah is my friend. "Sure. Yeah." *Anything.*

I can tell he's considering his words by the way he stares down at his feet, lifting the toes, then setting them down again, hands still tucked under his armpits. "I need to get proof of her age," he murmurs, and my heart stutters. Then he shrugs like this is run-of-the-mill. "Legal stuff, you know. For my lawyer. The, uh, charges are . . . different depending on age, and, well, we just need to be prepared for Monday's arraignment, when I have to appear in court."

At the look on my face, he rushes on. "Not that it'll come to anything—criminal charges and all that—but Jim, my, uh, lawyer, wants to know where we stand. What they're going to try to pin on us. So maybe you could text her or talk to her or, you know, find a written form of hers with her birth date spelled out? I know you've got Cats Club early this Sunday, right, to hide Easter eggs?"

Find a form with her birth date? As in, steal one?

"Um." I shake my head to clear it, wondering how today could've possibly turned into all this: Dad arrested, best friend vanished, Kyle watching Dad get hauled off in cuffs, Mom bailing him out. Jail and lawyers. Criminal charges that depend on a girl's age and stealing forms with printed birth dates.

The snake has returned, dark and feral as it twines around my intestines.

Dad must mistake my headshake for a lack of willingness because he steps forward, an arm's length from my bed, a pained expression twisting his face. "I know it's . . . awkward to ask, but I need you, Em. Could you do this one small thing for me? Please?"

In my belly the snake coils tight, hissing, but what choice do I have?

Slowly I nod, whispering, "What do you need me to do?"

"Could you text her?" he asks, voice hopeful. "So we could get it in writing?"

I'm dizzy with his request. How the hell can I pull this off? I already know how old Hannah is, that it was raining on her half-birthday, that, after some convincing, her mom had agreed to let her have a mini unicorn-and-rainbow-themed party, unironically, for just the two of us. I remember the giant slice of soft yellow cake I'd eaten, picking dots of melted gold wax from the creamy chocolate frosting. Hannah'd taken so long to blow out her candles—a number one and number five—that they'd melted halfway down by the time she'd gotten around to huffing them out in their dining room as I'd cheered and her mother had shaken her head but not without a reluctant smile on her face. My pulse had thundered, watching all that gold wax drip down to the frosting below, so much so that I'd wanted to lean over the cake and blow out the flames myself just to halt that waxy avalanche.

Hannah was always doing stuff like that, dragging out moments just to see how far she could push it. As her best friend, I know this about her and so much more, so how the hell could I ask her how old she is, in a text no less, without it being awkward, like our friendship is that superficial? Like every single personal detail of her life's history isn't already etched into my brain? How can Dad possibly expect me to ask her for this, all for his lawyer?

I flip my phone over, not quite meaning to but also needing to know. My heart skips a beat. There it is, unread in my notifications, sent several hours ago: a text from Hannah, just like I knew it would be.

"I don't . . . ," I begin, staring at the notification, suddenly wanting Dad to leave so I can read the text in peace, to take his favor-asking elsewhere and stop crowding my room when he shouldn't even be up here alone. He glances at the phone I'm cradling, and it's like I've said it aloud because he retreats to the doorway, leaning into the frame again.

Guilt floods me. He's looking at me with such wild desperation that I'm sure he doesn't want to ask me to do this any more than I want to do it. But he needs me to. He needs me.

In this moment I realize he must already know about the text, must've seen the alert. It's why he's up here handing me back my phone and asking for my help. Because he knows Hannah and I are still linked, despite all that's happened.

He *needs* me.

"Okay," I hear myself whisper. When he doesn't move, I add, "I'll . . . I'll ask her."

He straightens at this, nodding with a grin so full of gratitude and exhaustion and relief that it hurts to look at. "Thanks, Emma-Bean," he says, half turning, rapping his knuckles against the doorjamb. "I knew you'd come through for me. I love you, Bean."

Then he's gone, the image of his silhouette leaning against the doorframe burned into my mind. The imprint of it awakens the dark shadow of a memory deep within me, but I shove the image down hard. I'm tired. So very tired.

I expect to hear his footsteps cross the landing to the guest bedroom, but instead I hear the gentle *thud-thud-thud* of his socked feet descending the stairs. Guess he's sleeping in the same room as Mom tonight, in the bedroom directly below mine.

As soon as his footsteps retreat, I scramble to unlock my phone and read Hannah's text. It's just one lone text, but it tilts the Earth back on its axis: Em I didn't get you in trouble did I?? I heard your mom!! Maybe we should lay low till Sunday?? You're coming to Cats then right?! MISS YOUR FACE!!!!!

As I read her words, everything—everything—else melts away. She's worried she got me in trouble. She misses my face. We'll see each other at our Cats meeting on Sunday.

Except . . . her text doesn't feel quite right. While Hannah's prone to exaggeration and over-the-top antics, even for her this feels a little forced, overly enthused, especially after how awkward she was on the phone earlier.

I sigh the thought away. It's been a total nightmare of an insane day. If anything, it means she's just trying harder to let me know we're still friends. Best friends. And even though we may need to lie low like she said—till things calm down a bit—we're okay. That much hasn't changed, and it won't.

It can't.

But apparently I'm not super great at the "lie low" part because I punch out a three-word response and hit send before I can stop myself.

You still awake?

There aren't many nights where I fall asleep without sharing at least a few back-and-forth texts with Hannah, or even a whispered, laughing-under-the-sheets phone call. I'm hoping tonight won't be any different; I need it not to be, after all that's happened.

As I wait for a response from her, I flip the phone in my hands, relieved to be holding it again, its shimmery case soft and familiar. But even after several long minutes in the dark, pulling the covers over my head to cocoon myself in the glow of the blue-white screen, I'm met with only silence.

I guess the lying low has already started, which makes me wonder how the hell I'm going to keep my promise to Dad and find proof of Hannah's age, all before his court appearance on Monday. Sunday may be my only chance, though I'm already dreading it with everything I have. Because, despite whatever Hannah said to get my dad in trouble, asking for this from her still feels like a betrayal.

You remember drowning moths

You remember, three summers ago, when you decided to remodel your bedroom, which was shortly after moving to Prosper and a few weeks following the splinter incident. Now that you lived a mere town away from your aunt Jane, you wanted to impress her when she next came to visit. But, above all, you wanted to build a sanctuary—a safe haven—in the fresh, unhampered space of your new home where you hoped things could be different, less complicated.

You remember it was early August, blazing hot and sticky, which was unusual for the Oregon coast, or so everyone said. It was a heat that ballooned during the day and stretched late into the evening. Yet, indifferent to the high temperature, you worked tirelessly, preparing your haven from morning till night. First you discovered an online solution to your splintery floorboards, which you eagerly shared with your father. The very next day he drove you to the tiny hardware store in town that smelled like chicken feed and fertilizer, where he rented a rolling floor-sander and helped you run the unwieldy machine over the worn planks in your room.

You remember thick clouds of wood dust funneling into the air, caking your goggles and face masks as the two of you ground away any aspiring splinters. Your father had even worked out a deal with your landlord regarding "upkeep" so your family could deduct all renovation expenses from that month's rent, and only then did you allow yourself to stop feeling guilty about the cost. But though your father had vowed to sand down all the floors in the house, he'd run out of time owing to work, returning the sander late after finishing only your room.

You remember your father also helping you pick out the proper floor varnish (glossy shine) and wall paint (eggshell interior). And though he monitored your daily progress, hovering just outside your door, he told you this was your project and you'd be expected to do most of the work yourself. You knew this was a test of pride, of maturity, that he'd given you, which you vowed to pass with flying colors. Starting with the old wallpaper, you peeled it away in strips like tree bark, just as he'd demonstrated, and primed the raw wood underneath. You painted the walls a delicate lavender that reminded you of your visit to the teahouse Aunt Jane had surprised you with as a "welcome to town" treat, a place you now frequented with her as often as invited.

You also remember the night several weeks into the project when you stayed up late to varnish the floorboards with multiple thick layers, wanting them to gleam like honey. Your door stood ajar, and you propped the screenless window open with a wooden paint stirrer to ventilate the room. You'd accidentally varnished yourself into a corner, though, so there you sat, trapped on the window ledge till the latest coat of lacquer could dry enough for you to tiptoe to freedom. Meanwhile moths, attracted by the light inside, kept flying through the open window and dive-bombing onto the sticky floorboards. There they flailed around in vain, further saturating their powdery bodies in varnish. Unable to save them, you stretched your limbs to put each one out of its misery, then attempted to gloss over the gray-brown trails of struggle and death they left behind.

When at last their numbers grew too great and outside your reach, you remember giving up, straddling the ledge of the open window with half your body outside, watching the moths expire. You were far enough from the open ground below to scare the hell out of yourself because if you leaned sideways even a bit, your stomach would drop and pulse with anxiety, but you knew that if you jumped or fell, you probably wouldn't die. More likely, you'd just break both your legs, or at least an ankle.

Still, you played it over and over in your mind—the scene where you'd hurtle your body out the window, leaping into the black oblivion beyond. For a moment you'd float, suspended in midair where nothing could touch you, as the moths passed you by and flew inside to drown.

pretend

Saturday

"Up, up, up!"

I wake to Mom's voice. Her face looms in my doorway, already fully painted for the day.

If the level of light outside my window is any indication, it's way too early to be awake on a Saturday, and I'm not sure which surprises me more: Mom having climbed the stairs to my room—since she often never makes it past the stairs landing, always yelling up at me from there—or her announcing in such a fake-cheery voice, "Get dressed for the Easter egg hunt!"

I frown at her, puzzled, even as a yawn takes over my mouth. "But isn't Easter tomorrow?"

Her lips tighten like they always do when I've overstepped or asked one too many questions, and her tone sharpens. "Your father has somewhere to be tomorrow morning, so we're celebrating early. Now get up or we're starting without you."

I flail out of bed as she leaves, feeling a strange swirl of anticipation and confusion. Where does Dad have to be tomorrow, and on a major holiday? But as I pull on a pair of jeans, Easter excitement takes over and worms its way into my blood. I *love* holidays, and here in our house we take them very seriously, especially the candy part.

Opening my phone's music app, I hit shuffle on my latest playlist, heart skipping a beat when a Corey Starr song bursts out in full volume. Thumbing it to just audible, the upbeat melody creeps into my bones, and I allow myself a moment of wild dancing, envisioning Hannah dancing in a frenzy beside me.

Energized, I bound downstairs, then slow as I catch sight of Dad standing rigid in the dining room, one wooden arm around Mom. They're both smiling after Kyle, who's bouncing around the house, but Mom's face is pinched and Dad's whole expression looks slack, like he's somewhere else entirely. I gather fast that today is a day of pretend excitement, for Kyle's sake.

Kyle, however, doesn't need any pretending. The promise of candy squirreled away inside shiny plastic eggs just waiting for him to find them is enough to shield him from the negative energy humming throughout the house, at least for now, for which I'm thankful.

We have a "happy family" breakfast with honeyed ham, scrambled eggs, and French toast—per our usual Easter tradition—though I can't help but wonder, as I shovel piles of syrupy goodness into my mouth, how we can afford all this food, especially with Mom just having posted bail. But traditions must live on at all costs, apparently, because soon Dad goes outside to hide the plastic eggs while Mom stays inside with us to stoke Kyle's excitement and make sure he won't peek. The heavy vibes she's radiating contrast hugely with the bright colors painted across her face, but despite this, the enthusiasm in her voice sounds so convincing that even I forget for a bit that the fun is all an act.

Then Mom's phone shatters the illusion, its loud ringtone blasting us from where we sit at the kitchen table. As she stands, she hesitates a beat too long to mask her worry before catching herself and snapping a big fake grin back into place. I know the smile is for Kyle—a comfort—while her hard eyes are for me—a warning.

Mom snatches up the phone, her "Hello?" spun with sugar, and then her heavy eyebrows spike and pink lips flatten. "I'll go get him," she says, stomping from the room and calling out the back door, "Brian. Phone."

That's right, the cops still have his phone. And I know that voice of Mom's well. It's red in tone and means *Now!* layered with *Or else!* My pulse beats in my throat as I realize Mom's voice has another shade to it. Mist-gray. Fear.

Dad returns, looking wary, kicking off muck boots wet with dew in the middle of the back entryway. He eyes the phone in Mom's hand before reaching for it, his "Hello?" quiet. He's just about walked past us toward the living room and the stairs before retracing his steps to the bedroom he's supposed to share with Mom. The door closes behind him with a small but definite *click*.

"I'll hide the rest of the eggs," Mom says into the silence before slamming the back door behind her.

I sit, feeling trapped between the two closed doors—our parents' door with fear and countless unknowns lurking on the other side, and the back door with this unspoken game of play-pretend and tradition that we must uphold no matter what, waiting to be resumed. Kyle's eyes are drawn to the uncertainty behind Mom and Dad's door, his hands fidgeting without Benny. Mom made him leave his LEGOs in his room so he wouldn't lose them in the grass outside. Now he tugs at the sleeve of his sweater, pulling it over his hand and stretching it beyond return.

"Hey." I nudge his small shoulder. "Wanna hear a funny joke?"

He pauses his tugging and nods.

"What's invisible and smells like carrots?" It's a childish joke that Hannah told me at lunch on Thursday, probably because it's so immature. But at the thought of her now, an ache tightens in my ribs like I've been sprinting. I wish I could've known on Thursday to savor the normal with her, but then I catch myself and resume my silly expression for Kyle.

Kyle starts up his sleeve-pulling again, though not quite as hard. He thinks about it for almost a full minute. "Rabbit breath?"

I feel my eyebrows rise, impressed. "Wow, good answer. But not quite. I'll give you a hint: like breath, but it comes out the other end."

Kyle breaks into a massive grin. "Rabbit farts!" He snorts at his own answer, snot from his runny nose shooting down his cheek.

"Gross!" I yell as he uses his too-long sleeve to smear it across his entire face. A snot bubble forms over one nostril before popping, and we dissolve into laughter, Kyle because anything about farts or snot makes him laugh, and me because hearing Kyle hiccup with laughter pulls at my heart in a way that's almost too painful to bear. Score two for fart jokes. I think again about grabbing cold medicine for him, but we ran out last night, and I know mentioning this to Mom would just overwhelm her with everything else going on. Still, I wish I could help make him feel better.

Kyle stops laughing then, concern twisting his face. At first I'm afraid he's read the worry in my eyes, but then he asks, "Are the police gonna take Dad away again?"

I imagine Kyle yesterday, home with Dad. I picture police sirens blaring in the distance, then growing steadily louder. Two patrol cars peel into the driveway like they do on TV, their lights strobing red and blue off the trees, the side of our house. A swarm of cops pound on the front door, not knowing or probably caring that we never use that one. They demand to see Brian Clark before presenting him with a warrant and telling him he's under arrest. In the entryway, Kyle grips Dad's leg, Kyle's expression confused, terrified. He squeezes LEGO Benny in his fist—the same one he'd been clutching in the car when he and Mom came to get me.

Dad demands, *What's going on?* even as two of the cops push past him and into the house. Kyle backs away, tripping on the stairs, watching in horror as the remaining officers shove Dad against the open front door and handcuff him in his pajamas and slippers, telling him he has the right to remain silent. *It's okay*, Dad whispers to Kyle as Kyle starts to cry, even as Dad's face is smushed against the brass door knocker. Then they lead Dad out to the driveway, an officer on each side gripping his upper arms, before opening the back door of a police cruiser, ducking Dad's head inside, and driving away, lights still flashing.

One officer stays with a sobbing Kyle as the others search the house. This officer phones Mom at work and tells her to come home. As they wait for her return, the officer with Kyle removes his gun belt and places it in the next room before Kyle will even look at him. With all the softness and kindness of someone who has kids of his own, he coaxes Kyle to show him his favorite toys— LEGOs, of course—until Mom arrives. The officer sits cross-legged on the floor, playing space battle even as the other officers tear up our house. But this officer makes sure his sound effects are loud enough to drown out most of the crashes and bangs from the search so Kyle won't be as scared.

At least that's how I hope it all went down, that at least one officer took the time to notice what must've been Kyle's massive cloud of panic. Because the thought of his distress going unnoticed till Mom pulled up at my school makes me feel sick.

Are the police gonna take Dad away again? My heart hurts at Kyle's question, and I want to tell him no, that the police will never dare come here again. I want to tell him that everything will be all right, that we're safe now, that he never has to worry or feel any pain again whatsoever. But I can't lie to him. Instead, I offer up the only truth I have, hoping to distract him from his original question.

"Hey." Kneeling down beside his chair, I trap his eyes with mine, needing him to know I'm serious. He's kicking his feet into my chest, but I know it's compulsive, not meant to hurt. I grip his hole-riddled socks, warm in my hands, and still his movement even as I feel his feet fight me. "Kyle, I'm not going anywhere, okay? You couldn't get rid of me even if you tried. Mom either. Okay?"

Kyle's still frowning, though the creases around his eyes and forehead have smoothed out a little. "Promise?" he asks.

I raise my right hand, left palm over my heart. "I promise on the sacred oath of rabbit farts." This earns me the flicker of a smile.

The back door bangs open, and we both jump. Mom calls out, "All set. Have at it."

I want to ask if we should wait for Dad but don't want to draw Kyle's attention back to his absence. Instead I help Kyle off his chair, then tuck his holey-socked feet into dirt-spattered boots. I'm about to march him out the back door when Mom catches my arm. "Don't get greedy," she demands. "You're too old for this anyway."

Anger flares in me. Like she needs to tell me not to take any-thing away from Kyle. *Anything.* Like I ever would. Like I don't already know I've outgrown these childish activities or am some-how unaware we're all playing "pretend happy holiday" for Kyle's sake, not mine. But I just nod so Mom will let go of my arm, and then Kyle and I can resume the routine: find our basket first, then collect eggs. Normally the candy alone would get me almost as excited as Kyle, but today far bigger things are knocking around in my brain: closed doors and mint green Tic Tacs, complicated favors and unanswered texts.

I wonder where Hannah is now, how the egg-dyeing party went, who Dad's talking to on Mom's phone behind that closed door and whether he could go back to jail. I wonder what the Cats Club meeting will bring tomorrow, if anyone besides Hannah will know Dad got arrested, how things will be between Hannah and me when we see each other at last, and most of all what "lying low" will look like around everyone else. But above even that, I want to know exactly what Hannah said to get the cops called.

I think again about the promise I made to Dad last night. The last thing I want to do is taint my time with Hannah by fulfilling his uncomfortable request, but I promised. Still, thinking about our friendship with all this madness going on feels like stepping out onto a lake that you're not sure is fully frozen yet. Like, any wrong step and you're plunging in, your only warning coming milliseconds before with the sound of the ice cracking beneath your feet.

The white basket with purple plastic grass—my basket—swings in my hand, though I don't even remember picking it up. And I don't stop to pick up the many eggs Kyle's run past. Instead I watch as he tears around the side of the trampoline and through tall grass, eggs flying out the end of his basket just as fast as he's collecting them. I glance behind me to see if anyone's watching, wondering if Mom will think I'm not playing along well enough.

When I turn back around, my gaze wanders across the field and settles on the barn in the distance, surrounded by electric fences. It's where Hannah and I escape to sometimes for privacy when she comes over. When she was allowed to come over, anyway.

Cautiously, I slip my phone from my pocket, but there's still no response from Hannah. I scan the log of our texts from last night:

Hers: **Em I didn't get you in trouble did I?? I heard your mom!! Maybe we should lay low till Sunday?? You're coming to Cats then right?! MISS YOUR FACE!!!!!**

And mine: **You still awake?** It'd been a mistake to send it, disregarding her request to play it cool.

I glance behind me again and see Mom slip from the house. Jamming my phone into my pocket, I know I've been caught, but—*strange*—she doesn't even glance in my direction before exiting through the side gate.

Curious, I creep across the yard and over to the gate, struggling to unlatch it with the basket in my hand, then swing it open just wide enough to peer around the corner of the house. Mom's making her way down the gravel driveway and toward our mailbox.

A frown pulls at my lips. Mom never gets the mail. She always has me grab it after I get off the school bus or will send me down to fetch it on Saturdays. So she must be expecting something for her to come out here herself. Something important. Something she maybe doesn't want me to see.

Mom stops in front of the mailbox but doesn't open it, instead reaching underneath into the plastic newspaper basket. Even from where I stand several hundred paces away, I can see her clearly as she pulls the paper free and unwraps it to look at the front page, her hand flying to her mouth as she studies it. I duck back around the side of the house, though right before I do, my brain takes note of the careful way Mom folds the paper before carrying it back inside, tucked under one arm like a top secret military order.

Easing the gate closed and hurrying back into the yard, I scramble for a shiny green egg to chuck into my basket. But when Mom drifts back in, she doesn't seem to see me—see anything at all—as she heads into the house.

Heart thundering, I tiptoe up the porch. Through the glare of the dining room window, I stand off to the side and watch as Mom unfolds the newspaper over the table. Dad's joined her, Mom's phone still pressed to his ear. They look at the paper together, Mom pointing something out, her mouth tight as she speaks. Then she folds it back up and takes it toward the kitchen as Dad wanders back into their room, and I just know she's going to throw the newspaper away.

I press myself against the side of the house so Mom won't see me from inside and try not to shudder as spiderwebs cling to my hair. But I can only stare at the window she and Dad just exited, looking past the ripply waves in the old glass, the fly buzzing in the lower corner, and wonder what fresh nightmare this is.

"You only got one egg."

Kyle stands at the base of the porch in the overgrown flower bed, peering up at me.

"You only *have* one egg, not *got*," I correct, pulse still drumming overtime, and then I hop from the porch and muss his hair. "Not to mention, you flung half your eggs right back out of your basket."

He ducks from my hand. "Yeah, but I got them again. Here, have some." He shoves his basket at me. It overflows with boxes of neon Peeps, mini cartons of egg-shaped gum, and a jumble of plastic eggs.

I take his basket in my hand, feeling its weight against the weightlessness of my own, and give Kyle the sweetest smile my heart can manage, hoping he can read my enormous *thank-you* in it that has nothing whatsoever to do with candy.

All the while, in my head, I vow to find out exactly what is on that newspaper.

You remember a loving mother

You remember many years back in San Francisco, before Kyle burst into your lives as a colossal, wailing blessing, your mother was your homeschool teacher, role model, and best friend. You remember waking to a shower of sunlight from a retracted curtain and a melodious "Good morning to you!" song that eased you from any lingering sleep. Every morning, she would dress you in girlie T-shirts and headbands, or—on special occasions—the flouncy dresses she had made from frilly patterns and bolts of floral fabric, sewn by the German seamstress in apartment 4C. Your mother would then plait your long hair into two dainty pigtails and apply strawberry lip gloss to your lips, then step back to admire her handiwork, smiling in a way that let you know how very much she loved you.

You remember that, for breakfast each morning, she'd scramble cheesy eggs for you, gooey and soft, just how you liked them. And on Fridays—designated "treat" days—she'd prepare for you your beloved waffles, baked to golden-brown perfection with mini pools of syrup poured into each square and doused in powdered sugar. And after breakfast, you remember sitting with her at the freshly wiped kitchen table, where she'd teach you about science using Mentos and bottled Coke, or fractions with construction-paper pie-slice cutouts, or how to write perfect cursive like hers.

And you remember when you'd inevitably grow frustrated—your paper pie slices not perfectly aligning or your cursive letters too cramped—and she would rub circles on your back and tell you how math had never come easily to her, how her own cursive used to be "abysmal" as well, according to her own mother. Then she'd relay stories of how her mother had made her sit hour upon hour after school practicing each letter a thousand times until she'd perfected them all. How she had been tasked to balance books on top of her head for proper posture until she could glide across the room without dropping a single one, just as they used to do with female royalty back in the day. How she had been taught to paint on her face every day until she understood why—to let the world know she took it seriously and to be taken seriously in return. After which, your mother would reassure you that "practice makes perfect" if you only tried hard enough. Then she'd nudge a fresh page in your direction, and you would start your cursive over yet again, daunted but also eager to bask in her approving smile once more.

You remember how she would take you to the San Francisco Public Library each week, allowing you to roam free while she browsed the romance section. And you wouldn't resurface until your arms were weighed down with a stack of books as tall as your conviction to beat the summer reading challenge for the third year in a row—all one hundred books on the list. And though your mother frowned at the girl sleuth books in your pile, she would allow them to pass so long as you added in some of her favorites—*Little House on the Prairie* and the American Girl series—which you didn't really like though you'd never admit it.

And you remember how sometimes, afterward, she would take you to McDonald's and let you order whatever you wanted, which was always a Happy Meal. You remember the one time you tried to order something from the adult menu, she had looked down at you with such exquisite sadness on her face that you pretended you were only joking, and could you please have an apple pie with your Happy Meal?

But then you remember that whenever she would hug you, all the worries of the universe would fall away—in the arms of your beautiful mother, who looked at you like you were the shooting star she'd wished upon.

You don't remember, however, the exact moment your mother's affection for you started to wane. Only that you woke one day to a shadow crossing her face that would not clear—no more "Good morning!" sunshine melodies, no more frilly outfits. Just a new life in a gangly, prepubescent body, a tangle of frizzy hair that would never plait right, and a frown twisting your mother's mouth that let you know her endearment for you had grown conditional. If only you could perfect your cursive or hug her fiercely enough, surely you could convince her to love you all the time . . . couldn't you?

weight

After the egg hunt, I'm sitting on Kyle's bunk bed with him, head ducked low to avoid the top bunk. I take a sip from my can of root beer before cracking open another plastic egg to dump into his Ziploc. My own Ziploc's half full and resting against my leg, packed with Whoppers malt balls, shiny jelly beans, marshmallowy Peeps, and oval gumballs speckled to look like birds' eggs.

I'm emptying the last plastic egg when he eyes my soda, perched precariously on a thin wooden railing beside me. "Can I have a drink?" he asks.

"You already drank all yours," I say, stretching my socked foot across the bed to toe the empty can beside him.

"But I'm still thirsty!" he whines.

I sigh and hand him my can. "Just one sip, okay? And not a big one."

Dad appears at the door and catches my eye. "Emma-Bean? Your mother and I need to talk to you."

Panic flutters in my chest as questions pop into my mind like bubbles—*Talk about what?* and *Why just me?*—but I don't ask, somehow knowing that, this weekend of all weekends, questions are frowned upon and will only bring on disapproval. Besides, I know the answers to my questions anyway, at least in part, and I'm not about to mention Hannah's name.

"Me too?" Kyle asks, but Dad shakes his head.

"Just your sister."

I glance at Kyle's hand, wanting my root beer back before I leave, knowing it'll be empty by the time I return, but I don't ask for it, telling myself it's not important.

I feel Kyle's eyes trail me as I follow Dad out of Kyle's room. I watch Dad closely for hints of what's to come as he and I move through the house and out the back door.

I've never seen Mom on the trampoline before, and it's unnerving somehow. But there she sits, cross-legged in the middle of a stretchy sea of black, her weight pulling her down into its center.

As Dad and I clamber on, I can feel Mom's discomfort humming around her like a swarm of gnats, especially once Dad starts to explain how he's hired his lawyer friend, Jim, who he's meeting with tomorrow morning to go over possible legal next-steps, which is why we had to celebrate Easter early.

As soon as he finishes, Mom blurts out, "I am going to stand with your father and support him through this. I know he is innocent of all accusations, and I know his name will be cleared once this whole thing goes away." It comes out in a long, flat string, as if the words had tumbled around in her head like rocks till they were smooth and dull. I wonder how long she's been holding them in.

We've all slid closer toward one another into the trampoline's spongy center, our gravity pulling us together like magnets. I push my hands behind me, driving my palms into the taut slope of the fabric to keep from slipping any more.

Mom's not done yet. "That slut friend of yours will be exposed for the liar she is."

Her words—so close to my face—land like a spatter of hot oil, and I flinch away. It's like she's saved up all her emotion to cram into that one sentence.

It's true, then. Something really is happening. Something big. Which is painfully obvious, only nothing has felt entirely *real* until now, like one giant, disturbing fairy tale.

But this is real. One hundred percent real. Hannah versus Dad. Will this turn into a whole legal thing, with Dad having to go on trial? *Will I be forced to testify?* The thought makes me sick. Now more than ever I wish I could talk to Hannah, to hear what she's thinking, how she's feeling, what all she knows. This whole year it's been Hannah and me. And that can't change, even though it's clear Mom blames me for Dad's arrest since Hannah's my best friend. Of course, I suspected this—knew it, in fact, since the car ride home— though I'd still hoped that Mom wouldn't hold me responsible. But then again, Mom's never approved of my friendship with Hannah. Even before this mess, Mom was always commenting on how disrespectful Hannah is, despite the fact that Hannah's just not afraid to express her opinion, even if it doesn't match someone else's. But she was never rude about it. She did say "shit" in front of Mom once, who'd later raged over how "vulgar" it was. Mom's never liked swearing, *especially* from me, though I've heard a few choice words dropping from her and Dad's mouths at times.

Not to mention, Mom never let up about how "inappropriate," how "bizarre" it was for a sophomore like Hannah to want to hang out with a lowly freshman like me, even though I told Mom that Hannah'd said she admired my "brain smarts." Still, that hardly seemed like Mom's real reason for disliking Hannah either, especially since Dad's so much older than Mom is—by, like, eleven years, not just one. The two of them got together when Mom just turned eighteen and Dad was twenty-nine. So if anything, *that's* a weird age gap, not Hannah's and my friendship.

And yet, Mom must feel so very justified about her past opinions of Hannah now, given how things have turned out.

Like some sort of bad joke, the three of us slide even closer on the trampoline, our bodies now pressed against one another when everything about Mom is screaming *Stay away!* The hard plastic tread of Dad's muck boot pokes my shin while Mom's kneecap presses into mine. I try again to hoist myself back but get only the start of a friction burn.

". . . will just have to tell them the truth when you go in on Tuesday," Mom insists.

I shake my head to clear it, pausing in my efforts to find purchase. "Tuesday? What's Tuesday?"

"Your interview at the children's advocacy center, Tuesday morning," Mom says with impatience.

"Interview?" I ask, panic rising. "What interview? And what's an advocacy center?" She'd said it like it were obvious, something we'd already discussed, and like I was being difficult on purpose.

Mom waves her hand, dismissive. "Where that Kathleen woman works. Her team wants to speak with you for lord knows what reason, so you're going to march your butt in there and tell her that your little 'friend' lied." Lifting her arms for air quotes unbalances us all, and we rock into one another. Flustered, Mom continues, "And, frankly, you owe your father that much after the horrible things she said about him."

I shrink back, desperate to ask who this "team" is that I'll have to talk to—*Like the police? An interrogation?*—or what it even is that they want to talk about. Plus, when did Mom find all this out? When was she planning on filling me in? And why doesn't Kathleen just relay to everyone that I don't know anything because clearly I didn't have a single important fact to tell her? All of a sudden, I feel claustrophobic, pressed in on all sides. But Mom's still not done.

"I don't know what they think you can tell them that I can't. But would that Kathleen woman listen? No. Like I don't know what goes on in my own house?"

When I turn, Dad's eyes—an arm's length from mine—bore into me. In that moment, Mom could be anywhere else, raging on about anything, because the backyard holds just Dad and me, sitting on a trampoline that sags under our collective weight.

The snake in my belly flits its tongue, just to remind me it's still there. As if I could forget.

Then Mom's shooing me away, saying she has more to discuss with Dad. I scramble off the trampoline, relieved.

Only when I'm safe inside the house again do I let my brain drift back over what I just learned: interview. I'm going in for an interview in three days. What could they possibly want from me?

Suddenly, talking to Hannah at Cats Club tomorrow feels so much more important. If I can find out what she said, what she accused Dad of exactly, then maybe it'll help me prepare for whatever's coming during this interview.

Hannah, please be there tomorrow. I need you.

You remember date nights and gifts

You remember the chore chart from your childhood covered in glittery red heart stickers that you'd started around third grade. It hung taped inside a kitchen cupboard in your family's San Francisco apartment, earning one sticker for every day you did all your homework and chores without complaint. You remember ten stickers entitled you to a movie night at home with your film of choice, complete with air-popped popcorn and so much melted butter drizzled on top, it would turn the popcorn kernels into soggy wet clumps, just as you liked it. But you remember even more clearly what thirty stickers offered: a date night with your dad, a whole evening out on the San Francisco town where you could have him all to yourself.

You remember choosing the thirty-sticker date night every time because, even at three times the effort to earn, it was well worth the extra hours you got to spend with your father, just the two of you. You remember how you'd ride the Muni Metro or BART together to the Cheesecake Factory in Union Square for strawberry shortcake topped with vanilla ice cream and whipped cream, or to the In-N-Out down by Pier 39 for a Double-Double cheeseburger with whole grilled onions and a strawberry shake. Each time, you'd eat your fill in a smooth booth seat before requesting a quick stop at the wharf or the Bay Bridge or anywhere and everywhere else, just to make the evening stretch a bit longer.

As you grew older, you remember how the heart stickers became report cards and the date nights turned to gifts. And after you moved, you remember the silver box he'd handed you two Christmases ago that housed a delicate bracelet with clear purple stones that had made your heart swell. But you also remember how this was after he'd given your mom a box of new silverware, which had made her cry and not in a good way. She'd glared down at the bracelet he'd clasped onto your wrist until you'd tucked it away under long sleeves, vowing never to wear it in front of her again.

And most recently of all, you remember the fourteen long-stemmed roses in a square vase tied with a pink satin ribbon that he'd sent at the start of high school for your birthday back in late August, one bloom to celebrate each year of your life. You remember the embarrassed pride you'd felt after retrieving the bouquet from the front office at the start of lunch and carrying them through the halls while everyone stared.

You are special, each date, each gift, each bloom whispered into your ear. *You are loved, Emma-Bean.* And you loved your father so much in return, more than you loved anyone else in the whole wide world. You knew you'd do anything for him.

run-in

In the afternoon Dad leaves the house, and when he comes back, he's brought home a silky green plant with big white flowers for Mom, which he must've bought in town. It's put Mom in a great mood, and now she won't stop staring at it, even placing it in the middle of the dining room table as we all sit around and piece together an early dinner of tacos. Mom went so far as to clean the table herself just for the plant. The fake citrusy scent of disinfectant still lingers in the air.

I inspect the plant again, its black plastic pot resting on top of a crocheted hot pad Aunt Jane made. There's a neon price tag slapped against the pot's side: HOWARD'S HARDWARE, $19.97. It makes me wonder if Howard read the headlines this morning, which I still haven't seen but know must feature Dad and what he's been accused of. Did Howard, or his wife, Jen, who helps out in the store, look at Dad any differently, watching him as he searched for the perfect plant before he brought it up to the counter? Did they talk about him after he left? How soon until everyone in this town knows, if they don't already?

Kyle pushes his food around his plate, taking small mouse bites of tortilla when prompted, but he's not the only one. Everyone's quiet tonight, not eating much.

"Let's go get ice cream!" Mom says, pushing away her plate because, in this family, there's always room for ice cream. Kyle's head snaps up, his face eager.

Dad begins to excuse himself, telling Mom he has several phone calls to make. The fact is, Mom's phone has been ringing all day for Dad. And all day Dad's disappeared, closing himself in their room. The one time I'd answered when Mom was busy, it'd been Dean Meyers, the dean from Stirling Community College and Dad's boss, who thought I was my mom.

Teresa, he'd begun, *I just saw the paper. What's going on? Is Brian there?*

Just a minute, I'd said, then called for Dad without bothering to correct Dean Meyers.

It seemed like everyone we knew was calling, asking about the newspaper. Asking what had happened, how this could've happened. They wanted to know who was accusing him, and even though Dad wasn't supposed to talk about the case or even say her name because she's a minor and protected and all that, I imagine her name slipping from his lips in the dark of his room anyway. *Hannah, Emma's friend. I tried to help her, tried to be the father figure I thought she needed, tried to pay attention to her, and this is what she did. Turned it into awful lies. Who knows why. Maybe she was just looking for more attention than any one person could give her, even someone well-meaning. You've got to feel sorry for a girl like that, in a way.*

Finally, just before dinner, the phone calls had petered off. But Mom's not about to let Dad stay home on the phone anymore. Her mouth pinches together, eating up her faded lipstick, before she tells him that the calls can wait until tomorrow. And now, with

Kyle looking at them like Christmas in ice-cream form has come early, Dad relents with a sigh.

Mom nods, satisfied. "Kids, be ready to go in ten minutes. You"—she points to me—"clear the table."

We take Mom's car into town, driving in relative silence before pulling onto Main Street and into the parking lot next to Sprinkles & Cream. The way Kyle runs to the entrance and flings open the jangling door reminds me just how small he is, especially when compared to the door towering above him.

I'm about to follow Kyle inside when Mom calls my name. "I need you to run to Tucker's," she says, referring to our one and only grocery store. "We're out of bagels. And milk." She rummages in her wallet, then sighs and tells me to charge it to our tab, which is a strange quirk about this town that was not at all true of San Francisco. Here in Prosper you don't need cash or even a credit card. You can just charge things to your account, then the owner will send you a bill for the balance. It's how most places work around here, including the sole hardware store, the gas station, and even the corner market that sells mostly candy and snacks, cold drinks, and dollar hot dogs.

I swallow down a complaint. Even though there aren't that many people out right now, the last thing I want to do is walk across town and see how many townsfolk stare at me or whisper that I'm *Brian Clark's daughter, and didn't you see the article in the paper this morning?* But I swallow my dread and nod, shoving my hands into my sweatshirt pockets and making for Tucker's.

The door sensor buzzes as I enter, and I flash a quick smile at Jacoby, the owner, who's standing at his register, before I dart down an aisle. I grab the first bag of everything bagels I see—Dad's favorite—then head for the refrigerated section in the back.

I'm almost to the glass case lined with cartons of milk and juice when I see who's standing right in front of it. Mrs. Garber. Hannah's mom.

Like my mom, Mrs. Garber has a face hidden behind layers of makeup, but unlike my mom, Mrs. Garber doesn't seem to try to hide the fact that she's wearing a lot of makeup, all the colors popping off her features like a tropical coral reef. More than once I've heard Mom call Mrs. Garber "tacky," even though they probably wear the same amount of product. Or maybe Mom was talking about Mrs. Garber's skirts, which she wears formfitting, though not unlike Mom's pant-suits. *Honestly, at her age,* Mom would say with an eye roll.

Mrs. Garber has her back to me, her cart piled high with several of Hannah's favorite foods—a frost-covered box of Eggo waffles, an orange net bag of tangerines, boxes of Fruit Roll-Ups, Honey Maid Cinnamon Graham Crackers, Goldfish crackers, and, next to her purse in the child's fold-down seat, a small mound of foil-covered strawberry Yoplait yogurts. Unlike ours, the Garber house is organized—by their housekeeper, Helen, since Mrs. Garber is always working—and their pantry is stuffed with colorful brand-name snacks. When I'd visit almost every day after school, Mrs. Garber would let us take whole armfuls of them up to Hannah's room, pretending like she didn't mind, even though her eyes wouldn't stop watching my hands carrying the snacks.

Mrs. Garber's on her phone, I realize, when she says in a low voice, "As well as can be expected." She pulls open a fridge door, sounding tired. "Things have been . . . hard for her since the news came out. She's been in her room all day, quiet."

Hannah. She's talking about Hannah.

Mrs. Garber grabs a half-gallon of skim milk, letting the door swing shut as she turns. "God, how that vile man could . . ."

There's nowhere to hide as her eyes lock onto mine. We both stand frozen, her with the plastic jug of milk, me with the bag of bagels slipping in my grip. I squeeze tighter so it won't fall.

"Emma," Mrs. Garber says with a tight nod, her phone almost dropping from her ear before she remembers it's there and catches it just in time, ending the call without a goodbye. She tosses the milk jug into her cart, which lands halfway in her purse, but she doesn't seem to notice, already shoving at the cart. It lurches, one wheel stuck sideways until it finally rights itself, and she hurries away.

My mind's buzzing as I grab for the milk, then bolt toward the front, only hoping I can make it through the line before Mrs. Garber reaches the register. And I don't know if Jacoby won't look at me because he's busy writing up a receipt for our tab or because he knows about Dad, but I'm out the door in a flash without waiting for a grocery bag and only a quick "Thanks!" thrown behind me.

Mom's angry when I show up with bagels and a carton of grapefruit juice I'd somehow managed to grab instead of milk, but thank goodness she believes me when I say Tucker's was out. Only Dad seems to notice something's wrong when I turn down a waffle cone piled high with vanilla and chocolate swirl like Kyle got, but he doesn't say anything, just keeps catching my eye and sending a covert smile my way. Then I feel bad because of course Dad has enough to worry about without trying to make me feel better. I tell myself to snap out of it since we have almost the whole place to ourselves, so I try to become hyper-chatty like Hannah would till Mom tells me to calm myself.

When we're leaving the shop, a man I recognize from Dad's Rotary meetings stops Dad in the parking lot. They have a hushed conversation near our car while I'm buckling Kyle into his booster seat. Then the man slaps Dad's arm, and I hear him say, "Well, best of luck to you, Brian. Could've happened to any one of us these days. No one's safe no more, but you'll get through this soon enough. You're a decent man, and everyone here knows it."

"Thanks, Tom," Dad says, and I hear the gratitude in his voice, the relief. "This town's been such a haven for my family and me. I really hope that doesn't change with all this nonsense."

As Dad starts the car and backs out of the lot, I realize with dawning clarity that everyone's already taken their sides, either against us or against Hannah. In a small town like this, there's apparently no room for middle ground.

You remember tall tales

You remember your father telling the best stories from his childhood, and how at every opportunity you would beg him for another one. One time in San Francisco, you remember waiting outside your mother's work for her to get off her shift. You held your father's hand, pleading with him to please tell you another tale from when he was a kid.

Which story? he asked.

Any one! you said.

And you remember how he told you about the time in elementary school when he; his older sister, Jane; and two of their friends had dug a tunnel in the playground behind a bush so the teachers couldn't see. The four of them had used the metal spoons and forks from their lunch boxes, he said, to dig away at the ground. After each lunch, when they'd return to class filthy and dirt-covered, the teachers would ask them what they had been up to, but they would just shrug their shoulders and reply, *Playing.*

The four of them continued to dig throughout their lunch periods, he explained, until the tunnel was so large that all four people could fit inside it. After a while, though, they each grew tired of the tunnel, abandoning it for other lunchtime pursuits. But then one day some other kids found the tunnel, and while they played inside it, it collapsed on them, suffocating and killing them all.

You remember when your father had finished his story, your mother was just coming out of work, flinging her coat around her shoulders. But you remember barely managing a *hello* since images were playing over and over in your head, ones of complete darkness, mouthfuls of dirt, and screams silenced by caving ground.

But you also remember a few years later, when you were visiting Aunt Jane over winter break. You two were alone in the kitchen, you were helping chop tomatoes for the dinner salad, and you noticed how upset your aunt seemed because you always picked up on such things. When you asked her if she was okay, she stared at you for a long time, almost without seeing you. Finally, she shook her head and confided that a student from the fifth-grade class she taught had just died in a car accident and that she was feeling very sad.

Like the kids from your elementary school, you remember saying, happy to have something to add. *The ones who died in the tunnel.*

Died in a tunnel? she asked, confusion coloring her voice.

Yeah, from when you and Dad were little, you prompted, *when you built that tunnel at lunchtime while the teachers weren't looking. And then you guys forgot about it, and it collapsed on those kids.*

But you remember how your aunt was looking at you in a strange way that made you fidget.

Sorry, M&M's, she said at last. *I'm not sure what you're talking about. Your dad and I did dig holes, but in our backyard, if that's what you mean? But they were never more than a foot or two deep. And he and I never had lunchtime together. I was always three classes ahead of him.*

You remember how she kept looking at you until you said, *Oh, I got confused. Mixed it up with something else.* But you knew with every ping of—Sadness? Loss?—in your heart that you hadn't gotten it mixed up, that your father had told you about a tunnel he'd dug and the kids who had died in there. You were sure of it.

And of course the story wasn't true, you chided yourself. Kids don't die in underground tunnels dug at lunch with metal forks and spoons. The teachers would have noticed them digging and stopped them, obviously. And of course your aunt Jane and father were too far apart in age to share a lunchtime. You'd have to be unfathomably naive to believe a story like that.

But you remember how deeply you had believed him, how you had felt such grief, such fear and sympathy for the final moments of the young kids' lives as they suffocated in a tunnel that had never existed. You'd believed every story your father had told you: about the booby traps he'd rigged to get revenge on mean neighbor kids, about how he'd always get picked last for every sports team until he hit that home run during PE and showed them all, about the inventions he'd made to do his chores for him. You'd been so proud of him, proud that such a cool kid had turned into your father.

Then you remember thinking that if the tunnel story wasn't true, what else had he made up that you'd believed? And the answer mattered more to you than you could ever admit, especially to yourself.

secrets

As it grows dark outside, we all sit down in the living room to watch *It's the Easter Beagle, Charlie Brown!* with Mom and Dad on the green couch I hate, and Kyle and me on the other.

Two minutes into the movie Dad excuses himself, mumbling something about getting up early, Mom's eyes trailing him as he rises. Dad hesitates before heading to their shared bedroom, and it dawns on me that the only time he's really talked to me today had been earlier to ask if I'd texted Hannah yet. I told him I thought maybe asking her in person tomorrow at Cats Club would seem more natural, thinking but not adding that I still had no idea how to pull it off without sounding suspect. He'd nodded somberly, then walked away.

Now Mom rises from the couch, kisses the top of Kyle's head, and follows Dad.

I wait about ten minutes, counting the time in my head as Snoopy dances across the screen, and then I rise slowly, like Kyle's asleep and I'm trying not to wake him.

But no luck. Kyle's eyes snap to mine.

"Popcorn," I say by way of explanation, even though I don't eat popcorn anymore, and I'm almost positive we don't have any. Still, Kyle relaxes.

I steal through the darkened house, careful about my foot-steps as I pass Mom and Dad's closed door. And in the kitchen I find what I'm looking for exactly where I expected to, and it's not popcorn.

Mom had tried to bury it, but the trash can is only so deep, and the newspaper couldn't get very far. I slip it free, cringing as I brush away the taco remains from dinner.

Pushing aside the dirty dishes on the counter, I unfold the newspaper, anxiety sparking through me as flecks of shredded cheese and salsa fly from the paper.

Then I see it, printed across the front page.

Looking at the headline feels like the moment just after I'd accidentally touched an electric fence. Any mental preparations I'd attempted don't even begin to dull the nerve-zapping shock of what I'm seeing.

Dad's picture stares up at me from the front page. It's a mug shot, I realize, though his face is a copy several times removed from the original. His normally vibrant blue eyes look watery and distant, and his hair stands up like a mad scientist's, looking even more disastrous than when he'd come home. A printer smudge mars his left shoulder, though thank goodness you can't tell he's in pajamas.

But it's the caption that packs the biggest jolt: BRIAN CLARK, 43, OF PROSPER, OR, ARRESTED ON ALLEGATIONS OF CHILD MOLESTATION.

Flipping, I search the rest of the food-splattered pages, but the newspaper doesn't offer up any more info.

Child molestation. On the front page, with Dad's picture. This is huge news anywhere but especially in such a small town, and it's news the whole county must've seen. Plus, since everyone knows

everyone in Prosper, they'll know it's my dad. The thought brings
back the snake, twining its dark, scaly body around my heart and
constricting. No matter where we go, people will have read this.
And who knows which of them will assume it's true?

A noise sounds from Mom and Dad's room, and I freeze, but
no one comes out. I shove the newspaper in the trash. In a daze,
I wipe the salsa and cheese off the counter with a gross sponge
that makes my fingers smell bad. After washing my hands twice,
sweeping the floor three times, then riffling through the cupboards for microwave bags of popcorn I know don't exist, at last I
turn off the light. Yet my guilt sends my gaze back over the stack
of dinner dishes now sitting in the dark—dishes that, for once, I
can't summon the energy to clean and whose murky, silhouetted
outline haunts me all the way to the living room.

"No popcorn," I explain to Kyle.

Just as I'm drooping back onto the couch, something on
the armrest glows bright—my phone with a new text message. I
scramble to unlock the phone, almost sending it flying.

The text is from Hannah, just like I prayed it would be.

**Emmer-lemmer-ding-dong! Sorry I didn't respond to your text
last night!! Mom's been Queen Pain In Ass and guarding my phone.
Still not allowed but ha!! She's gone for a bit. Hope your Easter
tomorrow is full of chocolate bunny turds and sour candy up to your
nonexistent boobs! See you tomorrow at Cats!!!! (don't text back)**

I jump to my feet and sprint upstairs to my room, ignoring
Kyle's "Where you going?" Swinging my door shut, I pace, reading
the text again and again. With each read-through, the "don't text
back" flips my stomach in another somersault. After a minute, I
have the whole thing memorized.

Setting the phone down, I leap onto my bed, knowing this text from Hannah feels overly exuberant too, but also wondering if I can catch her before Cats Club tomorrow morning. We're supposed to hide the eggs that the club dyed in Bellflower Park, but it's not like I can tell Hannah I want to meet early, let alone get written proof of her age, if I can't even text her back.

I don't realize I'm clutching the Ziploc filled with my Easter candy till its crinkling pulls my focus. My hand is plunged deep inside the bag, closed around a fistful of shiny beans and chocolate spheres. Overflowing with candy, my palm draws closer, filling my mouth with the snap of cold chocolate and the sweet crunch of jelly-bean shell.

(don't text back)

Rising quickly, I begin a mental plan of action, ticking off each step as it comes to me. I'll go back downstairs and wait till the movie is over. Then I'll make sure Kyle brushes his teeth.

Fist by mechanical fist, the bag in my hand grows lighter. Swallow by mechanical swallow, the contents of my stomach expand.

(don't text back)

I'll find Kyle clean pajamas and read him the next chapter of his Ninjago book. A small bubble of calm rises in me at the control I feel from making these plans. I'll make sure Kyle's in bed, then come back upstairs, and even though I can't re-vacuum all the cracks in my floor or risk disturbing Mom and Dad below me, I can still sweep under my bed, and dust, and reorganize my nightstand and dresser. Then I'll pick out what I'm going to wear tomorrow, and what I'll say to Hannah. My Corey Starr shirt, I decide, so Hannah won't forget how much we have in common. That we're on the same team, always.

(don't text back)

I pop the last of the candy into my mouth—an explosion of black licorice. I'm already starting to feel a little sick, but it's worth it for the ringing in my ears and numbness quieting my brain. Tossing the empty bag in the trash, I replay Hannah's text again and again because she texted me back. Her mother was just being ridiculous. Hannah still wants to be friends—of course she does—and I'll see her tomorrow at Cats Club.

It will all be fine. Better than fine. Normal.

At least, that's the fairy tale I'm telling myself. Because I don't want to live in a world where my best friend is telling me not to text her back so her mother won't find out since her mother hates our family. It's the same world in which I promised Dad an insane favor that I have to follow through on tomorrow morning, despite the possibility that doing so could further damage my friendship with Hannah.

What did you tell everyone, Hannah?

I try to conjure up a happy memory to slip into, to teleport myself away from here, but like a broken loop, my brain keeps flashing to an image of my journal and its gap of missing pages. And for the first time, for just a fleeting second, I allow myself to remember that maybe Hannah's not the only one with secrets.

You remember four words

You remember the journal your aunt Jane gave you for your thirteenth birthday on the eve of eighth grade, your second year at Prosper Junior High. It was a small, cream-colored book that fit into the palm of your hand, with light pink roses swirling over the cover and gold lines embossed across the gilded pages. You remember feeling overcome by its beauty, stunned into silence after unwrapping it at the dining room table in front of your family.

In her card to you, Aunt Jane had written, *Write your heart out, M&M's,* and she beamed at you from where she sat across the way.

And written your heart out, you had.

Long after everyone had gone to sleep that night, you remember crawling into bed and flipping to a random page, holding a pen over one of the middle lines, thin and shimmery as a spider's web. There you wrote four words before staring at the page, the truth of your words seeping into your conscious mind just as sure as the ink to paper. You remember ripping the page out, feeling a similar tear mirrored inside you as you did.

But you'd pressed harder with the pen than you had intended, desperation driving your fist, and you could see the imprint of your words on the page underneath and the page underneath that. Just to be sure, you tore out more pages, thirteen in all, at the time one for every year of your pathetic life. All these you shredded into tiny, indecipherable pieces that you buried deep in the trash before looping the bag closed and dragging it out to the garbage bin in the dead of night.

You remember that you couldn't stop sobbing, even after the fragments of paper—of truth acknowledged—were tucked away where no one would ever find them. The journal was ruined now, the jagged void a disfiguring scar, but you kept it in spite of this, over time filling in the remaining pages with bizarre, fantastical fairy tales. Because you couldn't bear the thought of throwing away the gilded paper, the exquisite rose cover, even if you hadn't—couldn't have—trusted it with your secret.

"The Girl and the Cursed Painting"

Once upon a time there lived a girl—a poor, hardworking girl who resided on a small farm with her father. Every morning she would rise with the crow of the rooster to milk their scrawny cow, collect the frail eggs from their single hen, and turn their scant supply of wheat into a small, edible morsel for the evening's meal. Her father was a painter and made a meager living selling landscapes by the river in the town square. The town itself held little color; thus, the paintings were drab things with burnt umber hills and obsidian black rivers, and hardly a splash of bright pigment amongst them. The paintings stood as an unwelcome reminder of the dreariness of the town; hence, the painter and his paintings went ignored.

Upon the morning of the girl's thirteenth birthday, the father gathered his paintings and headed for town as he did every day. But it was to be no ordinary day, for after the painter had set out his wares, a wealthy eccentric gentleman strode through the dull town, tossing several heavy coins into the painter's tin without sparing him so much as a backward glance or bothering to collect a painting for his generosity. The painter, unable to bear the weight of such a fortune, rushed to the market, his muddied canvases forgotten. There in the market, the painter's eager hands amassed all the sumptuous goods they could hold—exotic peaches and plums, ripe to bursting; fragrant loaves of bread infused with roasted garlic; the finest brilliant-hued paints and soft bristle brushes; yards upon yards of thick canvas awaiting trimming and stretching over wooden frames.

It was in the final market stall, stacked to its roof with exquisite fabric, that the painter spent the last of his hefty coin. Seeing the man's paint-scarred hands, the female merchant recognized him. His presence brought to her mind images of a pale young girl scattering chicken feed on hard ground, whose worn dress was as colorless as her father's landscapes. Touched by a small sorrow, the woman fingered the single coin due to the painter, saying, "Perhaps a little something for the young miss?" Though he hadn't meant to, in his excited haste all thoughts of his daughter had escaped him. His eyes now scanned the cramped stall before falling on a rosy satin ribbon draped over a spool of thread.

"This," the painter said, thrusting the ribbon atop his hoard of heaped goods. Thereby, the painter brought home a small gift for his daughter's birthday.

Upon receiving the gift, the girl rejoiced, for the satiny richness of the rose-colored ribbon was the finest thing she had ever owned. The girl plaited her hair high upon her head as was fashionable with the young women in town, weaving in the beautiful ribbon. When she had finished, the painter looked upon his daughter with renewed focus. "Daughter," he said, "come here. Let me have a look at you." And look upon her he did, taking in every inch of her small figure with his painter's eye. The girl felt very pleased, for never before had her father deemed her worthy of such fervent attention, even as he sat her upon a stool to pose, adjusting her form so that her large eyes peered at him from over one shoulder. She sat very straight and still, smoothing the folds of her dress as she did, afraid her father would deem her too plain, restless, unworthy of his consideration if he gazed upon her for much longer.

But this was not so. For night after night, the painter rendered on canvas upon canvas the image of the young girl. And dawn after dawn, he carried his paintings into the town to sell, still damp. In this way, the painter's fortune amassed, for not a single day passed where a sole painting remained. Word had spread of the sweet girl with the brilliant eyes and rose-colored ribbon. Lords and ladies traveled from far and wide to admire the painter's work, and thus every noble citizen in the land came to desire a painting.

Day by passing day, the painter's fortune steadily grew. Yet with each new sack of coin, the painter became increasingly distrustful, afraid someone would steal the girl from him, and that his newfound fame and fortune would be lost. So great was this suspicion that one day he shut the girl in a shed deep in the woods—"To keep you safe, my dove," he said—and never let her out. Night after night, he visited the shed bearing easel, paints, and a fresh canvas. And night after night, the girl sat atop her stool, remaining perfectly still, only tilting her chin this way or that when commanded in order to catch the most favorable light of the oil lamp.

Despite working late into the night, the painter could not paint fast enough, with each subsequent portrait selling faster than the previous. Every soul who looked upon the painted girl became entranced, the plush ribbon wholly at odds with the youth of the girl's face and plainness of her dress. And, as not a soul had laid eyes upon the girl for many a fortnight, their curiosity and intrigue grew.

One afternoon a wandering wood nymph happened upon the

shed in the woods and heard the girl crying. The girl missed her scrawny milk cow and hen, her chipped teakettle and measly garden. What's more, the girl feared the dark shadows that leaned against the windows and the low-hanging branches that dragged stiff fingers across the roof. But most of all, the girl feared that her ribbon was fading in the dim light, that one day her father would discover she was unworthy of his attentions and fail to return. She feared she would die, alone and forgotten, in her solitary prison. When the wood nymph's strange face peered through a window, so surprised was the girl that she stopped crying at once.

"Why cry you, little one?" asked the wood nymph in a voice as rough as tree bark.

"I . . . ," sputtered the girl, "I cry for I am trapped in here, unable to free myself. I wish to return to my home and my father, to be rid of this horrid shed forever."

"Ah," said the wood nymph, "perhaps of assistance I may be."

What the girl did not know was that wood nymphs are tricksters by trade, motivated by curiosity and an insatiable desire for chaos. This particular wood nymph had witnessed the painter's greed and the townsfolk's seeming indifference to the girl's disappearance; thereby, the wood nymph desired to know how far this greed and blindness would stretch. But the girl, unsuspecting and desperate as she was, readily accepted the wood nymph's merciful offer of assistance.

"This must you do, little one," instructed the wood nymph. "Very, very still sits you when next your father comes to paint. Then free of here and back to home you shall be for all eternity."

The girl nodded, eager to escape, and with a crackling laugh, the wood nymph vanished.

That very night, when the painter returned to the shed, the girl sat stiller than she ever had before. And this time, with every brushstroke, bits of the girl began to fade away—a wisp of hair here, the hem of dress there. This went unnoticed by the painter, for so overcome was he by his work that he painted in a fervor as never before, unceasing throughout the night until the glimmering rays of dawn shone above the horizon. By this time the girl had disappeared entirely from the stool, but her father paid no heed, for what stood before him, stretched across the broadest canvas yet, was a masterpiece of perfection. The girl had been replicated wholly, down to the delicate curl of her ribbon and the melancholy weight of her brilliant eyes.

The painter rushed into town, broad canvas in hand, with his daughter—unbeknownst to him—trapped inside; all he knew was that never in his life had he created such a magnificent portrait. When the assembled crowd beheld this final painting, a fight broke out amongst them, for all those present coveted it. Thus the crafty painter concocted a plan. He would erect the canvas above the hearth in his humble home and charge visitors to gaze upon its splendor.

And so it came to be. Voyeur upon voyeur arrived to stand before the portrait, studying the superb detail in the folds of her girlish skirts, the bounce of her dark curls, the unspoken allure between full lips and innocent face. All the while the girl remained imprisoned in her silence. Only her eyes could she move, eyes she fixed on each new visitor, pleading for them to witness her plight. And in turn, the many spectators felt the uncanny sense that the young girl's gaze held them captive, trailing them about the room. Finally, unable to stand before the painting any longer, they would flee the miserable cottage that was falling into such grand disrepair without the daughter there to care for it. And yet their unease lingered, chasing at their heels all the way to their respective homes, where they would latch their gates, bolt their doors, and comfort themselves with cake and drink, forcing down their disquiet until it gradually relinquished its grip.

And in the woods could be heard the cackling laughter of a wood nymph who knew the secret of the curse: if one single bystander were to so much as remark upon the strangeness of the eyes, the unsettled feeling inside the house, or the mysterious disappearance of the young girl, then the curse would be broken. Yet not a word of acknowledgment was ever uttered, just as the wood nymph knew it would unfold.

And thus the girl with the satiny rose ribbon, alluring eyes, and threadbare dress remained inside the confines of a majestic, gilded frame, trapped amongst the weaves of canvas, the brushstrokes of thickly laid paint, for all eternity.

interception

Sunday

I peek through my bedroom window, gazing out over the foggy fields. It's still a bit dark—way earlier than I'm normally up—but today's a big day.

Today I get to see Hannah.

And yet, if I'm going to make it out of this house unheard and unseen, I must be careful and quiet.

Ten minutes ago, I'd silenced my alarm as soon as it'd gone off and dressed slowly in the dark, afraid to take multiple trips across my bedroom floor or make any sudden moves for fear of the squeaking floorboards waking my parents in the room below mine. Now, hair combed, teeth brushed, and even a swipe of mascara and face powder means it's time to sneak out. Last, I grab for my small purse, looping it across my chest.

Dad will know where I went, I'm pretty sure, but Mom? It's understood that if she finds me leaving for Cats Club to "help hide eggs," she'd never let me go. Because Hannah will be there.

Butterflies zip around my stomach at the thought of not only getting to see Hannah, but also of fulfilling my mission for Dad. I still haven't worked out how I'm going to manage it, but I guess I'll worry about that later because my phone says it's 7:24 a.m. The egg hiding starts at eight a.m., the community hunt at nine a.m.

sharp, and I've got four-point-eight miles of biking to get there.

I creep down the stairs, slowing when I pass Kyle's door, but no sounds come from inside. He's always been a good sleeper.

I'm tying my blue club sweatshirt around my waist and am almost through the dining room when I hear the sound of water running in the kitchen. Another step forward brings Mom into sight, filling the coffeepot at the sink. *Crap.* I have to walk through the back entryway and open the door to leave, so there's no way she won't see me go.

I'm debating whether or not to chance the noisy front door and slip around the back for my bike when Mom turns, catching me hovering. She jumps, nearly dropping the coffeepot.

"Christ, Emma. The hell are you doing, skulking around?"

"Just . . . Just going for a bike ride." It's not a total lie. Still, I only manage to say it to her left ear.

Water sloshes in the coffeepot Mom's holding as she steps closer, glaring down at my Corey Starr shirt like it's a swear word before taking in my makeup and combed hair.

"I sure hope this 'bike ride' doesn't involve Cats Club," she says, heated.

My mouth goes dry.

"Really, Em?" Mom gives me a disgusted look, then dumps the water into the back of the coffee maker, splashing some down the side. She ignores the spill, shoving the pot onto its cradle and flicking the on switch before folding her arms and turning to face me. "How could you possibly think sneaking off to see your little friend is okay, what with everything that's going on? With everything she said against your father?"

Telling her why I'm going isn't really an option. I doubt Dad's filled her in that I'm gathering data on Hannah for him. Plus, for whatever reason, I don't want to let Mom in on the why. Maybe it's because it feels like a secret, even though Dad never specifically stated it was, but with Dad it's just understood that Mom shouldn't know everything. That's how it's always been. Or maybe I don't want to tell Mom because it confirms I'll be seeing Hannah today, which would most definitely piss Mom off.

"Well?" she demands, still waiting for an answer even as the wet coffeepot starts to hiss on the burner.

I'm saved from having to argue my case when their bedroom door swings open. Dad emerges, knotting the belt on his forest-green bathrobe, his hair a morning disaster.

"What's going on?" he asks, stepping forward, his expression almost pulling off neutral. He slings one arm around my shoulders, squeezing us together in the doorway.

Mom's full-on glaring now. "Apparently Emma thinks she can go traipsing around wherever the hell she wants. I just caught her trying to sneak out to her club thing to go hang out with her little friend." Mom's face looks almost triumphant as she jabs an accusing finger at me, like she's just scored a point against me in Dad's eyes. I realize she hasn't actually said Hannah's name out loud since Dad's arrest.

Dad drops his arm from around my shoulders and runs a tired hand through his hair. "I told her she could go," he says, voice low.

I go very still. This isn't entirely true. He'd asked me to get info from Hannah and even mentioned today's club event. And I'd told him it might be more natural to talk to her in person, but I didn't ask to go, and he didn't tell me I could. Asking him outright had felt like a test of loyalty I couldn't hope to pass. Because seeing

Hannah . . . I want it too badly, and I somehow knew he'd be able to tell. So I figured I'd just go this morning and get the info he wanted. After I returned, he'd be so thrilled, he'd write the trip off as a good choice, necessary, even.

"You what?" Mom demands, redirecting her indignation at Dad, her arms pinching tighter across her chest.

"I told her she could go," he repeats, voice firm, chin lifting. "I didn't see the harm in her hiding a few eggs to help out, especially since she had to miss the party on Friday."

Now I fully freeze in place, fighting to keep my expression neutral. Me going this morning has nothing to do with the party, or hiding eggs, and he knows it. Also, it's definitely not lost on me that he didn't say anything about Hannah or what he asked me to do, which makes me glad I trusted my instincts and didn't mention it either.

The coffeepot gurgles and sputters as the water heats. I have to leave now or I'll really be late and the club will already be heading over to the field. Then I'll have to walk there by myself, with everyone staring.

Mom's really worked up, jaw clenched. "Why would you say she could go when—"

"T." Dad cuts her off, calling her by the first initial of her name, like he always does when he's trying to soften her, though this time it comes out sharp. "I told Em she could go, so she can go. That's the end of this discussion."

Mom's whole face is red, but Dad ignores her and turns to me, giving me a quick hug. I try not to flinch away as his hairy chest, exposed through the half-open robe, sponges against my cheek.

"Have fun, Emma-Bean. Let me know how it goes."

I feel his words as a deep rumble in my ear, though I definitely don't miss the deeper meaning or the hope in them.

"I will," I promise before pulling away and scooting past Mom, who looks like she's about to explode, and then I flee outside into the safety of the misty morning air.

The wind whips hair around my helmet as I tear out of the driveway on my bike, tires spewing rocks onto the pavement. I pedal hard toward town, my purse bouncing against my butt as I ride. All the while, relief washes over me like the cool breeze, blasting my face and making my eyes water. I'm on my way to Hannah at last.

I remember when we first declared ourselves best friends. It was two weeks into our friendship when, out of the blue, she asked straight up, *Emma, will you be my best friend?* It was such a vulnerable, even childish thing to say, and yet I couldn't respond fast enough: *Yes!*

Now the memory tugs a small grin from my lips. But just as I'm dodging a pothole in the road, Alice's face—my ex–best friend from San Francisco—swims in front of me. I double down on my pedaling, pumping my legs hard till I've all but cleared Alice from my mind.

I promise myself that what's happening with Hannah won't be like what happened with Alice.

It can't be. I won't let it.

You remember having to move

You remember why you had to leave San Francisco.

Before then, things were still good in the Clark household. Your mother still cleaned the house, still smiled at you and your father, and he in turn still smiled back at her. But you remember most how lovingly he'd smile at all the young girls in the Sunday school he helped teach every weekend without fail. You remember that one girl in particular, Alice, seemed to capture his attention. *She reminds me so much of you*, he'd told you once, which had made you feel both a little envious of her but also proud.

You remember when your father asked you to befriend Alice, to play with her and have her over since, as your father confided in you, her own family treated her poorly. And so you did, inviting her to tea parties in your living room or to build forts with you in the guava tree, the two of you becoming fast friends.

You remember realizing rather quickly that your father was right. You and Alice were preternaturally alike, your resemblance almost uncanny—she, ten to your eleven years—Alice, with her small, childlike face and blunt bob much like yours at the time, to the point that strangers never believed you when you insisted you weren't sisters, let alone twins.

And you remember how Alice started to spend the night more and more frequently, so enthused was she to get away from

her own home. You felt elated, relieved, to have a true friend . . .
Until you didn't.

You remember when the whispering started, allegations that
you didn't quite understand . . .

Until you did.

But you didn't want to hear them—couldn't—and buried them
away, along with the fact that your father had been called into the
pastor's office and asked to leave the church. He'd been told he was
no longer welcome, your family was no longer welcome, despite
years of volunteer work fundraising for mission trips or new chairs
for the congregation, your mother acting as treasurer and your father
helping teach Sunday school every weekend without fail.

And most of all you remember how crushed your father
seemed after this, how differently he acted. Not as quick to grin
or laugh. *Lost religion,* Mom had whispered into her phone one
day at breakfast like you couldn't hear. And you remember thinking that losing religion must be like dying, for your father seemed
almost weightless in his grief, a mere apparition floating through
every room of your apartment for days upon weeks . . . until the
day your parents announced that your family was moving north.

You remember them sitting you and little Kyle down on the green
couch, snapping their plastic smiles into place and cooing at the two
of you about how much better life would be in the country—the fresh
air, the lack of traffic. A new beginning. For everyone. So great was
your relief at having your father back that you welcomed with open
arms the idea of moving, of going far, far away, despite having to leave
Alice behind. Because, even then, you knew that you'd already lost her.

Yet you never asked—never had to ask—if the allegations you
were all fleeing from were true. And no one had ever asked—never
thought to ask—what you might have seen.

intruder

By the time I arrive at Club Hall, I'm a sweaty mess from ped-aling so hard, and my brain feels like scrambled eggs. I've had the whole ride to play out every possible scenario: *What if Hannah doesn't make it because her mom won't let her leave the house? Or, worse, what if she's here but doesn't want to talk to me, doesn't think we should be friends after all?*

The snake in my belly is back, crimson eyes and slitted pupils ever watchful as I swing my helmet free and lock up my bike at the base of the stairs. It's a few minutes after eight, but I can still hear movement and the murmur of voices inside the hall, which must mean they haven't left to hide the eggs yet. Stalling for time, I glance beyond the parking lot to the baseball field at Bellflower Park. It's empty.

Here goes nothing.

I sprint up the stairs, hand pressed to my purse to stop it from bouncing. And when I open the door, everyone goes quiet, several blank faces turning to stare at me. The smell of hard-boiled eggs and old pizza hits my nostrils, no doubt left over from Friday night. And though Club Hall's been straightened up since the party, it's not as clean as usual. Cardboard egg cartons are stacked high on one table, the old sheet below streaked with egg dye. The floor looks like it hasn't been swept well, covered in an alarming amount of dirt, glitter, and stray popcorn kernels. Sweeping's normally my job, but of course I wasn't here to do it. And now everyone's looking stunned to see me standing here at all.

Shontelle—Justin's mom and our parent club leader—sets down an egg carton onto a large stack without taking her eyes, wide with surprise, off me. Our assistant club leader, Barb, pauses with her pen still aimed at the cartons she appears to be counting, her face twisted in similar confusion.

Everyone else is seated around a table, all seven club members either cutting sheets of paper into quarters or piling the cut papers into stacks. They're flyers, I realize, for the Memorial Day barbecue we're throwing next month. Everyone must've decorated them at the party as well, judging by the highlighter, marker, and dried glitter glue covering them. A small pang hits my heart, and though it's juvenile, especially in this awkward stare-fest moment, it's yet another reminder that I missed out on all the shared fun and future secret jokes.

My cheeks flame hot at their attention as I scan everyone's faces. I'm used to seeing these people every single day at school, plus once a week and for special events here. Though I'm definitely not popular, they've all accepted me for the most part, especially in the privacy of the club.

But now, Sequoia's and Bobby's expressions match Shontelle's. There's Amy and Breeyan and Kirsten looking as confused as assistant leader Barb. Even Justin's staring at me like I'm an intruder. Like any of them can catch whatever I have by me walking through the door.

Last, my eyes find Hannah at the far end of the table. Her

surprise clears in an instant—*Did she not actually believe I'd come?*—as she drops a stack of flyers to blow me her customary triple air-kiss. But even though she's done this a million times, something about it feels off. Maybe it's her expression—*too hyper*—or her movements—*too buoyant*. Still, my nervousness melts a little. At least there's one person not making me feel like an outsider. Then again, Hannah's always given me a place to belong.

Hannah hops up from the table and rushes over, slinging an arm around my neck. "Emma-lemma!" She glances down at my Corey Starr shirt and laughs, and only then do I realize she's wearing the same one, which maybe means she didn't make Friday's party either. "Twins!"

Everyone seems to take their cue from Hannah because they unfreeze, Shontelle and Barb gliding over to say they weren't expecting me but rushing to add they're glad to see me. It almost sounds true.

Turning to our leaders, Hannah asks, "Can Em and I take the first batch of eggs over to hide?" She scoops up a carton from the table with her free hand.

Shontelle and Barb give each other an obvious *What do we do?* look. Finally, Shontelle starts, "I guess it's about that time. . . ." Calling over to the table, she adds, "Okay, everyone, that's enough flyers for now. Clean up the scissors, please, then why don't you all follow Hannah and Emma over to the field? Each of you, grab two cartons to hide, but make sure the grass is clear of any trash before you start. Sequoia, grab gloves from the supply room. Bobby, your turn for garbage bag duty. Get one from the kitchen. We'll . . . be right behind you."

Shontelle gives Barb another conspicuous look, and it's clear they're hanging back to talk about me. They weren't expecting me to come today, and now they don't seem to know how to act. Shontelle's always been the first to give me hugs, and Barb's always complimented me on my hard work, but now they're both acting like my being here is weird. Maybe it is. Maybe everyone thinks so. *Should I not have come?*

Hannah doesn't give me any more time to think about it, swatting my arm and scooping up a second carton. "C'mon, Em! Let's go!"

Chairs scrape the floor as everyone stands, stacking flyers that rain glitter or scooping scissors back into bins. Hannah's flyer pile sits abandoned.

I force my gaze from the thick dusting of glitter on the table before gesturing to my purse. "Lemme just . . ." Rushing to the supply room, I shove it into my cubby and hurry after Hannah, grabbing two egg cartons from the stack and almost dropping one in my haste. She's already halfway out the door, beckoning me wildly.

Only when the door to Club Hall has shut behind us and we're thudding down the stairs does she bump my shoulder with hers and lean in to whisper, "Hey, how are you?" She sounds almost breathless with excitement. "I just knew you would come today. I just knew it!"

Hannah always radiates frantic energy, but today's feels even more manic than usual. Still, my relief is enormous at how almost-ordinary she's acting, how happy she seems to see me, despite her momentary surprise earlier. Her enthusiasm catches in my chest like a matchstick.

"Of course I'm here!" I manage, feigning normalcy despite my heart pounding with reassurance and nerves. "And you? You look like you swallowed a whole bottle of Prozac!"

It's a weak joke, but Hannah laughs.

"Practically!" she exclaims, and I'm suddenly proud of the joke. I rarely make them, and rarer still are they any good.

We shiver in the cold fog—me more so now that my sweat has cooled. Call it superstition, but I don't dare put on my club sweatshirt and cover up Corey's face, one half of our matching shirts. Crossing the empty parking lot, we veer for the field as Hannah gushes, "I've been dying to talk to you all weekend, but my mom was being . . . unreasonable."

It's a tiny hesitation, but Hannah doesn't meet my eye as she says it, and straightaway my brain sounds off: *What did her mom say? That we shouldn't hang out anymore? Is Hannah trying to gloss over the terrible things her mother spewed about me, about Dad?*

"But forget her!" Hannah rushes on. "I have big news. Like, BIG, big news! And, oh my gosh, you're just not going to believe this, but I can't wait any longer. . . ." She thrusts her egg cartons at me, which I barely manage to stack on my own before she lets go and jams her hand in the back pocket of her jeans.

The door to the hall swings open behind us, and everyone thuds down the front stairs, pulling on club sweatshirts and following in our wake. Hannah, meanwhile, has extracted a harmonica-sized, crumpled white envelope. "Here, take this!"

Shoving it at me, she realizes too late I can't do anything while juggling four egg cartons. She grabs all of them, but the bottom one droops dangerously, and before I can react, a tie-dyed egg falls out, splatting on the asphalt with a sick wet crunch that makes my stomach somersault.

"Whoops!" she laughs, soccer-kicking the egg against the chain-link fence edging the parking lot. Though she rebalances the cartons in her arms like a baby, her focus stays locked on me and the envelope she'd just handed over.

I turn it around. It's unsealed, the flap open, exposing rectangle-shaped paper with print across the front. Like a ticket.

All I see are the words "COREY" and "Theater" before Hannah squeals beside me. "Aah! I got us tickets to see Corey Starr in Portland!"

Stunned, I rip the ticket from the envelope. Sure enough, that's exactly what it is—a concert ticket to see Corey Starr. I blink a few times, then belatedly start jumping up and down with Hannah as my brain catches up. I'm going to see Corey Starr. *We're* going to see Corey Starr. We squeal together in delight, even though everyone behind us must think we're nuts. For once, I almost don't care. In fact, I hope they're all watching us—Justin included—and seeing how normal we're acting. At least, I hope that's what they all see.

Still, I lower my voice. "Oh my god, oh my god, oh my god! You got us tickets!"

The "us" tastes like a Starburst melting onto my tongue. We're going to see Corey Starr, together—I scan the ticket again—three weeks from now! I squeeze Hannah in a sideways hug, afraid more eggs will plummet but not enough to stop myself. This is what we've dreamed of ever since meeting and discovering our secret shared love for Corey.

"But how?" I ask, gripping the ticket so hard, I further crinkle its envelope. "I mean, they were all sold out!"

Several months ago I'd sat with Hannah in front of her computer, her mom's Visa card info already entered into the online form, both our fingers hovering over the purchase button. I had no idea how I was going to cover the cost of the general admission ticket, let alone the front-row tickets Hannah'd been eyeing. Still, she told me we'd figure it out, and I believed her. But even though we'd counted down the remaining seconds aloud, punching the enter key at the exact moment the tickets went on sale, we'd somehow been too late.

Hannah shrugs now, wearing the same wild grin I know must be on my face as well. "Mom got them." With one hand, she whips out a matching ticket from the same pocket of her jeans. "Two of them! Off StubHub yesterday. She knew how sad I was." Her eyes flick to me, and right away I think of Mrs. Garber's words in Tucker's yesterday: *Things have been . . . hard for her since the news came out. She's been in her room all day, quiet.*

"Sad about not getting tickets, I mean," Hannah blurts, though it's a bad cover-up, even for her. There's a reason Mrs. Garber decided to splurge on resale tickets now.

"Which means they were waaay more expensive," Hannah continues, "but Mom said it'll be my birthday present this year. And I've decided it'll also be yours. From me, of course. Just a bit early, or very late, I guess!"

And yet, our birthdays aren't till August, four months away. Not to mention, Hannah already gave me the Corey Starr poster and my succulent, Hector, for my half-birthday. So I know better. Plus, Hannah's "I've decided" makes me wonder if her mom even knows Hannah's doing this right now—giving *me* the other ticket for a concert that's three weeks away.

I try to shove the thought aside because right now I'm dancing through the mist beside my best friend like immature sprites, and we're both holding tickets to *the* concert of the ages, which means that we must be okay. That fact alone floods my bones with relief.

"Oh my god, I can't believe it!" I gush. "We're going to see Corey Starr! In person!" I let my excitement overwhelm me and allow myself to forget, for the tiniest sliver of happy moments, that the whole world is so off right now, because Hannah and I will keep hanging out, no matter what anyone thinks.

Hannah touches her ticket to mine, making a *muah!* kissy sound, and we both squeal again, jumping together in a clumsy hug before her eyes dart behind us, gauging our audience. But I don't dare, not wanting to see whatever judgment is written across their faces as I take my egg cartons back from Hannah.

I'm still out of breath when we reach the chain-link fence surrounding the baseball field. Lifting the U-shaped latch, I swing the gate open for Hannah, sucking in the smell of morning dew and fresh cut grass. Hannah steps through, both of us grinning like fools.

When I finally turn, the entire club is all staring eyes and whispering mouths, just as I feared.

They know about Dad. Even Justin does. Apparently everyone and their golden retriever read the paper around here, and even if they don't, they have family, friends, and neighbors who do. News this big wouldn't go unnoticed. Only, do they know it was Hannah who accused Dad?

That slut friend of yours will be exposed for the liar she is, Mom repeats in my head.

With a huge effort, I renew the wattage on my grin. *See?* its brilliance says to all their suspicious faces as they approach, even as I slide the ticket into my back pocket. *Everything's normal.*

Suddenly I picture Mrs. Garber on the phone, calling everyone she knows to tell them what a terrible friend Hannah has.

Maybe this is the excuse she's been looking for to get rid of me at last and convince Hannah that I'm a horrible person. Maybe she's already tried to talk to Hannah and that's why Hannah's pretending so hard that everything's fine, handing me tickets to our favorite singer like nothing has happened.

What I do know is this: whatever Mrs. Garber does when she finds out Hannah gave me this ticket, it won't be pretty.

My smile falters as I step onto the field and let the gate swing half shut behind me. I watch Hannah skip across the grass like no one is watching. *Hannah makes up her own mind,* I tell myself. *What her mom thinks won't make a difference. What* anyone *thinks won't.* Maybe we could even sneak out the afternoon of the concert, or pretend we've got something else going on that night and find a ride up to Portland. We can find a way, can't we?

Tears prick my eyes, but I will them back and force myself across the grass, holding on to the egg cartons for dear life as I follow Hannah's lead. Because if I can let all the dark questions go unanswered in my brain, at least for now, then maybe everything can be okay.

Of course, I still have to ask her what happened, and why and how the cops were called, not to mention keep my promise to Dad. Which, glancing behind me, I realize I need to do fast, before our club leaders or anyone else can interrupt. My heart beats triple time at the thought, and nausea pools in my stomach.

You're betraying her.

It's the accusation I've been trying to ignore since Dad made his request, and, in the middle of the empty field, it goes off like a gunshot in my head.

You remember the stolen gift

You remember how you got your half of the heart necklace and Hannah the other half.

It was a Sunday in late November, and the two of you were wandering around tiny Main Street while the sky above threatened rain, faded Thanksgiving decor still on display in several window fronts. Hannah's mom had told her she couldn't drive you both to the shopping center, and Hannah had complained she was too bored to stand being inside her house for even one more minute. So you two had decided ice cream from Sprinkles & Cream and roaming downtown was the only solution.

You remember the ice cream had come first, the tacky remnants still coating the palm of your hand that'd held the double scoops (cookie dough and strawberry cheesecake) in a chocolate-dipped-with-sprinkles waffle cone. You remember closing your palm again and again, the sugary milk sticking your fingers together as you trailed behind Hannah down the black-gum-spattered sidewalk.

Last, you remember entering the boutique clothing store, Kit'z Korner, where the owner, Kit, sat behind the register with her outdated floofed-up hair and bedazzled denim jacket. You remember, also, the overwhelming scent of baby-powdery candles as you gazed at shelves cluttered with gaudy jewelry, animal print scarves, and cowboy boots in colors you hadn't been aware cowboy boots could come in. You'd never been inside this store before, both because—as you now confirmed—the price of a rhinestone-studded coyote T-shirt was far beyond your measly allowance, and you wouldn't dare wear anything so flashy.

But you remember how at home Hannah had seemed in the store, waving to Kit and greeting her by name, which Kit did in return. You remember the pang you felt at this familiarity, proving that Hannah had a life outside of you, that she did things when you weren't around. This reminder hurt in a way you couldn't fully articulate, though Hannah had either sensed this, or maybe just to explain, turned to you and said, *Mom comes in here a lot.* Her words had felt like cool peppermint balm on hot skin—exactly what you needed to hear.

Anything in particular you're looking for? you remember Kit asking Hannah while eyeing you up and down. And you remember pressing your hand to smooth your plain T-shirt over plain jeans that were neither interesting nor high quality.

Nothing really. Just looking, Hannah had replied in that sparkling, effervescent way she had with adults before Kit had smiled and turned back to her computer.

You remember wandering the store with Hannah, quietly exclaiming over items you didn't actually like, until you got to the jewelry. There, you found a set of gold-plated half-heart necklaces on separate chains that formed a completed heart when placed together, both attached to the same plastic jewelry square. One half-heart read BEST, the other FRIENDS, each with a tiny blue gem embedded below. You remember gushing to Hannah about how much you loved them, but then you noticed the price. More than two full months' allowance wasn't going to happen. You remember your grin slipping a little as Hannah watched you return the item to the rack.

A few minutes later and two blocks away from the store, you remember Hannah draping something cool and delicate around your throat. Looking down, you saw it was the BEST half of the heart necklaces.

"Get it? Since you're the 'best!'" Hannah said before asking you to help with hers. You remember your fingers trembling so hard from elation that you almost couldn't fasten the clasp.

When had she bought the necklace? you wondered. But you dismissed the thought, for so great was your gratitude and awe that Hannah Garber lived and breathed such magic.

But you remember most when, a week later, Hannah's mother had called yours, saying the boutique owner had a necklace set go missing after you and Hannah had left her store, the same necklace Mrs. Garber found around Hannah's neck and your mother around yours. And yet, even as your mother berated you for stealing, grounding you for a whole month, you knew you'd never correct her about the theft because if Hannah had shoplifted, you'd shoplifted as well.

Even so, afterward, you remember catching yourself reaching for it at your throat—the stolen necklace promising forever friendship that was no longer there.

evidence

It takes a while to get to the actual egg-hiding part because of all the trash we have to pick up first, which entails getting gloves from Sequoia, then making several trips to the garbage bag Bobby begrudgingly holds open by the dugout. Every time we approach, he tries to pawn off the bag-holding job on one of us, even as we toss away Bazooka gum wrappers, empty sunflower seed packets, and half-drunk Gatorade bottles. If Hannah weren't here, I might've gotten conned into it, but not today.

All the while, everyone watches Hannah and me, even Justin, who only lifts his chin in my direction as a greeting instead of his usual witty remark. Hannah also notices, not-so-subtly taking in the hushed conversations and quick glances in our direction, but she's always been better at ignoring that crap.

Once the trash is gone, Hannah and I take up residence by third base, setting down our cartons in the newly trimmed grass and carrying a few eggs at a time to hide. We shiver from both the cold and—despite myself—lingering excitement, but still I refuse to put on my sweatshirt. Hannah doesn't have hers, and if she's cold, then I will be too. She keeps grinning and making silly faces at me, each one a thrilling reminder of the concert.

There's still no sign of our leaders, though, when normally

they don't let us out of their sight, which unnerves me and keeps me on edge—that, and knowing I still have to talk to Hannah, now that everyone's spread out across the field.

The damp grass has made the egg dye bleed, and I'm standing by our cartons, stalling, trying to wipe a smear of dark purple from my palm when Hannah returns to scoop up more eggs.

"Hannah?" I begin, and even though it's against court orders to talk about it, even though it'll dissolve any lingering magic between us and it makes my stomach turn over, I ask, "What happened on Friday?"

Her gaze, which had turned to look up at me, suddenly skitters away.

"I'm not supposed to talk about it," Hannah says, and my breath catches. "But it's you, so duh!" she exclaims, though I notice the waver in her voice. Still, she rises to her feet with a new batch of eggs like nothing's changed—like it's a given she'll confide in me, and the court order and our parents presumably at war with one another isn't enough to keep us apart or wedge distance between us now. A part of me loves Hannah for this small gift. But there's also the part that feels an inky darkness stirring in the pit of my stomach. Something major has shifted in our world. It's everywhere, all over town: in both our homes, in Club Hall, even out here on this crappy field. I know Hannah can feel it as well—how could she not?—despite the fact that she's trying to cover it up.

So why won't she let on that things have changed?

Or maybe I'm as bad as she is, trying to grin back just as big. So long as Hannah's faking it, I can't help but fake it right alongside her. It's tearing up my insides, yet it's also easier somehow.

Still, her gaze won't meet mine, and it's this lack of eye contact that gives her away.

"Mom came and got me," she says at last, just to the left of my shoulder. "She was really upset about some . . . some things I wrote. In my journal." She glances at me. "The one you . . ." Hannah trails off, but I already know the end of that sentence: *the one you got me.* Shrugging, she drops her gaze to her hands and huffs out a humorless laugh. "Mom was snooping, of course. She found it in my room and must've read it because she turned it over to the cops. Then she pulled me out of school to go talk to them about it."

The journal I'd given Hannah, taken to the cops by Hannah's mom, now submitted into evidence, probably. I absorb this information in my chest. Another bull's-eye.

I can picture the journal, sitting on Hannah's nightstand, its pages lined in gold, and shooting stars blazing across the front. I know it well because it's a distant twin to the one my aunt gave me that the cops also took. Except . . .

I know for a fact Hannah's never written in it. Or she hadn't, anyway—her mom's far too nosy for Hannah to write down any real secrets. In truth, when I'd given the journal to Hannah, she'd even joked that she'd only write things like *I'm the best daughter in the world* or something else in a code we had yet to develop. Anything but real secrets since she knew her mother would be reading whatever she wrote down. Yet, here were her secrets laid out in spite of that, now in the hands of the cops.

"The police asked me if it was mine, if what's in it was true." Hannah's voice is low.

"And what did you say?" I ask, throat tight.

Hannah tries to shrug away the weight of the question, but

her whispered reply gives her away. "That I wrote it," she says. "That it's true."

Now it's Hannah's turn to stare as I avert my gaze.

"I didn't know Mom would be *that* snoopy." She half lowers, half drops the eggs on the ground and steps forward when I won't look at her. "The things in that journal . . . I didn't know—"

"What did you say about him? In your journal? To them?" I try to ask, but it comes out more like a demand.

Hannah doesn't need me to clarify who "he" is, instead reaching for my arm, eyes boring into mine, face full of such bottomless sadness. It's agonizing to look at, so I retrain my focus on the gray sky outlining her hair.

"You were right. We shouldn't be talking about this," I say at last, pulling my arm free on the pretense of scooping up more eggs. "They told us not to." Even though I'm the one who brought it up.

"I know, but, Emma?" It's a plea.

"They want to talk to me, too," I blurt, and don't know why I do. It's probably treason to Mom and Dad even to mention it, and I just told Hannah we shouldn't be talking about the case. "Tuesday morning. At some center," I babble on, unable to stop.

Hannah nods like she'd expected this, like she knew this was coming but didn't bother to warn me. *Again.* And maybe she did know. So what else is she keeping from me, even now?

"Your birthday," I add quickly. "And your age. I need it in writing for . . . something. Will you text it to me? I'll text you, asking you to remind me how old you are and when your birthday is, and you text me back with it, okay?"

My lip quivers as we stare at each other, me in agony, her in confusion. I'm overwhelmed again, so here comes the tear parade, trying to force its way through.

After a minute her face clears, and I realize she's figured it out, but she won't say his name, and, again, I don't either. It's understood the text is for him.

"Sure," Hannah says, and shrugs again, though her voice has gone hollow and distant, like a balloon that's been cut free and is drifting away. "I can do it now, if you want."

Her repeat shrug, and mine in return, try to bluff that this isn't a big deal—as if I haven't just showed her my cards of loyalty, where one dark spade sits right in the middle. But then again, it was her journal that started all this, wasn't it? Maybe this is her way to try to make it right. I blink against the sudden warmth flooding my eyes.

She nods once to herself, decided, then fishes my phone out of my back pocket and enters my passcode.

"So, birth date and age?" She almost pulls off nonchalant, though the request repeated sounds so screwed up. Because it is screwed up.

"Yeah." I squeeze my eyes shut. "Sorry. Thanks. I . . ." The sorry admits guilt, but even if she doesn't know what it's for exactly, she already knows who it's for.

"No problem," she replies, eyes on the screen as she types. Handing it back to me, she pulls her own phone from her back pocket and gapes at it. "Oh."

"What?" I ask, but she waves me off.

"Just . . . Mom being crazy like always." An awkward laugh. "I . . ." She punches out a text, muttering a "sorry" of her own.

"No problem," I echo.

When she's done, we stare at each other, her pursed lips and furrowed brow mirroring mine, neither of us sure what to do about the deepening divide between us even as we stand here watching. All the energy from the concert ticket excitement of fifteen minutes past has completely evaporated, so we just keep smiling hollow smiles before snatching up our remaining eggs, both of us rendered speechless for once.

Our hands are empty, and my heart has almost broken in half, when at last Hannah whispers my name.

"Em?"

"Yeah?" Every single nerve in my body waits on her next words.

"We'll always be friends, right?"

The question, unexpected but perfect, cracks open my chest and spills warm, liquid sunshine inside, sealing my heart back together.

For the first time since Friday, I feel like I can breathe again.

"Yes," I say. "Always, Hannah." And I mean it with every bone in my body.

You remember electric shocks

You remember taking a stroll with Hannah to the barn behind your house, both of you dressed to the nines in outgrown formal gowns despite the chilly winter air. The two of you knew it was immature, ridiculous even, to be dolled up for a walk in the dusty countryside, but that was all the more reason to do it—*because* it was outrageous—and, besides, who knew who might see you in your fancy dresses? Quite possibly the field hand, Curt, who worked the surrounding acres, coming to stack more baled hay in the loft with his too-tight Wranglers and eyes for Hannah. You remember wondering if the bright cherry lipstick you'd both put on was for him as well, but when you arrived at the barn, you'd found only scratchy hay and dusty light filtering in through the slats.

That was when Hannah had suggested taking your adventuring into the cow pastures beyond, to which you readily agreed. The fields were empty, freshly mowed and baled, and besides, wasn't the whole world wide open for you two alone?

You remember hiking up your fancy dresses and heading for the woods beyond the fields and the electric fence line without a clear destination in sight other than *forward*.

It was you who reached the fence first. Though you and Hannah never openly competed with each other, you remember feeling an inward twinge of pride that you could always be faster than her, having more expertly navigated the uneven, hoofprint-riddled ground.

But, you later remember thinking, had you been listening properly, perhaps you would've heard the warning hum of the fence. Yet you were both too preoccupied to notice, prancing about and singing at the top of your lungs. You'd just assumed it'd been turned off, or maybe you hadn't even thought that far ahead, your only mission being to haul yourselves in your tight-fitting dresses up and over to the other side. And even though you knew better, you remember reaching out and wrapping your fingers around the thick metal wire of the fence without checking, without any hesitation whatsoever.

You remember the electric shock of the fence zapping through you with such force, you shot backward, tumbling and landing hard on the packed, bumpy earth with only clumps of dry hay to cushion your fall. In your daze, pulse hammering through your veins, you felt too stunned to even be embarrassed as you stared at the live fence like it had betrayed you, only now hearing the electric hum of the wires that ran the length of the field. You remember how your blood felt like it was boiling and the strange metallic taste that filled your mouth.

And you remember Hannah—half laughing, half in tears—rushing to your side and flopping onto the ground beside you, not caring if her own dress got soiled as she checked to make sure you were all right.

Because, unlike the fence, Hannah would never betray you, would never leave you alone in the dirt.

tricked

Everyone finishes "hiding" all the eggs in the park—aka dropping them into the grass—twenty minutes before the community egg hunt is set to start. Now we wander back to the hall in a big mob, following Shontelle, who came to fetch us at last.

Bobby's trailing behind as usual, complaining to anyone who'll listen how heavy the trash bag is and why did he get stuck with garbage duty again? The sounds of his grumblings and the half-dragging trash bag fill our ears, and I silently thank him, relieved that the conversation and everyone's roving eyes seem to have moved on from Hannah and me, for now.

Hannah's walking beside me through the parking lot, our shoulders bumping into each other's on purpose. I half smile down at my hands that are stained a muddy brown, picturing all the little kids who are about to get serious dye on themselves and feeling bummed Kyle won't be one of them. There's no way Mom would bring him today with half the town coming, even though he'd love it.

We'll always be friends, right?

Remembering Hannah's question is enough to rekindle my full smile. Though she may be outgoing, most of the time Hannah keeps her innermost feelings tucked away, buried deep so that no one gets to see them, not even me most of the time. For her to have asked such a vulnerable question means she really needed the reassurance. I only hope I did a good enough job of putting her mind at ease because I needed her to ask that question as much as she must've needed the answer.

I'm trying to think of something witty to fill our silence when a car approaches. I assume it's an overly enthusiastic egg-hunter parent till Mrs. Garber's charcoal-gray Honda SUV turns in front of us. She doesn't pull into a parking spot, though, instead coming to a stop right in our path.

At the sight of her mother's car, Hannah automatically slows her pace and steps sideways, away from me, so that she's walking next to Sequoia and Breeyan.

A twinge of hurt jolts through me as Mrs. Garber rolls down the passenger window. "Hannah! Get in!"

Hannah flicks her gaze sideways to me—a wordless apology—then looks away just as fast. She'd filled me in earlier that we're all expected to stick around to hand out Memorial Day barbecue flyers to egg-hunt goers. Then we have to clean up the hall before attending a debrief meeting. Mrs. Garber's at least an hour early, time I thought I'd still have with Hannah.

With a dramatic eye roll that's as much for me as anyone, Hannah heads for the Honda's passenger door.

"Come along." Shontelle ushers us toward the hall, but I've stopped in my tracks. The group streams around me, around Mrs. Garber's SUV, though their necks crane as their gazes trail behind. It must be obvious to them as well why Mrs. Garber's here early.

The Honda idles just ten feet in front of where I stand, but over the shuffling of feet, I catch only snippets of Hannah's conversation with her mother. I don't need to hear much, though, to know Hannah's getting worked up, gesturing wildly and clearly arguing. Words like "Mom!" and "being ridiculous!" reach my ears. Just a fraction of Mrs. Garber is visible through the open passenger window, and only because she's leaning forward to argue back.

I feel pressure on my shoulder blade—Shontelle's hand. She's doubled back to urge me forward. All of a sudden, I get it. Shontelle and Barb called Hannah's mom. It's why they stayed behind at the hall, discussing what to do about me. Then they told Mrs. Garber I was here, and that's how she knew to come early, why Hannah had received what must've been a barrage of angry texts from her mom back there in the park.

A pang of betrayal creeps up my spine as I turn to stare at Shontelle, but maybe I should've seen this coming. No one expected me to show up today—not Shontelle nor Barb and definitely not nosy, suspicious Mrs. Garber—since they all must've assumed my parents would stop me from attending.

For a split second I wish Mom had succeeded this morning. Then I replay Hannah's words once more—*we'll always be friends, right?*—and I know I'd been correct in coming today. She needed to see me just as much as I needed to see her.

When I turn back, Mrs. Garber's eyes are locked on mine. As her gaze bores into me, all my fears are confirmed. She's never liked me. And now she has the perfect reason not to. Who wants their daughter to be friends with the daughter of a pervert? At least, that's how she must see Dad.

Hannah turns back to me, expression pained, and then she opens the car door and climbs in, closing it without another glance in my direction.

"Let's get inside," Shontelle's saying in my ear because I

haven't started moving. Everyone else has drifted past, even whiny Bobby dragging his trash bag. I want to jerk away from Shontelle, but I don't, instead letting her lead me back toward the hall. And yet I can't stand the thought of staying. I want to get the hell away from here, especially from Shontelle and Barb, who decided ratting me out was their best course of action and robbed me of a precious hour with Hannah, like I don't deserve to be here. Like I should just disappear and make everyone's life easier.

"I think I should go," I mutter, watching the Honda drive off with Hannah trapped inside, her face turned away. This is probably what I should've said from the beginning.

Either way, Shontelle looks relieved. "All right, Em. Whatever you feel is best."

Traitor! After everything I've done for this worthless club. Staying late to help scrub the hall clean each week, or taking on extra community service shifts when everyone else inevitably flakes out, or fundraising twice as much money as anyone else, including Breeyan, whose parents donate the entire portion she's supposed to raise so she doesn't have to do any work.

Now I'm the last person to reenter the hall behind Shontelle. I feel her eyes follow as I beeline for the supplies room where I left my purse. Slinging it over my shoulder, I turn to leave, but Breeyan has just materialized in the doorway, blocking my path and watching me, expectant. Behind her stand Sequoia and—*oh god*—Justin.

What do they want?

When she sees me notice her, Breeyan plasters on the sugar-sweet smile she always wears when she wants something, though both Sequoia's and Justin's expressions stay near-unreadable. *Curious, maybe? Uncomfortable?*

My fingers squeeze my purse strap, and I brace myself, but what comes out of Breeyan's mouth throws me off: "The other members and I were in the field talking about how old our parents are."

I blink once, twice. "Okay . . . ," I begin when she doesn't offer up more.

"And we think you have the youngest mom here, out of everyone. Do you think so?"

"I . . . I guess so?" I respond, caught off guard. "She's pretty young."

"How old are your parents, exactly? Like, your mom's in her early thirties still, right?"

Breeyan's insistence, coupled with the fact that this is about my parents, starts up a warning beacon in my brain. "Thirty-two," I say slowly. "But she'll be thirty-three soon."

"And your dad?"

Her eagerness intensifies, eyes turning laser-focused, which transforms my mind's warning beacon into a full-on blaring siren. I can't help but feel that this is where she'd been aiming to go all along, but why?

"My dad's a bit older. Like, forty-three?" I phrase it as a question, even though I know Dad's age exactly, just like I know that some people think the eleven-year age gap between him and my mom is strange.

Is this what Breeyan's trying to get at? That my dad's creepy for being a little older than my mom? Because the look on Breeyan's face right now reads *triumph*.

Dread floods my spine. I have no idea what I just handed over, but it must've been something big owing to the satisfaction in her smirk. I didn't give away anything important or relevant to the case against Dad, did I?

"That's what we thought," Breeyan says, voice dripping syrup. "Guess you're not staying for the egg hunt?" She gestures to my purse, but it's more fact than question.

"I gotta get home," I reply, and move past them, not caring that it's a little aggressive and rude. Breeyan's behavior is unnerving me.

So's the way Justin's not quite looking at me, like he can't bring himself to, even as he gives me a small wave and a whispered, "Later, Em." What do my parents' ages have to do with anything?

I'm stepping out the front door, not even saying goodbye to Shontelle or Barb, when my phone vibrates in my pocket. I just know with every molecule of my DNA that it's a text from Hannah. She'll apologize and explain why she behaved so strangely and separated herself from me in front of her mom—that it's all just part of the "lying low" plan. That it's only for right now.

But the text isn't from Hannah.

It's from Dad.

Parked behind the Petersons' shed. Meet me here when you're done.

Thoughts torpedo my brain:

Why is Dad here?

He knows I have my bike.

What does he want?

Is something wrong?

My hands shake as I unlock my bike and walk it in that direction, only two blocks away. A few steps in, though, I stop, remembering the concert ticket. Sliding it out of my back pocket, I slip it safely into my purse. If Dad were to see it . . . it's definitely not something I can explain.

What does he want? my brain repeats.

But as my brain tries to puzzle out this mystery, it solves another. I'm halfway to the shed when I at last understand Breeyan's age-asking thing. Not Mom's age. Dad's. Forty-three. It's the age attributed to Brian Clark on the front page of yesterday's paper.

It had nothing whatsoever to do with Mom or whose parents were youngest. Breeyan, Sequoia, and Justin had just tricked me into confirming their suspicions, finding a way to ask without having to. What they really wanted to know was if the man who was in the newspaper headlines—who was arrested for child molestation—was my dad, a fact I'd just verified for them.

You remember not being a good friend

You remember the second time Hannah's mother had decided you weren't a good friend, which, prior to your father's arrest, had only happened twice that you knew of—once over the stolen necklace, the second time over the pack of cigarettes Mrs. Garber found in Hannah's room, back in February.

You remember them being Hannah's idea—the cigarettes— ones she'd snuck from her father's construction jacket during her last visit to his house and then brought to school to present to you at lunchtime on a flattened, fingerless-gloved palm. You remember the feeling, a tinge of excitement and unease, as you took in the honeycomb of orange butts all lined up in their pack, before your head whipped around to see if anyone was watching.

And you remember that same day, while Hannah's mom was still at work, how the two of you had smoked a single cigarette behind the shed in Hannah's backyard. You remember making it through just a few puffs before rolling nausea and a coughing fit overcame you, but mostly you remember laughing so hard with Hannah after you'd gotten your lungs back. Then you both had mad-dashed into the house to guzzle mouthwash and spritz yourselves with flowery perfume.

You remember wiping the whole ordeal from your minds. So

thoroughly done with smoking were you that it was a complete surprise when, days later, Mrs. Garber stood waiting on Hannah's front porch as you two walked up after school under a shared umbrella in the light rain. You remember Mrs. Garber's arms crossed fiercely over her chest, the pack of cigarettes growing more and more visible in her hand as you neared. And you remember inferring straightaway what had happened—she'd found the pack in Hannah's room while "cleaning" again.

You remember Mrs. Garber not believing the story Hannah had invented on the spot, that she'd just been hiding the cigarettes from her father so he wouldn't smoke them, that she took a pack every time she left his house to throw away. But most of all, you remember the way Mrs. Garber's eyes had grown ice-cold as she turned to you and said, *Perhaps it's best if you went home now.* Because you knew the feelings behind this look had always been there, lurking just under the surface, waiting for the opportunity to strike.

You remember how the next day at lunch, your insides had gone liquid with fear when Hannah confided that her mother had called you a "bad egg" and suggested that the two of you should stop spending so much time together. But you also remember your immeasurable relief at the fiery way Hannah had shot down her mother's words with such picnic-table-blasting righteous indignation, you knew beyond a blissful shadow of a doubt the ice in Mrs. Garber's eyes hadn't reached her daughter's.

And you remember when Mrs. Garber had called your parents, how you'd repeated the same story to them: *We didn't smoke them. The pack was still full. Hannah doesn't like that her dad smokes, so she steals them from him and throws them away.* You remember thinking how clearly your mother had seen through the lie, though your father had seemed oblivious, nodding his head after you'd finished your desperate story.

That's understandable, he'd said. *Cigarette smoking's nasty business. Hannah's just looking out for a father who doesn't know how to look out for himself. Sad, really.* Yet his statement called to mind the tobacco pipe your own father smoked, albeit infrequently.

In that moment, you remember realizing two things.

First, that you weren't grounded, because your father always sided with Hannah. If Hannah was over and suggested ordering pizza for dinner, pizza it was, even though your family never had food delivered since your father called it a waste of money. If Hannah mentioned a movie she wanted to see, you found yourself in the only theater in town, your laps piled with popcorn and candies and drinks that would have never been purchased if she hadn't suggested it.

And second, you realized just how excited your father always seemed at the mere mention of Hannah's name. How eager to please her he always was, going out of his way more for her in recent weeks than he'd done for you.

The first realization shot such envy through your blood, despite fighting your hardest against it because envying your best friend felt unforgivable.

The second realization knocked you off-kilter, made you feel almost light-headed, because it, too, felt like envy of the most wicked and dangerous kind.

And worse still—what proved above all else that you were the most despicable friend that ever lived—you didn't even warn her.

warning

The Petersons' shed is bigger than a normal shed—more like a falling-down half-barn a couple blocks from Club Hall—though it's in the opposite direction of downtown, thank goodness. With the Easter egg hunters about to descend, it's pretty obvious why Dad wants me to meet him here. He doesn't want us to be seen.

My footsteps falter, bike rolling to a stop when I spot his beat-up Chevy truck parked snug beside the shed. With rust eating into the truck's driver-side door, both wheel wells, and hood, it looks right at home beside the shed's rusty tin roof. Not to mention, both truck and shed look ready to give out at any minute, except the truck engine's still rattling and Dad's in the driver's seat.

What's he *doing* here?

I wheel my bike forward as he hand-cranks the window down, looking exhausted. "Hey, Bean." My skin prickles with nervous anticipation, and I wonder how his meeting with his lawyer went.

"Hey, Dad, what's up?" I say, because *Why are you here?* feels too harsh.

"Was just in town and thought you could use a ride," he replies, though I can see how much effort this "casual, upbeat" tone is costing him. Something's up.

"Oh, well, my bike . . ." I lift the handlebars till the front wheel leaves the pavement, as if he couldn't see it before. I'm stalling, of course. He's not supposed to be here, let alone drive me anywhere unsupervised. I try not to let the reluctance show on my face.

"Pop it in the back." He hooks a thumb behind him before adding, "Here, I'll help." As he climbs out of the cab, I chance a quick look over my shoulder. No one's seen us—yet.

Dad's already lifting the bike from my grip when I blurt out, "Won't you get in trouble?"

His pause is almost microscopic enough to miss as he lays the bike in the truck bed, but when he turns, his pained eyes give him away.

My guts hollow out. It was a mistake to bring that up. It's not like he could've forgotten the rules anyway. But is he also wondering just how far a thousand yards stretches? Or calculating if we've made the cutoff between here and Club Hall or Bellflower Park, which is about to be full of kids?

I'm afraid for a second he can read my thoughts, but then his face clears, and he gives me what he must think is a reassuring grin. "Hey, let your old man worry about that, all right? You shouldn't have to, Bean."

I manage a nod and walk around to the passenger side, though I definitely notice he's used my nickname twice already. If he's trying this hard to be normal or casual, it must mean neither is true.

The truck dips when he climbs back in, bald spot visible as he leans over to unlock my door.

Hauling myself in, I'm careful not to poke a finger through the thin seat fabric or into the rip where the crumbling yellow foam is already exposed. I do manage to knock into a paper bag sitting between us, but Dad rights it, his whole body angled toward me as the truck rumbles in idle around us.

"How was Cats Club?" he asks, and I know he means Hannah.

"I got her age, in a text," I exclaim, pulling my phone out to show him, feeling both terribly proud and deeply ashamed.

Hey when's your birthday again? Age?

Dork!! I'm 15! Birthday's August 17th, which you should remember cuz yours is ten days after!!

It's my first time reading both texts Hannah sent—first from my phone, then hers. They anchor me with guilt, reminding me how much deep emotion you can hide behind a text, how much lightheartedness you can fake.

Dad's relief at seeing the texts is almost embarrassing. "That's great, Bean. Just great. My lawyer will love this. Mind if I . . . ?"

I let him have the phone, and he takes a screenshot before sending it to himself or his lawyer.

"Thanks for doing that." He hands the phone back. "It's really important, you know?"

Nodding, I try to swallow around the knot in my throat, then jump when something touches my knee. It's Dad, patting it in thanks. I try to hide my flinch by twisting around and reaching for my seat belt before clicking it into place, but I haven't fooled anyone. He retreats to his side of the truck again, and a second wave of guilt washes over me. I know I just hurt his feelings.

"I, uh, got you something, Emma-Bean." Dad holds up the paper bag, voice soft and almost shy.

"Oh yeah?" I force brightness into my tone. The idea of him stopping to buy me a gift both makes my chest warm with pleasure—*he was thinking of me*—and tighten with something like melancholy.

From the paper bag, he pulls out a small black gift box the size of a stack of Post-its and hands it to me. It's from the little jewelry store in town, their name "Meteorite" printed in scrawly gold font across the top.

"Got it a while back, but I've been saving it. Go on," he prompts, and I pull off the lid.

Nestled on a square of fluffy cotton is a pair of tiny silver velociraptor earrings. I love them immediately.

"Oh, wow. Thanks, Dad!" I gush. "They're amazing!" I give him an awkward, wearing-a-seat-belt hug, and he holds on tight, one corner of the box pressing hard into my chest. I do love the earrings, though I have no idea what the velociraptors are supposed to mean. I've never had a thing for dinosaurs, and a big part of me wonders if he gave them to me today only because I got the info he wanted from Hannah. Would he have gifted them to me if I hadn't? The silver tarnishes a bit in my mind.

"I thought you'd like them," he whispers into my hair.

"I do. I really do."

Finally, Dad lets go and grins over at me, and I return his smile. Seeming gratified, he shifts the truck into reverse with a squeal of the transmission.

The truck's too old for mirrors on the sun visors, so I put the earrings in by feel as Dad pulls away. I know he'll be pleased I like them so much I'm wearing them already, but it's a gift from him, so of course I do. At least, I want to.

We take the back road out of town, and I only have to duck once, as we pass the Boyers' station wagon. When I sit back up, I notice a tiny ladybug crawling around the glove box keyhole. I'm still watching the little creature scuttle about when we hit Gorge

Road, which will bring us the few miles to home. It's taken me this long to gather my courage, and I clench the gift box as I ask, "How'd it go with your lawyer friend today?"

Dad must've expected the question because he's ready with an answer. "Not great, to be honest. Seems like this thing has the potential to go to trial."

I swallow hard as he continues, "Have to admit, Bean, I'm scared. Jim, my lawyer, warned me that the district attorney . . . She's a real monster. Out for blood." A heavy sigh. "As if that's not bad enough, I also just got word from Dean Meyers that he's putting me on unpaid leave till this whole mess is sorted out, which you know we can't afford. Not with your mother's salary." He shakes his head, running a frantic hand through his hair. "I'm still . . . trying to figure out how this could've happened, you know? Wrap my head around the fact that my whole life could be ruined by the fabricated stories of one girl."

Hannah. My friend.

His words hang heavy in the air, and I can feel him looking at me, wanting me to face him. Instead, I keep my eyes on the ladybug—as red and shiny as a maraschino cherry, black as onyx—one wing half unfolded under her shell, tiny legs scuttling up the dash.

I'm still trying to find my voice when Dad continues. "Have I ever told you about my friend, the guy whose stepdaughter accused him of molesting her?"

The lined page of a journal flashes through my mind as I recoil at the word, the way Dad's voice softened when he came to it as if trying to lessen its impact. I've never heard him use the word before, and it sends my pulse skittering.

"He got *forty years* in prison because of it." Dad hits the steering wheel with his palm to emphasize. "And all it took was one girl lying to her mother, and her mother believing it. It was his word against his stepdaughter's, and the judge decided to believe *her* lies." Dad's getting worked up, voice rising, expression darkening. "He was a good man. One of the best. Hardworking and dependable, provided for his family. He'd never do anything to hurt his stepdaughter. *Ever.* He's not a bad guy, you know?"

He removes his eyes from the road again, but I still don't meet his gaze, keeping my own locked on the ladybug, now crawling near the air vent.

Maybe she'll get lost in there, I think. *Fall down and not be able to find her way out. I should help her.* But I don't move. I can't.

"Even if he had done a fraction of what they 'claim'"—Dad air-quotes, elbows pressed to the wheel to guide it—"is forty years a just punishment? To rip him from his family? Lock him away for the rest of his life?"

Dad's gesturing has grown frantic, consumed by outrage, yet all I want is to scoop up the ladybug and set her on the cotton inside the box I'm still holding. But I can't reach for her, or for my ears that feel fever-hot now, pinched where I put the earrings on too tight. If I do either, Dad will think I'm not listening or taking what he says to heart. Nothing could be further from the truth.

"Listen, I know you love Hannah."

Her name on his lips tears my gaze to his, right as he signals to turn into our driveway.

"I loved her too, as a father of sorts."

The blinker *click click click*s as the truck slows before turning off the main road and crunching over our gravel driveway.

"But her invented stories could affect my life—our lives—forever. They already have. Do you understand that?"

I drop my eyes to the box, knuckles white around it, and nod.

"I'm not blaming you, of course," he continues, "but your friendship with Hannah comes with the responsibility to make sure the truth gets known on Tuesday. Okay?"

The interview. Of course, the interview. I realize suddenly that I don't know if Hannah will have one as well, only that she didn't seem surprised that one was scheduled for me. So maybe she's already been interviewed, on the day she got pulled out of school, perhaps, after she talked to the police.

I nod again to Dad, knowing that even though he says he doesn't blame me, what he really means is: *This is your friend, your fault.* That, along with *Make it right.*

"What friend was it?" I ask once we've rolled to a stop in front of the house and Dad's cut the engine.

"What?"

"Your friend who went to prison. Who was it?"

There's a faint edge to his voice when he answers. "You don't know him, but that's not the point, Em. I'm trying to tell you how important this all is, what's at stake for me. Do you understand that or not?"

My "yes" is quiet, just audible over the groaning and clunking of the engine cooling.

Dad pats my knee again, the warmth of his hand spreading like liquid fire up my leg. Desperation has replaced any irritation in his tone by the time he adds, "Listen, I know Tuesday's going to be scary for you, but you have the chance to help me clear my name. I need you to help me do that, Bean. For our family. For me."

I nod again, tracing a finger over the swirly font on the box lid. "I know."

"And *I* know you won't let me down." His hand disappears from my knee as he reaches for the door handle, and then he pauses. "But, Em?" He waits till I turn to face him. "Maybe it's best if you and Hannah don't see each other anymore after today, okay?"

The lump in my throat expands, and I fight to breathe. I think of Hannah stepping away from me when her mom came to pick her up. Her saying we should "lie low" for a bit, and not texting me back, looking around to see who all was watching us in the park.

But then I also remember the concert ticket tucked out of sight in my purse like a secret vow and the desperate plea in her voice when she asked, *We'll always be friends, right?*

I nod again because I know Dad expects me to obey, even though it means agreeing to a promise I don't know how to keep.

After a long pause, he says, "Roger was his name—my friend. A man torn from his family *forever*, and for what? Just *think* of it, Em."

And I do, long after he's patted my knee one final time and swept from the truck, still humming with righteous indignation.

I wait till he's disappeared inside the gate, then loosen the velociraptor earrings one by one.

Sadness blooms inside me—a wild snarl of prickly vines.

Gathering up my purse, the gift box, and the paper bag, I've almost shut the truck's door behind me when I remember the ladybug. I go back to rescue her, but she's already disappeared.

You remember a statistic

You remember your father coming home each day from the college where he worked—first in San Francisco, and then near Prosper—abuzz with facts to share. Back then he was always pulling you aside, feeding you bits of information he'd encountered during his workday like decadent secrets only the two of you could appreciate: how ham radios worked, why lightning conducts electricity, or, like that one day during your eighth-grade year, a statistic he'd learned from his readings in developmental psychology.

That out of all the abuses a person could face—physical, verbal, or even sexual—the person could heal from any one of them without lasting impact, except for neglect, which could damage the individual irrevocably.

You remember the way his tongue had slipped on the *s* of sexual, how it sounded serpentine and grotesque in his mouth and made your insides squirm in a way that forced you to avert your gaze. And then he wrapped you in a hug so fierce, so attentive, the opposite of the villainous NEGLECT he spoke of—the true evil—as if to fight off all the doubt volting like electric currents through your body.

Because you were loved, not neglected.

You were fine.

Just fine.

Just fine. . . .

missing

"Where the hell did all the cups go?" Mom's peering into kitchen cupboards as the last rays of sunshine fade away outside.

I flip on the overhead light, then resume my position at the sink, pushing my sleeves back up to my elbows and searching the soapy water for yet another dish.

I feel like I should know the answer to Mom's question since I usually do the dishes around here, but I have no idea where the cups might be.

"You didn't break more of them, did you?" Mom demands.

I'm pretty sure I haven't, not like the teetering stack I'd tried to carry to the cupboard a month back that had exploded across the floor. "I don't think so."

"You don't think so?" Mom echoes. "Or you don't know? Which one is it?"

"I don't know," I protest. "Really."

She throws her hands up. "Well, go find them, Em."

But clearly, the cups don't want to be found. They're not in the sink, or in any of the cupboards, or even on the table. They're not in Mom and Dad's room, which is piled high with dirty clothes and smells astringent, like Mom's hair spray, and they're not in my room either. I already knew this, of course, because I was just in there, revacuuming the floorboard cracks to perfection, since

I didn't get the chance last night and since I knew there must be a few grains of sand or strands of hair I'd missed. And there had been both, unmistakable through the clear plastic vacuum receptacle. Then I'd been forced to double-check once more that my books were alphabetized correctly, which, thank goodness I did, because they weren't. I'd messed one up, so I'd had to recheck them all three more times before moving onto refolding all my T-shirts because maybe I hadn't done that right before either, and how many officers' hands had touched them, anyway?

As I move my search to the guest bedroom, I peer in, not bothering to flip on a light, and spot a lone cup on the nightstand next to the unmade bed. I hate this room with its heavy, closed curtains and endless shadows, so I hurry inside and snatch up the glass because otherwise I'll never hear the end of it from Mom. And even though his pipe is nowhere in sight, the smell of stale tobacco smoke chases me into the hallway.

I skip over Dad's closed office door, seeing a bar of light glowing beneath and hearing his murmured voice, probably on another phone call since it's not like he has a computer to be on anymore or work to do for his job. Still, he's been shut inside that room since we returned home, which means avoiding the three of us like the plague and not even coming out for dinner. Mom made me bring him up a plate of food, and he hadn't looked all that busy then, aside from uttering a "sure" and "understood" into the phone while gesturing at me to drop the plate and be quick about it. But either way, I hadn't seen the cups in there earlier, so there's only one other place they could be.

Just as I've thudded down the stairs holding the water glass from the guest room, my phone rings.

Hannah.

THE SECRETS WE KEEP • 159

But still no luck. It's Aunt Jane.

I try to calm my running-down-the-stairs breathing before I answer, then cringe when my "Hello?" goes all high-pitched and makes me sound like I'm twelve.

"Hi, M&M's!" Aunt Jane's voice is bright, though a bit more subdued than normal.

"Hi, Aunt Jane!" I exclaim right back, genuinely glad to hear from her, even though she's not Hannah. I realize it's the first time my aunt and I have spoken since Dad's arrest. "How are you?" I press the phone between my ear and shoulder to free up a hand, then knock softly on Kyle's door. I feel like it's a sign of respect to knock, which is important, even for little brothers. Come to think of it, I haven't seen him for a while, though I assume he must be in here since the light's on and it's dark outside now.

"Sweetie, I'm just . . ." Aunt Jane starts before her voice hitches and she starts over. "I wanted to check in, what with all that's going on. Are you okay? I know things are probably pretty tough right now. . . ."

When there's no reply from inside Kyle's room, I push open the door but don't see him, my eyes landing instead on his LEGO sheets covering the bottom bunk. Kyle only uses the bottom bunk since he's afraid of the top. I used to sleep up there once upon a time, back when I still shared a room with Kyle. But that was in our old apartment before Dad told me I was too old to share a room and needed my own. A small part of me sometimes wishes Kyle and I still shared a room, even if he can be annoying, and his LEGOs take over every square inch, and he's the opposite of clean. Still, falling asleep to the sound of his breathing in the bunk below mine would always calm me.

"I'm fine," I say automatically when I realize Aunt Jane's stopped talking. "I mean . . ."

I don't want her to think I'm blowing off how serious things are, but they're so tangled and overwhelming. During our summers together, I felt like I could tell Aunt Jane almost anything—"troubles with making friends" or "problems at school" kinds of things. But this stuff with Dad is different, and maybe Aunt Jane also blames me for what's happening. Still, I don't dare ask. Dad's her baby brother, and Hannah's my best friend. I know I couldn't stomach it if Aunt Jane did hold me responsible.

"Things are hard, but we'll be okay," I finish, unsure if I sound like an adult or an automated voice from a telemarketer.

All the while, I scan the room where LEGO creations take up every flat surface—Kyle's dresser, table, desk, floor. Entire sets and figures stand frozen, midmotion, in little clusters that replicate the exact images on the box fronts because he likes them that way.

On one windowsill, LEGO knights march in a uniform line.

And on the other windowsill . . . are all the missing cups. But it's what's inside them that gives my gut a sick twist.

". . . and the teahouse?" Aunt Jane is asking. "Does that sound like a good idea?"

"The teahouse?" I haven't been listening.

The cups are all lined up in a neat row, each holding jelly beans sorted by color—pink strawberry in one, lemon yellow in another, followed by lime green, purple grape, white pineapple, and black licorice. The twist in my stomach wrenches once more as it dawns on me how long it must've taken him to do all that sorting. Worse still, despite how foggy it's been, all the jelly beans Kyle so painstakingly collected and color-coded have melted together, fusing into sticky balls of colorful goo in the heat of the window.

Kyle's candy bag sits on the floor nearby, chocolate balls and Peeps untouched.

I didn't realize how bad his compulsions have gotten. I knew he was particular about certain things, like I am about having things clean and orderly, but this? I glance back to the cups, the melting, wondering if he meant to sacrifice his candy like that. . . .

". . . next weekend," Aunt Jane is saying. "But only if you want to!"

I force my brain to tune back in, and after a second it does. Aunt Jane's asking if I want to go to our special place, the teahouse by her home. And I absolutely want to, even if the last time we went, Hannah was there too. I need to tell my aunt that of course I'd love to go, but I can't stop thinking about how crushed Kyle will be when he notices his jelly beans have liquefied, how pissed Mom will be when she discovers them for herself. Only her anger won't be aimed at Kyle, never at him. It is I who will have failed—to "find the cups, even though they were in plain sight," or in "allowing him to put the jelly beans in there in the first place," or maybe by "not properly watching him" when he did it himself. Still, what can I do? Nothing, and I'm not about to undo Kyle's hard work now. Or what's left of it, anyway.

"I'd love to go. Next weekend," I hear myself say, because I would, even if having fun feels wrong right now with everything in our lives seeming so broken and uncertain. But this invite might also mean that maybe Aunt Jane isn't that upset with me.

Something sounds behind me, and I pivot, gaze skittering around Kyle's room.

"I'm so glad, M&M's!" she says. "It'll be so good to see you."

It was nothing, I tell myself. I imagined it. "You too, Aunt Jane. Thank you so much."

I'm already turning to go, steeling myself for Mom's wrath as I offer her a single water glass and no explanation for the rest. Then I hear the noise again, coming from the corner.

"But Aunt Jane? I've got to run. Talk to you soon?"

I never end phone calls so abruptly. I don't really know how, always waiting for the other person to get off so I don't accidentally step on toes or hurt feelings. But right now, I have to take that chance because that's not just any noise. It's a small, muffled sob.

Kyle's in here. And he's crying.

You remember choking

You remember the get-together in your backyard last summer, two months before Hannah moved to Prosper. It was Fourth of July weekend and one of the rare times your mother had agreed to have people over for a barbecue—your father's coworker, his wife, and their two small children—just like an ordinary family.

That sunny afternoon, even your mother was in a good mood, an expression of genuine contentment on her face as she drank spiked lemonade and chatted with the wife. And once burgers and hot dogs were consumed and all three kids had cleared away at the call of ice cream, you remember watching your father and his coworker jump on the trampoline, laughing and launching each other higher and higher into the air. You remember trying to laugh as well, but something in your brain warned you that they were going far too high.

You remember the moment your father's legs slipped out from underneath him, how he bounced hard to the middle and, launched by his friend's subsequent jump, how your father had flailed wildly, nearing the trampoline's metal-ringed edge. You remember knowing he would fly off, hurt himself, but you were only right about the latter since your father landed on his neck on that metal-ringed edge with all his weight behind him. You remember watching as if in slow motion: the knot of his spine hitting first, legs rolling up the length of his body, the momentum of his weight forcing him into too tight a ball for a man of his size.

You remember clutching an American flag paper plate with a scoop of wilting Neapolitan ice cream as your father's face contorted with panic and pain. You remember each choking, gagging breath he tried to suck into frozen lungs, tears streaming down his mottled cheeks as your own breath snagged somewhere inside you. You remember his coworker kneeling beside him, urging him to remain calm, to breathe as everyone fell deathly silent and turned to watch. You remember the moment he at last connected breath to lungs, filling his chest with the gasp of a drowning man. You remember the next ragged suck for air and the next as more tears marred his flushed face. And when you looked around, you caught sight of a tiny, frozen Kyle, his plate of ice cream sagging in his hand, spilling its soggy guts onto the mangy grass. You remember your mother, tears of her own streaking an otherwise picture-perfect complexion.

You remember your father's coworker helping him to his feet, leading your stooped father into the shade of the porch to cool down and rest. You remember slipping away, taking your plate of ice cream around the side of the house and sitting on the front stoop, using your knees as a trembling table. You remember staring past the oozing lump on your plate, contemplating what your life would look like if your father had died just now. And you remember most the feeling of relief that filled your belly at the thought, cool as the center of the ice cream ball in front of you—

free

—followed swiftly by a flood of guilt too hot to bear.

crying

I'd thought Kyle's room was empty, but I should've known where to look.

In the corner there's a three-foot gap between the end of his bunk bed and the wall. Even if the tiny sniffles coming from the darkened corner weren't giving him away right now, it's also Kyle's go-to hiding place for hide-and-seek.

He cries hard, a little forced, then pauses to see if I've heard. I know he's not faking his sadness, just making sure I'm paying attention to him.

I approach the wet hiccuping sounds until his small head of light brown hair comes into view, and then I put on my softest stern voice. "Kyle, what's wrong?"

A renewed wave of crying answers.

Setting the cup and phone down, I pull my body between the wooden slats of the bottom bunk and squeeze myself beside a balled-up Kyle. He's squished into the corner, head bent, fists jammed with LEGOs.

I take one look at the white-knuckled fists, then begin to talk. By instinct, I avoid bringing up anything from the past few days, reaching back to my "boring" school day on Friday, before the cops came screaming down our driveway, before I walked out to the school curb and our lives changed forever.

I tell him about how I got an A-plus on my world history quiz where I had to memorize the name and location of every single country on Earth—195 in all—*plus* all their capitals; how next week in that same class we get to pick our favorite civilization we've learned about this year and do an art project on it. I tell Kyle I'm picking Ancient Egypt so I can make a mummy out of sugar, cheesecloth, and an old Barbie. I'll mummify her, then place her in a sarcophagus, which is a stone coffin, that I'll also make, which will open and everything, and that I'll paint to look old and like it's made out of rock. Then, if there's time, I'll also make tiny containers to hold all her pretend organs like the canopic jars they used with real mummified people back in the day.

I don't tell him I was supposed to do this project with Hannah, that even though we don't have World Civ at the same time, we got special permission from the teacher to collab on it together after school. But I'm not sure if that's the case anymore—if it's still okay or now forbidden. What I do say is that I'll have to cut off the Barbie's plastic blond hair first, before I mummify her, and that Kyle's more than welcome to help if he wants to. I tell him he can even use my grown-up scissors if he's careful.

Kyle's crying slows.

I tell him about lunch on Friday, and how Brooke—your basic, stereotypical mean girl—dumped a huge plate of French fries and ketchup into her lap, all over her new white skirt. I don't say this was after Hannah disappeared from class but before I'd searched and searched for her in the school hallways when she wasn't at her locker, texting her with no response. Instead, I tell Kyle about the way Brooke had leapt up from her seat, shrieking, a huge red ketchup patch staining her front, and how I'd laughed and laughed but only on the inside.

A smile tugs at Kyle's lips.

When I get to the end of Friday's school day, to our white Nissan parked at the curb, I mentally backtrack a month or so, to the last time I went over to Hannah's house—even though I feel a twinge when I mention her name. I tell him how the two of us had played the board game Tombstone on her bedroom floor, and how I'd won every single round.

At the mention of Hannah and Tombstone, Kyle's face finally turns toward mine. His cheeks are still pink and splotchy, but he's listening—he adores Hannah and Tombstone almost as much as I do. And though he's aware something is wrong, something big, he doesn't know enough to realize that Hannah's banished from this house forever and that the mere mention of her name in front of our parents is now a curse. At least, he doesn't know yet, anyway.

Kyle runs a sleeve across his still-runny nose as I tell him about our three rounds of Tombstone, making up any detail I can't quite recall, especially about the ghost hunters: the weapons and supplies each one carries, their strengths and weaknesses, and how Griselda the Vanquisher is the best one because she can throw ghost vaporizer bombs *and* carry a protective charm.

Kyle sits very still, absorbing every detail, as the streaks of tears begin to dry on his cheeks.

"And now it's your turn," I tell him. "How was your day?"

Fresh tears spring to his eyes. "Not very good."

"Which part wasn't very good? Are you sad about something?"

Kyle hesitates, then nods.

"What are you sad about?"

As I'm talking, I massage Kyle's hands, gently prying LEGO pieces one at a time from his fists and setting each one on the floor beside us without ever looking down. I leave only Benny in Kyle's fist because removing him would definitely draw my brother's attention.

Kyle stares through the small pile of extracted LEGOs as he answers. "I'm a bad boy." He almost makes it through the sentence without his voice cracking. "Dad got arrested because I'm a bad boy."

His answer doesn't quite fit the question I'd asked, but the way he blurts it out makes me realize he's been holding on to the thought for a while, possibly this whole time. The realization cuts. "Don't be ridiculous, Kyle. Why would you say that?"

"I'm not ridiculous," he says, pouting.

"No, of course you're not. I didn't mean that. What I meant was 'silly.' Don't be silly, okay? But why would you think that?"

His tears return, fists reclenching into rocks around Benny.

This time it takes me several minutes to ease an answer out of him. Finally, he manages, "I didn't listen to my teacher on Thursday. Or do my counting worksheet. Or write good letters."

I laugh—my relief launching from me like a harsh bark.

"Don't laugh!" Kyle yells, tears spilling over.

I can't help it; I laugh again, and it tastes delicious. Like cookie dough ice cream in the chocolate-dipped, sprinkle-covered waffle cones Hannah and I would always order together in town. "I'm laughing because you're being silly again, Kyle. None of those things got Dad arrested. You did not get Dad arrested."

"Then who did?"

Hannah. Me.

"Well, sometimes bad things happen to good people," I say,

evading. "Aren't you a good person?" When he doesn't answer, I nudge his shoulder. "Well, aren't you?"

He nods.

"And do bad things happen to you sometimes?"

He nods again.

"See? Sometimes bad things just happen, but that doesn't mean it's your fault, okay?" I hope my face looks confident.

Hannah. Me.

Kyle pauses for a second, then nods.

"So it's settled. It's not your fault, and you aren't going to think that ever again, okay?"

"Will Dad go back to jail?" he asks.

It's my turn to pause. He's ruminating on this and has been since yesterday's Pretend Happy Easter, so clearly the answer I'd given him then hadn't been enough. I hurry to fill the silence, knowing that this time I can't distract him away from a proper explanation. "No, of course not. Dad can't go back to jail. He needs to take care of us, right?" I feel the lie bloom in the center of my chest, but I ignore the expanding pressure, telling myself it's worth the hope I'm gifting Kyle. It's worth the worry I'm erasing so that he can let go of the thought that's so obviously plaguing him, even if only for now.

After a beat Kyle nods once more.

"So he wouldn't do that," I rush on. "Let anyone take him away from us. Not ever again. He's not going anywhere, okay?" The blossoming lie grows thorns.

Kyle's looking down, which is maybe why he doesn't see the fib. "Okay," he whispers.

Again, I throw as much cheer as I can into my voice. "All

righty, then. Now that that's settled, what do you say we get out of this dark space and go play some LEGOs, huh? My butt's falling asleep!"

Kyle lets out a tiny breath of a laugh. It hits me in the chest right next to my lie, and I don't think I've ever heard a more beautiful sound. The warmth of it feeds my generosity. "And I'll read you an extra chapter of Ninjago tonight, okay? Would that make you feel better?"

Kyle nods his most vigorous nod yet, and then we gather up all the LEGO pieces and climb out from the corner, my body growing heavier with every passing second.

I just promised Kyle that Dad won't go back to jail, and with my interview looming in less than two days, I can think of only one way to keep that promise to Kyle, to Dad.

Hannah. Me. No longer.

I leave Kyle to play, taking small comfort in the fact that his frown is a little less intense, his grip looser on his LEGO guys. When I return to the kitchen, Mom yells about how long it took me to find one single cup. I finish helping her with the dishes, then wait till she retires to her room so I can make school lunches unobserved for tomorrow—turkey for me and PB and J for Kyle. Mom always grabs a bagel from the bakery near her work since she says my lunches are "subpar," though I start to make one for Dad like I always do until I remember he's not going to work. And, of course, tomorrow he has court, which I know is in the morning, but I'm not sure how long he'll be there. Plus, Mom is going too, so maybe I should make her one as well? My brain locks up, and I can't decide, but I also don't want to disturb either of them to ask, so I spend the next several minutes agonizing, putting the lunch fixings away only to pull them back out again. Finally, I settle on making just Dad a lunch but stack his Craisins and tortilla chips on top of his sandwich in the fridge instead of putting it all into a paper bag so he can see it's there. I don't know if he'll eat it, or if Mom will be mad I didn't make her one this time, and I know my brain will loop back to this all night with growing conviction and panic that I made the wrong decision.

Next, I make sure Kyle's changed into pj's and brushed his teeth before I read him an extra chapter like I promised.

At last, I trudge up to my room and close the door, noticing that Dad's not in his study anymore.

I jolt at a buzzing sound, then realize it's a text notification, but it's only a heart emoji from Aunt Jane, not Hannah. Pulling the concert ticket from my purse where I'd stashed it earlier, I stare down at the print—*Corey Starr. Roseland Theater.* The address. The date: three weeks from now. The time: *7 p.m.*

Holding the ticket, I realize I don't know what to do or how to choose. Hannah's the greatest thing to ever happen to me, but Dad just told me I can't be friends with her anymore. Besides, how can I honestly hang out with her if she's the reason my family's falling apart? Why Dad's lost his job and has to hire a lawyer for a case that may go to trial; why Kyle was just crying, terrified Dad will have to go back to jail; why Mom's furious with me, even more so than usual. Because Hannah was *my* best friend.

Is. She *is* my best friend.

I don't have to choose, my brain lies as I stare across the room at Hector's sad, sand-less pot that I still need to somehow refill.

Turning away, I pull open the side pocket of my backpack and zip the ticket in with my highlighters. Alongside the ticket, I try to shut away all thoughts of my police-confiscated journal as well as Hannah's, that she wrote in and her mother found. This last part twinges *something* in my brain, but I push that away also, too tired to linger there.

Instead, I crawl under the covers and try to lose myself in *Grimm Tales* for the rest of the night while every part of me dreads going to school tomorrow. After Breeyan's *Aren't your parents super young?* stunt from earlier, I'm now certain everyone knows about my dad.

But above them all knowing, I dread the thought of seeing Hannah tomorrow and having to navigate the hair-thin, slippery line between maintaining my friendship with her and my father's insistence that she and I stop being friends. Yet, as I think it, I wonder if this town will even give me a choice.

You remember the knife

You remember the knife you kept under your pillow since last Halloween—a plastic-handled steak knife with a serrated edge that no one would miss because it was so old. And in the dark of your room, when the world pressed too mightily against your breastbone, you would pull it out, watch its metal blade reflect the tiny glint of light from the streetlamp a field away. Hold it against the blue veins of your pale wrist. Will yourself to saw deep enough.

The knife was for you alone, though you only ever made superficial cuts, ones that always healed in a day or two, concealed by the many rows of glass-beaded wrap bracelets you'd made with Hannah at Cats Club. This helped you convince yourself that maybe—just maybe—you didn't really want to die.

"The Girl and the Haunting Shadows"

Once upon a time there lived a girl—a loyal, timid girl who resided with her stepmother in a modest stone cottage. The cottage sat at the edge of a dark forest, and, above all else, the girl feared these woods, for she had been raised with the knowledge that these sinister trees had snatched her father away many years ago. That fateful day, or so it was told, the heavy shadows within the forest had lured the girl's father inside and consumed him with darkness. From the moment he had entered the towering oaks, he was never seen nor heard from again.

Since the father's tragic demise, the stepmother had taken to her bed until their coin had dwindled and the girl was forced to sell most of their worldly possessions. And even then, the stepmother made no effort to leave the cottage in order to provide for herself and her stepdaughter.

With every passing day, the stepmother would shout what a terrible burden the girl was. To atone for this, the girl would gather wild herbs, toadstools, roots, and flowers from the edge of the forest. She would cook them into meals or sell them in the village market, alongside the small eggs and mealy vegetables she collected from their three hens and simple garden.

All this she did in the company of her most beloved

companion—a small yellow songbird, vivid as a buttercup in full sunlight. The girl had rescued this bird from a hunter's snare, and in return, the songbird kept her company while she worked outdoors, flitting in and out of the dark woods unaffected or else perching on the girl's shoulder, all the while trilling a melody so sweet it seemed to banish all gloom. Only the stepmother loathed the bird, slamming windows shut whenever it sang too near the cottage.

One day, in the company of her songbird, as the girl gathered wild strawberries near the woods' edge, an unusual sight caught her eye. There, amongst the fallen leaves in a small copse of trees, was a toadstool larger and more magnificent than any she had seen before. Its cap was a rich shade of violet, its stalk a hand's width tall. Large orange spots dotted it like many staring eyes.

Overcome with curiosity and forgetting herself entirely, the girl ventured into the woods, plucking the majestic toadstool from the damp earth. The shrill cry of the songbird returned her to the present just in time, and she realized with mounting terror that the shadows of the forest all but surrounded her. One shadow stood out from the rest, in a shape reminiscent of her father, with sharp claws and haunting eyes. The girl cried out in fright.

Yet, no sooner had she opened her mouth than her beloved songbird swooped inside, where she promptly swallowed it. Astonished, the girl felt a strange fluttering in her heart where her songbird thrummed, warm and very much alive. There, it sang its melancholy tune, driving back the shadows that could no longer quite reach the girl.

Scooping up the toadstool, the girl ran, pursued by the shadows all the way to the back gate of her cottage. She did not slow until she and the songbird in her heart were safely inside once more. "Thank you, songbird," whispered she. "I promise to release you just as soon as I'm able."

At the sight of the stepmother, however, the bird shrilled louder than ever. Yet the stepmother only had eyes for the toadstool. "Devil's Cap," she croaked. "Where did you get such a thing?"

"At the edge of the woods," replied the girl.

"Those are used in the darkest of potions," replied the stepmother, eyes shining with greed. "They are very rare and valuable. Go now and sell that to the old witch. She will pay you handsomely."

And thus, with the songbird still fluttering in her breast, the girl went straightaway to the far side of the village where the old witch lived. When the girl showed the witch what she had brought, the witch paid her in heavy coin, enough that the girl and her stepmother could live comfortably throughout the long winter.

But as the girl turned to leave, the old witch pointed a bony finger at the girl's heart. Speaking in a voice as brittle as dry bone, the witch said, "Girl with shadows in her past, present, future. Once, your faithful companion has saved you from the black depths of the forest. Yet if you are to survive twice—nay, thrice—you must keep your feathered companion at your heart, for its song is your sole defense against the forest of shadows. Upon your final return, release your companion by saying so. But make haste, girl, for birds were not meant to live in cages."

At these words, the girl felt perplexed. She had no intention of keeping the songbird trapped, and she needn't survive the woods, for she would never enter them again. To her heart, the girl vowed silently, *Songbird, I promise to release you just as soon as I'm able.*

But the old witch had not yet finished. "Beware too, girl, all you take from the black wood, for it demands a sacrifice. And above all else, beware the shadows lurking nearest home."

With that, the girl took her leave, pondering the meaning of the old witch's words all the way to the cottage; however, she needn't wait long, for when the stepmother saw the heavy coin in the girl's hand, her eyes shone brighter with greed.

"Girl," replied the stepmother, scarcely audible over the shrill cry of the songbird. "Return to the woods at once and fetch another toadstool."

Remembering how the shadows with haunting eyes had nearly consumed her, the girl shook with fear. "But, Mama, this coin will keep us full in bread and cheese throughout winter. And the shadows frighten me, Papa's amongst them!"

"There are no shadows, you silly girl!" cried the stepmother. "Only that horrid bird's beastly song, driving me mad! Now off with you, and dare not return till you have fetched another."

Obedient yet afraid, the girl ventured to the back gate where the dark shadows waited. To her heart, she pleaded silently, *Songbird, please protect me once more. The shadows are after me. You will be safe. I promise to release you just as soon as I'm able.*

In response, the songbird burst into melody. Emboldened, the girl stepped outside the gate, and, once more, the shadows did not close around her forthright. Thus, the girl entered the woods for a second time, venturing deeper than before as the songbird sang its melodious tune to keep the shadows at bay. Soon, the girl discovered another Devil's Cap, larger and grander than the first.

Yet, upon their return journey, the songbird's tune grew softer, for so weary was the small creature. All the while, the shadows grew closer, nearly reaching the girl's skirts. And when the girl finally took leave of the woods, the shadows did not halt at the back gate, instead pursuing her all the way to the cottage door where she could scarcely outrun them.

Inside, instead of a joyful reunion at the sight of the second Devil's Cap, the stepmother's eyes brimmed with deeper greed yet. "Such a small trifle you bring back?" replied she. "Go and fetch a larger one at once."

"But, Mama, the shadows! And Papa's amongst them!"

"There are no shadows, you silly girl! Only that horrid bird's beastly song. Now go, and dare not return till you have fetched another."

The girl's heart grew heavy at this, for she understood that if she were to venture into the woods for a third time, the journey would prove too great a burden for her beloved songbird, for the small creature had grown so weak. And yet the girl knew she could not refuse her stepmother, for so vast had become her greed.

Thus, the girl hurried from her cottage door for a third and final time, even as the songbird's melody grew fainter still, hardly bold enough to drive off the shadows nipping at her heels. To her heart, the girl pleaded silently, *Songbird, please protect me this one final time. The shadows are after me. You will be safe. I promise to release you just as soon as I'm able.*

Thus, thrice the girl journeyed into the woods, farther and deeper than before. And no sooner had she plucked the grandest of the Devil's Cap from the earth did the songbird fall quiet, its small heart scarcely beating beside her own. So taxed was the small creature, it stood on the brink of death. Without the songbird's melody, the shadows crept nearer, pulling at the girl's skirts.

Suddenly, the girl knew that if she were to use the last of the songbird's melody to deliver herself safely home, her most beloved and loyal companion would surely die. The girl also understood that, upon her return, the stepmother would undoubtedly send her into the woods once more, this time to be consumed by shadows without the bird's protection, for so insatiable was the stepmother's greed and insistence that the shadows did not exist.

In this moment of greatest despair, with her bird companion growing ever frailer and the shadows moving in, the words of the old witch came back to the girl: *Beware . . . all you take from the black wood, for it demands a sacrifice. And above all else, beware the shadows lurking nearest home.*

At long last, the girl understood. The shadows were not near her home; they had already crept inside, a fact to which her songbird had tried to warn her, crying its shrill cry each time they were in the stepmother's presence. In both these woods and her cottage, the girl was in the gravest of dangers and could not escape.

And yet . . .

Release your companion by saying so.

The girl also realized there was someone she could save. Even as the shadows tugged at her sleeves and pulled at her hair, the girl spoke aloud these words: "Songbird, I release you."

Something tore at the girl's breast moments before the tiny bird shot from her mouth and flew in stuttering circles above her head.

As the shadows closed in, wrapping their icy fingers around the girl and dragging her down, she watched in perfect wonder as her most cherished companion—the small songbird, vivid as a buttercup in full sunlight—flew beyond the treetops and disappeared to safety.

mean

Monday

The school bus bounces through the thick fog and over yet another pothole as it heads for town. Our district is small enough that the elementary, junior high, and high school all share the same bus—dropping off the little kids first, then the sixth through twelfth graders since the junior high and high school are neighboring buildings. Plus, on any given day, usually only half the bus seats are full. And though it's been almost a whole academic year, Mom still worries Kyle won't be able to find his classroom by himself, so every day, I get off at Kyle's stop, walk him to class, then jog the five blocks to the high school before the second bell rings. Which is going to be tougher today since Hank, the bus driver, is running behind schedule, having picked us up almost seven minutes late.

I'm in my usual seat in the back row, my feet tucked up under me as I lean into the window. Per usual, I keep an eye trained mid-bus where Kyle also sits by a window, his head bobbing with each bump. And, as always, he insists on sitting by himself, even though he usually has trouble with the older kids.

Today my eyelids feel too heavy, my body sagging with fatigue, which makes watching him tough. Last night's relentless thoughts have left me bone-tired, and the idea of sleep feels so alluring, lingering just behind my eyelids, growing closer as the bus engine drones on. But when we near the light gray house with black trim, I force myself upright, blinking hard.

Yet thankfully, for once, there must be a swirl of luck in the clouds because Derek doesn't stand outside, waiting to catch the bus. Though Derek's only ten, he's one of Kyle's biggest tormentors, seeking Kyle out in every situation to stick him with cruel insults or the tip of a sharpened pencil, just hard enough to hurt but not hard enough to leave a mark. Every time I confront him, he slinks away, but only because I'm older, and just for that moment, and sometimes not even then. Everyone knows that the one person Derek fears is his mother, in case the bruises seeping from under Derek's sleeves or the frequent "accidents" that take him out of school for days aren't proof enough. But in this town, everyone seems to have adopted a strict "mind your own business" policy, except, of course, in the case of my dad.

We sail past Derek's house with a speed that indicates even bus-driver Hank is breathing a sigh of relief that Derek didn't show.

I let my eyes close again, basking in the luxury of it, because now I don't need to open them again till we reach Hannah's house.

At the thought of her, a small tug of worry pulls at my chest. I hung out with Hannah just yesterday, but that was before her mom picked her up. I still can't get over it—the way Hannah wouldn't look at me, sidestepping away as soon as her mom appeared. Or the look Mrs. Garber gave me when we locked eyes, like she was angry but also scared, maybe even of me. Or Breeyan, Sequoia, and Justin, all pretending to be so interested in my parents' ages so they didn't have to ask straight-out if my dad was the one arrested on salacious allegations. And they must all know who the accuser is too, otherwise why would they be scrutinizing Hannah's and my every move yesterday? The thought takes with it the few spool-lengths of energy I woke up with.

I glance back at Kyle. From what I can see around the other bus riders, he appears to be drawing random shapes on the fogged glass, whispering to Benny and holding the LEGO guy up to see his handiwork. The rocking of the bus tugs at my eyelids until at last I give in, letting the image of Kyle pinch out of sight.

I wake with a start when I hear my name, then spring to my feet. The bus is idling in front of the elementary school, and all the little kids are off the bus with only the older kids remaining. I search for Hannah's familiar strawberry-blond waves, but I don't see her. It's just people I don't have classes with, all staring at me probably because I've managed to drool all over. Hannah must not have taken the bus today. She usually gets her mom to take her so she can sleep a little later, but I'd hoped she'd make an exception this morning.

Snatching up my backpack from where it's slid under the seat, I dash off the bus and fling a small "Bye!" in response to Hank's "Have a good day now, Emma."

My eyes lock on Kyle, who stands off to one side, peering out through a serious expression. Sighing in relief that he hasn't wandered far, I make my way over, noticing as I do a milky stain on the front of his blue sweater. It looks vaguely like a lopsided heart, tipped on its side, one half pooled into the other. I hate anything asymmetrical, almost more than stains on sweaters.

"What did you get on your sweater?" I ask, snapping him out of his daze.

Kyle glances down, almost going cross-eyed and bottom lip jutting out as he pulls at his sweater to examine the stain. He shrugs. "Yogurt."

I should've known judging from the smears in both corners of his mouth. Not to mention, I was the one who'd gotten him the yogurt this morning to go with his cereal, since we're still out of milk, and Mom and Dad had to leave early for Dad's arraignment. And with only one yogurt left, I'd eaten my own cereal with applesauce, which hadn't even been half bad.

"Then why didn't you grab a new sweater before we left?" I ask, though I already know the answer, too—there weren't any other clean sweaters. I'd spotted the red sleeve of my own sweater hanging from the overflowing hampers in the laundry room on my way out the back door. Plus, I should've seen him spill his yogurt, or noticed while we waited for the bus, but my mind had been overloaded.

Kyle shrugs again.

I feel the anxiety start to expand my chest like a water balloon filling too fast. "Well, now we'll have to go get you cleaned up." And quick, so I'm not late to my own classes.

We enter the elementary school's main building, and I'm about to steer him into a bathroom when Kyle plants his feet.

"I can't go in there!" he insists, horrified. "That's the girls' bathroom!"

"Kyle, who cares? Besides, it's just for a second so I can get a paper towel."

"But it's the *girls'* bathroom!" he wails.

My brain fills with "gender's a societal construct" counterarguments, but I'm running out of time, and I don't know if he'd get it anyway. "Kyle, the bell's about to ring! Now come *on*!" I tug on his backpack as the balloon in my chest expands, stretching thin.

"I'm not going!" He fights, twisting his backpack and almost dropping Benny in the process.

"Well, how the hell am I supposed to clean your sweater if you won't come with me?" I tug again, the word "hell" I'd just used against Kyle tasting like pennies on my tongue. But my pulling is in vain because Kyle wrenches free and takes off down the hall toward his class.

"Kyle, stop!" I hiss.

Nearly-tardy students and their parents stare at me, because I'm trying to keep my voice down and failing or because they read newspapers, I don't know.

"Kyle!" I call again, then jog to catch up. Spinning him around, I demand, "What are you doing? We have to get you cleaned up!"

"I don't care," he says without looking at me, though I know he does care.

"Fine," I say, halting, short of breath. "Whatever. Look like a slob, then!" I watch as his golden-brown head of hair weaves around the hallway stragglers before disappearing inside his classroom.

Guilt clutches at me. I was so mean to Kyle just now, raising my voice and calling him a slob. Imagining the tipped-over heart still staining his sweater fills me with bottomless sadness.

Now I doubt I'll have time to find Hannah before school and talk to her. It'll have to wait till third period. But I *need* to talk to her, for so many reasons. I was up half the night thinking about each and every reason—because of tomorrow's interview, yes, but most of all, because of her journal. I've only just allowed myself to acknowledge that things don't quite add up there, so I need her to say it to my face.

I turn and sprint, flying out the front door, wishing with everything I've got that I could outrun my thoughts.

You remember falling from trees

You remember climbing a tree a few years back with your younger brother. It was the large, shadowy tree that grew beside the house that would scratch its skeletal fingers against your bedroom window on particularly blustery evenings. The same tree that towered over your white picket fence and made you think about the boy who had died out at the ranch where you had camped with your father . . . (But then you didn't want to remember that trip anymore, so you grasped that last memory in your fist and hurled it away.)

You remember your brother had climbed higher in the tree than you and stood on a tiny branch that looked far too thin for his weight, his bare toes curled over the edge. He wore a red bandanna around his head like a pirate because that's what you were playing, and the tree was the tall, tall mast of his ship. The sight of his delicate toes on such a slight branch conjured up the image of the branch snapping beneath your own feet and your body plummeting to the ground. You remember this gave you an idea for a funny joke. So you bent your knees and hung from the branch at your brother's feet with one hand so it looked like that one hand was your sole lifeline to the tree. The other hand you reached up to him, gasping as if startled.

When his eyes snapped to yours, you put on your most terri-fied voice. *Kyle! Kyle!* you pleaded. *I'm falling! Please help me!* You remember you did a magnificent job of pretending to dangle help-lessly, if you do say so yourself.

You remember his eyes widening in alarm, wider than you had ever seen them grow, as his small hand reached down for yours, squeezing it tight as he yelled, *Sis! Don't fall!* As if his tiny hand could save you, could hold you up against the entire weight of the world, the inevitable gravity of such a drop.

You remember realizing in that instant just how terrified you had made him, and how quickly you stood up on the branch at your feet, not meeting his eyes as you dusted off your palms, telling him that you had just been kidding. You even tried to lighten your voice to explain the joke that had never been funny. When recognition of your betrayal dawned across his face, you remember how he began to bawl, his inconsolable tears rendering you the most terrible sister—the most terrible girl—that had ever lived. And looking at your brother sobbing under his crooked red bandanna, Pirate Cap-tain of the Tall-Masted Tree, you asked yourself how you could have possibly thought it would be comical to deceive him.

Kyle, I'm so sorry. I didn't mean to scare you, you remember say-ing in your softest voice. But he kept on crying and crying until his whole face went red and he shook with such violence, you feared he really would fall from the tree. And you remember the weight of your guilt—an anchor with chain wrapped three times round your ankle—that should have yanked you from that tree, too, and dashed you to the sparse grass and jutting tree roots below.

Above all, you remember how, for months afterward, every time you recalled that moment, the memory sent waves of guilt coursing through you that never diminished in size or intensity. And for a long, long time, it remained one of the saddest memories you could recall—despite everything that came before and after. From then on, you vowed to be a sister who would never ever hurt her little brother, who would protect him from the cruelty of sadness, of the world, at all costs.

betrayal

After what feels like days, third period arrives at last. I make it to geometry just as the bell sounds, which seems to be a reoccurring theme today.

My eyes go straight to Hannah, who beckons me to come sit by her despite the fact that it's my regular seat. Permission granted, I guess? I force a grin even though I'm annoyed that all the normal life stuff seems to now need confirmation, whereas before Friday, everything between Hannah and me was a given. Still, some of my worry disappears with Hannah's ecstatic smile, even though it's a shade too wide again.

I sit at my desk, the one with a faded Millennium Falcon sticker stuck on top, and glance at a distracted-looking Mr. Barnham before meeting Hannah's eyes. We've got a few seconds to talk.

"Hey, I was waiting for you all morning," Hannah says, voice as energetic as her smile. "Where were you?"

Yesterday I found Hannah's enthusiasm a little confusing. Today my irritation flares at the sound of it.

"Oh, just dealing with Kyle." I shrug. "You know, little brothers."

As an only child, she doesn't, but nods anyway.

"I like your earrings!" she exclaims. "Those new?"

My fingers draw to one ear, feeling the miniature velociraptor.

The lost ladybug and Dad's indignant fury spring to mind. I don't respond.

Mr. Barnham's "All right, class!" booms out, and Hannah turns to me in a rush.

"Guess we'll have to make plans at lunch!" Her expression goes exaggerated-enthused, clearly overcompensating for my lack of eagerness.

"Plans?" I echo.

She feigns exasperation. "Um, the concert, dorkface! It's only three weeks away, in case you've forgotten!"

Hannah's always calling me pretend-insult names, and "dork-face" is tame compared to many of her others, but today it just feels obnoxious, not to mention immature.

"Right," I say with a fraction of her passion, even though I know I should be trying harder. Why am I being like this?

Her upbeat expression falters as a cloud of confusion passes over, before returning full force. Then she does an exaggerated eye roll before turning to face front, and I just about lose it. It's not just her annoying name-calling or fake enthusiasm. It's the concert, and the fact that she's not only tainting today us with all this phony sincerity, but she's also doing it to three-weeks-from-now us as well. Who knows where Dad's court case is even going to be by then—in trial already? In front of a judge and jury? Then what?

Her mom wants her to have absolutely nothing to do with me, a fact I'm now certain of after seeing Mrs. Garber yesterday. That, and she has zero idea Hannah gave me the concert ticket. So why won't Hannah just admit it? Why all this pretend planning and pretense like we can go anywhere together, let alone to this ridiculous concert, when it's obviously impossible? In case she somehow forgot, her mom's breathing down her neck and Dad's breathing down mine, both saying it's for the best that Hannah and I don't hang out anymore. Hannah hasn't told me her mom's said this as of late, but if it was the case before Dad got arrested, it's certainly the case now.

As I pull out my homework and pass it toward the front of the room, tossing it too hard to Leo in front of me, I realize this: come lunchtime, Hannah and I are most definitely going to discuss the concert, though not in any way she's expecting.

"So this is the hotel I found. Check it out! It's right beside the venue!"

Hannah's got her phone out and is expecting me to lean in. We've just sat at our customary picnic table, one we invited ourselves to back in September until the original owners vacated. Our lunches are not even unpacked, and already she's back to concert planning. Since we met up at our lockers, I've said no more than two words, but it doesn't seem to matter. Clearly, someone spent most of her anatomy period mapping out every second of our concert-going, and there's no stopping her.

"Em." An edge of exasperation cuts through her voice at last. "You're not even looking. This place is amazing!"

It took her long enough to realize that my enthusiasm didn't quite match up to hers. And yet, all it would take is for me to lean in and *ooh* and *aah* like I normally would. To tell her how rad I think the lobby is or how cool that they have a pool or to make some joke about sneaking alcohol from the minibar. But I can't bring myself to do it.

"I kinda need to eat, Hannah, given that it's lunchtime?" It comes out far harsher than I mean it to, loaded with all the anger of the words I'm still not saying.

Hannah pulls her eyes from her phone, small frown lines knitting her brow. "We have a whole forty minutes to eat, Em. But that's not what's important right now. We need to nail down a hotel so that we can then—"

"So that we can what, Hannah?" This time there's no trace of warmth in my voice. "Pretend like we're going to actually stay there, in some amazing hotel?"

Hannah's looking at me like she doesn't recognize me, but that makes two of us. I've never talked to Hannah like this. I've never had thoughts of her with any real resentment attached, but every word coming out of my mouth right now is dripping in anger.

"What do you mean?" she asks, and her genuine confusion flames my fury to an all-time high. Has she really convinced herself so completely that everything is fine, perfectly *normal*, that even when I call her out, she has no idea what I'm saying?

For days now, we've both been kidding ourselves, acting like things could ever be ordinary between us again. Yet, at least *I* knew what we were doing—pulling the wool over our own eyes—but did Hannah? Did she not understand that it was all a lie? That it wasn't—couldn't ever be—real? That, sooner or later, our little game of "faking normal" had to end? Well, there's no time like the present.

I shove my lunch bag aside. "Hannah, does your mom know you gave me that second ticket?"

Her pause is infinitesimal, gaze skittering away. "It doesn't matter."

"It *does*, Hannah! It matters a hell of a lot."

"She doesn't need to know," Hannah says, arms crossing, defensive. "It's *my* present."

"That she bought you," I add. "For far too much money. Because you were 'sad.'"

I air-quote the word, which is mean, but I can't stop myself. Even so, I'm only toeing around Dad's arrest, though it still catches her off guard. She must also be thinking back to Friday and this agonizing past weekend because her face goes from surprised-hurt to blank as she looks away.

"Plus, who's going to drive us there?" I demand. "Your mom, maybe? Or mine?"

Hannah flinches. "I mean, there's a bus—"

I shove my lunch bag off the table. It goes flying, and everyone stares; they were probably already staring, but I don't care. I don't even *care*.

"Hannah, they aren't going to let us go, okay? They were never going to. Not together, not now, not *ever*. You saw the look your mom gave me yesterday. She hates me; she thinks I'm trash and that you and I shouldn't be friends. She's always thought that, so don't try and tell me she doesn't, okay? So there's no way this worthless concert is going to happen, and you sure as hell should know that by now because I certainly do!" I slam my palm into my chest at these last words, breathing hard.

Hannah stares at me for a long time, eyes brimming with tears. I watch as both eyes overflow and drip tears down her face. She doesn't wipe them away. In a tiny voice that feels like someone else's entirely, she whispers, "I know, Em."

My heart cracks at this small truth, and I feel my anger start to whisk away. Then she adds, "But what's the harm in pretending, right?"

Fury rebuilds in me like a rising storm. I've had all the

play-pretend bullshit I can stand for an entire *lifetime*.

"Hannah, why did you really write that stuff in your journal?"

There it is. The biggest white lie between us, spilled out of me and into the open at last.

I've known all along that Hannah never writes in journals, that it's never made any sense for her to have written anything import-ant down, especially about my dad, given how nosy her mom can be. The truth is, in the back of my mind, ever since Hannah said it was her journal that started all this, I think I've known the real reason. I just couldn't admit it. Digging any deeper would've cost me too much—then I'd really have had to choose.

But I've finally asked the question, and there's no taking it back now. And if there's ever been one thing about Hannah I admire most, it's that, in the end, she'll always answer a direct question honestly.

Hannah's hazel eyes drill into me, all traces of her enthusiasm gone, which is how I know that when she speaks, it's going to be the truth.

"Because I knew my mom would find my journal." Her gaze bores a hole right through me, and then she shrugs, though it's anything but casual. "I knew Mom would make it stop when I didn't know how to. At least, that's why my therapist says I did it, but I don't think she's wrong."

Dizzy, I absorb every word in my chest like a Robin Hood, arrow-splitting bull's-eye. Apparently Hannah also has a therapist now, though that's hardly her biggest revelation.

"When . . . ?" is all I can manage. *When did you write that stuff? When did your mother find your journal?* Which all comes back to: *How long have I not known?*

But Hannah knows me intimately, knows what I'm asking

without me even having to finish. "A few weeks ago." It's a mere whisper, gaze dropping, both of us fully aware that every single day in between—every single day that she could've told me but didn't—has been a betrayal. "She found the journal a few weeks ago, not on Friday, like I told you yesterday. It's why I've been acting so weird lately," she says. "Why I haven't been able to come to your house. I couldn't, Em, ever since Mom dragged me into the police station, and showed them the journal, and they asked me to help them investigate . . . him."

Him. My father. She still can't even say his name.

"After that, Mom didn't want me hanging out with you at all, even at school." Hannah's eyes swim with apology. "But I told her it wasn't your fault, that you didn't have anything to do with it. That it was all him. That he's . . ." She breaks off, unable or unwilling to go there before continuing in a rush. "Plus, the police said we should act as normal as possible, so she finally agreed that I could still hang out with you, but only at school, even though I wanted it to be more. Then she pulled me out of class on Friday when she knew they were going to . . . go get him."

"You've been . . . helping the police"—I swallow—"investigate *for weeks*?" It takes me several tries to choke it all out, my brain working overtime to process every fragment. "You wrote in your journal, *on purpose*, for your mom to find so that they would *arrest him*? You've only been hanging out with me lately so I wouldn't be *suspicious*? And you left school early so you wouldn't have to witness the devastation from *your* dirty work?"

My head swims with the truth of it all.

"Em, that's not . . ."

But I hardly hear her.

Weeks of lies. She's been helping them destroy Dad's life. My life. Kyle's and Mom's. For *weeks*.

Does she have any idea what she's done?

I stare at her, someone I thought I knew, but who's clearly a total stranger. Which begs the question, what else has she been keeping from me? What the hell else don't I know? She's been lying to me this entire time when I thought we never—*never*—could lie to each other.

But here she was, pretending her mother "accidentally" found her journal that she "accidentally" wrote a bunch of terrible things about my dad in while I was foolish enough to believe that this scenario was totally plausible, just a little *whoopsie!* in an otherwise rock-solid friendship.

Well, screw that noise. Because no real friend would work with the cops to destroy your family, no matter what, and they wouldn't lie to your face while they did it either, smiling evil counterfeit grins and giving you worthless concert tickets to see your favorite singer, all so they could feel better about burning your entire life to the ground.

"I have to go." I snatch my lunch bag from the dirt and sling my backpack onto my shoulder, then turn so she won't see me cry.

"Emma?" Hannah waits for me to look at her.

At long last, I do, rooted to the ground next to our picnic table, feeling the cold meanness written across my face.

I see the tears falling down her cheeks too, feel the sadness radiating from her—so big, I can't see its edges. It's the same kind drowning my own heart, but that I can't let myself show.

"We're still friends, right?" Hannah pleads, a desperate echo of yesterday's question.

"How could we be?"

I watch my words cut into her.

On purpose. For weeks.

How many conversations have we had while she was doing the police's bidding? Spying for them? Asking questions so she could get it on the record? Is that why she'd been so quick to hand over that text with her birth date? Because it had alleviated some of her guilt to be on the other side, being stolen from instead of being the thief?

A huge wave of relief washes over me now, for all the things even Hannah and I have never talked about. The police will never know what I know, what I saw—any of it—because I'm not like her. I don't give away my best friend's secrets. Not to anyone, not ever.

Her hand grips my arm, snapping my eyes to hers, frantic and on edge. "Emma, please. How can I fix this? I'm so sorry. I didn't mean to hurt you. I was just trying to help. Help us both, maybe?"

Anger and serpentine panic thrash through me at her almost-question. But I don't respond, tearing my gaze from hers and wrenching my arm free, abandoning Hannah at the picnic table along with all she thinks she knows about me or my family. Because she's gravely mistaken. I don't need her help with anything. Anything at all, ever again.

As I rush away from her, I can't shake a single image from my mind—a gold heart friendship necklace broken into two jagged halves, right down the middle, like a warning I'd been too foolish to heed.

You remember back rubs

You remember your father giving you back rubs.

Your shoulders were always so tense with stress from attending public school for the first time, not to mention the tote you stuffed with books and lugged in and out of the Prosper Library on Main Street each week. Your father would often come up behind you—in the kitchen as you washed dishes or in the hallway as you passed each other—and knead at the knots forever present.

This time, though, you found yourself in your parents' room lying facedown on their dark maroon bedspread as your father pressed his thumbs into—slid his fingers across—your back. But you told yourself that it was okay because your mother was in the room with you two, seated at her desk in front of the computer.

Until she wasn't.

You remember her leaving to help Kyle change. Kyle had still been taking naps at the time and, judging by his wail, had just woken to another accident in his Pull-Ups. That was when your father had asked you to take off your shirt, explaining to you that the fabric was "too bunchy." And though you were reluctant, you relented. He had asked you to, after all. You remember trying to relax, wearing only your shorts and the training bra you'd thankfully just started wearing.

Yet you remember a few minutes later when he asked you to take off your bra as well, arguing that it was "getting in the way." And even though it twisted something in your gut to comply, again you relented because "no" was not a word you could wield against your own father. You remember how, as you removed it, you fought to protect your modesty, covering yourself as best you could until you were able to press your small chest into the bedspread and jam both arms at your sides so he couldn't see even a sliver of bare breast.

But then you remember a short while later when he began to run his fingers down your sides. The touch made you squirm. *Does that tickle?* he'd asked, throaty excitement in his voice. When you didn't respond, he did it harder, more frenzied until you were forced to flip over and expose your naked breasts in your fight to free yourself. You remember grabbing up your shirt and hugging it to your chest, pretending to laugh because he was laughing, pretending it was hilarious so that you didn't cry, didn't show him how uncomfortable you felt, how sick to your stomach, how afraid.

You remember your mother returning then, demanding to know what the two of you were doing, and how your father had answered for you both: *Just trading back rubs. She's always so tense.* You remember how there was still a trace of laughter, of glee, in his voice, despite the rage written across your mother's face.

And you remember how, without another word, your mother had turned her back on you—on your half-naked body huddled next to her grotesquely grinning husband—and snapped the door shut behind her, willing herself not to see it, to unsee it at all costs. . . .

hate

I keep my eyes trained down as I move through the school grounds, as far from Hannah as I can get. My body hums with frantic energy I can't seem to shake, and I bite my lip hard to keep myself from remembering, from crying anymore, but the words reel again and again through my mind.

We're still friends, right?

How could we be?

As soon as I step through the school library doors, it feels like a haven, and I wipe at my eyes.

Ms. Saeed sometimes lets us come here during our class period to research an assignment, but it's been a while. Hannah's not a big reader, so I haven't been in here during lunch since just before winter break, when Hannah was out with bronchitis for a week and a half. But now I realize how grateful I am that it holds almost no association with Hannah except for her absence. I've desperately missed the smell of crisp copy paper and musty old pages, colorful book spines lining the shelves, and most of all, the librarian, Ms. Patterson.

Ms. P's the nicest person I know, but more than that, this is the only place I could think of to go. It was my lifeline throughout junior high, and it sure feels like one now, though I don't know if Ms. P will still be here. But she must be if the door's unlocked.

Sure enough, when I round the corner, Ms. P stands behind her desk, her face registering surprise at the sight of me that quickly morphs into kindness.

"Why, hello, dear!" she calls out, setting her rose-pink purse down on her chair. Somehow she always manages to sound both formal and warm. Today she's all sophisticated grace with her pearl jewelry and dress the color of creamy pink flowers that matches her purse and complexion.

Not for the first time, I wonder how Ms. P can manage to always be so happy, especially since everyone whispers about how she's had a life full of tragedy. First, years and years ago, both her teenage sons died in a car crash on the way to the lake with their friends. Then, maybe ten years back, her husband had a heart attack and died, even as she held him in her arms, but at least that was from old age.

Yet, every time I've seen her, Ms. P has been smiling a smile as white as her pearls, the last present Mr. Patterson gave her before he died, which she never takes off. Even now, all the wrinkles around her mouth look like water ripples gliding away from her smile, and though it's completely absurd, I want so badly to dive into that smile, curl up in its warmth, and fall asleep forever. I almost cry again, just at the thought.

"I'm so very glad you caught me, Emma," Ms. P is saying. "I was about to lock up. Will you be joining me for lunch today, then?"

I nod, trying not to think about why I'm here. *Will I have to spend every lunch alone all over again?* The thought of it, of *her*, pushes tears to my eyes that I blink back hard, though I don't know if Ms. P can see well enough to tell.

"If that's all right, Ms. Patterson?" It comes out scratchy.

"Wonderful!" She claps her hands together, then moves to sit down. "Of course it's all right. It's been quite a while since I've last been blessed with your company. How are things going, my dear?"

As I move in closer, I wonder suddenly if the police shared what happened with the school—all the teachers, librarians, coaches, and staff. Probably. Which then makes me wonder if Ms. P's question really is as casual as it sounds or if it's got secret feelers that whisper *I know about your father and Hannah.*

How could Hannah use the journal *I* gave her to write down all that heinous stuff about him? Now I need to go into that "advocacy center" tomorrow and fix what *she's* done—tell the police and social worker Kathleen and whoever else that Hannah was lying and that none of it happened. *Why would she do this to me?*

For *weeks.*

I realize Ms. P is still waiting for an answer, and I'm not sure how to respond, so I just shrug. Then I'm afraid that was rude, so I add, "I'm fine, I guess."

"I'm so very glad to hear it. Come, sit with me." She gestures to her desk, then to the shelves around her. "Or did you want to peruse the books first?"

It's what I'd do back in junior high and the first month of high school, plus the one-point-five weeks Hannah was out sick—browse the stacks, then bring back anything resembling a fairy tale or retelling so Ms. P and I could chat about it while we ate together. It'd been so nice, and now I feel horrible for not having visited sooner, going to the public library after final bell instead, since this library is only open during school hours. The rest of the time, I'd spend—

Spent.

—in Hannah's company.

And maybe I've even avoided coming here out of guilt for having ditched Ms. P, especially after she did me such a colossal favor in giving me a place to belong whenever I had nowhere else to go. Like now.

And while I'd love to check out the books today if I had the energy, I want to sit inside Ms. P's smile even more. I drag a chair over from a nearby table and place my lunch bag on her desk. Ms. P takes out her lunch as well—her usual Tupperware container with far too many vegetables.

Pulling out my soggy sandwich, I frown down at the jelly leaking out the sides. "Oh no," I whisper.

"What's wrong, dear?" Ms. P asks, a fork stuck in her vegetable pile.

"I, uh, mixed up my lunch with Kyle's." I hold up the PB and J as evidence. "He doesn't eat turkey, which is what he wound up with." I should've paid more attention. How had I messed this up too? I'd run to his school right now and trade if I could, but his lunchtime's passed anyway.

The red-eyed snake writhes through me at the thought of Kyle going hungry, though I fight to ignore it. If I cry now, Ms. P will definitely notice. And it's not just that. It's the feeling that my life and my family are falling apart, and I'm somehow the cause.

I tuck the PB and J back in the paper sack to save for Kyle. He'll be so hungry on the bus ride home. Which leaves me with—I spread the rest of my lunch out—a giant bag of Craisins and some stale, smashed tortilla chips, probably from when they fell off the picnic table. My thoughts are yanked back to Hannah, and why I'm here instead of out there with her.

When I glance up, Ms. P's watching me, so I snatch up a tortilla chip and take a bite, thinking I should say something but not knowing what.

She's the first to break the silence. "How has your freshman year gone so far, dear? School treating you okay?"

"It's okay," I say, careful to wipe chip crumbs from my mouth.

"Don't feel like hanging out with your friends today?"

My face flames hot and both ears blaze. I shrug, this time chancing Ms. P thinking I'm impolite. "Friends" is generous since it's pretty clear I only have—*had*—one.

God, why do I keep crying? What's wrong with me?

Ms. P must notice my discomfort because she changes the subject, for which I'm eternally grateful. She chats about recent popular books and then—my favorite—stolen books. There's the usual most popular theft, *Guinness World Records*, for some unknown reason, which she says she can never keep on the shelf. Also, more recently, an art book went missing—which Ms. P presumes is because of the nude paintings—plus a book about ghost sightings.

As she talks, I keep drifting in and out of the conversation, dragged back into repeated thoughts of Hannah—*How could we be?*—and Dad in court today, my interview tomorrow, then Hannah again, and I have to fight my way back up and out of my head. Several times, my hand creeps over to the corner of Ms. P's desk, straightening her Post-its, pens, time stamper, tray of paper clips before I have to force myself to stop. Ms. P either doesn't notice or is kind enough to pretend not to.

One such time, though, Ms. P lets out an "Oh!" that makes me jump, and I know I've been caught. "Speaking of books," she adds, "I almost forgot. There's a new one that just arrived that I think you'll enjoy."

I sit up straighter, relieved to not be reprimanded but also feeling important as Ms. P slips a book from a nearby filing cabinet.

"I keep all the new materials in there that I haven't yet cataloged," she explains, handing the book to me.

It's thick and violet-colored with shiny black floral designs and embossed script. I run my finger over the loopy cursive title: *Fairy Tales of the Heart*, then leaf through the pages, stopping on an illustration that looks like a stained glass window where a beautiful maiden weaves colorful silk in a castle tower.

"Wow. This is incredible!" I say.

As I page through the stories, I think Kyle might even like them, or at least the nonviolent ones. I'll skim them first to pick the more kid-friendly of the bunch, or maybe I'll just note the gruesome parts so I can alter them while reading aloud.

"I thought you might appreciate that," Ms. P says. "I acquired it specifically for you, so it seems only fitting that you be the first to read it."

"Really?" I squeeze the book to me like a precious treasure. I'm amazed and so touched that she thought of me, especially given how long it's been since I've visited.

She beams. "Really."

"Thanks, Ms. Patterson. This means . . . so much to me."

"Are you still writing your own fairy tales?" she asks.

"Um, I . . ."

Now that the police have the fairy tales, my having told Ms. P that I was writing them feels like a secret I maybe shouldn't have shared.

206 • CASSIE GUSTAFSON

"...I stopped," I finish weakly.

"Well, that's a shame. I do hope you find your way back to them someday." Then she surprises me with "Why do you think you like them so much?"

When I glance up, she adds, "Fairy tales, I mean. What draws you to them?"

I've never really thought about it before. I guess I like imagining that the real world could be as they are, where things are always black and white or good versus evil. Where the rules and punishments are harsh but just, cruel witches get shoved into ovens for trying to eat little children, and misunderstood beasts turn out not to be the real monsters. Spoiler alert—it's the handsome brutes. Or, in the case of the darker originals, where cruel young maidens' eyes are pecked out for how terribly they treat their stepsisters, or menacing wolves' bellies are cut open to free little girls and their grandmothers. Evil stepmothers are forced to wear red-hot shoes made of iron and dance till they die, and creepy little men who like to collect small children end up ripping themselves in half in fits of rage. Unlike the real world, fairy tales don't shy away from the darker stuff. They show it how it really is—bleak and messy and scary and uncomfortable. Yet they do it in a way the reader can handle.

But of course I can't say this to Ms. Patterson. I'm about to give her some invented answer when the warning bell shrills. Thankful for the excuse, I turn the book over in my hands, then raise my voice to be heard over the last of the bell. "How do I check this out? There's no barcode yet."

Ms. P returns her empty Tupperware to her cooler bag. "I trust you implicitly. You'll bring it back when you're done. And I'll be eager to hear how you liked it."

Her words glow warm in my chest: *You are welcome here.* "Thank you! I most definitely will."

Wait till I show . . . My grin flickers, all momentary enthusiasm vanishing as I shove *her*—the traitor—from my mind again. Picking up my backpack, I tuck the uneaten PB and J inside and slip the book under one arm. "Thanks for having lunch with me today, Ms. Patterson." It comes out sounding shy.

Ms. P runs her fingers over her pearls. "Anytime, dear. You know where to find me."

I nod, then rush out, disappearing into the chaos of the hallway.

Nearing my locker, before I can even prepare myself for the possibility of it, there she is, like she was trying to be found. I halt in my tracks.

What would my parents say if they knew Hannah and I had talked today? More than that, that regardless of the promise I'd made Dad and the fact that I'd been nasty to Hannah from the moment I saw her in class, some part of me had desperately wanted us to still remain friends until I'd found out what she'd done. That even right now, I have the ticket she gave me in my backpack for a concert I pretended I could attend with her, despite knowing it was disloyal to Mom and Dad, especially now, with tomorrow's interview looming that I'm forced to endure because of her. Who lies to her best friend and works with the cops for *weeks* to try to break apart her best friend's family? Who does that?

That slut friend of yours will be exposed for the liar she is, Mom repeats in my head.

Hannah moves toward me, her expression tentative but still bewilderingly hopeful. She passes her own locker, closing in, looking like she's about to stop and say something. But she can't stop.

She can't say something. Because I *have* to do this tomorrow for my family.

"I hate you." I mouth the words to her with such force, I almost say them out loud, feeling my whole face twist with rage as I do. I've summoned the dirtiest, most loathing look I can muster, sloshing everything—the evil look, the mouthed words—all over her like a bucket of hate paint.

It hits her square in the face. I witness the exact moment it makes contact because she stops dead in the middle of the hallway, students streaming around her, buffeting her, but she doesn't budge. Any glimmers of hope in her expression crumble and fall, leaving behind the most heartbroken expression I've ever seen.

She's not pretending now.

For a moment it's just us, two ex–best friends frozen in time. The hurt radiating from her is so raw, so real, it seems impossible she was ever wearing a mask of pretend. A single tear forms in the corner of her eye, overfills, and slips down her cheek. She buffs it away. Then she's moving fast, passing me in an instant.

As Hannah disappears, I feel the hate slide right off my face. *What did I do? Why did I do that?*

I swallow hard.

I had to—*didn't I?*—choose my family, start preparing for tomorrow, go in there and undo all the damage Hannah's caused. This is all her fault . . . *isn't it?*

So why does it feel like my body is fracturing? Her face just now, the immense devastation in it, was something I felt in every cell of my being.

Slowly, numbly, I swing my backpack in front of me and slip the fairy tale book inside. Next I open the small side pocket and pull out the concert ticket. It's bent, a little smashed, but I smooth it flat between my palms, then walk over to Hannah's locker. Tears drip from my chin as I slide the ticket through the slat, imagining it flutter on its way down.

It's over.

It's better this way, my thoughts whisper, trying like hell to convince myself of it. But how is anything better without Hannah? When has it ever been better without her?

She turned Dad in!

Stop it! It doesn't matter. She's gone, and there's no undoing that now. I made a decision, and I have to stick with it. I made a promise to Kyle, to Dad. What other choice did I have?

Glancing one last time at her locker, I allow myself to imagine the ticket resting inside, one that meant we could still be friends. Then I walk away.

We're not friends anymore.

How could we be?

You remember moldy cheese

You remember a conversation between Hannah and your father back in early November.

You were in the kitchen, having just told Hannah you'd find a snack for the two of you. You'd left her up in your room after dumping off your backpack so she wouldn't see or smell the state of the fridge or the pile of unwashed dishes stacked across the counter. You knew that cheese and crackers were the closest thing you had to a decent snack—something like what Hannah's mother would serve if you were at Hannah's house. But you also knew from an earlier investigation that the sole block of orange cheese in the fridge had mold on it. You suspected the crackers were also stale, though they turned out to be okay. And you even managed to whittle the mold from the cheese without leaving too many holes.

You remember thinking it might be fun to take Hannah back down to the barn since she seemed to love it down there, or maybe it was handsome farmhand Curt she liked. Either way, you'd only been gone five minutes—seven tops—by this point, but it was then that you heard the voices coming from upstairs.

You stilled, listening hard, knife suspended over tiny squares of misshapen cheese that had fallen over like dominos. You heard

Hannah, whom you'd known about, and your father, whom you hadn't. Their voices filtered down through the vent in the upstairs hallway and across the dining room, the back entryway, and into the kitchen. Your heart sank, drowning in festering possibility.

You remember you couldn't hear what the voices said. Yet something about the energetic clip and upbeat cadence of Hannah's tone that your father's voice matched caused you to slice through the cheese faster than was safe for fingertips. Because if it was anything like the last time you caught Hannah and your father talking alone, you knew you needed to hurry.

Tossing cheese and crackers at random onto the plate you'd just scrubbed clean, you hurried through the kitchen, dining room, living room to stand hovering at the base of the stairs.

You could just see the figure of your father leaning into the doorframe of your room, having an animated chat with Hannah. You hadn't even realized he was home in his study and cursed yourself for your lack of vigilance, normally razor sharp, because of course his truck was in the shop.

You remember climbing the stairs with a heavy heart and even heavier footsteps so that they'd both hear you coming, because the words you were hearing stirred the nausea coursing through your gut.

You remember your father speaking, answering a question you hadn't heard asked. *How do you do it? Well, ah, I've never really described it before, but . . . Well, it's one of those things you just do and get good at from practice. But don't worry. You'll learn soon. There are plenty of willing male recipients at your school, I'm sure.*

Yeah, but all the boys in our school are so gross! Aren't they, Em? Hannah looked past your father at you for confirmation.

You remember nodding. *Gross. They're all gross. So gross. Beyond gross.* And you remember wanting to be somewhere far, far away from those stairs instead of climbing them, witnessing your father discuss such things with your best friend because your best friend had asked your father how. Because you hadn't seen your father that eager in a long time, leaned into the doorframe toward Hannah while grinning like an idiot. Because his eyes roved from Hannah's wide-eyed face to her tight tank top showing off breasts that could have belonged to a senior. Because Hannah's slight chest lift let slip that she knew where his lingering gaze fell.

You remember the way his body angled against the doorjamb, reminding you of an apology you'd rather not remember.

You remember the last time Hannah had talked to your father, which you'd also rather forget.

You remember the way she pressed her hip into the dresser by the door, arms crossed under her breasts, emphasizing rather than shielding, because she didn't know. Didn't know. Didn't. Know.

I brought cheese and crackers! you said, bounding past your father. You had hoped your voice would snip the invisible thread between father and best friend that held them smiling at each other in a way that made your skin crawl.

But no one moved.

No one spoke.

The silence stretched across lifetimes.

Well, I'll leave you girls to it, your father replied, breaking the thread at last. *Nice to see you, Hannah. We'll talk again soon. And . . . let me know if you have any more questions.*

You remember hating the soft, almost gentle way he'd said her name. You remember slamming down the plate on your night-stand harder than you'd intended. You remember worrying about the "again" and "soon" parts, but feeling ten pounds lighter because he was leaving, crossing the hallway, retreating into his study.

But before he could close the door, you heard rather than saw the grin in Hannah's voice when she replied, *Looking forward to it, Brian! Have a good day!*

You remember staring down at the plate in your hand where several crackers had slid off and into your nightstand drawer that Hannah must've opened, the crackers coming to rest on top of your journal—the cream-colored one with pink roses and a gaping wound of retracted words. The one that you'd since written only fairy tales in because you had nothing else whatsoever to say. Nothing, anyway, that could ever fit between its crisp, pristine pages that smelled vaguely of lilacs and a happy girl's life.

attack

When I slip into Honors English after lunch, I half expect Han-nah not to be there. She's not. Her desk beside mine is empty, a hollowness I feel in my bones.

But then several minutes after the bell's already rung, the door bangs open, interrupting Ms. Saeed's lecture on storytelling.

Hannah steps through the door. Her head's down, and she won't look at anyone. Still, it's clear even from across the room that she's been crying, her makeup smeared under her eyes, face mottled red. Hannah is the queen of *Who cares?* but that usually doesn't extend to anything so vulnerable.

My whole body aches at her pain, and for one agonizing min-ute, I hold my breath, wondering if I should talk to her or what I could even say as she sits beside me for an entire class. But she doesn't come near me, instead lowering herself into the wobbly, half-broken desk in the very back that no one ever uses.

I see Brooke elbow Kat, the two of them shooting each other *delighted by the scandal* looks, making me hate them both even more.

"All good, Hannah?" Ms. Saeed asks from the front of the room, eyes keen. Hannah gives a short nod, though I doubt she's convinced anyone. Still, Ms. Saeed doesn't mention a late pass, instead picking up where she left off—a kindness to Hannah.

"As I was saying," Ms. Saeed continues, "short stories are nothing more than a string of words in a specific order. But why do they work?" She taps the book of short stories in her hand. "Because words have meaning outside of their individual definitions. Place them together in the right context, and they can entertain or injure, delight or humiliate."

I hate you. The hallway scene replays fresh and raw in my mind like it's happening all over again.

Heat scalds my chest as if Ms. Saeed's called me out in front of the whole class, and I curl into myself. It's been ages since we've gone to church or even so much as mentioned religion in our house, but in a flash I'm back in the pews of our old congregation in San Fran, where somehow that Sunday's Bible School sermon always seemed to perfectly mirror my sins of that week.

"As Mark Twain once said"—Ms. Saeed grabs a whiteboard pen and begins to scrawl—"'Writing is easy. All you have to do is cross out the wrong words.'"

Of course Hannah wouldn't sit by me. I told her we shouldn't be friends, that I hated her. How could I think it would be any different?

"In fact," Ms. Saeed continues, turning back to us and tapping the air with her marker, "does anyone know one of the most famous six-word stories ever written?"

"Six words? You can't write a story in six words!" Rory protests to my right, arms crossed over the bib of her neon overalls.

My pulse races at the sudden noise. Yet, while most teachers would treat an outburst like this as a sign of disrespect, Ms. Saeed loves "open discussion."

"Sure you can," she shoots back. "It's been done, and by some old white dude you may have heard of. Ernest Hemingway ring a bell? Or, at least, that's who the story's credited to."

"Well, what was it, then?" Mikai asks from the front row. Ms. Saeed smirks at us all, her raised eyebrows promising to let us in on the secret. She returns to the board and, with a dramatic flourish of her wrist, starts to print in slow, meticulous lettering, her body blocking most of it.

On a normal day, I'd lean forward and collect every single one of Ms. Saeed's words in my cupped hands like dewdrops. But today, words feel like toothpick-sized splinters.

She steps away, giving us a clear view of her perfect handwriting. *For sale: baby shoes. Never worn.*

The class is silent for a moment, absorbing, and then there's an uproar with shouts of "That's not a short story!" and "Whoa!" But it only takes one raised hand from our teacher for the class to fall silent again. That's been her bargain from day one. She'll give us respect if we'll repay the favor.

"One at a time," she instructs. Her brown eyes turn to me. "Miss Clark, what do you think? Is this a short story?"

For the first time in the history of this class, I drop my gaze and shrug. Judging by the rustling and whispers, everyone's astounded that I failed to answer one of Ms. Saeed's questions. I know they all think my usual eagerness in class is annoying, which Hannah always said was envy for my "brain smarts," something even she'd claim to feel at times since math and English come so easily to me. But now I can sense them registering how "off" Hannah and I are acting, taking our ignoring each other as confirmation of Hannah's and my friendship breakup over dad's arrest—and for once, they're right.

When I dare look up, face scalding, Ms. Saeed's expression is unreadable. Disappointment, maybe? Something else? But she's already calling on Brent.

"How about you, Mr. Parker? What do you think?"

He shrugs, then nods. "Yeah, I'd say so."

"Back it up," she replies, arms pedaling backward in a circle like she always does when she wants one of us to elaborate and support our ideas.

Brent shrugs again. "Well, because it tells a story. Conveys emotion. Word count doesn't matter if you make the reader feel something, right? Plus, there's plot there, internal and external, so it covers the bases. And it makes the reader ask questions, want to know more, but is also complete as is."

Ms. Saeed's eyes light up, and she presses a hand to her heart. "Well now, did I just teleport into a college-level English class? Preach, Mr. Parker!"

Despite everything, a vine of envy twists through me.

"I have nothing left to teach you!" she jokes to Brent, then addressing the class at large, adds, "On that magical note, pull out your class journals. Today's assignment is—"

"Write a six-word short story?" Kat interjects.

"No, that's your homework, but good guess. Right now, I want you to think on this idea of 'words matter.' I want you to write four words, not six. Just four words to your past self, telling that younger version of you what you most needed to hear in that moment of your life, okay? And this is going to take funneling, right? Throw a bunch of words at it, then start whittling it down. Meanwhile, I'll be coming around with your essays. Okay, ready?" She claps her hands. "Set, go!"

There's a flurry of movement as everyone unzips bags, grabbing for notebooks and pens. The class goes quiet like it always does during journaling time, the only sounds more rustling paper and scratching pens. Normally this is my favorite part of English, but today when I pull out my notebook, nothing happens. I feel dried out, like a marker left out in the sun.

I glance back at Hannah, who's hiding her face behind the hand pressed to her forehead.

What would I tell my past self that I most needed to hear? Better yet, what would I tell my current self?

Finally I write *Suck it up, buttercup!!!!* knowing that later I'll have to tear out the page so Ms. Saeed doesn't see. But then that's messy and uneven, meaning I'll also have to tear out its counter page so it's not obvious a page is missing.

But now that I've begun, I can't stop myself from scribbling down another line onto the already ruined page:

You don't have choice.

But of course that's cheating. "Don't have choice" isn't proper English. It should be five words, so just leaving out the article doesn't count. How foolish can you get? I scratch it out too hard, even though I'll have to tear out more pages to cover the marks.

From nowhere, my hand writes on its own:

You didn't see anything.

I underline the last word several times, swallowing hard. Shielding my notebook with my arm, I glance around to make sure no one's seen what I've written. Everyone's bent over their own notebooks, and Ms. Saeed's across the room returning essays. I chance another glance back at Hannah. She looks wrecked, shoulders slumped and hair curtaining her face, hiding her from view. I can see enough, though, to know she's not writing in her notebook.

Good. She's written enough down in notebooks, hasn't she?

My pen tip stabs the paper.

She didn't even attempt to hide the fact that she'd done it on purpose.

Advice to my past self? Here's some.

In the largest letters yet, that are uneven, shaky, ugly, I carve: *DON'T TRUST HANNAH GARBER!!!*

I outline each letter again and again, trying to make it prettier, smoother, but also trying to etch it into my brain where it should've been all along.

I almost jump out of my skin when Ms. Saeed drops my essay on my desk. It hits my arm and starts to slide away. Scrambling to catch the loose essay, I'm forced to uncover my notebook.

"Whoops!" Ms. Saeed says, and all eyes in the room pivot to her. "Sorry about that, Emma." But her gaze is on my notebook, on the words I wrote, the crater I've made in the page.

"No problem," I mumble, rushing to cover it.

Her eyes linger, but I don't meet them.

"Well done," she says at last, tapping my essay.

I mutter a thanks, then wait till she's moved on to glance at it. A giant *98%!* is printed on top. But where did I go wrong? What did I mess up? Tearing through the pages, I find the mistake on the last page in my closing line: "Gertrude Stein was an undeniable literary genius, far to ahead of her time for her life's literary work to be adequately appreciated."

Red pen circles "far to," and Ms. Saeed's perfect script explains in the margin: *Should read "too" here. Think of it like this: the two os are excessive, just like the word's meaning—"too much" and "also."*

But I know the difference between "to" and "too," and I know its dual meaning. I could use the word both ways in a sentence right now: "This day is too much, and my life is too." So how could I have made such a careless mistake?

Glancing back at my notebook, I take in the words: *DON'T TRUST HANNAH GARBER!!!*

How could I ever have trusted her? She lied to me. Betrayed me. Messed up my family forever, and for what?

My brain's looping again, and I have to stop or I'll implode right here in the middle of class with everyone watching. With Hannah watching.

Don't think about Hannah. Don't think about Hannah.

I remember . . .

I remember . . .

I remember Hannah coming over.

I remember moldy cheese.

No!

I remember . . . Christmastime. Yes!

I remember lights and candy canes and popcorn, a green couch . . .

NO! NOT THAT!

Nothing's safe. Everything's ruined. There are no memories left that haven't been tainted.

I don't realize I'm crying till the tears drip onto my notebook and blur the gel ink, the exclamation marks slipping away in a wet swirl of navy.

Stop crying, Em. They'll see.

But when I go to suck in air, there isn't any. Something catches in my chest and won't release.

Breathe. Why can't I breathe?

It's like the wind's knocked out of me, but how? I try sucking in oxygen but can't.

What's happening?

Breathe!

Why can't I breathe?

Is this real?

Wild panic thrashes through me, and I throw my chair back and stand. Wrapping both hands around my throat, I try to force air through.

Breathe!

Am I dying?

Faces stare up at me. I turn, eyes meeting Hannah's. Is that terror reflected? Pain? But my vision's swimming, sunbursts popping. I'm falling backward into a dark, endless tunnel. . . .

I can't hear what happens next, only feel Ms. Saeed lead me by the shoulders out of class. Somewhere on the way to the main building, the nurse meets us. She tries to coax air into lungs that won't take it. Darkness swoons before me. I step once, twice, before my vision distorts, knees hit grass.

There, in the middle of the school lawn, I shatter into a million pieces. Endless tiny fragments of all I've seen and felt but have had to pretend don't exist. Fragments of my whole family counting on me not to screw up and break us apart. And the sharpest one of all—knowing that I've already lost Hannah Garber forever, which feels like absolutely everything.

When Mom comes to get me, at first I think it'll be okay, that she's not mad. As the EMTs finally remove the oxygen mask from my face and heart rate monitor from my finger, one of them explains to her in a serious tone that I just had a severe panic attack, hyperventilated, and passed out on the lawn. All the while, as she listens, she's full of concerned expressions and *Oh my!*'s and *How awful!*'s, especially in front of Ms. Saeed, who's returned holding my back-pack with my notebook tucked inside.

Mom's face only slips once toward the end when Ms. Saeed leans in to give me a hug, an expression I catch behind Ms. Saeed's back. Maybe no one else would see the simmering resentment in it, but I do, particularly when Ms. Saeed whispers something to me that Mom can't quite hear: "I'm here should you ever need to talk, Emma. I mean it. It's going to be okay. *You* will be okay."

The grave concern in her warm brown eyes tells me all I need to know—Ms. Saeed knows about Dad. The realization feels like stepping on glass.

Ms. Saeed holds my gaze longer than comfortable, especially with Mom watching, then squeezes my hand and slips out of the office, giving me a nod of encouragement before closing the door.

Only after Mom has signed the release forms and promised to make sure I rest—not to mention "talk it over" with Dad about making me an appointment with the school therapist—are we at last allowed to leave. But we're not even to the car before her anger bubbles over. "I do not have time for your attention-seeking antics, Emma. And on today of all days! I had to leave your father in court to come get you. How could you be this selfish?"

Of course, the arraignment. I'm too afraid to ask how it went or even to speak at all.

I calm my thoughts by squeezing the fingers of one hand hard in the other, imagining myself cleaning the whole house when I get home, as penance for Mom having to come get me. And I can double-check my room for sand and loose hair again, just in case I missed any because there has to be some.

All the while, my brain loops on Mom's words: Was I just trying to get attention in class? Hannah's, too, even after everything? I'd certainly succeeded whether I'd wanted to or not. All those staring faces . . .

But no. What I'd wanted today was to be invisible, for Hannah to stop crying so I wouldn't have to feel so guilty, and for tomorrow to not have to happen at all.

I swing my backpack onto the passenger-side floor and climb in, only then remembering what I'd written in my notebook. Slipping it from my bag, careful to angle it away from Mom, I open the notebook to the last page. Angry words scream out, the second line scribbled out entirely:

Suck it up, buttercup!!!!

You don't have choice.

You didn't see anything.

DON'T TRUST HANNAH GARBER!!!

This last line is blurred with a few patches transposed onto the opposite page by my tears.

Did Ms. Saeed see all this? She must've when she put the notebook in my bag, if not earlier. Or maybe the notebook closed itself, which I'm hoping for but not counting on. Cringing, I wonder what she must think after watching me freak out, then seeing these crazy scribbles.

As we drive away from the school, Mom's foot once again pressed firmly against the accelerator, questions crowd my mind. But there's one question that stands out above all the rest: How do I go back in time and make those last two four-word pleas I wrote come true?

You remember knowing

You remember the night before Christmas Eve when you were watching *The Santa Clause* with Hannah from the gray couch while your father sat on the green one. You remember leaving to find more candy canes and to pop more popcorn—the latter of which you'd burned ever so slightly—before returning to the living room bearing treats, only to witness the scene that now played out before you. In your absence, Hannah had moved to the faux suede green couch to sit beside your father.

You remember staring, unnoticed by them, at the back of the two silhouetted figures of your father and best friend entwined on that couch, the soft glow of the Christmas tree a pixelated blur in the background. A blaring announcer's voice from a car commercial on the TV filled the room, its flickering, frenetic images casting shadows over your father and best friend as they leaned together, heads resting on each other, a white snowflake-covered blanket spread over them. You remember how his shoulders moved, angled in a way that whispered of hands caressing under the blanket, in her lap.

You remember tiptoeing behind them, popcorn bowl pressed to your chest, before fleeing up the stairs, the booming TV muffling your retreat as you took the steps two at a time. You remember how, once in the safety of your room, your legs crumbled, knees hitting hard wood as candy canes cracked and popcorn flew around you. Acid churned in your stomach, pushing bile up your throat, blocking words you wished you could speak aloud, wished you could *shriek*.

You remember your well-trained ears snagging on the sound of gravel crunching in the driveway, exceeding the sound of the television. You remember a car door slamming, the TV clicking off. You remember the green couch sighing its relief, released from the burden of bearing witness, as the voices of your mother and little brother floated in through the back door.

You remember your mother calling out in a too-loud voice, "Girls! I brought you hot chocolate!"—a voice ensuring that nothing was happening.

You remember covering your ears, but your mind was an unrelenting tempest as it screamed and Screamed and SCREAMED....

stolen

School's long since let out as I stand across the street from our house, arms folded against the chill, waiting for the bus to drop off Kyle. Mom had to go meet Dad at his lawyer friend's office, then leave from there to close up at work, so she'd told me to make sure I met Kyle at the bus stop. Of course, even if she hadn't said a word, we both know I'd be here waiting for him.

When Kyle finally shuffles off the bus, I notice deep lines creasing his brow.

"Hey," I murmur, extending my hand even as I recall our fallout from this morning and glancing at his yogurt-heart-stained sweater. I was hoping he wouldn't remember, but as soon as I speak, he faces away, toward the closing bus doors. Guess that answers that.

The stop signs unfold from the sides of the bus and flash their red warning as I take Kyle's hand in mine, but he pulls it back.

Trying to ignore bus-driver Hank watching us, waiting for us to cross the street so he can leave, I bend down and turn Kyle to face me. "Kyle," I say, trying to sound patient despite my hurt feelings. "You need to hold my hand when we cross the street, even if you're mad at me."

His small chin is still angled away from me, but his hand

creeps toward mine. I grab it, and he lets it go limp, a sign he's following orders but not happy about it.

When we're back on our side of the road and the bus is retreating, I try again. "What's up, chicken butt?" But I accidentally nudge him too hard when I half trip over a rock in our driveway. Kyle staggers but rights himself without reply.

We're halfway down the drive when I make one last attempt. "Hey, Kyle? I'm really sorry for this morning, okay? I didn't mean to get mad." But it's not until I've glanced away from his face for long enough that I spot the void, the real reason Kyle's acting so off.

"Where's Benny?" I ask, twisting around him to stare at his other empty fist, the one that's always reserved for his favorite LEGO guy.

Kyle shrugs, though his face pinches to keep himself from crying.

"Kyle, where's Benny?" I ask, more insistent.

This time all the face-pinching in the world couldn't halt his tears. They stream down his cheeks and drip from his chin before sinking into the blue yarn of his sweater.

I pull him to a stop and kneel down, one knee biting into gravel as I fold him into my arms. His wet tears drip down my neck, breath shuddering through him.

"Oh, Kyle," I say, because there are no words to comfort him. I know before I ask that, even without Derek at school today, some of the other kids must've stolen Benny. But I ask anyway. "What happened?"

Kyle pulls away from me, face pink, eyes blazing. "It's your fault they took him!"

His abrupt movement unbalances me, and I teeter forward before catching myself with a palm on hard gravel. "What do you mean, my fault?"

"If you hadn't made me late today, then I would have remembered to put Benny in my cubby, and then they wouldn't have taken him at recess, and I would still have him. It's your fault he's gone!"

His words sting, but I can't argue with them. "Kyle, who took Benny? When? And I'm so sorry he's gone. I didn't know. . . . I'll . . . I'll get you a new Benny. A better one!"

"I don't want a new one!" he yells, storming away. "I want my old one back! You're the worst sister ever!" Kyle yanks at the latch to the back gate but can't manage to slide it.

"Let me!" I rush forward, brushing away loose gravel, but with a mighty pull that takes all his strength, Kyle drags the latch out of place and wrenches the gate open, disappearing inside. My heart constricts, knowing he's going to hide in his room and mourn his missing Benny for the rest of the day. And when our parents finally do get home, they'll be so preoccupied, they won't even notice to ask why he's sad. I hope I can find a way to make it up to him.

Exhaling hard, I feel the weight of today press down on my bones, but for once I'm too tired to cry.

I've just dragged myself to the gate and am shutting it behind me when I hear Dad's truck rumbling closer, then turning into our driveway. He must be free from court and lawyer things, for now at least. I can only hope the arraignment went okay, though after everything that's gone wrong these last four days, I'm not holding my breath. *A man torn from his family* forever, *and for what?* he'd warned me yesterday. *Just* think *of it, Em.* I hurry into the house so I don't have to see him just yet.

Halfway to my room, a text pings onto my phone, quickening my pulse, but it's from Aunt Jane: *Love you, M&M's! Know your interview's tomorrow so wishing you luck. Call me if you need anything or want to talk in the meantime!*

It's a kind text. Yet as I stare down at it, all I can think is: *Is this another warning?*

You remember remorse

You remember the day after the "couch incident" between Hannah and your father. It was Christmas Eve, and your family had driven to your father's uncle's house where the frenetic energy of eighteen people permeated the space, and a dinner table the length of an entire room was laid with fine china and poinsettia decor.

You remember having watched your father intently since sunup, observing how quiet and reserved he'd grown overnight. Whereas the evening before he'd acted tipsy-giddy and almost manic in his exuberance, now he'd withdrawn into himself, hardly eating or speaking to anyone. As family members prattled on in a vortex of clattering and conversation, you remember how his eyes stayed trained on his half-full plate of turkey dinner, how they'd only rise partway but never meet each speaker's gaze.

You remember wondering if anyone else noticed how broken he seemed. Could they feel it in the air, that everything had changed?

Above all, you remember how melancholy his remorse made you feel, though in that moment you didn't want to articulate to yourself why, and it would be many months before you could even begin to.

Yet, at that dinner, staring at your father drowning in his own sea of unfathomable guilt, you remember wondering if there were many different kinds of love. Love conditional, love dangerous, love blind. Because then your own love must lurk in the shadows, where your shaking hands hoarded each tiny, splintered silence.

chase

After arriving home, I'd heard Dad go straight to my parents' bedroom and close the door. Probable translation: the arraignment hadn't gone well. From what I'd read online last night about arraignments—before getting too overwhelmed and having to stop—what I'm guessing went down today is this: they read the charges against him aloud, in front of a judge; he showed the judge that he had a lawyer representing him; he entered a plea to the charges, his plea being "not guilty." At least, that's what I figure he'd plead based on the little I overheard Mom and Dad discussing before they left this morning.

Now I try to will my brain to stop looping because it keeps returning to thoughts of her, and I can't think about her anymore. Hannah and I are over for good, and there's no changing that now. This fact alone would be enough to wholly deplete me, and that's without counting my panic attack in English and fight with Kyle.

Kyle hasn't talked to me since the driveway. He's been hiding in his room, door slammed shut, and even though I know I should, I can't summon the energy to go fix things with him, mostly because I know that I can't make it right today, no matter what I say. I'd left the now-soggy, bagged PB and J from lunch at his door as a peace offering, not knowing when he'd find it but knowing he'd sure be hungry when he did.

Somehow, despite my utter exhaustion, I've managed to force myself to drag the vacuum hose—at least once, knowing I'm risking disturbing Dad—down every crack in my floorboards, around every corner of my room, even under my bed and dresser. It doesn't matter that there wasn't much visible dirt or hair. I could *feel* it there. Then, tiptoeing around as recompense for the noise, I've run a damp rag over the top of my dresser, bookshelf, and nightstand to get rid of any lingering dust. I've even spritzed and buffed my mirror and windows till they're streak-free, taken my little rug outside for a good shake, and rearranged all the posters on my wall, making sure the edges are taped back up precision-straight. This last part I had to do after taking down the Corey Starr poster because, without it, there was a giant blank space on the wall. That poster used to be the first thing I'd see after waking—an instant, nerve-sparking reminder of Hannah—but since that's no longer a good thing, I didn't even bother un-taping it before ripping it off the wall. I'd had to come back for the corners, which had torn clean off. Now the poster's a crumpled ball in the trash like it'd never happened, like Hannah and I never happened.

And now that everything's in its rightful place, even if that place is the trash for some things, a feeling like calm settles over me. I try to breathe in the clean order of it all—of crisp lines and empty cracks. She's nowhere, and I tell myself I'm glad. Even my Corey shirt and Hector the succulent in his gold pot had gotten tossed, though I'd felt like a murderer and gently lowered both into the trash bin instead of chucking them. Not that it'll make a difference to their fate in the end.

All the while, I've been inhaling the sugary, birthday-cake-scented candle I'd lit as soon as I'd come up to my room this afternoon. And after setting it on my dresser, I'd rotated the candle so the peeling cupcake label faced away and the creamy yellow wax pressing against the glass faced forward like a smooth, decadent treat. I'd gotten it in my Christmas stocking, presumably from Mom's work, with rainbow glitter embedded in the wax like confetti sprinkles. Today's the first time I've burned the candle since Dad's arrest. I used to burn it every time Hannah would come over, but anything that's even hinted at Hannah's existence these past few days has felt forbidden or disloyal somehow. Now I figure that, since Hannah's no longer in the picture, it can't be traitorous anymore.

I toss my backpack onto the freshly made bed and climb on, laying out my day planner, schoolbooks, three-ring binder, and homework sheets in tidy rows. I place the *Fairy Tales of the Heart* book Ms. P gave me on my nightstand, parallel to the edges, my insides warming at the thought of cracking open the stiff binding and slipping inside its crisp pages, but that's for later, only after I've finished my homework for the next two days, or as much as I can do. After each of my classes today—up until my mental breakdown in English anyway—I'd told my teachers I'd be absent tomorrow without offering an explanation. Not a single one of them looked even remotely surprised, one even wishing me "good luck" before catching himself, which was basically confirmation that they all know about the interview.

As I line up my highlighters and pens by color, I know I need to distract myself and decide to start with World Civ, my least favorite subject minus the Barbie mummy project I plan to do. Or maybe I'm punishing myself for all I've done wrong these past few days, weeks, months. Still, I better get started since there's a whole day of missed classwork to make up for. But every time I try, my brain keeps reminding me why I won't be at school tomorrow, and dread falls over me like a collapsed blanket fort, smothering me into stillness.

The image of Easter candy flashes in my mind, and I welcome the distraction, stomach flipping in anticipation before I remember that I ate it already, mowing it all down in a single day. Sighing, I've just about resigned myself to opening my World Civ textbook when I recall the carton of grapefruit juice in the fridge, the one I'd accidentally grabbed instead of milk at Tucker's on Saturday. All of a sudden, I can't think about anything else. The juice reminds me of my most favorite candy—sour grapefruit wedges—which are best eaten when they're a little stale since it makes them crunchy on the outside and gooey soft in the middle. I can almost taste the bittersweet tang as I rush downstairs.

I tell myself I'll only be gone for two minutes.

And I would've been—mug brimming with grapefruit juice, having already chugged a full glass of it down right there in front of the fridge—had I not, on my return trip, happened to glance through Mom and Dad's mostly closed door.

I stop and creep nearer, noting Dad seated at Mom's desk where the home computer used to live before the cops made off with it. But that's not what'd made me pause, I realize. It's the sound of keyboard keys clacking, the fact that Dad's still typing away somehow, even though the home computer and his laptop and iPad were confiscated. Then I spy Mom's ancient, chunky laptop, plugged into the ethernet cord instead of connected to the Wi-Fi for some reason. Dad's peering at a web page that looks like . . . an email account maybe? Or some sort of chat room? Either way, he's clearly on the internet, which he's most certainly not allowed to be on. Doesn't he even care that he could get thrown back in jail if caught?

I don't realize I've stepped even closer till a single floorboard gives me away. Dad's head whips around to where I stand, and I have no choice but to clear my throat and announce my presence—"Dad?"—like I meant to come over here all along, like I haven't seen.

By the time I ease the door open all the way, he's managed to slam the laptop closed and lean forward, moving one elbow to rest on top of it like it's part of the desk and nothing important at all.

"Hey," I say.

"Hey, Emma-Bean." Dad flashes me a tired smile that he must hope will hide the alarm written across his face. "I was just thinking," he offers for no reason.

"Okay." I shrug, scrambling for something to say, taking a gulp of the grapefruit juice before it sloshes over the side of the mug. "I just wanted to check on you. Make sure you were okay after today?"

I'm expecting him to be sad, maybe, or even scared, so the anger that bristles through him surprises me.

"Today didn't go so hot," he admits. "My lawyer talked to the DA—that bitch prosecutor I was telling you about?" I wince, but he waits for my nod of confirmation before continuing. "Well, she informed Jim—my lawyer—that she's seeking the maximum sentence against me. Practically laughed out loud when I pleaded 'not guilty.' Jim thinks she's got a vendetta against men, trying to burn us all to the ground, but still, he's nervous. Says this woman hardly ever loses a case." Dad's face transforms, spent of anger, replaced with a mask of fear that hollows out his features. He runs a shaky hand through his hair. "It's . . . not looking good."

Maybe I'm imagining it, but everything Dad's said recently sounds rehearsed, like over-recited monologues that've lost some meaning. But even so, I absorb his words like tiny, anchored weights. "I'm so sorry, Dad. That's awful."

Then he sits up straight, looking almost eager. "Hannah say anything to you? At school?"

"We're not friends anymore." I say it down to the pink frothy juice in my mug, noting how bitter my words sound, unlike yesterday when I'd so willingly handed over Hannah's birth date just like he'd asked. Yesterday I'd jumped at the chance to prove my loyalty, to please him. But today's not yesterday, I guess.

I try to remind myself that he's had a hard day, that I need to be kind, but then I think of Hannah's face, crumpling in agony when I'd mouthed hateful words at her, and my heart bursts all over again. Between doing Dad's bidding yesterday and what I'd said to her today, maybe she's not the only one who's done the betraying here.

She turned Dad in, my brain insists. *She worked with the police for weeks.* Clearly that's worse than anything I've done. But the stab to the gut I'd felt earlier when she'd told me what she'd done has been replaced by a twinge of something else, something unnameable.

"It's for the best," Dad's saying in a counterfeit-solemn tone. Yet it doesn't even begin to hide his relief that my friendship with Hannah is over.

Sudden fury flames through my blood. I turn away fast so he can't read my face, but then he adds, "She's no good, Bean. I knew it all along. Could see it a mile away."

My body stills.

Ears ring.

White-hot rage lights up my spine.

So that's why he ruined my friendship with Hannah just like he did with Alice? Because she's 'no good?' Because he could see it a mile away? Why the hell can't he just leave my friends alone so they can stay *my* friends? So I can have a normal freaking life with normal freaking friendships? Who does he even think he's kidding right now? Maybe he's somehow forgotten, but I'm the only one he can't hide the truth from. The least he could do is remember that.

Words erupt from me like lava. "Why were you using Mom's laptop just now? You're not supposed to be on the internet. It's *illegal.*"

He's stunned into silence, looking like I've slapped him.

My throat goes as dry as dust. Blood pounds in my ears, pulsing through the hand that's clenching the mug. In all my life— every single one of my fourteen years—I have never *ever* talked to my dad like that. Never dared, except for one time when I told him to leave my room. And though that'd ended badly, right now's different. Worse. Bone-chillingly terrifying.

At first I think he's going to deny being on the internet, tell me I didn't see what I saw. But I guess he finally realizes better than that, knows he can't talk his way out of this one. Not to me. Still, I don't give him the chance as I whirl around and flee.

"Emma," he barks in a voice so stern, it would normally stop my heart and render me immobile.

But I don't stop—not this time—sloshing juice as I race through the living room and up the stairs. And I'm only steps away from my room, from safety, when I hear his pounding footsteps chasing after me.

You remember disappointing him

You remember being in your room the week before Valentine's Day in your eighth-grade year. You were changing out of your school jeans and shirt and into your loungy pants and tank top so you could do your homework in comfort. It was something you did, quick and efficient, having laid out your clothes on your bed ahead of time. But just as you pulled off your shirt, like the devil's clockwork, you heard his footsteps in the hall. Inexplicably but without fail, he always seemed to sense the exact moment your shirt lifted past your ears in a fleeting confusion of hair and darkness.

You remember him bursting in, not saying anything, just standing mute in the doorway and leering at you like this was all a sick joke only he thought was funny.

You remember trying to wrench your shirt back on, yelling, "Get out!" which you'd surprised yourself in doing. But for good measure, you did it again. "Get out!"

And so deep was your fear, your dismay, that you tried to force the door shut on him, pooling every ounce of pent-up resentment into your shoulders, into the strength of your push, from all the times before when you'd bit your tongue instead of speaking, hard enough to draw blood.

But then you remember his shove in return, a force so violent that it flung the door wide, sending you flying backward and sprawling across the floor.

You remember his face, crimson with fury, as he screamed, "Don't ever try to shut me out again!" You remember watching, speechless, horrified, as he stormed away and stomped down the stairs. The wrath he left in his wake let you know how very wrong you'd been to challenge him, how deeply you'd just disappointed him. This made you sad in ways you couldn't begin to express because you didn't know how to make it all okay, how to make him love you again. . . .

But then again, maybe you did know, didn't you?

burn

I burst into my room but catch myself just before slamming the door in Dad's face like last time. Besides, it wouldn't stop him anyway.

Backing against my bookshelf, I squeeze the sticky mug in both hands like it can somehow shield me as I watch Dad clear the landing. He's breathing hard, vein popping in his neck as he comes for me, stepping over the threshold of my room like it's nothing but a chalk line.

I know he'll scream at me about back-talking and disrespect, that he's the father and how dare I question his authority. So it comes as a shock when he stops dead in his tracks and turns toward my dresser to where the cupcake candle sits. But where there had just been flame, smoke rises from the wick like a curling memory. It must've blown out when I ran past.

I watch the tension coil in his body, moving from anger to utter rage, and I think he must somehow know it's the candle I burn when Hannah's over. But this level of fury? Sweat erupts over my skin as my brain flails to understand, braces for impact. Because if I thought he was mad before . . .

He raises his hand, and I flinch, but he only jabs at the smoking candle. "What the hell were you thinking, leaving a candle unattended?"

When I don't say anything, floundering to catch up, to make myself smaller, he rages on. "What, you just walked out of this room, to spy on me, and you didn't bother to blow it out? You could've burned the whole goddamned house down, Emma, with your negligence."

He advances on me, seething, and I'm too disoriented to react, brain trying to switch gears from what just happened downstairs to this. Still, like always, my chest absorbs the words, some piece of me noting how much sharper they feel compared even to Mom's most cutting remarks.

"In seconds, *seconds*, we could've lost everything." He's closing the gap between us, mere paces away. "This house, all our possessions—if we didn't die in the process. Is that what you want?"

I lean back, bookshelf pressing into my backbone. Guilt zaps through me, but I don't move, don't speak.

"Is it?" he insists, a foot from me. "To put your family in danger? For us to be homeless?"

I can't answer.

But what about you? Putting us in danger? my brain spits back. But I don't dare say it aloud. I've done enough back-talking today.

"How could you be so irresponsible, so stupid?"

I go utterly still as his words land like a whiplash across my cheek.

I'm still reeling when Dad turns and grabs for the candle on the dresser. But he's barely seized it when he stumbles back and drops it with a crash, shaking his hand from the blistering heat. I shrink away as glass and hot wax explode across the floor and its many coats of gloss. My hands shoot to my mouth, pink juice splashing down my front. Moths pop into my mind, their powdery bodies thrashing in sticky varnish. I picture them coated in the yellow wax that now seeps into the cracks between the floor-boards, ones I'd just vacuumed clean. It's splattered across the front of my dresser and down Dad's pants as his words pound their hoofbeats through my brain: *so irresponsible, so stupid.* Dad's never called me stupid before. Ever. Just the opposite. He's always praising my intelligence, rewarding me for my good grades.

Like with the backpacking trip.

But he's right. Leaving the candle lit was careless. Danger-ous, even. So was contradicting him downstairs. We could've lost everything. Because of me. And we still could. Because of me.

Dad's out the door, barking, "Clean it up!" before the stam-pede in my mind has time to burst through the gates. I stand there, mug suspended in one hand. In front of me, the jagged shards of the candle sink into hot wax, the scent of spongy vanilla cake with white frosting and confetti sprinkles still lingering in the air like a ghost of happier times.

So stupid.

So stupid.

So stupid.

You remember slamming dishes

You remember doing dishes in the kitchen with your father.
He washed them while you dried and put them away. This was
early January, a few weeks after you had walked in on him and
Hannah entwined under that blanket on the couch.

Your mother came in then, telling you to start the spaghetti
for dinner. But you had a pile of homework to finish and told your
mother as much, to which she replied, *And I had a hard day at
work. We all have to do things we don't want to do.*

Whatever, you muttered, unable to help the annoyance, the
resentment that slipped into that single word, pooling around its
sharp edges.

You remember the energy shifting in the room a mere exhale
before your father slammed the frying pan he'd been washing
against the divider in the sink—once, twice, too many times
to count, and with such force that it warped, conforming to an
alarming curved shape. You remember jumping back, dropping
the towel in your hand, as with each smash he screamed at you
to respect your mother. Why did you have to act like that? Be
so disrespectful? Why couldn't you just listen and obey for once
without talking back? Why did you have to make everything
more difficult?

You remember cowering at his raised voice, flinching with each accusation, each deafening crack of metal on porcelain as the pan jerked up and down in his fist. The surprise of it sent panicked tears streaking down your face, chest weighted with the understanding that this was your fault, that you'd failed once again to be an obedient, deferential daughter. That you should've tried harder. Why couldn't you have just tried harder?

But even through your terror, you remember most the voice whispering in your ear that he dare speak to you about disrespect.

You remember standing with your mother in mutual, stunned silence as the pan finally slowed, then fell from his grasp with a crash on top of a mound of soapy dishes. Chest heaving, anger spent at last, your father stood there for several long moments before muttering that he was sorry for having lost his temper. And when he pulled you in for a hug, you remember resisting the embrace, still frightened by his brute strength, wondering with each bang of his heart against your eardrum if the searing heat of his chest held additional unspent anger. And when he turned to hug your mother, mumbling further words of apology, you noticed that she was also crying. It was the first time you'd seen them hug—touch—in a very long time. In that moment, you felt so relieved, lucky, even, that he had never ever hit you or Kyle. Because he loved you. He did. And wasn't neglect the very worst of all abuses?

You remember finding the warped pan in the trash later that night. You remember shoving it to the bottom of the bag by its handle, getting the slime of cold spaghetti sauce up your forearm for your efforts, but at least it was hidden from sight. At least it was gone.

Over.

Done.

You remember this all happened mere months before the police came and arrested your father for an unspeakable crime.

"The Girl and the Buried Secret"

Once upon a time there lived a girl—a quiet, reticent girl who kept to herself. Unbeknownst to all, the girl had a secret, a secret so vile that it had turned her insides black with an inexplicable illness. The girl knew she needed to rid herself of the secret as her frail body could harbor it no longer, though she also knew that freeing herself of it would require an impossible sacrifice.

In the garden behind her home, in the shade of her favorite oak tree beneath her childhood swing, the girl dug a hole under the pink rosebush. As she dug, the roses reached out their thorny fingers, whipping at her face and arms. They called out to her, "Stop, girl! This is no place for your secret!"

Silent and steadfast, the girl kept digging, silver spade slicing into dark earth, not even slowing for the curious earthworms whose thrashing bodies she cut in two. The girl dug on, long past the afternoon that dragged its shadow across the yard, past tiny speckled stars that popped into existence in the sky above, past the wheezing in her chest and the fatigue weighing her arms.

Only when her spade struck bedrock and would go no farther did the girl plant her secret. Into the earth's yawning mouth, the girl tucked a black mahogany box sealed with a gold lock. Its insides, she knew, were lined with red velvet and filled to the brim with her unspoken words. It was where she had kept the secret since its inception. Against her breastbone burned the lock's lone key.

Only once the hole had been filled, earth piled high on top of her secret, did the girl stand. Stretching her bone-wearied limbs, she listened to the cicadas chirrup in the cool night air. To them alone she whispered, "My secret will be safe now." Turning her back on her tree, her roses, her swing lilting in the evening breeze, the girl toiled back inside. Bolting the great door behind her, she vowed never to return to her garden.

Numbers fell from the clock, and still the girl kept her promise, never venturing near where her secret lay buried. And yet a sense of fear crept endlessly upon the girl, wrapping its skeletal fingers around her thin shoulders. Instead of gaining strength with each passing day since burying her secret, the girl grew steadily paler, the wheezing in her chest more pronounced.

From time to time, she labored to rise from her bed and peek out her bedroom window. Daily the roses called to her. "Please," they begged, "please, unburden us from your secret!" But she ignored them, and when their strangled cries became too much, she snapped the window shut, bolting it as well.

Months peeled free from the calendar, and still the girl held steadfast to the key around her neck. Over time, the roses grew silent, though a steady change befell them. The girl watched from her window as, inch by choking inch, the roses consumed her swing and tree, wrapping their thick, thorny branches around rope and trunk. She felt as, inch by diminishing inch, her body grew weaker, frailer.

One breathless winter day, the girl glanced again through her window. She had grown her thinnest yet, bones jutting out like knobs from under her skin. And what she saw beyond the smudged glass froze the breath shuddering through her lungs. Hastening down the stairs as quickly as she was able, the girl pulled at the back door that led to her garden, but the door would not budge. Time had warped and weathered the door, sealing it shut. The girl pulled and pried at it until finally, with the creak of a thousand ages, the door wrenched free. She rushed into her garden.

The girl knew that to bury her secret required a tremendous sacrifice—that of her childhood garden—and still she could not prepare herself for the changes of what had once been her sanctuary. Where soft moss had once grown at her feet, only a cracked and barren land remained. Where once her massive oak tree had towered its large branches overhead, protecting her from the elements, only a stark and leafless giant stood. Where her swing had once hung, only a half-collapsed jumble of rotted wood and twine lingered.

Only the roses flourished.

In her absence, the roses had shed their delicate pink hue, transforming into something murky and monstrous. The now-obsidian roses stared out at her from their jumble of thorns like many vacant eyes.

"What has happened?" she whispered to the roses. "What has become of you?"

From the ground beneath the roses came a voice, multiplied yet unified, feral and vicious. "You did this to us."

The girl shook with shame and fear. "But how could I have known?"

In lieu of a reply, the roses extended their mighty stalks and chased the girl, snarling after her, "You did this."

The girl hurried into the house and slammed the door, separating herself from the cruelty of time and festered secrets. Wheezing, she fastened bolt after bolt upon the door to shield her from the garden she no longer recognized, for it had decayed into something predatory and savage.

As time slipped steadfastly away, the girl kept watch over the roses, waiting for them to die, for their death was imminent. She had smelled it on their charcoal petals as they'd chased her, their floral fragrance replaced by pungent earth and rotten corpse. By now she herself had whittled down to little more than bone, with skin as pale as a ghost. "It will all be over," she wheezed, "once the roses are dead. Then my secret will truly be safe."

But it was not so.

For one by one as the roses died, their many midnight petals dried up and turned white as ivory. A black mold spread across them.

Pages, the girl thought with growing horror. *The petals look like pages. From a diary. My diary.*

The girl spoke a petrifying yet unyielding truth. For as the dying blooms crumpled and collapsed to the ground, they scattered forth heaps of pages. Before long, endless sheets of paper filled the garden, tangling themselves in the rosebush and dancing on the breeze. Though the girl longed to catch them and stash them away, she could only watch from her vantage at the window as they cartwheeled through the air and slipped beyond her walls.

Glowering faces surfaced above the brick wall. "What is the meaning of this?" the townsfolk demanded, fists clenching dozens of rose-corpse pages. "How dare you sully our community with such filth! You should be ashamed of yourself!"

Their furious cries did fill the girl with shame, but above all, their cries struck the girl's heart with the icy spear of dread—for here was her secret, spreading across the land for all to read, and she had grown so very weak. . . .

Desperate, unfastening each screeching bolt in turn, the girl pried open the back door, rushing to the rosebush as fast as her sickly body would allow.

By now all the roses had died. All that remained of them was a snarling heap of thick stalks and thorns, choking the life from the old oak tree. The remains of the rosebush towered over her, as sinister and sharp as the nightmares that plagued her troubled sleep.

Hesitant and afraid, the girl approached the thorny mass, dropping to her knees in front of it. "Please," she begged. "Please make it stop. They will find out. They will know."

In a voice made of gravel, the thorny mass croaked, "I cannot make it stop. For I did not make it start."

Tears slipped from the girl's eyes like endless strands of pearls. "But what should I do—what can I do—to stop this?"

"I would tell you," replied the thorny mass, "but you already know the answer. . . ."

leaving

Tuesday

I wake to my alarm, instant dread pooling into my stomach around the oily black snake forever living inside me.

Today's the day.

Last night I'd managed to catch Mom at the bottom of the stairs and ask her what time this morning's interview is, even though I knew she'd be mad at me for bringing it up despite the fact that I needed to know.

Nine a.m. today. I have to be there by nine a.m., less than two hours from now. Well, *we* do. I was also able to gather that Mom's taking me and has to stay till it's done. Dad's, of course, not allowed anywhere near the center, let alone allowed to drive me, and for once I'm glad I'll be going with Mom. After last night's incident with the candle, I hadn't come back downstairs again besides talking to Mom on the stairs, not even to eat dinner or read Kyle a bedtime story. I figured Kyle would still be mad at me about his stolen Benny anyway.

But now I know I should've tried to be there for Kyle—he must be scared or at least sense the raw emotion in the air, or else feel that big things are happening all around him—but I hadn't wanted to risk running into Dad again. I'd told Mom I was sick and couldn't help with dinner, and thankfully she had let me off the hook, if nothing else because she was still pissed about being called to come get me from school, pissed also that she has to take me this morning.

Now I sit up in bed and glance again at my phone screen. It's only 7:07 a.m., but the center's thirty minutes away according to Google Maps; plus, I know I'll need extra time to put myself together and straighten out my thoughts.

I didn't sleep well last night, staying up way too late reading half the fairy tales from the book Ms. Patterson had given me. Several of the story lines had even gotten me thinking about ones I'd written a while back.

There was one in particular, from *Fairy Tales of the Heart*, that I reread multiple times about an evil tree that devours the hearts of passersby. It'd reminded me of one of my fairy tales, about a girl and her childhood rose garden, one that I'd never quite finished because I didn't know how it should end.

Writing those fairy tales always felt like wandering down a dark path with a million forks in it, blindly hoping you picked the right one again and again. But if you chose wrong, you had to keep going back, figuring out which fork had led you astray. Sometimes I delighted in the discovery, while other times it all seemed like more work than it was worth. Still, I'd completed enough stories with solid-ish endings involving cursed paintings or carnivorous shadows, but no ending ever felt quite right for this one: the girl and her secret. And last night, for the first time in a long time, I found myself staying up late thinking about it. That, and I kept picturing Kathleen or the police today, throwing printouts of my fairy tales in my face and demanding to know what they really mean. Because what if they aren't just silly stories after all?

Full stop! I shout in my mind. It's the same path my brain kept trying to take me down last night, but it's too dark and haunted with sharp-clawed monsters lurking in the shadows, just waiting for me to wander past. I won't go down that lane. I can't.

But, strange enough, even after all that reading and thinking last night, I didn't dream about any of those fairy tales. Instead, my brain had invented a new one involving slightly burnt popcorn kernels, a fake suede green couch, and a blaring car commercial. And the whole time, Dream Me was mute and immobile, unable to utter a sound like my lips were glued shut and my feet were sewn to the floorboards, as if I'd been dropped into a Brothers Grimm fairy tale. The dark, original ones with all the gore.

I am *terrified* of going to the center today, of saying the wrong thing, and especially of having to state on the record that Hannah lied about all the things she'd told them. This last part feels like the ultimate act of betrayal to her, but I don't have any other choice. Besides, I need to get used to it being "Hannah versus Emma" instead of "twin souls united," particularly if this thing goes to trial. Not to mention, she was disloyal first, right? Wasn't she the one who started this whole nightmare?

Wasn't she?

I throw off my comforter and move to my dresser, stepping around the spot on the floor where the candle had shattered. I'd swept up the glass and tried to scrape all the wax off the floor but hadn't known how without scratching the varnish. Then I'd gotten to a dark spot where a moth had clearly died, and I'd stopped trying. That's when I'd crawled into bed with my book. Still, I hate the creamy yellow film the wax has left behind, marring my glossy floors and caking under my fingernails like bar soap. It's enough to send almost unbearable panic jolting through me, but there's nothing to be done about it now. I'd gotten most of the wax out from under my nails, at least.

As I root through my drawers for something presentable to wear, I wonder if I'll have to take a lie detector test or if the cops will interrogate me in a dark room without any bathroom breaks like you see on TV. It's enough to make me queasy. Maybe Kathleen will be there as well since Mom mentioned her with a "team." Will she take pity on me? When I tell them Hannah's lying, will they even believe me?

Before the snake can wriggle up my throat and choke me, I close my eyes and squeeze the shirt I'm holding, reminding myself who I'm doing this for: Dad so he won't go back to jail, Kyle so I can keep my promise to him, and even Mom so she doesn't have to be a single parent while Dad's locked away, so I won't have ruined the last chance for her to still love me. So they will all still love me, and we can stay together as a family, because I don't know what I'd do if I lost them, too. I owe my family this much for inviting Hannah into our house in the first place, not to mention giving her the journal that started this whole mess.

I swipe furiously at my tears. *You have to do this, Em. You want to.*

But even as I dress and try to smooth my hair flat, I can't get Hannah out of my head, or the blast of hurt on her face when I told her I hated her. I can only imagine how she felt when she saw the concert ticket in her locker. Did it feel as permanent a breakup for her in that moment as it did for me when I'd let go of the ticket and listened to its small landing inside?

256 • CASSIE GUSTAFSON

I spend another hour wandering around my room, fretting, not going downstairs even though I can hear the sounds of everyone waking up—Mom and Dad's door swinging open, Kyle's small feet thudding toward the kitchen, the clinks and murmurs over breakfast. No one bothers me or tells me it's time to eat, and I feel both relieved and a bit sad, maybe even a little guilty. I should be down there having breakfast with my family, not hiding up here, waiting to slip out. But I can't face Dad right now. He probably told Mom to give me space because I'm guessing he's still mad.

At last, footsteps echo on the stairs, and my chest tightens as I wait for Dad's stern face to surface, but it's not him.

Mom enters my room, looking exhausted beyond words, a steaming mug of coffee in her hand.

"Ready?" Her voice is soft, her whole face drawn even though it's been painted to look awake. When I nod—"Almost"—she turns and shuffles back downstairs.

Dad's waiting in the dining room with Kyle, but he doesn't seem upset at all. Instead, he looks sorry.

"Hey, Bean," he says, wrapping me in a hug so tight, all I can smell is his spicy deodorant. I know this is his apology for getting angry yesterday, for breaking my candle.

"Hi, Dad." I feel almost dizzy, relieved we're okay.

When he pulls back, he flashes me an anxious, hopeful expression, and I know it's because he's counting on me to set things right this morning. I smile back my most earnest smile because I want him to know that I understand how important today is and that I won't mess it up.

"I know you're probably nervous, Em," he adds, "but you

shouldn't be. There's nothing to be nervous about when you're doing the right thing."

"I know," I whisper even as the snake flip-flops in my belly like it's been poked.

"Are you leaving?" Kyle asks, confusion and worry clouding his face. He's sitting at the table, a half-eaten stack of freezer waffles in front of him.

I ruffle his hair. "Just for a bit."

"Are you going to come back?" he asks.

I bend down and give him a big squeeze, not letting go even when I feel his small hands get syrup in my hair.

"I'll always come back," I tell him, voice muffling into his sleeve. Then I repeat, "You couldn't get rid of me even if you tried, okay?"

He nods, pulling away, though the frown lines around his mouth and forehead stay scrunched.

"Em?" Mom says, and it's the gentleness in her voice that makes me turn. "It's time to go."

Mom and I gather our things, and I'm just shutting the back door behind us when Dad calls out, "Love you, Bean!"

"Love you too," I whisper. But the door has already closed.

You remember showers interrupted, locks denied

You remember being in the shower and hearing the bathroom door creak open for the first time. You remember the shower curtain ripping aside and your father's face appearing in its place. You remember how he ogled your naked twelve-year-old body, not saying anything, just grinning a Cheshire cat's grin that could almost be considered playful were it not so hungry.

Dad! you remember yelling, even as your heart raced. You tried to twist your legs together, cover yourself with your hands. Anything to keep him from seeing you—all of you—wet and soapy and developing in ways that were terrifying.

You remember him asking, *What?*—feigning ignorance as if he couldn't fathom your discomfort. *We're family,* he murmured, too close. *Seeing each other this way is natural.*

You remember the way he said it, giddy in a way that felt immoral. Because you knew normal fathers shouldn't do this. Shouldn't make their daughters feel grotesque, alien in their own skin, never wanting to show their faces again—let alone their developing bodies—for fear of unleashing a grin of that caliber.

You remember right then and there, with your father's eyes roving over your naked flesh, vowing to only shower when you absolutely had to.

. . .

You remember, shortly after the shower incident, working up the courage to tell him you wanted privacy, stating this away from Mom's listening ears. She would ask too many questions, you feared, then find a way to blame you for the answers. Or maybe you actually dreaded her not asking enough questions at all.

You remember approaching your father and requesting two locks—one for your room and the other for the bathroom because, as you explained it, you "didn't want Kyle barging in." But you both knew who you were really trying to keep at bay.

And you remember most how your father shook his head in refusal, playing along in some game you wanted no part of, saying, "It's dangerous to lock your room from the inside. What if there was a fire? You could get hurt, Bean. And I love you too much to ever allow that to happen."

Just like that, you knew—that no matter the game, no matter the rules—you had already lost.

heat

Mom's silent on the drive to the center, but she doesn't seem mad for once, just utterly exhausted.

I stay quiet for most of the ride as well, not wanting to bother her but also grateful for the silence. That is, until I get stuck in my head, trying to figure out what I'm going to say, and start feeling queasy again.

The sky looks ominous today, like the clouds overhead might rip a seam and dump their contents at any moment. I half wish they would just to get it over with.

Twenty minutes into the thirty-minute drive, I decide that I'll simply tell them Hannah was never alone in our house with Dad, that I was always there with the two of them, and that nothing could've happened without me seeing it. It's almost entirely true. And I'll just insist like I did with Kathleen that Dad's a great dad and wouldn't hurt a fly.

So irresponsible! So stupid!

Exploding glass. Oozing wax.

Clean it up!

"How was work yesterday?" I ask Mom at last, both to break through the silence and the noise in my head.

She's just exiting the freeway, which makes my heart skip a

beat. I glance at her GPS. Only four minutes till arrival.

"You mean after your little incident at school?" she asks, though I'm relieved when her voice is weary, not angry.

"Yeah," I say, trying to keep my voice cheery. "Before I freaked out for no reason."

This must appease her because she sighs deeply, deflating as she rolls to a stop at the traffic light. "It was work. We had a bride come in for a consultation, but, get this, it turns out it was her actual wedding night. Her friend let it slip, but only after we'd done all her makeup for free *and* she didn't buy a single thing from the shop. Can you believe that? I might've been suspicious except for the fact that no one ever gets married on a Monday night. Who gets married on a Monday night?"

"The same person who tricks people into doing their wedding makeup for free?" I offer.

I'm rewarded with a quick smile from Mom as she makes a left turn, and I almost jump when her fingers knock into mine until I realize she's reaching for my hand. When she catches it, giving my fingers a squeeze like she used to when I was little, I melt into the warmth of it. For a glorious moment, I revel in our joined hands. Then she seems to catch herself and pulls away, her mood again turning somber and subdued.

"You know I gave up my youth to raise you, Emma. And my beauty. The best years of my life." She doesn't look at me when she says it, though it's as if she's repeated these words to herself on an endless loop. "So I sure hope you know how critical today is. That this isn't a joke."

More than she could possibly know. Her gaze is dead ahead, but I stare right at her so she can sense my seriousness as

I nod, the heat of her hand still humming across my knuckles.

"If anything would've happened, I would've known," she whispers out of the blue, so soft I almost don't catch it. Maybe I wouldn't have if I hadn't been watching her so intently.

I drop my eyes, a sudden, chilly gust of sadness blowing through the car, and I'm not sure if she's telling herself this or me.

But then we're turning into a parking lot and pulling to a stop in front of a plain, single-storied brick building that must be the advocacy center. And just like that, I've run out of time.

You remember strip poker

You remember the night back in eighth grade when Kyle fell asleep early, and your mother had an office party. It was the night your father gave you your first Mike's Hard Lemonade and sat you down at the kitchen table to play cards. You remember how special, how grown up, you felt, sipping that sharp, strawberry-flavored syrup.

You remember a little while into your poker game when he grew mischievous, confiding, *The normal way is boring. We should play the fun way.* You remember relenting, even after you found out that the "fun way" involved taking off an article of clothing for every hand of cards you lost. A war raged on in your sugar-saturated and increasingly tipsy brain, waged on guilt, the desire to please, and a sharp, clawing feeling that insisted Normal Families didn't do this type of thing. Yet by then you'd already lost your shirt, your bra. Topless, you tried to cover your small, bare breasts with clumsy hands, but he told you that you were "cheating" and you had to leave yourself exposed.

You remember your mother coming home shortly after and yelling one long condemnation that doused you and your father in equal culpability. *What the hell are you two doing? Get your shirt back on, Em!* You remember darting out of the room, clutching your shirt to your chest while hearing your father begin to mount his defense even as you fled. In this moment you remember the wall of shame that hit you because your mother had called attention to the wrongness of it all, a wrongness that you had participated in by doing as your father had asked, a wrongness you'd felt in every sparking nerve of your body from the moment you'd first sat at that table but had tried to shove away.

Yet mixed in with these dark emotions, you remember a glimmer of light—relief—because for the first time in a very long time, when your mother looked at you, she actually saw you. You knew she would know how to finally set things right.

hostile

I follow Mom through the glass front door and into a small waiting room with beige walls and cherrywood paneling. Across the way, a bald man sits at a front desk that's behind a sliding glass divider. He holds up a finger in a *wait one minute* gesture, glancing away from his computer screen just long enough to flash us a courteous smile before resuming whatever he's doing. Mom huffs, but I'm glad for the borrowed time, any extra seconds I can steal before I have to go in there.

I eye the two closed doors to either side of the front desk, wondering which one I'll have to enter. Turning, I take in the waiting area with its large front window and scraggly plant on the ledge that looks out over the half-full parking lot. Below the window are four squat, red plastic chairs that look like giant Duplo blocks, all tucked under an equally squat blue-and-yellow table. Next to it is a small bookshelf, and even though I doubt there are any books for someone my age, my fingers still itch to comb through them. But of course I don't.

I feel someone watching me and scan the vinyl black chairs lining the room. Sitting in the far corner is the only other soul in this waiting area: Aunt Jane.

I stare at her, startled, as she rises and beams at me. I had no idea she was coming today, didn't even notice her car in the lot.

Mom, though, looks completely unsurprised as they greet each other. I guess Aunt Jane being here is yet another thing Mom decided I didn't need to know about today. It makes my mouth go dry thinking about why Aunt Jane must be here—to make sure I tell them Hannah was lying about her brother.

Aunt Jane scoops me into a big hug, breathing, "Hi, M's," into my hair. Her breath smells like coffee and that flavored hazelnut creamer she always douses it with. "Ooh, it's so good to see you."

"You too, Auntie," I whisper back, softening into her hug. I'm not sure if today's going to be easier or harder because she's here, but I think I'm glad she came. Either way, it doesn't change what I have to do, just drives home the fact that I need to do it, in case I required another reminder.

"You ready?" she asks, and I nod the small lie against her collarbone. Truth is, I'm ready for it to all be over. I wish so hard it was.

The front desk window slides open behind us, and I pull away from Aunt Jane to watch Mom approach it. Mom's face is drawn, her mouth a tight line and tone "controlled annoyed" as she gives the bald man our names. The fact that she's not trying harder to hide her irritation this early on sets me on edge.

I scan the signs taped to the glass about not smoking or leaving your children unattended, then spot the decals stuck to the wall behind the man's head—fluffy pink roses in full bloom. My "girl and her garden" fairy tale comes flooding back, and I picture the girl kneeling in the dirt, begging the roses to *please make it stop. They will find out. They will know.*

The door to the right opens, and I shrink back. Two people

step through, one a curvy, dark-haired woman with warm brown skin who looks to be a bit older than Mom, and the other younger with one temple shaved, a thick black braid, and a tanned white complexion.

"Emma?" the older woman asks me in a slight Indian accent. She's wearing a pleasant, social-worker-Kathleen smile on her face and seems to be the one in charge.

My pulse double-taps in my throat. Shoving my hands into my pockets, I nod once.

The woman in charge makes eye contact with Mom next, then Aunt Jane—"Teresa? Jane?"—before gesturing us all through the door. "Come in. Please."

As we step through, I realize I've been expecting a long hallway dotted with doors or even something resembling an interrogation room from the movies, but it's just another waiting room, though it's twice the size of the last with at least three times the decoration and color: large armchairs, an adult-sized table, safari animal decals, and vibrant drawings encircling the walls.

Once we've all entered and the door's closed behind us, the older woman presses a hand to her chest. "I'm Paula, the forensic interviewer, which is just a fancy way of saying the person who's going to be talking with you today, Emma."

As Paula's eyes find mine, I think, *This is the woman who's interviewing me?* She sure doesn't look like a police officer in her black pants, light blue blouse with doves, and dangly silver earrings. Paula does have a picture ID draped around her neck where a photo of her smiling face beams out, but it's not a police badge, and she's definitely not in a uniform. And she seems almost . . . friendly? But then I stop, reminding myself she's not my friend.

Not even close. She wants to lock my dad away, and I can't let her.

Paula gestures beside her. "This is Silvi, our family advocate. They are here to help you fill out your paperwork and make sure you get all your questions answered. They'll also be taking you on a tour after some initial paperwork and our briefing with you, Teresa."

I register Silvi's nonbinary pronouns and realize I misgendered them in my head earlier. Mentally correcting my error, I remind myself that people are far more complex than society often seems to allow for.

Silvi steps forward with a folder tucked under one arm. I take in their striped rainbow dress with gold moons printed all over it that match the tiny gold moon studs in their ears. Even with their own photo ID badge, it's definitely not a uniform either. Silvi raises their free hand. "Hi, everyone."

Aunt Jane and I both return the greeting. And when my aunt sticks out her hand to shake Paula's and Silvi's, I copy her lead, even though I really don't want to because my palms are sweating like crazy and I know they'll both be able to tell. Despite why I'm here, I still want them to like me. They're kind enough not to react to my clammy hand.

As Mom shakes their hands, I feel resistance pulsing from her like a force field. She clearly wants nothing to do with this place, aggravated over having to be here at all. Worse, I'm sure Paula and Silvi can tell, and I find myself grinning harder, as if I can somehow make up for it. Here Mom was lecturing me in the car on how "critical" today was, and then she acts like this?

"Like Paula said," Silvi continues, "let me know if you have any questions or concerns, and I'll do my very best to answer them.

But first let me introduce you to this room." Flipping their braid over one shoulder, they gesture around. "So this is the family room. It's our special waiting area for children, teens, and their families. And just so you know, we'll have this room to ourselves today, so feel free to leave your belongings behind. They'll be perfectly safe."

As Silvi speaks, I take in the space in more detail, feeling more and more out of place. This space is set up for kids. The walls are bright yellow, plastered in cartoony jungle animal decals I know Kyle would love, plus a Thomas the Tank Engine train table complete with wooden tracks and tiny magnetic railway cars.

The only thing that looks remotely promising is on the far wall—another overflowing bookshelf that I so badly want to go look at but don't dare. Also, strung together and looping the entire room above our heads are rows upon rows of colorful signs made out of construction paper. Some have plain edges, some have fancy cutout ones, but each is unique, plastered in everything from stickers and finger paints to glitter and rainbow pom-poms. Words like "BOLD," "TRUTH," and "STRONG" jump out. I feel a twist in my gut, each word like an accusation.

Silvi must catch me staring because they gesture upward. "And these are the survivors' flags. Every child or teen is given the opportunity to make one after their interview."

Aunt Jane nods, looking appreciative, but Mom crosses her arms. Paula's eyes draw to Mom's movement, though her expression stays neutral. How could Mom be acting so hostile in front of them? Doesn't she care how she's making us look right now; know that, today of all days, she needs to cooperate, or at least pretend to?

Silvi's eyes catch mine. "You can also make one, Emma, if you want."

The truth is, some ridiculous part of me does want to. I love crafting almost as much as I love reading fairy tales, but they'd called them *survivors' flags*. There's no way I can make one without giving people the wrong idea.

Like Mom's read my thoughts, she says, "Let's not get ahead of ourselves." Her tone is cool, and this time everyone turns to look at her. Aunt Jane's expression clouds.

I feel myself scrunch inward, face flaming as I try to catch Mom's eye and somehow communicate to her that I don't want to make some silly little flag. I remember why I'm here, and it's not to play with stickers or glitter glue. But she won't look at me, so instead I attempt a belated grin for Silvi and Paula in a *Sure, I'd love to make an idiotic flag!* way so they won't also think I am rude or can't be trusted.

Paula and Silvi swap a quick glance before Paula fills the silence, directing her words at Mom. "I'll take you to meet the rest of my team soon, Teresa. But first we'll need you to fill out some paperwork." She nods to Silvi, who hands Mom the small folder they've been carrying and leads her over to a chair across the room.

Dread ices my veins. So I did hear Mom correctly back on the trampoline. There's going to be a whole team grilling me like an actual interrogation. Real cops, too, maybe. For a minute I consider verifying with Paula what "team" means exactly but decide against it. I don't want to look nervous or like I've got something to hide. And mixed in with my nerves, I feel something else start to stir. Anger. Why didn't Mom tell me what to expect today? Why leave me so utterly in the dark about everything?

Then Paula's gesturing my aunt and me to sit in nearby chairs before taking the seat opposite us. Like she's just read my mind, she asks, "Emma, did your mother explain what to expect from today? How the day will unfold?"

Aunt Jane's nodding beside me, clearly in the know, but I just stare before shaking my head. Then I wonder if I should've lied, if I've made Mom look bad just now, or worse than she's already made herself look. They all must think Mom's horrible, but I want to tell them that she's not normally like this. Well, not quite this bad. She's just really stressed, and understandably so.

But Paula doesn't skip a beat, nodding like she expected that answer. "In that case, let me give you a quick rundown, okay? As I mentioned earlier, Silvi, my team, and I will discuss with your mother how the interview will be conducted. Then Silvi will take you all on a tour of the center so you can get the lay of the land. Then, Emma, I'll come collect you for our interview. You know, just a chat where I ask you some questions. And after that, depending on the outcome, you may have a quick medical exam with Dr. Rocco— she's our specially trained pediatrician on call, and she's very nice. At the end, we'll all debrief together. Does that make sense?"

But my brain is stuck, looping on "medical exam," because why would I have to do one of those, and depending on what "outcome?"

I look over at Mom, who's seated a few chairs away, but she's frowning down at paperwork and didn't hear. Still, this is apparently repeat info that Paula said she'd already told Mom. So Mom knew I might have a medical exam, and she didn't even bother to warn me? Didn't think I'd want to know about it? That I *deserved* to know about it?

"Why would Emma have to undergo an exam?" Aunt Jane asks, and I'm so grateful she has. "I thought this was just an interview."

"So, as I mentioned to Teresa on the phone," Paula explains, "for every teen or child seen here at the center, it's recommended they also receive a medical exam, not only for evidentiary purposes, but, as we always say, it's often the first step in healing for abused individuals to know that their body is okay, that they are safe. If, you know, abuse did occur," she adds almost as an afterthought.

This attempt at what she must consider reassurance doesn't stop the panic thrashing through me. The medical exam doesn't sound like any old checkup—not with words like "evidentiary" in there. They're looking for *evidence*, on my *body*. Does this mean that if I say the wrong thing, they're going to make me do this exam? Because no matter what Paula says, this interview isn't the friendly chat she's trying to portray it as.

Paula glances up, then rises to her feet, and I turn to see Mom and Silvi already standing.

"Teresa," Paula says, "Silvi and I will take you to meet the team now, if you're ready?"

Mom sighs. Holding on to her purse like a rifle on a strap, she follows Paula, who uses her ID card to open the door. Silvi holds the door for them, then turns back to us. "I'll be back to take you on that tour in no time!" they enthuse before closing the door behind them.

Hannah's eager face pops into my head, and for the first time I imagine her here in this building, inside these walls. Did she sit in this exact chair I'm sitting in now? My eyes slip over the many flags, and I try to find hers here, wondering if she even made one. I wonder, too, what she would've said and how she would've acted. If she was nervous, I doubt she would've shown it. I can hear her proclaim it all over again: *Pretend they're all cockroaches, and picture yourself squashing them into the dirt when they're mean.*

My gaze drops to the carpet—charcoal with lighter lines running through it like noodles—and I jump a foot when Aunt Jane coughs. Even though it's just the two of us in here now, the normal, relaxed attitude we always have around each other has disappeared, replaced by a veil of discomfort between us that's as strange as our surroundings.

We sit in silence, and I keep trying to drag my thoughts away from Hannah. But it's like Hannah's the deserted island in that movie *Cast Away*, and I'm Tom Hanks on his makeshift life raft trying desperately to escape, except giant waves keep crashing over me and pulling me back to her, splintered raft and all.

Out of the blue, Aunt Jane asks, "Hey, M's, you remember that one time at the beach cabin when you got stung by that crazy yellow jacket?"

I toe the noodle-y carpet, the corner of my mouth pulling up. "Yeah, I remember. We'd just gone blackberry picking, right? And I still had all that berry juice on my hands, and I was carrying a giant bucketful, too. I guess I must've kicked his nest in the sand or something? Or maybe he wanted my berries because he sure went after me."

Aunt Jane's nodding. "Stung you seven times in the gut, the nasty little beast."

"Till you rescued me," I add. "Threw sand at it till you knocked it out of the air, then stomped it to death."

She flashes a fake-evil smile. "It was my pleasure, M&M's. Not sure what made me think of that. Only, I'd never heard your dad so upset, furious that the yellow jacket had hurt you. . . ." Her grin falters as she trails off.

274 • CASSIE GUSTAFSON

An uneasy feeling creeps up my spine as I watch her expression flatten out, then fill with worry lines.

At last she turns to me, a fierce intensity in her eyes as she clutches at my hand. "Em, is there anything I don't know that I should? About your dad, I mean? You know you can tell me anything, right? Anything at all?"

Something stabs through my heart. All this time, she's never asked. Never knew to ask, probably. But how could I even begin to answer that question now?

The door behind us unlocks with a *click*. Our gazes snap to it as it's pushed open from the inside, effectively shutting down any further conversation with Aunt Jane.

You remember the before (aka: trip preparations)

You remember several years ago, when you were freshly eleven, how your father took you shopping for your first-ever overnight backpacking trip together. The closest you'd come to backpacking in the past had been the few car camping trips you'd taken as a family, which, according to your father, was "sissy stuff" compared to how technical a real backpacking trip could be. But since you had just received your latest report card—full of As and A-pluses, with a single A-minus that even your father hadn't seemed too disappointed in—and since your father had deemed you mature enough to handle this new undertaking, this backpacking trip was to be your reward. You remember pride ballooning inside you at having earned such a special trip with your father.

You remember in the time leading up to the trip how the two of you had run through each preparation like a sacred ritual, though, admittedly, the sudden resurgence of one-on-one attention had overwhelmed you at first. As of late, work had snagged much of your father's concentration, but now—inside the cavernous REI sporting goods store near the Bay Bridge that smelled like beef jerky and bike tires—he directed his entire focus on you as you tried on dozens of sleek overnight backpacks, sturdy hiking boots, and quick-dry socks. He helped you cinch down various straps to see how each pack balanced on your small hips, instructed you to walk around the store in pair after pair of boots to see if they pinched, and explained in detail what every nook and cranny of the pack was meant for—from water bladder pouches, to drinking tube throughways, to sunglasses loops and sleeping pad bungees. It was all stuff he'd learned from a wilderness class he'd taken several years back, information he seemed eager to pass on to you.

You remember it took you almost half an hour to choose a single backpack, but the whole time, your father never grew impatient. The one you at long last settled on was deep purple—your favorite color—with black straps, a rigid frame, and a spongy back support that fit snug against your spine like the softest of foam mattress toppers. And so enamored were you with your new hiking boots that you removed them from the box and tissue paper as you rode the light-rail so you could lace them up while your father watched out for your next stop, which was the used outdoor goods store a few miles away. All the while, you remember allowing yourself to feel only a fraction of guilt—for now—over how much every brand-new item he'd just bought you had cost, and you even managed to block out the voice that told you how furious, how worried, Mom would be once she saw the resulting credit card bill.

At the next place you stocked up on provisions—dehydrated foods, a water purifier, and a used orange camping pad, plus a green sleeping bag for you. Your father let you pick out the desserts, so you chose bags of freeze-dried ice cream and apple crumble, one for each of the two nights you'd have alone with your father. He explained that this was the type of food astronauts ate in space, and you remember feeling awed, wondering how one person could know so many amazing things. Finally, you helped pick out a small, lightweight tent with a single strip of duct tape on the side where a tear had been patched, a tent that would fit the two of you, but only just.

You remember how, back on the light-rail, he pulled a packet of dehydrated mint chip ice cream from a shopping bag, an extra he'd snuck in without you seeing. Then he snapped it in half and handed you the bigger piece. *Don't tell your mother,* he'd said with a wink, which felt strange because your mother often let you have sweet things. Unless guests were over, then she would tell you to wait till after dinner or you would spoil your appetite.

You remember the delightful crunch of that filmy ice cream, the way it melted against your tongue, how you savored it for as long as you could, just as you were savoring this whole day with the man you were immensely proud to call your father. So great was your anticipation for your upcoming trip together that your small frame could hardly bear the enormity of it.

interrogation

Silvi holds the door open for Mom, who pushes past them like an angry bull, reentering the waiting room where Aunt Jane and I sit. Mom may be attempting to rein in her indignation but only just.

Silvi, for their part, seems to have lost a bit of chipper edge as they let the door swing shut behind the two of them, tapping the clipboard they're carrying. Still, they beam at Aunt Jane and me as we rise to our feet.

"We're ready for the tour now," Silvi says to Aunt Jane and me. "We want you to see the medical exam room, therapy rooms, and finally the interview room where you'll be talking with Paula today." As an aside to me, they add, "It can be less scary that way, knowing where you're going to be."

Aunt Jane goes to Mom, putting a hand on her arm and talking in a low voice I can't make out, but Mom doesn't respond, her eyes finding mine. She approaches, voice low and seething. "Well, I just got to meet the district attorney who's prosecuting your father, *and* some police detective, so that was lovely, as was seeing that social worker again."

A plum jacket flashes into my mind as I catch up with Mom's words. District attorney, *and* police detective, *and* social worker Kathleen—*that's* the team?

"Sounds like a lot," I whisper.

"Oh, it was. And you'll be video recorded, and they'll be watching your every move, so you better behave yourself."

I nod because it's all I can do over the chaos in my mind. The district attorney is here—the horrible woman who wants to put Dad away for a long time. And a police detective, maybe even one of the officers who searched my house and read the private stories in my journal.

Silvi must sense trouble because they ask in a raised, cheery voice, "Shall we begin?" Scanning their badge at the same door, Silvi holds it open and waits for the three of us to file past. We're dumped into a short, sky-blue hallway lined with doors painted in bright shades. It's colorful, but no less daunting.

"So this is our medical wing," Silvi explains, gesturing widely and walking backward down the hall. "Our board-certified pediatricians are on call twenty-four seven, and today's physician is Dr. Rocco. She's very friendly. And this . . ."

I'd been taking in a large banner filled with rain-forest animals next to a weight scale and height chart, but I pull my gaze away to watch Silvi duck into a small room.

". . . is the exam room where you'll have your medical."

If I have one, I mentally correct Silvi when, by some miracle, Mom doesn't.

We all squeeze in behind Silvi, entering the space that looks just like a checkup room at a doctor's office, complete with an exam table covered in tissue paper, random medical equipment on rollers, and a framed picture of puppies peering out of laced-up tennis shoes. There's even a rocking chair in one corner, so I guess that's unusual. Plus, dangling from one of the metal rollers next to a stethoscope is a pair of bugged-out glasses with a light on top that look like something a mad scientist would wear.

Silvi follows my line of vision and picks them up. "The doctor does wear special eyewear to make sure they don't miss anything, but you can look at them if you'd like." Silvi tries to hand the glasses to me, but I shake my head, feeling suddenly too cramped in this tight space.

"Is the exam also recorded?" Mom's voice drips sarcasm, and I wish I could shake her. *You're making this so much worse!*

It's a throwaway remark, but Silvi nods, taking in the question while returning the glasses to their spot. "Only if there's anything of note, then the doctor will videotape for evidentiary purposes. But the videotape isn't running normally."

That word again: "evidentiary." This new info does nothing to lessen my nerves as I retreat into the hallway. I pray I'm not being rude, but I had to get out of there. How's seeing all this beforehand supposed to make me feel any better? Now I have actual visuals to hold on to and anticipate, like those grotesque magnified glasses. *What all could they see?*

Thankfully Silvi seems done with that room, taking up their post at the front of the group and leading us past a closed door that they explain is Dr. Rocco's office. A phone rings down the hall, and we follow its sound to the far end where Silvi rounds the corner and stops in front of another open room. Gesturing inside, they say, "So in addition to the medical checkups, we also do on-site therapy, specifically trauma-focused cognitive behavioral therapy, which is the research-supported approach to helping kids overcome abuse. And one of our clinicians—this is her office."

I'm behind Mom and Aunt Jane, so I only spot turquoise

walls, a decaled Dr. Seuss quote, and a zebra-print chair before Silvi adds, "So, Emma, you could come back here and talk, should you want to or should it be recommended."

I half duck like Silvi's thrown something at me, then swallow and nod, stepping away as everyone moves on to the next door.

"And here's the other therapy room," Silvi continues. "In fact, Claudia's in today."

I catch a glimpse of a round woman sitting at a desk, holding a phone away from her ear to return Silvi's greeting. Hand-painted mini canvases circle the room, depicting rainbows, potted daisies, and a sunset, all clearly made by little kids.

Silvi introduces us, and Claudia smiles at me, hovering in the back. "Hi, Emma. So nice to meet you."

Silvi adds, "Should you need a referral, this is who you'd be seeing, Emma."

"But only if deemed necessary," Mom cuts in.

Again, Silvi doesn't miss a beat. "Yes, that's right, Teresa." Rounding the corner, we all walk down another hall, and I realize we've gone in a horseshoe.

"And finally, this is the interview room."

I expect to see Paula and her "team" inside, but the room is empty. It's small and, unlike all the other rooms, subdued. Still, it's friendlier than I was expecting an interrogation room to be, with gray walls and a large decal of a dandelion blowing seeds that turn into a swarm of butterflies. Two cushiony teal chairs sit around a small white table that's stacked with a packet of markers, some loose pens, and two mini canisters of what look like new Play-Doh resting on a pile of blank paper.

Besides a beige filing cabinet on the far wall and two prints of famous-looking flower paintings, there's nothing else in the room. No other toys or flags or books. And there's not enough room or chairs for Paula plus a whole team to sit in here with me. But didn't Mom say something about it being recorded, about me being watched? There isn't a camera, though.

Even though I'm confused, I breathe a sigh of relief.

"Doesn't look so bad, huh, M's?" Aunt Jane asks in a whisper, squeezing my shoulders. Then louder she asks, "What's the Play-Doh for?"

"Oh, it's just there should Emma want to do something with her hands while she talks with Paula," Silvi answers.

That's when I spot it on the far wall beneath one of the flower paintings—something that looks like a white light switch cover, except that instead of a light switch in the middle, there's a shiny black rounded screen.

Camera.

The snake twines its way up my spine, its pupils deadly slits in those ruby eyes.

Silvi asks, "Any more questions?" directing this at me. "Or anyone need to use the bathroom before we head back?" They gesture across the hall to a yellow door marked RESTROOM, but I shake my head hard because I don't need to pee and, even though there are far too many questions rattling through my brain, I'm not about to ask a single one.

"Great, let's return to the waiting room, then."

I glance at the far end of the hall, spotting a closed, unmarked green door. Mom's words replay in my head once more: *You'll be video recorded, and they'll be watching your every move.* . . . In an instant, it all makes sense, especially after Mom shoots daggers toward the door before following after Silvi. The team is behind there—the DA, the police detective, and Kathleen with her endless probing questions, all waiting to hear what I have to say. They'll be monitoring me from inside that room.

Dazed, I'm about to follow Silvi, who's retracing our path back, when I spot another surprise. It's beyond the green door and bathroom, on the far wall at the hallway's end surrounding another exit. I stop in my tracks, and Mom rams into me.

"Sorry," I mumble.

"Oh yes. I almost forgot," Silvi says, returning and gesturing to this wall, which is covered from floor to ceiling in overlapping handprints of every color. But the prints don't stop there. They spill out from the one wall and back into the hallway, too many for a single wall to contain.

"In addition to the survivors' flags," Silvi continues, "anyone who sits for an interview is invited to put their handprint here."

I stare at the dozens upon dozens of handprints in all sizes, imagining the cold squish of paint against my palm and hardness of the wall as I press my palm to it before carefully rolling each finger into existence. Peeking down at my hand, I stretch it out, seeing how much larger it is than most on the wall. I couldn't put my handprint on there either. Just like the rest of this place, I don't belong—too old with too much to lose. Don't Paula and Silvi know that? They talk about playing arts and crafts with survivors' flags or stamping handprints on walls like a little kid, but do they have any idea how much is resting on my shoulders? That my family is counting on me to hold us all together?

Wet, hot emotion knots in my throat.

Don't you dare freak out. Not here. Not like yesterday.

Just then the mysterious green door opens, and Paula slips gracefully from it, closing the door behind her in such a way that I can't see inside. It as good as confirms my suspicions that the "team" sits in there, even now preparing to scrutinize my every move during the interview.

"I was just about to take everyone back to the waiting room," Silvi explains to Paula. "Unless you're ready for Emma now?"

"Yes," Paula confirms, her expression pleasant but neutral. "You ready, Emma?"

I nod past the knot in my throat as Aunt Jane gives my shoulders another tight squeeze. "You'll do great, M's. Just go in there and tell the truth." I nod again, afraid to speak and no longer sure what "truth" means anymore.

Mom moves toward me, but Silvi matches her step. "If you'll just follow me, Teresa," Silvi says, "I'll bring you back to the waiting room where we can go over resources available to you."

"I still don't understand why I can't stay with Emma during her interrogation. I'm her mother, for god's sake."

It's physically painful how close Mom is to losing her cool, which Paula and Silvi must note, given the look they exchange. Yet Paula doesn't miss a beat. "Interview, Teresa. It's only an interview, not an interrogation. And I'll take good care of her. Also, now's a great time to discuss with Silvi any services you may need, like therapy, should that prove necessary."

I don't know whose face is redder—Mom's or mine—but at last Mom turns and follows Silvi back down the hall. Before Aunt Jane goes, she flashes me two thumbs up, mouthing, "Good luck!" but it doesn't mask the worry weighing down her mouth.

I watch them all go, feeling close to tears already, wondering how in the world I'm supposed to get through a whole interview without crying, without messing up.

When I glance over, Paula's watching Mom's retreat with a keen gaze, but then she's turning to me, her expression clearing. Opening the interview room with her badge, she gestures me inside with a "You first," like this is a kindness.

My eyes go straight to the camera, to the faces I know are observing us from the other side. Inside me, the snake flicks its tongue, fully alert and ravenous, as Paula closes the door behind us.

You remember that trip

You remember that it almost rained the first day of the back-packing trip, but it didn't. What would have happened if it had, you wonder, or were the events of that trip inevitable, not reliant on any single fated time, or location, or weather forecast?

You remember driving with your father out to his grandfather's cattle ranch nestled deep in the hills of California, ominous clouds chasing you the whole way. They lingered above, as weighty as marbles in delicate silk, even as your father, seemingly undeterred, parked at the end of a winding dirt road. The two of you hoisted on your packs, your journey together begun, stopping only to readjust your pack once, then to cross a freezing stream. You remember removing your boots and shoving your socks inside, tying the laces together and hanging the boots around the back of your neck like your father showed you. Then you carefully picked your way across the slippery pebbles in rushing, toe-numbing water, the pull of the current and weight of your pack threatening to topple you. But your father was there, talking you through each step, throwing out a hand to help you right yourself when you stumbled.

Once safely across, you remember hiking several more miles, reveling in the press of your pack against your shoulders and hips, the lukewarm sips of water hinting at plastic, the crunch of dry leaves underfoot. Each turn in the path stole your breath. You remember thinking you had never in your life seen anything so beautiful as those rolling hills, those whispering trees. You had never before smelled such clean air with whiffs of evergreen and limestone and earth dancing through it. You remember wanting it to last forever, but instead of forever, you had just two nights alone with your father.

Your mind has since misplaced, in all the fractured chaos that was to follow, what must have been blessed normalcy that first night. For you remember only that second night—vividly—with superhuman powers of memory. After all, it was the events of this second night alone that crept past your defenses and shattered your mind from inside its own walls, a night spent in the yard of your great-grandfather's now-deserted farmhouse.

On that second day, you remember first arriving at the old farmhouse, feeling weightless after dropping your heavy packs onto the front porch before setting out to explore the surrounding area. You remember your father leading you through empty fields and up a hill to the overgrown grave of a little boy who had died on the property. Staring at the small tombstone set into the earth, you did the math between the years of his birth and death, coming up with just under eight years, which you told your father. You must have done the math quickly because your father beamed at you, rubbing the top of your head like you were five and not eleven. *Smart girl.*

You remember your father narrating the story of how it happened—the boy falling from his tree house in the front yard and plunging onto the white picket fence below, its sharp points piercing through him. It was a story your aunt confirmed when you dared to ask her later, though you knew you were poking at a warm, breathing monster by even mentioning the trip, but you needed to make sure that this wasn't like the tunnel story. That it was true.

And as you stood by the unkempt grave next to your father, your own guts churned at the thought of a sharp picket puncturing them. You pictured your body draped backward over the fence, harpooned in place, helpless and awaiting death as you gasped your final breaths.

You remember that when you hiked back to the house, you looked in the massive tree for a tree house that was no longer there. As you ran your fingers over the rough edges of pickets, you noticed how all the tips were now rounded. Though they could have been worn smooth from age, you didn't think so. And when you examined the pickets below the tree, you didn't find anything unusual. No blood, no gore. No sign whatsoever of such a terrible tragedy. But you remember thinking there should have been some marker, some indication, that Death had dragged a tender soul from here, still warm. Then you stood straight and unmoving, thinking that perhaps you did feel a tinge of melancholy pulling at the tattered edges of the wind. *The spirit of the boy*, you thought, *who died too young*.

Later you remember setting up the camp stove while your father erected the tent, right under the tree where it'd happened. You made dinner together—dehydrated beef Stroganoff that actually tasted good even if the noodles were still a bit crunchy. While you ate your portion from a tin cup with a hard plastic spoon, your father explained about all the things you could scavenge from the yard if you ran out of food. *Fiddleheads from ferns, the inner side of bark. Even snails,* your father had insisted, and because you teased that you didn't believe him, he told you he'd prove it.

So the two of you rounded up a few garden snails and cooked camp-side escargot. The snail felt rubbery and slimy in your mouth, even though you had sautéed it in extra margarine. Your father was always having you try strange things like ant lemonade, a mix of regular lemonade with black ants added in to make it sour. The hard part had been catching the ants, then shaking them into the lemonade when their microscopic legs were so good at sticking to jars. Or fish eyes, taken from the rainbow trout you had caught on your last family camping trip, which he had paid you five dollars to eat. But you'd been forced to eat another when you'd hidden the first inside a marshmallow and swallowed it whole. This second one you'd had to pop between your teeth, to taste. *My daughter won't be squeamish,* he'd insisted, to which you'd readily agreed, his radiating pride having made those earned five dollars well worth it.

But even though you were used to eating weird things to impress your father, you remember only managing a few chews of the garden snail before spitting the whole thing to the ground, laughing and gagging. This time, though, not toughing it out was okay because he did the same.

Washing away the greasy slime with hot chocolate dotted with mini freeze-dried marshmallows, you remember feeling perfectly content, knowing you two were in this together, mirrored father and daughter souls reflecting each other in such a vast, lonely wilderness. And once the fire crumbled to coals and the sky above exploded with stars, you remember crawling into the tiny two-person tent with your father, clothed in your warm sweatpants and thick brown hiking socks. As with the day before, it had become your nightly ritual to massage each other's sore back muscles, and you had plenty from that second day of hauling your pack. You remember how you massaged his back first, and when it came time for your turn . . . Well, that isn't something you want to remember any more of right now.

Strange, how deep some memories burrow and cut, in their dark descent, all the way down.

poison

I expect Paula to have a legal pad and an earpiece like private investigators do in movies, but she doesn't have either. Guess the camera mic's that good. I also expect her to turn intense and aggressive, leaning forward, ready to lunge on any slipup, but again, no. She seems relaxed, movements slow and unhurried like before. If anything, maybe even more so since shutting us both in here. She must be waiting, working up to that.

We've sat down in the two teal chairs, and I try to remind myself to sit up straight. I want everyone watching to know I'm taking this seriously and am to be trusted no matter who they think my dad is or how my mom's acted today.

"Are you comfortable?" Paula asks, and I assume she's talking about the chairs, so I nod.

"Great." She crosses one leg over the other. "Before we start, I want to let you know we're being recorded, okay? Do you see that right there?"

Shocked she'd admitted to it, I follow her finger to the camera across the way that I'd spotted earlier.

"There's a camera on that far wall, and one on the ceiling as well," she continues, pointing skyward.

I glance up, and, holy crap, there it is. I'd missed that one. My palms start to sweat again, and I rub them together. But why's she telling me this? To try to gain my trust? Because she saw me spot one earlier, or heard Mom telling me about the recording, and decided to own it up front?

"Who's watching us?" I ask, testing her, like I don't already know.

But Paula doesn't hesitate. "Great question, Emma. There's a group of my colleagues in the next room listening in to help me make sure I don't forget anything."

"What kind of colleagues?"

"Well, as I explained to your mother, there's Kathleen, a social worker, whom I believe you've already met when she came to your house?"

My mind flashes to Kathleen sitting on my bed, nearly whacking her head on the sloped ceiling and me feeling evil-glad.

"Yeah," I confirm with a trace of guilt.

"Also, there's a detective from the police department here today, along with the district attorney, just to help me do my job right."

My mouth feels like a desert. Even though Mom had warned me about this, and I'd believed her, having Paula verify it freaks me out. The police detective could even be the same one Hannah was helping with the investigation, which further confirms that all these people watching me in this exact moment are just waiting for me to make one tiny mistake so they can lock Dad up and throw away the key.

"What will happen with them?" I ask. "The recordings from today?"

"So the detective will take them with him, and they'll be entered into police evidence."

For the case against Dad is what she's not saying. I once saw, on a murder documentary, this guy getting crucified over what he'd said during a taped interrogation. Is an "interview" really so different?

Paula leans forward, dangly earrings swinging like pendulums. "But I want to remind you, Emma, that everyone's only here to help me make sure I ask all the right questions. They're on my team, but they're on yours as well."

She's wrong, of course. *My* team is Dad's team. It's Kyle's, Mom's, and Aunt Jane's. Still, I give her a small nod, though I vow with all my heart to stay vigilant. I will not give them anything they can use against Dad.

Paula flips her dark hair behind her shoulder. "Great. So, before we begin, let's go over some important ground rules, so we know we're on the same page."

"'Kay."

"First"—she holds up a thumb—"I want you to know it's totally fine if you don't understand a question or if you don't know the answer, all right? You just say so."

She waits for another nod, and I give it.

"Second"—she raises her pointer finger beside her thumb—"in here today we're only going to talk about things that really happened, all right? No make-believe stuff of any kind. True things only."

"Okay," I say.

"Third"—she raises another finger—"I wasn't there during any of the situations I'm going to ask you about, so I don't know the answer to any of these questions, which is why I'm asking them, okay?"

I nod again.

"Finally"—all fingers minus her pinkie are raised—"if you need to take a break or use the bathroom at any time, you let me know, Emma, and we'll pause, all right?"

"All right."

"Great. All of that makes sense?"

I unstick myself from the chair and sit forward. "Um, so, if I don't have anything to tell you, like if I don't know the answer to something you ask me, then I just tell you that I don't know?"

"That's exactly right. So my job"—she presses a palm to her chest—"is to ask you questions, and your job"—she gestures at me—"is to answer what you know, but if you don't know the answer to any of my questions, you just tell me that you don't know. I am not here to force any information out of you, understand? I'm not a police officer, and this is not an interrogation. Nothing of the sort."

I swallow and nod. If she's telling the truth, this sure doesn't sound like an interrogation. And if it's not, maybe I can actually do this? Hope sparks in me before being snuffed out by the thought: *But what if she's lying to put me at ease and get me talking?*

"Lastly, feel free to doodle or play with Play-Doh if you want. Sometimes those being interviewed find it comforting."

I stare at the tube of purple Play-Doh, already smelling its salty dough, feeling its soft squish, but instead of reaching for it, I shake my head.

"All right, but feel free to change your mind at any time, Emma. Are you ready to start, then?"

I realize I've started curling into myself again and sit up straight, giving Paula a tight nod.

"Great. So first, can you tell me how school is going for you?"

It's not a tough question, but it is. I swallow hard, thinking of Hannah's tears, the evil looks Brooke and Kat had given each other in class yesterday when Hannah wouldn't sit next to me, the fact that I have no friend to go back to other than Ms. Patterson. Eventually, I shrug. "Fine, I guess."

She nods, like that was a legit answer. "And what would you say is your favorite subject?"

"English lit, especially when we read legends or fairy tales. I like to write them too. Just . . . silly nonsense I make up, is all . . ." I can only hope everyone listening is buying it. "They're not real, though, you know. Just stories . . ." I've overdone it, and I clamp my lips together.

But Paula doesn't miss a beat. "They sound interesting." When I don't elaborate, she asks, "And what would you say you like most about yourself, Emma? Your favorite attribute."

It's kind of a weird question, but my answer is immediate. "That I'm smart."

"I can see that."

"And I know why I'm here today."

The tiniest flicker of surprise crosses her face, the first human crack I've seen from her, though she smooths it out immediately. She probably wasn't expecting me to get down to business so fast. "Why do you think you're here today, Emma?"

"Because my best friend lied?" I blurt. "Ex–best friend," I correct. "Lied about my dad. Saying he . . . did bad things to her."

"And what's the name of this ex–best friend?" she asks.

"Hannah Garber."

"How old is Hannah?"

"Fifteen, just a year and ten days older than me."

"And how long have you two known each other?"

"Forever. Well, actually, just seven months? But it . . . feels like much longer."

"Emma, you said earlier that Hannah lied, saying your father 'did bad things to her.' Can you tell me what it is that Hannah claims your father did?"

"That he touched her." Heat blasts through my body. "Touched her 'there,' I mean."

Paula reaches for a pen, then pulls a sheet of paper from the bottom of the stack, rocking the Play-Doh containers on top. I'm expecting a blank page but see instead a printout of a very basic black-and-white human body, arms and legs spread like a starfish, though it's missing any sex organs. Paula points her capped pen to it, holding it up for me but also for the camera as she draws an imaginary circle around the whole thing. "Using this anatomical picture, can you tell me exactly where Hannah says your father touched her?"

"Well, she says here." I jab at the crotch area. Wait, Hannah never specifically told me this. Still, there's no going back now. "But . . . But it's not true!" I rush on.

"Would you mind drawing an *x* in the area Hannah says she was touched, just for our records?"

She sets the paper down and hands me the pen, which slides in my sweaty palm. Gripping harder, I press the pen to the crotch, wondering if I'm making a further mistake by recording this. I mark a big *x* before shoving the paper back at Paula. But I pressed too hard, I realize, and now the imprint of an *x* is etched into the top paper of the stack like yet another accusation.

I stare at its ghostly imprint as I add, "But like I said, Hannah's lying. My dad never did that."

"And why do you say that?"

My eyes meet hers. She needs to believe me. "Because I was with her every time she was over at my house. The whole time. I never left her side besides to, like, pee." Face flaming, I glance away. "And Dad was never alone with her either. Not once."

She nods like she believes me. Am I actually pulling this off?

I keep going. "But even if he was alone with her, which he wasn't, he never would've touched her like that. He's not like that."

"You never saw him do anything inappropriate with her, anything of a sexual nature?"

I swallow hard past the lie. "No."

"And has he ever done something like that to you? Anything inappropriate or that made you feel uncomfortable in any way?"

"I . . ." The smell of pine, of lingering campfire. "No." It's a microscopic sound.

Paula leans forward. "You seem stressed, Emma."

My whole body's sweating. I'd been foolish enough to think she couldn't tell. Sliding against the chair, swimming in my own panic, I watch her left earring catch the light as it swings. I can't speak, the words stuck to my tongue like rotten leaves.

"Are you worried about something, Emma? Worried, maybe, that someone you know might get in trouble if you talk with me today?"

A phone rings in the distance as I swallow again.

"I gotta pee," I blurt, leaping to my feet. It's rude, but I have to get out of here. I can't stay in here any longer.

"Of course," Paula says, standing.

I lunge at the door Paula opens, not even trying to cover up the butt-sweat mark on the chair I know I've left behind.

"It's right across from us." Paula points, but I'm already halfway to it.

Bursting through the bathroom door, I slam it behind me. Pressing my back to it, I try to will my pounding heart to calm, but it's slamming against my rib cage. I know I can't stay in here forever, but I also can't go back in there. How naive I'd been to bring up the reason I'm here. Who knows how long it would've taken Paula to get there with her basic, feel-good questions, and I could've bought myself some time. Instead, I brought out the dynamite *and* lit the fuse myself. Now there's no time to outrun the fiery blast.

I pace, around and around. Past the toilet, sink, towel dispenser, diaper changing station, door. Again and again I loop, the orange walls swimming around me as I circle, a flyer advertising a self-defense class turning melty.

When I'm dizzy beyond belief, I splash water on my face, the whole room spinning at breakneck speed, but at least I know what I have to do. Go back in there and repeat what I said the first time: *No, I'm not worried someone I know could get in trouble. I'm not stressed, either. I'm just trying to set the record straight so everyone will know the truth: my dad is innocent.* It's the only way I know how to save my family.

Tears burn into existence, but I scrub them away. I've been gone too long, need to get back. Yanking a towel free, I dry my face.

It's time.

But when I step back into the hallway and cross over to the

interview room, I expect to find Paula still in there. Instead, glancing down the hall to the far end, I see her staring up at the wall of handprints. I hesitate, then join her.

"They're something, huh?" she asks, gaze flitting. "Sometimes when I'm feeling a bit down, I look at all these handprints, and it makes me feel better somehow. So much strength in these kiddos, these teens. So much courage. They really are something."

"Yeah." I scan the wall, not sure what else to say. This close up, I can make out individual lines in palms and fingerprints, but also first names signed in permanent marker beside each hand, some written in fancy cursive or loopy print, but most in blocky, little-kid lettering.

Cody. Akiko. Eric.

Maria. Kim. Zephyr.

Daveed. Suzanne. Joan.

"Well, I'm going to head back in there, but you take as long as you need out here. I mean that."

I nod and watch her reenter the room.

It's as I turn back that I spot it at last, tucked in the left corner toward the top of the wall, unassuming and almost camouflaged. But it's no less there—a handprint the size of my own, stamped in our favorite shade of magenta with her name printed across the palm in bubbly, overly enthused print: *Hannah.*

I don't even realize I've lifted my hand till it's covering hers, the edges of her thumb, fingers, palm aligning perfectly with mine. Something breaks free in my chest, and I close my eyes, leaning into the wall and picturing Hannah standing right here, making this print after telling her story. This time, as in the hallway at school, she wasn't acting fake-hyper, and she wasn't pretending.

As tears slide down my face, warm emotion crashes over me, and I start to understand. Understand that when I looked at Hannah in that hallway and mouthed "I hate you"—that was a lie. Because in that moment, I hated Hannah like you hate a mirror.

Instead of "I hate you," what I really meant was "We're the same."

What you've been through, so have I.

Me and Hannah, Hannah and me.

Now, finally—*finally*—for the first time since finding out she got my father arrested, I get it. I realize why I thought I hated her so much.

It's so unbelievably simple, I could laugh even as I sob. And as I stand here, palm still pressed to the brilliant purple handprint of my ex–best friend in the whole wide world, I do just that. A tiny, desperate laugh burbles up from deep within me, past all the endless tears and feral gardens, caged birds and jet-black snakes seeping their poison inside me.

Hannah Garber did what she had to do; she did what I couldn't, even if she was only guessing about me.

Tell someone to make it stop. For both of us.

You remember that one night

You don't remember rubbing his back that night in the tent, but you must have because then he was rubbing yours.

You remember lying on your stomach, slowly melting onto your sleeping bag and nearing the world of dreams. But an instant later, you tensed, on full alert. His thumbs had slipped lower, over your sweats but farther down the back of your waistband. As you held your breath, they inched down, down, down until he began to knead the muscles of your glutes.

You remember stiffening, his whispered "Relax" into the darkness, and you tried to because those muscles really were sore. He was just being a good father, you knew. This is what backpacking must entail.

You remember repeating these reassurances in your head even as he told you to turn over and started rubbing your upper pectoral muscles, which were tight from your pack straps' relentless tugging. But then he moved on to your legs, massaging up your inner thighs, then back down again, up and back down again, never quite high enough to . . .

Until the third time advancing up your thigh. You remember how this time his fingers maintained their ascending creep until his hands reached the space between your legs, and a white-hot bolt of lightning erupted through your entire being. You remember lying there, corpse-still, the lightning quickly souring to nausea as you grappled to comprehend what was happening—Where were you, precisely? Who exactly was that beside you? Why were his fingers massaging you in that way, because wasn't he your father?—until something outside you, or perhaps deep within you, vised your legs together like iron. Some part of you feared angering him, but was it even you who had done it?

You remember his hands jerking away, the relief that flooded you wholly.

It had worked.

This time.

You don't remember anything else from that night, only the thick, choking fear clinging to you like mist—that you had angered your father, that he would turn against you, but above all else, that his roaming hands would reach for you again.

Later you fell asleep. Perhaps it took mere minutes or perhaps several long hours of shame battling confusion battling the most insidious of dreads. But there you must have slept, next to your father in a tiny, two-person tent under a tree where a young boy had fallen to his death many years ago on a white picket fence that surrounded the old farmhouse that belonged to the Clark ancestors in the middle of the wilderness on your first backpacking trip that was your reward from your father for being an exemplary student with near-perfect grades.

You remember knowing; his remorse

You remember staring, unnoticed, at the back of the two sil-houetted figures of your father and best friend entwined on the couch, his hands caressing her under the blanket.

You remember tiptoeing behind them, popcorn bowl pressed to your chest, before fleeing up the stairs.

You remember your mother calling out in a too-loud voice, *Girls! I brought you hot chocolate!*—a voice that ensured nothing was happening.

You remember covering your ears, but your mind was an unrelenting tempest as it screamed and Screamed and SCREAMED:

It's happening to her, too.

You remember the next day when you began to wonder if there were many different kinds of love. Because then your own love must lurk in the shadows, where your shaking hands hoarded each tiny, splintered silence. And you especially remember watching him all that next day, observing how quiet and remorseful he'd grown.

But most of all, you remember thinking how much sorrier he looked for what he'd done to her than he ever had for what he'd done to you.

You remember darkness

You remember that, as it grew closer to bedtime each night, you'd linger over making lunches, taking extra care with the smoothness of the peanut butter on the bread, the precision of Craisin-to-baby-carrot ratio you'd tuck into plastic bags; you'd read a second chapter to Kyle and keep reading, even after you'd hear his soft snores begin and know you'd have to reread the same passages the following evening; and you'd spend a few minutes longer than strictly necessary slipping completed homework into respective folders, binders, backpack compartments before reorganizing your pens and pencils and highlighters case—again and again and again.

You remember that, all the while, the crimson-eyed snake in your stomach would thrash and flail, filling you with increasing regret for the extra food and dessert you'd consumed at dinner, and you'd curse yourself—again and again and again—for eating so much too quickly like always.

But you remember most, on the evenings when the shadows grew as long as a nightmare and the sky outside fell into a torment of dark, how he would stand in your doorway and call to you, softly at first, as you both pretended that you were asleep. Then, when he'd inevitably grow impatient, you remember how his voice would turn as hard and sharp as the knife you kept under your pillow, whose blade you'd only ever thought to use against yourself, just yourself, but never him.

And you remember how, inevitably, with the slowness of a waking maiden, you would slide your bare feet, one by one, from the warmth of soft sheets to the cool, varnished floor. And as your father would step aside, allowing you to traverse the dark hall in front of him and enter the guest bedroom first, you remember slipping headfirst into your fairy tales and dreaming of kingdoms in a land far, far away, that were so magical, so dazzlingly bright, they could banish even the cruelest of darknesses.

too

"I see that you're crying, Emma. Can you help me understand what's going on?"

I'm back in the interview room, sitting across from Paula, but I can't speak, can't tell her. I can hardly move. All I can do is clutch this purple canister of Play-Doh with everything I have and think of Hannah. Brave, fearless, unapologetic Hannah, who sat here where I'm sitting now as she told her truth. Our truth.

"Did someone ask you not to say something, Emma? To keep a secret?" Paula asks.

The lid pops from the Play-Doh and rolls away. My eyes flash to hers. Does she already know?

Slowly, slowly, I nod my head.

"And are you worried that if you talk to me today, that someone could get in trouble?"

I nod again, more vigorously.

"Who are you worried might get in trouble?"

"My . . ." I choke on the word. Swallow. Try again. "My dad."

"Tell me about that."

Silence.

"Emma, did your dad ask you to keep a secret?"

"Yes."

"What kind of secret?"

Silence.

"You said earlier you thought Hannah was lying about what happened."

"She's not."

"You don't think Hannah is lying about what happened?"

"No."

"And why do you say that?"

"Because . . . ," I say, barely audible through my sobs. "Because it happened to me, too."

Me too. Me too. Me too.

"What happened to you, too, Emma?"

"My dad, he . . . He touched me. Made me do things. Awful, messed-up things. I didn't want to, but he was my dad, and I loved him"—*love* him—"so much. . . ."

"How long . . . ?" Paula begins.

Years.

I'm made of tears, comprised of nothing but devastation and grief. Crushing this canister of Play-Doh so hard, the dough squishes out, smelling like salt and starch and a childhood forgotten. "When we moved, I thought it would stop, that he would stop, but he didn't. And then Hannah came, and it suddenly did for a while, and I was so relieved, like I could breathe again. But then he did that to her, and I finally realized. He hadn't stopped, he'd just switched. From me to her. And he was never going to stop. Not ever."

Snot bubbles from my nose, mixing with a river of tears, and I feel so ugly and broken, so foul. How could I ever have thought I could be a good daughter? A good sister, niece, best friend?

"I'm sorry! I'm so sorry!" I sob.

"What are you sorry about, Emma?"

I'm sorry, Dad. You'll soon know how greatly I've failed you, that I couldn't keep your secret anymore.

I'm sorry, Mom. You'll hate me forever once you find out, more than you already do, because now I've given you a reason to.

I'm sorry, Kyle, for breaking my promise to you about Dad not going back to jail.

I'm sorry, Aunt Jane, for getting your little brother into impossible trouble. Because there's no turning back after what I've said. It's out there now. No retractions.

But above all, I'm sorry, Hannah, for hurting you so badly, for betraying you so deeply. Causing that hopeful smile to slide off your face yesterday was the worst thing I've ever done in my entire life.

Until now. Because now everyone knows, both inside this room and the next, full of Paula's "team." Because I just shattered my whole family apart. Because I've been broken for so long, living with this infinite pain inside me all these years. Because when I looked at Hannah in that hallway and mouthed the words "I hate you," I was talking to myself.

Because I'm the most despicable friend that ever lived. I didn't stop it from happening to her, too.

"I didn't protect her," I say.

"Who didn't you protect?" Paula asks.

"Hannah. I didn't warn her. I had hoped it would be different with her—because she's stronger than me, more outspoken—but it wasn't. She didn't know. Had no way to know what would happen when she did those things in front of him. She was just responding to his attention like I used to. She didn't realize . . ."

Paula is talking, but I can't hear her. The howl in my ears is a scream. No, it's the room, closing in on us. No, it's me shrieking with everything I have, hands over ears, roaring into this space that is too small and contained. The sound that comes out is a wail of agony—a wound so deep I know I'll drown in it.

The sobbing and screeching become a lit hurricane inside me—outside me. Blasting its wet violence straight through my soul. Ripping, shredding, consuming till there's nothing left, not even a red-eyed, oily black snake. The cyclone at last dissipates, leaving behind only crumpled foundation, torn earth, and a bone-numbing hum.

"Emma?" I hear at last through the retreating vortex of noise.

Paula waits until I look up. She's leaning forward, hand resting on the stack of white paper like she'd reached for my hand but stopped herself. Her gaze is strong and steady, more intent than ever but also endlessly kind. In this gaze, I can tell she's not scared of me, or of anything I've told her today. And most astounding of all, I somehow know she doesn't think I'm a bad daughter, a bad person. I only wish I could sit in her eyes, pooled in their compassion, for the rest of my life. I know I'd be happy there. I'd be safe.

"If it's all right with you," Paula continues, focus unwavering, hand tapping the table, "I'm going to keep asking you questions, but if you need a break, it's important that you tell me."

I nod several times, a deranged bobblehead on a dashboard, feeling embarrassed beyond measure but also something like calm.

"When was the first time he abused you, Emma? Do you remember?"

I can never un-remember, no matter how hard I try. "Um,

there was this backpacking trip. . . ." And the words don't stop, pouring from me like they'll never end. I see the tent's duct-taped rain fly flapping above me. Hear the chirrup of the crickets. Feel his warm, rough hands. Smell his sweat mixed with musty sleeping bag. Fragment by fragment, I relive everything with my entire body like it's the first, second, third time. I tell it all—answering Paula's questions about place, time, where, how, with what. I draw pictures of the tent, the yard of the farmhouse, my bedroom in San Francisco, my bedroom in our current house, and the guest room across the hall. I point to the anatomical picture *here* and *here* and *here*, over and over and over. And I don't stop—can't stop—till my heart has drained dry and every last tarry black secret has dropped from my chest.

"I think we should stop here for now," Paula says at last. Has it been several minutes or hours or days? "We can save any follow-up questions or clarifications for our next meeting, which I'll schedule for early tomorrow or the next day. But in the meantime, I want to make sure we have time for me to answer any questions you may have, Emma."

"Can Hannah and I still be friends?"

I've blurted out the words before I even knew I was thinking them. But I already know the answer, and I'm crying too hard again to hear Paula's response.

Once I manage to calm myself, Paula rises and says, "I'm going to leave you for a quick moment and check in with my colleagues to see if I forgot anything. And while I'm gone, if you feel up for it, perhaps you could write down anything else you can think of. Anything that you didn't want to tell me or maybe couldn't remember at the time."

I watch her leave, then stare down at the blank sheet of paper on top of the stack now imprinted with so many *x*s, it looks like a warped pattern. In a flash, I realize there is something left to write. Someone, anyway.

Dear Hannah . . .

I tell her I'm so sorry I ended our friendship, sorry beyond words that I told her I hated her. I anguish over not having warned her about my dad, that I hadn't known how or even that I'd needed to. I confess that if I could do it all over again, I never would have brought her over, introduced her to him. I would've protected her like she had always protected me. I ask her to forgive me, if she can somehow find it in herself. Then, finally, I thank her for doing what I didn't know how to do, didn't know could even be done.

Unburying a secret.

You remember the next morning; an apology

You remember the morning following that night in the tent.
By sunrise the novelty of backpacking had worn off, and you began
to act out toward him in small, defiant ways. You huffed and rolled
your eyes when he asked you to grab the tent bag that had blown
across the yard, or to rinse the breakfast dishes in the stream, or to
repack your bag because you had put all the heavy things on top.

But it was this single question that most caught you off guard:
"Emma, what's gotten into you today?"

You remember thinking, *You know why,* because not even your
socially awkward father could be that ignorant, that aloof. And
for someone who always rewarded you for your intelligence, how
could he have thought you wouldn't know the most basic lesson of
all—good versus evil?

And yet, curiously, confusingly, you also remember not quite
wanting to go home just yet, not wanting the trip to end. You
had anticipated it for so long, this time alone with your father,
that having this coveted trip become a past event struck you with
some strange form of inexplicable grief. Your brain was at war
with itself, struggling to reconcile the incredible man you knew
and loved as your father with the impossible, twisted version you'd
discovered last night, and could it really have even happened at all?

You remember how on the drive home in his old truck with torn seats and worn shocks, you asked him if he could pull over so that the two of you could cook on the camp stove the Velveeta Shells & Cheese that you still had in your bag, the box that had weighed down your pack the whole trip but that you'd never eaten. He told you it would have to wait until you got home.

Because, unlike you, he suddenly seemed eager for the trip to end.

You remember that same evening when your father came to your room. You sat on your bed cross-legged, not facing him as he leaned against the doorframe.

You remember the two of you mumbling your way through small talk about your science homework, though both your minds were miles of dirt path away, stuck in a tent under the tree where a young boy had died. Yet, at long last, he said what he had come to say:

"I'm sorry for last night. For what happened."

You remember that your response came out just above a whisper: "It's okay." It wasn't and you both knew it, but you both wanted it to be—needed it to be—so badly. You remember thinking that he would tell your mother what had happened, that even if she'd be mad at you, that her knowing would mean it would never happen again. And you assumed that he did tell her, assumed that she knew. But now you believe he didn't, and yet it was still only a matter of time before she'd have to make a choice anyway, on whether or not to see, to know.

What you did find out, however, was that your father wasn't truly sorry. At least, not sorry enough to stop.

fault

I'm back in the special waiting room, sitting in the same chair as before, still shaking uncontrollably, still crying even though the interview and medical exam have been over for at least half an hour. In my hands I clutch the damp letter I'd written Hannah and folded countless times, not knowing when I'll send it but hoping I find the courage to. She deserves to know and to hear it from me.

And though the doctor had been professional, gentle, even, during my exam, I can't stop seeing her eyes, bright and bugged-out from her magnified glasses. Can't stop feeling the warm glow of her headlamp and gloved fingers roaming my body, over every part of me. Searching for physical marks that weren't there because they'd have to cut me open to see the scars.

Silvi's wrapped a soft blanket around me, and Paula's somewhere with Aunt Jane "talking about next-steps." At least, I think that's what Paula said. I haven't been able to take in much information after finding out about Mom.

All I know is that I came out of my exam and Mom was gone. She left me here. Because of what I said. What I told them.

Silvi and Paula have been so kind and patient with me today, but that doesn't stop it all from feeling so broken, especially me.

From what little I've pieced together, I was in my exam when

Silvi went out to talk to Mom, telling her that, based on new information, Dad could no longer be allowed in the house with Kyle or me for our own protection and that additional charges against him were going to be filed. I guess that's when Mom flipped out and caused a big scene. They wouldn't tell me what she said, but I know it was bad based off their reactions. And if Hannah had been a lying "slut," I can only imagine what Mom had called me. Then they must've whisked Aunt Jane away to talk because I haven't seen her since before my interview.

And now, I guess, I wait for . . . something. I know Silvi or Paula must've told me what, but I couldn't hear it, and now I don't have the energy to ask. What happens to teens whose parents abandon them at advocacy centers? Who hate you so much, they refuse to stay and make sure you're okay or even to scream at you to your face?

Silvi steps into my field of vision, holding out a sheet of snakeskin-green construction paper. I take it in trembling hands while still gripping Hannah's letter tight.

"Would you like to make one, Emma?"

I glance up at them, not understanding.

They gesture around at the survivors' flags that loop the room, each one its own unique expression—stickers, glitter, words. Everywhere I look are words. Again, I scan the dizzying circle for Hannah's flag, but there are so many. Too many.

All these kids and teens, I think. *All like me.* A strong wave of something like reassurance, hope, even, washes over me, but then I immediately feel sick. Having more kids and teens who understand what I'm feeling, what I've lived through—or worse—isn't a good thing. But I guess it does make me feel less alone.

Silvi sets a small box of art supplies on the side table next to me. "They're here if you want them."

When I don't move, they say, "Emma?"

I look up into their warm, solemn face.

"You did it."

"Did what?" I ask, all color drained from my voice.

"Survived."

Fresh tears gather and fall, gather and fall. Then I hear a door open and Paula's voice as she ushers someone back into the waiting room.

Mom, I think. She's returned. She was just mad, but she's come back for me anyway, to make sure I'm okay.

But it's not the door leading to the lobby, and the face I see isn't Mom's. Instead, Aunt Jane appears from the hallway behind Paula, her eyes bloodshot and swollen.

Paula leads her over to where I'm sitting, then flashes me a gentle smile. "Emma, I've filled your aunt in on some aspects of what's happened here today. At least, the parts I can legally share. Like I mentioned before, most everything you told me in that room remains confidential between you, me, and my team until we finish our interview in the next day or two and the police have finished their investigation, all right?"

I nod but don't break eye contact with Aunt Jane, who's staring at me with an expression of stunned horror. "I just . . . don't understand," she says, and ice-cold terror washes over me. She doesn't believe me.

"I'm not lying," I whisper. "I swear, Aunt Jane."

Her face breaks into the saddest smile I've ever seen. "No, of course you aren't, Em. I didn't for a second mean to suggest that. I'm just . . . trying to wrap my head around everything, is all."

"Are you mad at me?" I manage, voice cracking wide open.

Aunt Jane drops to her knee and wraps me in a tight embrace, her tears mixing with mine as she says, "Oh, hon, I'm so, so mad, but not at you. Never at you. I'm just absolutely furious this happened, that I didn't know."

"It's not your fault," I tell her.

She pulls back, balancing on her heels to look me dead in the eye. "Emma, those may be the most important words you have ever said in your life. And I need you to listen, okay? Because I'm going to say them back to you right now, and I need you to believe them yourself. Got it?"

I stare at her.

"It's not your fault," she says, and we're both sobbing.

"It's not your fault," she repeats, hugging me fiercely. "It's not your fault, Em. It never was. It's not your shame to carry. It's his. Can you believe me when I say that?"

"I can try," I whisper.

"That's a great start. That's really good. And I'm so, so proud of you, for everything."

Aunt Jane and I weep into each other's hair for a long time. When at last our tears are spent, Silvi and Paula pull her aside once more, saying they need to talk with her about "arrangements." They tell me I can listen in if I want to, but I'm too depleted.

Instead, I let my head fall back and sink into the soft cushions of the chair, closing my eyes against the fluorescent lights above.

Is it my fault for telling? It absolutely feels like it. But what other choice did I have to make it stop?

Tears slipped from the girl's eyes like endless strands of pearls. "But what should I do—what can I do—to stop this?"

My eyes fly open, and I snatch a neon purple gel pen from the

318 • CASSIE GUSTAFSON

art box, our favorite color. In shaky cursive across the entire piece of serpent-green paper, I write: *"The Girl and the Secret Unburied."* All of a sudden, it clicks into place, this fairy tale I didn't know how to end, and I lose myself in bolding and smoothing out the letters of this new title, adding tiny gold rose stickers to the page and drawing silhouettes of a large tree and snarling brambles around the perimeter. All the while, my mind tucks and pulls at the second half of the story line, weaving it into existence in my brain.

Only after Aunt Jane returns with Paula and Silvi do I find out my fate—I'm going to go stay with Aunt Jane for now.

My aunt turns to look at me, cheeks still shimmering with tears. And when she smiles, it's the return of the saddest smile I've ever seen, though her voice holds warmth. "Isn't that great news? Just you and me, M&M's!"

"What about Kyle?" I ask. "Is he coming too?"

Aunt Jane exchanges a quick look with Paula and Silvi. "He's . . . going to stay with your mom for the time being, but Silvi will be checking in on him to make sure he's doing okay. And since your father . . ." Her voice breaks, and Silvi steps forward.

"Since your father isn't going to be home anymore," Silvi finishes, "it will just be your mother and Kyle."

"Dad's getting arrested again?" I ask the obvious, and Silvi nods.

Staring down at my flag, I notice several teardrops have smudged the gel ink. I've marred it, making something almost beautiful turn ugly, but for once I don't want to crumple it into a ball and start over. This time, it brings me a shred of comfort, making a small piece of my sadness visible so that maybe others can feel less alone in their own loss, their bottomless sorrow.

"I can't leave him," I whisper. "I can't leave Kyle."

"It's only for right now," Paula adds. "We hope you two can reunite soon."

None of them have to say it, but I know why I can't stay with Kyle. I'm no longer welcome at our house. Mom doesn't want me anymore.

"And he'll get to come visit as often as he likes," Aunt Jane adds. "We'll be going over there tomorrow to grab some of your things, so you can say hi then."

This is really happening. I won't be able to live with Kyle anymore, or with Mom or Dad. I won't be able to go home. Dad isn't going home either. Not this time. I didn't know a heart could break so many times in a single day.

There's more paperwork, another debriefing, and then we're finally, *finally* allowed to go, though I have to return tomorrow afternoon for a follow-up interview.

Only after we've climbed into Aunt Jane's Jetta do I find the courage to ask, "Aunt Jane? Do you mind if we stop by the toy store on the way"—I catch myself before saying "home"—"on the way out? There's something I need to get for Kyle."

She flashes that same smile that doesn't reach her eyes, but she nods and dabs at her face with a tissue.

Her car smells like lemons and is clean and warm from the sun. I lean against the window, closing my eyes and feeling the soft rays of afternoon sunlight trickle over me.

A few blocks from the toy store, the final line of the fairy tale appears in my mind like magic, and I sigh an exhausted sigh of relief. At long last, I know how the story of the girl and her rose garden will end.

"The Girl and the Secret Unburied"

Tears slipped from the girl's eyes like endless strands of pearls. "But what should I do—what can I do—to stop this?"

"I would tell you," replied the thorny mass, "but you already know the answer. . . ."

For a long while the girl lay motionless on the ground, prostrate against the earth of her childhood haven. She felt the press of dirt to her knees, clasped hands against her forehead. She heard the gentle rustle of rose-corpse pages on the wind, the angry hum of townsfolk even now peering over her garden wall. And she might have stayed there for all eternity, were it not for the brilliant magenta butterfly that blew into the garden on a warm breeze, alighting on the girl's upturning palm. As the girl lay still for a long, long while, watching the butterfly wink its magnificence at her, everything else fell away. Finally, the butterfly took flight once more, disappearing over the heads of the onlookers but leaving behind an invisible trail of courage in its wake.

When at last the girl stood, it was on wobbly legs and a cracked conviction. Yet she knew what she had to do. For, in the depths of her heart, she had known it all along.

Gathering up her courage, she took a deep breath. One of

the rose-corpse pages had caught at her ankle, wrapping itself around her stocking. This she plucked up and smoothed against her skirts. Then, lifting the paper to her eyes, in front of all the staring faces, she began to read aloud from the page of secrets she had tried to bury so long ago. As she read, a passing wind caught at the inky words and pulled them from the paper while the page itself crumbled to soil beneath her fingers. When she had finished, she plucked another rose-corpse page from a townsperson's hand that dangled over the wall, and she read this, too, aloud. On and on she read until she could find no more pages. But still the thorny bush stood, as heavy before her as it was in her heart.

The noise of the onlookers fell away when, in her mind's eye, she saw the solid mahogany box, felt the press of satiny red velvet to her heart, heard the gentle click of the gold lock, setting tiny, unspoken words free.

Heaving a shaky sigh, she sank once more to her knees beneath the great thorny bush. And, as she had so many sunrises and sunsets before, she began to dig. This time her hand bore no spade. Fingers clawed into wet soil. Pebbles bit at her palms. Thorns scraped her face and arms. Yet on she dug as the many faces watched her.

It did not take long to reach the box, for she had known just where it lay. Dragging it free from the earth, she saw how much it had decayed with age, collapsing in, the lock nearly rusted through. And yet, pulling the tarnished key from her breast, she fit it to the lock and twisted it with a resolute *click*.

Out oozed the remaining pages, the tarry center of her secret.

Pausing, she looked down at the mess of wet pulp in her hands.

To read aloud her heart's blackest secret was to betray those she loved most.

She glanced into the faces around her. Some looked curious. Some looked bewildered. One looked angry.

To read aloud her heart's secret was to no longer betray herself.

And so, though her voice quivered and her body trembled with the weight of it all, Emma began to read aloud. Despite the irate face directed at her, a silent command to stop, she read on and on until these pages, too, dripped through her fingers.

Emma stood, heavier and lighter than she had ever stood before, wiping soiled hands on her skirts and across her tear-streaked cheeks. The faces around her spoke now, an incessant chatter she could not hear over the drumming of her own heart. One face, however, stayed quiet, filled with a silent rage. Frozen with fear.

Perhaps it's your turn to be afraid, Emma's heart said to him.

Only then did she notice it—a pale, thin light flickering across her brow.

Looking up, she saw that the thorny mass that had once been a rosebush had fallen away. In its wake sat an empty void of thorns and dust, releasing from its deadly clutches her beloved oak tree. Between the naked branches of the tree, the sun revealed itself, a sun that she had not seen in many long years. It glinted down at her, though it emitted no heat.

Deep in her soul, Emma knew her swing was gone, and her beloved oak would not survive the winter. The garden she had loved from her childhood would never be the same. Perhaps time would fill the holes left by the roses and the buried, now unburied, secret. Or perhaps not. Perhaps some holes were meant to stay holes.

Her heart held little triumph, but rather the acceptance of a childhood lost, though no longer buried in shame.

Yet, despite her grief, despite the ache in her heart as deep as the chasm before her, the girl turned her face to the sun and let the light stream over her.

safe

Wednesday

I'm standing before the back doorway of our house, not sure how to enter. It feels like some invisible string is pulling me back like a whispered warning: *Don't go in.*

Not even a minute ago, Mom had answered our knocking, but when she saw me standing there beside Aunt Jane, she'd turned away and left without a word. Aunt Jane had hurried after her, telling her to stop, saying they needed to talk, that she was being terrible, but Mom must've slammed her bedroom door in Aunt Jane's face because she had returned, expression pained, and told me she was going to go check on Kyle.

And still I stand here on the rear stoop, tired afternoon sunlight dappling the porch, a paper shopping sack clutched in my hand. I hadn't really believed it till this exact moment: This isn't my home anymore. I no longer live here.

At last, I put one foot in front of the other and step over the threshold, feeling the invisible line behind me stretch taut, then snap like a spiderweb's thread. Stealing through the downstairs of our house, I linger on every turn of the walls, every gouge in the wooden floor, every dried paint drip on cupboard doors. I touch my fingertips to old spice jars full of clumpy herbs, and across dusty picture frames and the sooty rims of half-burned candles.

All the while, I remember.

Through the entryway window, I look out over the yard once full of glistening Easter eggs. Past the sink where a pan was slammed so hard it warped. Past the cupboards of missing cups. Past the downstairs bathroom where I'd asked for a lock, held my breath while showering, strained to hear the sound of the knob twisting once more. Past the dining room table where I'd drunk my first Mike's Hard Lemonade and played a card game I didn't want to play. Past my parents' closed bedroom door where he'd given me that shirtless back rub and tickled me before Mom had walked in. Past the green couch where he and Hannah had sat together that one night, the blanket over their laps unable to hide his crimes.

In this house, I want to remember everything; I want to remember nothing.

Aunt Jane's in Kyle's room, trying to coax him from his hiding spot. I can hear him crying from where I stand in the doorway, his sobs carrying loud and clear from the gap behind his bed. And when I approach, dropping the store bag, pulling myself through the slats, and easing myself down beside where he sits as I have so many times before, I wonder if it's for the last time.

Mom won't change her mind, won't take me back no matter what. And though I'm here to get my stuff now, I understand that, once Mom clears her initial shock, she won't be letting me set foot in this house again.

Kyle's face is mottled, eyes red-rimmed and nose still bubbling snot.

"Aunt Jane is mean!" he cries.

I shake my head, confused. "Kyle, Aunt Jane isn't mean."

"Yes, she is! She's taking you away!"

"No, Ky, Aunt Jane is the nicest aunt in the whole world, and you want to know why? Because she's letting me stay with her, *and* she said you can come over whenever you want. Isn't that so cool?"

"But I don't want you to stay with Aunt Jane!" Kyle wails. "I want you to stay here with me!"

I grip his hands in mine. "I know you do, Kyle, and I want that too, but I'm not allowed to stay here. And at least this way, you can come visit me at Aunt Jane's every week. Wouldn't you like that?"

Kyle shakes his head hard, new tears spilling over.

"I know it doesn't seem like much fun now, but I promise you it will be. And even though things are going to be a little different, I'll get Aunt Jane to drop me off at your school every morning so I can still walk you to class, okay? And on weekends, we can have sleepovers, and you can bring your LEGOs! We'll stay up past our bedtimes eating licorice, watching movies, playing LEGOs, and reading all the Ninjago you want, okay? Does that sound good?"

It takes a long time, but at last he nods.

I nudge his shoulder. "You know what else sounds pretty great? The present I got for you."

His big eyes flash to mine, full of curiosity and excitement before he remembers he's upset and drops his gaze again.

"Plus, this is a present I know you're really, *really* going to like. The only problem is, it's in a bag I left out there, so you'll have to come out if you want it, 'kay?"

I let him think about this for a while, and then finally he mumbles, "Okay," and I help him to his feet.

He climbs out first, me following behind. From the crinkly paper sack embossed with the toy store logo, I pull out a small LEGO box with a brand-new Benny inside and hand it to Kyle.

Before he can protest, I cut in. "I know this isn't your old Benny, but listen up. I'm going to talk to your teacher and make sure she knows what's been going on with those mean boys so that it doesn't happen again. And I'll try my hardest to get Old Benny back. But I was thinking that maybe this Benny could keep you company in the meantime, just until we get Old Benny back. Sound good?"

His mouth stays pinched, but he nods, and I exhale with relief.

"Great. And maybe if you ask nicely, Aunt Jane can help you take him out of the package while I run up to my room. Would that be okay?"

Kyle nods again, forehead scrunched. My eyes land on the sticky rows of jelly bean cups, and I wonder how long it's going to take Mom to notice they're there.

I wait a moment to ease Aunt Jane into helping Kyle before I slip out the door. Then I climb the stairs where I once carried up a plate of crackers and cheese, the mold freshly whittled from it. I move past the guest bedroom where he'd lead me at night, where I'd fall headfirst into fairy tales and drift to lands far, far away.

Easing into my bedroom, I think about the doorframe of my room back in San Fran that he'd leaned against to apologize, but only the once, and this doorframe that he'd leaned against before asking me for an impossible favor. I take in the bright lavender walls covered in posters minus one, the floors coated with thick, glossy varnish and the remnants of moth suicides and shattered candle, the pirate captain tree just beyond the window whose ledge I'd straddled, wondering if pitching sideways and plummeting to the ground below would be easier than trying to hold myself up for even one more second.

Last, my gaze finds the pillow under which the knife no longer lives, then the bed where I'd held that knife all those nights, sobbing and imploring the universe, "Why?" all while pleading for the courage to cut deeper. The same bed where, a year and a half ago, I'd finally allowed myself to write those four words in my journal before ripping them out and destroying the evidence:

My dad molested me.

I've decided I don't want that journal back from the police anymore, with all its missing pages and dark fairy tales inside. After finishing the one about the buried secret last night, I think I'm done with writing them as well, at least for a while. It hurts too much.

Crossing over to my duffel, I reach deep inside and pull out the knife, small and serrated, the next best thing to a sharpened blade. Holding the edge up in the afternoon light, I notice the pink tint caught in the small crescent scoops. My own blood. I'll need to wash it before putting it away.

Instead, I linger and wonder over it all: that he's gone and that my life in this house with my parents really is over. As Aunt Jane assured me, I never have to see him again if I didn't want to, and I definitely don't know if I want to yet. All I know is that the guilt and all-consuming sorrow I feel now that he's gone is matched by a relief that's as sweet and soft and airy as cotton candy.

Trudging downstairs, knife in hand—for once, in plain sight—I move past Mom's closed door. I wonder if she'll ever speak to me again. I know she blames me for Dad's second arrest, and in that she's right. My testimony from yesterday and today got him thrown back behind bars. Yet Aunt Jane keeps telling me that, though I may be the cause for it, I'm absolutely not the reason, and that there's a big difference. I'm still trying to see it, though.

Slipping into the kitchen, I slide the knife back into its wooden block with five matching brethren, finally filling the void that used to stare out at me like an accusation. Returning the knife feels complicated but also satisfying somehow.

As I turn to go, my fingerprints glint off the matte hilt, a smudge of "I was here." I forgot to wipe the blood off as well and almost reach for the sponge to do it, then pull the knife free instead and place it in the sink for someone else to deal with.

My shoulders feel heavy, bearing an impossible weight—for doing the right thing, the wrong thing, incriminating a father I love wholly and not at all. The pain hits next, blasting in on a phantom wind, as I return upstairs to what used to be my room and sit on the edge of what used to be my bed because I have to keep reminding myself, this place doesn't belong to me anymore.

Opening my backpack, I pull out a piece of notebook paper, pretending it's my journal full of gilded pages. Across the middle, in neat cursive, I write four words to my younger self that I know I needed to hear. That, even in this moment, I still need to hear:

You are safe now.

I draw a heart, then tear the message from the page's center, folding the jagged scrap into the smallest imaginable shape. Then, kneeling before my window, I shove the shred of paper deep into the widest crack between my floorboards. I hope someday someone will find it and know that whoever wrote it is okay, that they are somewhere else, away from the person who hurt them.

Finally, I stuff my backpack and duffel with school supplies, library books, my favorite novels from the bookshelf, and as many clothes as will fit. Taking one last look around, I hoist my back-

330 • CASSIE GUSTAFSON

pack and swing my duffel over one shoulder. Last, I grab my Corey shirt from the trash and scoop up Hector into my arms. Hardly any sand remains in his broken pot, and a single snapped limb twinges me with guilt. I wrap Corey around Hector's pot and pull off the severed limb, sticking it next to him in the remnants of sand, hoping maybe it can grow into a baby Hector.

"Aunt Jane?" I ask softly, coming down the stairs, my bags and Hector's Corey-cradled pot in tow. I find her on the couch with Kyle. She's got her arm around him, and he's squeezing his new Benny in both hands.

"Do you mind if we stop at the beach on the way . . . on the way to your house?" I correct midstream. Calling Aunt Jane's place "home" still doesn't feel right. "It'll be quick. I just need to get some sand."

She smiles at me, though it's the version still trying to cover up a galaxy of sadness and not doing a great job. "Sure thing, M's. You about ready?"

I nod once. Because I am; because I'm not.

Tears stream down my face as I give Kyle one last hug, promising to read him the next Ninjago chapter over FaceTime tonight. Then I re-scoop up Hector/Corey and my duffel, walking out the back door and into my new, unknowable life.

mischief

The following Monday

It's lunchtime, and I'm sitting in the school courtyard beneath the protective branches of my crab-apple tree, for once not minding the smell of sunbaked garbage, or the fact that everyone is watching me. Their mouths all move with the same twitterings, anyway: *Emma Clark. Her father got arrested again last week, did you hear?* But, of course, everyone's already heard.

The only person to approach me all day has been Justin, who caught me after second period. "Hey, Em. I hear you're moving," he'd said. When I'd nodded, he'd run a hand through his curls, not meeting my eye. "Well, good luck. We'll sure miss you around here, especially in Cats. You were one of the best parts of that club, you know?" Then he'd bolted before my astonishment had time to wear off.

And now, halfway through the day, I'm at peace with the fact that I'm back to eating alone, at least for today, a feeling that solidified in me last night over Chinese takeout with Aunt Jane at her small two-person dining-room table. Because that's when it fully hit me: today is the last day I'll ever have to spend at Prosper High School. I'd stayed home the rest of last week to "adjust," as Aunt Jane had called it, with the exception of riding in Aunt Jane's car each morning to pick up Kyle and walk him to his classroom so I could keep the promise I made to him—for this one week, anyway.

(Aunt Jane had managed to convince Mom that bringing Kyle to school was "the least" my aunt could do to give Mom "this necessary break," though Aunt Jane didn't mention my involvement.) She'd also given me the option to attend my final day here before my official Tuesday start date at the high school closer to her house.

Our house, I mentally correct. *Our small, two-person dining-room table*, but it's in Aunt Jane's voice, not mine. Still, after less than a week, her home is almost starting to feel familiar, not quite the same disorienting gut punch when I first open my eyes in the morning, which I suppose is as much as I can ask for at this point. Still, a few days back, in my new room that used to be Aunt Jane's office, I wouldn't stop vacuuming the blue carpet, or straightening my new comforter again, or refolding my clothes in the small bureau over and over. Finally, Aunt Jane had dragged me out, and I'd collapsed into her arms, crying in her hallway for a long time.

As for today, Aunt Jane had seemed both surprised, and not, that I actually wanted to attend my last day here. I didn't tell her I felt like I had to, but I think she knew that without having to ask. I needed to say goodbye to Ms. Saeed and Ms. Patterson, and thank them both for all their endless small kindnesses, which I'll do with Ms. Saeed in English and right after the last bell with Ms. Patterson. I also wrote out a copy of my last fairy tale for Ms. Patterson, which I think she's going to like. As for lunchtime, I wanted to declare to all the staring eyes and whispering mouths that I'm not intimidated by them anymore—spiteful Brooke and Kat, sickly-sweet Breeyan, or any of the rest. Truth is, they can't hurt me any more than I've already been hurt.

At least, that's what I'm telling myself today as I don't even pretend to read or eat the lunch Aunt Jane so generously packed for me. Not yet, anyway. Mostly, I'm trying to take it all in—the finality of it. But I guess that, more than anything, I needed to see her one last time, my ex–best friend, even if we don't get to talk. I haven't communicated with Hannah since mailing her my letter late Wednesday night from Aunt Jane's mailbox—

our mailbox

—even though Aunt Jane had warned me not to expect Hannah to write back. Aunt Jane and I had also discussed what to do today if Hannah were to be here, if we were to run into each other.

Give her space, M&M's. She probably needs it. If she wants to talk, let her come to you, but also be prepared for the fact that she may not want to, or will be angry, even.

So I'd made it easy for Hannah in third-period geometry by taking a seat at the back of the class away from her. That way she wouldn't have to decide to be nice if she didn't want to. Then I'd been out the classroom door almost before the bell rang, not really giving her a chance either way. Truth be told, I'd been afraid of what her choice would be. Maybe I still am. Scared of what went through her mind as she read my letter too. *If* she read my letter.

And yet, too sudden for words, there she is: Hannah, marching out of the main building—*toward me?*—like she's on a mission.

Swallowing hard, I tear my gaze from her and glance off into the distance, to the chain-link fence surrounding the school. But in no time a dark mass materializes in front of me. Something solid hits my foot, and I jolt, heart thundering. Looking down, I see the plastic bottle of orange Crush soda that's just rolled against my shoe.

Hannah.

She's standing a few paces away, hands shoved deep in her

jeans pockets, wearing her no-bullshit expression, though the edges are laced with something I've never seen on Hannah's face before. Nervousness.

"I got your letter," she blurts, taking a step forward as she does.

"Oh," I say, unsure if she took the letter as the peace offering I'd intended, or something of the devil's work.

"My mom even let me read it," she says, stepping closer, shrinking the distance between us.

"Well, that was big of her, considering," I add, and mean it.

Her face shifts, and I try to brace myself for the brutal anger I've been expecting, but she doesn't yell. Rather, her voice drops to a low whisper that she leans in to deliver.

"I didn't know."

Her words hang between us in the air, zapping like sparklers.

"I mean, I suspected, but I didn't know. Not for sure." Her eyes fall away from mine, and something like shame, regret, flashes through them.

"You couldn't have," I say. "I—well—*Dad* made sure of that, didn't he?"

The word "Dad" grates against my tongue like sandpaper, feeling all wrong, too familiar, reminding me that I have yet to decide what to do about his label. Is he still "Dad" if I no longer want him to be? Or does the phrase "my father" distance me enough from the man who gave me life, then slowly ruined it by turning it perverse? Or should he be "Brian Clark," as cold and removed as the type set under his mug shot?

Tears prick my eyes. None of it fits. Nothing's easy anymore. But then again, maybe it never was.

I swipe at my cheeks, muttering, "Sorry," but it's automatic, and I don't know what I'm apologizing for or who I'm even apologizing to. But then again, I do know, don't I? "I'm sorry I didn't protect you, Hannah."

My eyes burn hotter still, overflowing with more tears, in sync with the ones now streaming down Hannah's face.

"I know," she says, then reaches for my hand, not letting go even as she moves to sit beside me, pressing her shoulder into mine, leaning her head against my own. Reinforcing her grip, she interlaces our fingers, giving my palm a tight squeeze.

I don't look at her, torn between the overwhelming desire to flood the silence and tell her how very much she means to me, while simultaneously feeling like I shouldn't say a single thing to risk breaking the delicate shell of this moment and losing it forever. My time with Hannah Garber is already running thin enough as it is without me rushing it.

I also half expect Hannah to crack some joke about our linked hands—to diffuse, with humor or sarcasm, the quiet intensity of our tears and intimacy of our nearness—but she doesn't. Instead, she turns, her hazel eyes a few inches from mine, weighted in a seriousness even I didn't know the true depths of. Then she asks like she's read my mind, "What now?"

"I don't know." My voice fissures, exposing grief and a deep, overwhelming unease. Does Hannah know how much she means to me? *Could she ever?*

"I don't know either," she confesses, and her admitted uncertainty about what lies ahead is the millionth thing I wasn't expecting from her today. It makes me love her all the more fiercely.

"But maybe we don't need to?" she continues. "Have to know, I mean? At least, not right now?"

Me and Hannah. Hannah and me. The earnest, desperate smile she is gifting me stills all the noise in my mind, granting me an intensely clear focus of her—the sun dappling through the crab-apple tree, turning her strawberry-blond hair into a blazing supernova crown. The smell of her warm breath—sweet, like fresh milk. The heat of her palm, her knuckles like friendship knots beside my own. Then she's leaning her head on my shoulder again, her words a vibration in my ear.

"We'll write each other letters all the time. We don't have to stop being friends just because you're transferring schools tomorrow. At least, that's what I heard was happening."

But she tires of her own words, or maybe she needs a subject change, because all of a sudden she's buzzing with unspent energy and pulling away, her eager grin slipping, unlinking our hands and reaching down for the orange Crush bottle that still rests by my shoe.

We both frown down at the unopened soda for a long while, watch the condensation *drip drip* down the label. Then, out of nowhere, I feel a small smile dart in and spread across my face. Into the silence between us, I add, "Careful opening that. It might explode."

She eyes me sideways. The grin spreads like magic, working its way from my mouth to play across her own. "I'm counting on it."

Her gaze holds mine, even as her smirk turns full-blown mischievous. Then, in a single, quick jerk of her hand, she twists open the bottle too fast. An orange geyser of soda bursts out, and, alongside it all the uncertainty of what will come next. An uncertainty that is—at least for now—overshadowed by the howls of laughter shared between two old friends.

Acknowledgments

Colossal THANKS to all the incredible humans who aided in the creation and production of this book, including:

My rock-star agent, Sara Crowe, who is the ultimate author champion and who found this book the absolute perfect home. I'm so lucky to work with you!

My incomparable editor, Krista Vitola, whose fierce advocacy for this story since Day One will always hold a Krista-shaped place in my heart, and whose patience, gentle guidance, and sage advice gave this book new wings on which to soar. Your belief in this story afforded me the strength to keep going, and I will forever be grateful to you for it!

My thesis adviser, Professor Irena Praitis, for gifting me a safe space in which to not only send those first fledgling pages, but also to sit in her office for countless hours as I worked through those early difficult chapters. This book would not exist without the immense generosity of your time and wisdom, and I will never forget your kindness. The academic world is blessed beyond measure to have you on faculty!

My second reader, Professor J. Chris Westgate, whose astute critique and generous praise of early pages boosted my confidence in this work and helped me confirm I was on the right track.

The whole crew at Pippin Properties for their relentless

support of kidlit authors and their works, including this one. And, of course, the whole team at Simon & Schuster Books for Young Readers, whose magical touch elevated this novel to new heights. Y'all are the greatest!

The supremely talented Beatriz Ramo and Krista Vossen for helping create the masterpiece that is the cover. It is utter perfection—embodying Emma's brave yet haunting journey perfectly—and I stand in awe of your collective genius!

Kathy Harvey-Brown for the generous gift of her time and insight on forensic interviews and children's advocacy centers, both of which play a pivotal role in helping keep our children safe from abuse. Additional thanks for the comprehensive tour and many answered questions! Caitlin Massey for her added insight into forensic investigators and children's advocacy centers. Thank you both for the imperative work you do! (Any errors in my depiction of interviews or advocacy centers are my own.)

My husband, Carl, who is still my favorite part of every day. (And our fluff-butt, Maui, too!) Your patience, understanding, and fierce hugs as I fought my way through drafting and editing this book made me fall in love with you all over again.

Ashley for navigating this publishing journey right by my side, and for being the world's greatest CP, friend, listener, and cheerer. (Long live our state-hopping escapades, white-noise debriefs, and hours on the phone with all the crunchy snacks!) Thank you for everything. I'd be utterly lost without you.

Lucy for bringing such light to my life even in dark times, and for being there when I need you most. And Jenn, for always holding space for me and forever accepting me as I am. Team JammyPack forever. **Special thanks to Lucy for the stellar close read, margins packed with all the amazing GIFs and words of encouragement!

Jessi and Clay, I cherish your love and kick-ass friendships immensely, including celebrating every victory—both large and small— together. **Special thanks to Jessi for the generous and insightful close read of this manuscript. I value your opinion immensely!

Jackie Harkness for answering my one million lawyer questions and for being a dear friend all these many years!

Sharon Bailey, whose close reading and immense enthusiasm for this manuscript lifted my spirits and helped me double down on my determination to see this book into the world.

My New England homegirls and guys. You know who you are—pirates, pilots, and mermaids alike! Thank you all for your love and support, and for everything from beach walks and outdoor movie nights to high teas and adventures near and far. I treasure each and every one of you—especially you, Tres Best Chicas!

My family—especially my sister, Megan; mother, Sonia; brothers, Daniel and Benjamin; and aunt, Cathy—for their endless cheerleading and support. I love you more than words can express! **Special thanks to Aunt Cathy for reading the novel, and for all her praise and support!

David Gustafson for reading an early draft and calling immediately with expert feedback and enthusiasm. (I sure needed both—thank you!)

The Wordsmith Workshops community, started by Cristin Terrill and Beth Revis. Thank you both for creating a dynamic community of writers I couldn't live without. And Mama Lynn, you were like a second mother to all who knew you, and your passing affected us deeply. You will forever be missed, though your light shines on in our hearts and writing.

My local writer kin. A profound thank you to all for the many write-ins, the sage advice, and the incredible gifts of your friendships, including Adi, Mary, Katie, Sara, and the whole "Plague Bagels" gang; Rebekah, Karina, and Beth—love you ladies!; Erin, Lita, and the Kidlit603 New Words community. And a special thanks to Jeff Deck for the weekly writing dates, invaluable publishing insight, and top-notch friendship!

The incredible writers whose work influenced my own and who bravely paved the path for us all to tackle the tough stuff, including (but not limited to) S. K. Ali, Laurie Halse Anderson, Stephen Chbosky, Akemi Dawn Bowman, Tiffany D. Jackson, Chanel Miller, Toni Morrison, Dave Pelzer, Jenny Torres Sanchez, Courtney C. Stevens, Courtney Summers, and Alice Walker.

And finally, for everyone else who has supported me throughout this Mr. Toad's Wild Writerly Ride in ways both great and small, I thank you endlessly from the bottom of my heart.

Resources List

988 Suicide and Crisis Lifeline
https://988lifeline.org/
1-800-273-8255 (hotline, available 24/7 in English and Spanish)
or dial 988

RAINN (Rape, Abuse & Incest National Network)
https://www.rainn.org/ (live chat and hotline, available 24/7)

National Sexual Assault Hotline
1-800-656-HOPE (4673)

National Sexual Violence Resource Center
https://www.nsvrc.org/

Stomp Out Bullying
https://www.stompoutbullying.org/
HelpChat Hours: Tuesday, seven p.m.–twelve a.m. EST

The (free + anonymous) Be Strong app for people in crisis
https://bestrong.global/
1-954-246-5807